SODOM

ROAD

EXIT

# AMBER DAWN

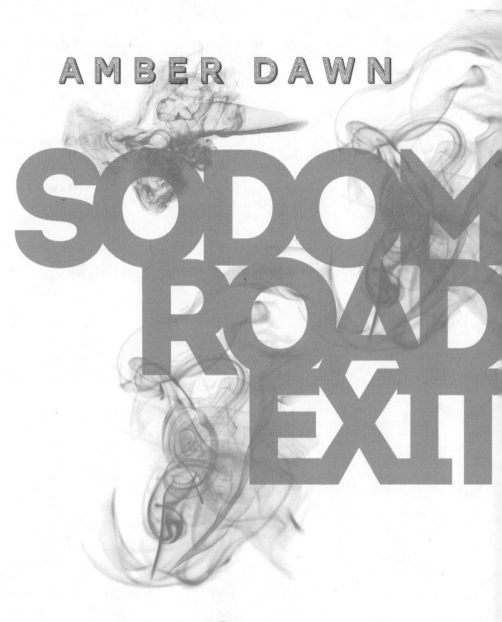

# SODOM ROAD EXIT

ARSENAL
PULP PRESS
VANCOUVER

SODOM ROAD EXIT
Copyright © 2018 by Amber Dawn

ARSENAL PULP PRESS
Suite 202 – 211 East Georgia St.
Vancouver, BC V6A 1Z6
Canada
*arsenalpulp.com*

The publisher gratefully acknowledges the support of the Canada Council for the Arts and the British Columbia Arts Council for its publishing program, and the Government of Canada, and the Government of British Columbia (through the Book Publishing Tax Credit Program), for its publishing activities.

This is a work of fiction. Any resemblance of characters to persons either living or deceased is purely coincidental.

Cover and text design by Oliver McPartlin
Edited by Susan Safyan
Printed and bound in Canada

Library and Archives Canada Cataloguing in Publication:
Dawn, Amber, 1974-, author
        Sodom Road exit / Amber Dawn.
Issued in print and electronic formats.
ISBN 978-1-55152-716-1 (softcover).—ISBN 978-1-55152-717-8 (epub)


        I. Title.

PS8607.A9598S63 2018          C813'.6          C2017-907212-9
                                               C2017-907213-7

Dedicated to everyone who has talked to me
about healing—theirs, mine and, yes, even healing the fallacious
world around us. I am a humble ear, listening.

PART
ONE

# Prologue: Spring 1990

The first photograph of the angel of Crystal Beach was taken by our own local newspaperman, Howie Foster. After stealthily drinking four lukewarm Labatt Blues in the back seat of his car, while his brother laboured for hours in the May sun, Howie mounted his pricey Canon camera atop his tripod and began snapping.

Was the erection of the Ricky Esposito Memorial Gazebo news-worthy enough to earn us the cover? Not likely, at least not during a holiday weekend, and especially not considering the gazebo technically stands on private property. We guessed that the enormous twenty- by twenty-foot hexagonal structure would be used for the occasional wedding, or maybe, if we felt ambitious, we'd offer it to a book club for summer meetings or the local seniors' choir if they wanted to sing show tunes in an outdoor bandstand. To be honest, we weren't really thinking about how the gazebo would be used, only that it needed to be built.

The reason Howie ran the gazebo story—the reason he was there rather than fraternizing with other red-nosed men in a nearby beer tent—was because he wanted to do right by his brother, Joe Foster, who was celebrating his tenth year sober. The cover photo and accompanying news article were Howie's ways of being an enthusiastic, albeit a condoling, witness to his brother's recovery.

The fact is, everyone who showed up that day showed up in service of somebody else. Tamara was there because she was falling in love with me, or she was falling in love with the feeling of love; in other words, the sex we were having was fucking blessed. My mother was worried—though not about me—that she'd be excluded from a notable event in our small community. Dr Rahn Johnson was there for my mother. Dolores Longboat was showing her steadfast friendship to Bobby. Hal and Bobby, Rose and I, well, we believed we had a higher calling. We were truly summoned by divine purpose. Or divine purpose is one way of looking at it. I might also say I had no choice.

The photo in *The Fort Erie Times*: front row, left to right; Rose Esposito, Barbara and Starla Martin, Tamara Matveev, Roberta Varin: and back row; Dolores Longboat, Wendel Swartz, Howard and Joey Foster, Rahn Johnson, Harvey Varin, and little Lucky (just "little Lucky") perched on top of Hal's shoulders. We were a wide-smile group; new buddies, recently consummated lovers, both blood and unconventional family, each of us allowing a day's worth of honest work to yoke us together. And in this way, the photo does not lie.

The article made no mention of angels. No ghosts. No miracles. No lady of blessed whatnot. No harbingers of transformation. Nothing supernatural at all. Those of us who had seen her were doing our best to keep her a secret. We were in awe of what we had seen and also mortified. Saying it aloud would have made it more real, too real and too soon. Therefore, the May 22 cover page headline read, "Memorial Gazebo Built with Salvaged Wood from Crystal Beach Amusement Park."

Days after the local paper ran our story, we studied the newsprint grain, the pixels. "Do you see her?" Her hourglass shape like an elegant smudge.

Since *The Fort Erie Times* article, there have been other photos, better-quality photos in more reputable newspapers. But this clipping is the one stuck to Barbara's fridge, another is taped to Rose's hall mirror, and a third is proudly framed and hangs from a beam of our revered Ricky Esposito Memorial Gazebo. Some claim to see her right away, others denounce her as a trick of light and shadow. Either way, it's unmistakably Etta standing beside me in the photo. The angel of Crystal Beach, Ontario. Her filmy arm stretched forward, as if someone has just asked her to dance.

# 1 Running a Balance

The anonymous woman in bed beside me adamantly shakes my shoulder. She had a name last night. She must have; as part of my hook-and-line, I complimented her "pretty name" and said, "It suits you." Unless a woman's name is Mavis, I normally compliment her pretty name.

"Your phone keeps ringing. Four times in a row. Maybe it's an emergency?" Not-Mavis is still naked. I, evidently, pulled a nightshirt on backward before completely passing out.

I don't have to look at my call display to know it's a 1-800 number. Debt collection agencies call early in the morning, and repeatedly. They're not supposed to call before nine a.m., or at least that's what other flunkies and bums tell me, but so far I've failed to convince the telephone goon squad to stop.

"I can't believe you slept right through it," she says.

"I took a sleeping pill."

"You took a sleeping pill? Are you crazy? We drank two bottles of wine last night."

Who said you could sleep over? What's wrong with your own bed? That's how I want to respond. But it's a bad idea to aggravate a naked woman. There are only two reasons for a woman to sleep naked next to someone she just met. One—she is extremely comfortable with herself. Two—she has hastily decided that she is comfortable with you. Either way, she is not a woman I want to fight with at the crack-of-my-ass in the morning.

"May as well seize the day," I say, slowly sitting up. I have an eyeball-socket headache. "Coffee? I know a cute place on DuPont."

In the elevator I get the feeling her name could be Tabatha or Tammy or Tiffany. Tatiana? I don't dare address her by any of these, as I'm likely wrong. Not-Mavis is wearing the perfect day-to-night dress. Was she anticipating doing the walk of shame this morning? It's leopard print, but, like, business leopard, with a mid-thigh hem and three-quarter sleeves. Her leather oxford shoes have been recently polished. I figure she's got five years on me. Or more. Might be pushing thirty. Knees are how I tell age. She's got beginner kninkles—knee wrinkles—frowning under each knee. I picture a cartoon eyes and a nose on her kneecaps. Sad-faced clowns.

We reach my lobby and both put on sunglasses. Ha! She was prepared to spend the night. Who carries sunglasses in an evening bag?

I take her to Gigi's Bakery because counter service will make this whole thanks-and-goodbye bit go more quickly. "Their Nutella croissants are divine. Let me buy you one," I offer.

We sit outside on wobbly bistro chairs sipping espresso. Not-Mavis breaks off a piece of her croissant and tosses it to a nearby pigeon. "I won't bother leaving my number," she says.

"Enjoyed yourself that much, eh?" Bitch, buy your own croissant from now on.

"No, no. I had a lot of fun." Not-Mavis squeezes my arm. I pull away, pretending to take a last sip from my already empty cup. "Josie and Zed warned me not to try to get a second date out of you."

"Josie and Zed?"

"You know. Your friends who set us up."

"I know who Josie and Zed are," I say, quietly, hoping that if I speak quietly she'll lower her volume too. "I'm just ... surprised they said that."

"I was looking for a discreet thing. Remember, I'm married."

This is exactly why I don't go to breakfast diners with one-night stands. If I had to wait for a waitress to take care of the bill right now, I'd die. The extra five minutes would kill me. I'd clunk Not-Mavis over the head with her tiny espresso cup and kill her too. And where do Josie and Zed get off? What am I, the dregs of casual sex, bottom-feeder of blind dates? I swear I'm never having another threesome with those two again.

I refuse to watch Not-Mavis walk away in her business leopard dress, and that's one of my favourite parts. The walking away part. Women's hips are spellbinding after they've been fucked. Men too, actually. Except there's often less hip and more shoulder sway with a guy's goodbye march. Weak moment, I turn to see Not-Mavis hail a cab as she reaches Spadina.

I follow in her wake. How long has it been since I've taken a taxi?

Loitering at the intersection, I count the yellow Checker cabs driving by. The best thing to do would be to go home and sleep for a few more hours. Unplug the phone. Pull the blinds. My right arm rises. A familiar thump thump thump pulses under my jaw as a cab pulls up to the curb. "Lawrence and Bridle Path."

The cabbie harumphs. He switches on the meter.

We pass jocks in University of Toronto's Varsity Blues hoodies walking toward campus in a small huddle. The football team hasn't won a Vanier Cup since 1965. They've been losing longer than I've been alive. Put that slogan on a hoodie: "Varsity Blues: losing since before I was born." Campus fables claim the team is cursed. I think about curses a lot. How we need something titillating to blame for all our failures. How blame itself is titillating.

Blame: Latin *blasphēmāre,* "to blaspheme." Titillate: verb, Latin *tītillāre,* "to tickle." Curse: noun, Latin *cursus,* "course," as in the direction taken. *Quod est super.* I no longer study Latin.

The Varsity Blues are no longer my team.

The cab is hot and smells sickeningly sweet like Vanilla Armor All. Why didn't I drink any water at the bakery? My hangover presses on my dry tongue. I crack the window.

Outside of Davisville station, we pass a busker with dyed green hair playing "Sweet Jane" on acoustic guitar. Not the Velvet Underground version, the Cowboy Junkies version. MuchMusic still plays that video like three times a day. My Pay-TV was cut off last Thursday.

Men in grey shorts jog along the shoulder of Sunnybrook Park. Further toward the hazy horizon line, a pair of horses and riders stand stationary in a field.

Today is my third trip to the Bridle Path—a.k.a. Millionaires Row—since I moved to Toronto. I have chosen a favourite house from one of the few that isn't hidden behind hedges and high iron gates. Twenty or more of my apartments could fit inside this house. A dozen of my apartment towers could sit on the property. The façade is flanked by Corinthian columns. Not those budget Tuscan columns, oh no, Corinthian columns. Gilded street lamps flag the driveway, like they are saying "welcome to a world of happiness and supremacy." Inside, I imagine a grand staircase centred around a chandelier, marble floors, and Persian carpets, a two-storey library and an Olympic-sized swimming pool. And maybe a taxidermy African elephant head mounted above a fireplace, or something equally ostentatious and devastating.

"You know which house you're supposed to go to, right?" asks the cabbie. He thinks I'm a what? A strip-o-gram? A call girl?

"No, sorry. We can head back. Midtown is good." My words come out gurgled. Wine phlegm gags the back of my throat.

The cabbie pulls over. "You pay for the ride here first. Then I'll drive you back." His meter reads $39.50. I swallow back spit as I pass him my Visa. Silently, I will him to simply ink my card through the imprinter and have me sign. He picks up his car phone for authorization. Run, I think. Run, as he punches in my card number. Run, as he waits on hold.

I tell him, "That's my good card. That one's good."

"Declined. You wanna talk to them?" I reach for the receiver. "The cord doesn't go as far as the back seat. Come up."

Again, I picture myself running. My imaginary superhero body bolts through a row of hedges and leaps over a wrought iron fence. In each of these yards there is likely a Doberman or a pet tiger or something I'd have to wrestle. And I can't actually wrestle. Delicate ankles. My superhero fantasy has real corporeal limits. I'm not much of a dreamer. And I already have a juvenile record for shoplifting. I open the passenger side door and slump defeated beside the cabbie. The Visa representative on the phone politely chides me, "If you were a customer who paid your minimum on time, I could make an exception. But you're running a balance month after month." The cabbie shifts his gear stick from neutral to drive. I make a head gesture that I'm sure appears to him like a nod, but really it's only my neck giving up the burden of carrying my stupid head.

He parks in the loading zone behind Crestwood private high school. I am relieved as he undoes his pants in the front seat. Front seat equals blowjob. Back seat equals more. Or at least that's what the boys in my hometown taught me.

My ears fill with vacuum noise as if the world has just been punctured and everything is being sucked through a small hole. I am spared from hearing the sounds he makes. I expect him to be a rough ride. Isn't that what happens when you cheat a cabbie? A head-pushing, hip-pumping rough ride? He only rubs his hands up and down my arms, dips his fingers under the back of my dress.

Afterwards, I sit forehead to knees on the curb in front of the private school in the richest zip code in the country. When the recess bell rings and teens in navy blue cardigans and grey slacks swarm the lawn, I quickly move along.

I head down York Mills Road, past the auto-body shops and Mr. Subs and self-storage lots. Past Sleep Country Mattress and the Rogers Cable headquarters. Past the biggest liquor store in the entire province. Hardly anyone walks York Mills Road. It's a thoroughfare. A driving route. I am an obvious outcast legging it along as station wagon after station wagon whips by me.

I reach the York Mills Station, which is where I should catch the TTC, but I'm not ready to share a small space, like a subway car, with other humans. I turn down Yonge. *The Guinness Book of World Records* says that Yonge Street is the longest street in the world. *The Guinness Book of World Records* is mistaken. The longest is the Pan-American Highway. I can fact check better then those Guinness dimwits. Although Yonge may as well be the longest, since now I've doomed myself to walk it.

I make myself stop at the Bedford Park Community Centre to use the women's washroom beside the pool. My body slips out of autopilot and back into present time and place. The tile floor is slippery. Mirrors are fogged from the perpetually running showers. Old women bathe and speak a language that sounds a lot like Italian, except I don't understand a word. I edge my head into a metal sink and slurp back cold water from the tap. The cold metal faucet lets me grip it tightly—it doesn't care about what I've done.

Further down Yonge, I welcome pedestrian density and transit hubs. I am delightfully nobody in the crowd. The shopping centre at Eglinton lets me know I've almost reached Midtown. For several blocks, the buildings turn to glass and steel and become disproportionately taller. This too is comforting—how small I am in comparison. Then, a few blocks later, I'm shouldered up to Mount Pleasant Cemetery. Cherry blossoms and magnolias are at the end of their bloom. Pink petals snow down on the headstones. Spring has been warm, too warm. I feel an eyeball headache coming on again.

It isn't until I pass Summerhill that I feel the surroundings are "mine" again. The corner grocery store that is just called Food is mine. Rows of red brick houses with rock-and-roll flags instead of curtains in the windows are mine. And finally, finally, my building on St. Georges, always with a VACANCY, BACH, 1 BED, 2 BED sign posted out front.

I slip my shoes off in the elevator. Swollen feet. Almost five hours have elapsed since Not-Mavis and I left my apartment. From the hallway, I can hear my phone ringing. It rings again as I hang up my keys. A third time as I collapse into my bed. You just paid for a cab ride with a blowjob, I remind myself. What's left to lose? I pick up the phone.

"Star? Star, I got this message on my machine." I can hear my mother's utter dismay from 150 kilometres away. "It said you owed a lot of money." Yes, this also is what other flunkies and bums warned me about—creditors will track down family members, growing their phone tree of harassment.

Again, there is a ubiquitous suction, a velocity so much bigger than me. Its master force pulls confessions from my cerebral cortex or whatever part of the mammal brain holds secrets: I dropped out of school. My student loans defaulted. I owe a fuck ton of money. And I hate myself.

# 2 Sodomite

"Sodom Road exit?"

Lampoonist question. I almost answer, *Yes sir*, before the driver comically clears his throat. His hired Lincoln's front grill is so bug blemished from countless trips between Toronto and the boondocks that clearly he knows exactly which route to take. Exiting on to Bowen or Bertie would add fifteen-odd minutes to the trip. The driver's question is for amusement's sake. Sodom Road is the joke of the Niagara Peninsula. Travel south on Queen Elizabeth Way and you can't miss the radiating letters under a bald sun, or at night, the reflective aluminum letters that rush to meet your headlights. They read "Sodom Rd. Crystal Beach," with an arrow pointing to the expansive stretch of overgrown brush. The road's name nods to the late 1880s when Crystal Beach was a religious colony and Chautauqua assembly. True story. The village was settled by Jesuits or maybe Methodists who soon found more secular entertainment and more profitable ventures than Bible Camp. The Holy Trinity was replaced by a dance hall, a vaudeville theatre, and a carousel. Hailed as the "Coney Island of the North." Pity Sodom Road was never renamed. I might enjoy returning home via Vaudeville Road. Painted Pony Parkway. Something nostalgia-worthy.

Will the driver also think it clever when Sodom Road becomes Gorham Road? Gorham (like Gomorrah) Road has never earned the same heckling. It's unfair—both Sodom and Gomorrah were cities of grievous sinners, both destroyed by fire and brimstone, and so shouldn't both share equal rights to innuendo? Lewd animal butt-lust sodomy is what stuck around our pitiful noosphere. Sodom. So be it. Welcome home.

I make no attempt at eye contact in the rear-view mirror. I can't be bothered with his grin. And I don't want to invite any other jokes he may have about the backwards track of my childhood.

Over the past week, friends and acquaintances spawned our gross jokes. My return to the village is considered foolish funny, not ha-ha funny—as if I would immediately be gifted a straw hat and oversized hammer upon arrival. Torontonians believe that anywhere outside of Toronto is a pantomime stage—a place where mute actors perform a dumb show.

My farewell party was an LSD dropping and viewing marathon of *The Prisoner*. I hemmed my bachelor apartment in with back alley mattresses and borrowed blankets. Acid was supposed to be tongue-in-cheek—as in, psychedelics are the type of drugs only found in 1960s television or in small-town Ontario—but everyone around The Annex actually showed up ready to trip. A clique of Ontario College of Arts and Design students brought several giant white latex balloons. "Contact imminent," they parroted. "Turn back before it's too late." One fawn-like girl I've never seen before walked in circles wearing only a white bikini with the number 6 painted on both breasts and butt cheeks. Where did they come from? "Starla fucking Martin," they greeted me by name, "don't leave us."

As the night wore on, I recognized fewer and fewer of their faces. This panicked me at first. My skin itched. I pulled at my hair, follicle by follicle. Fawn-girl appointed herself the bad-trip nurse and calmed me by instructing me in breathing. "In. In. In," she cooed, then, "Out. Out. Out." Hours later I was said to be shouting, "I'm not a number, I'm a free man."

A few wrote their phone numbers and some intoxicated proposi-tions on my bathroom wall. "Starla fucking Martin, you can't leave this city before sucking my cock"—one example, written in lipstick. Not one of them helped me pack and haul my stuff to the curb. In Toronto, it's every asshole for themself. No farewell kisses. Maybe adieu is only bid when you're going somewhere big.

Crystal Beach's population is 3,000 year-round residents, give or take.

Once upon a time, the village was famous. Or between the twenty-fourth of May and Labour Day we were famous. Known throughout Erie and Niagara Counties in New York State, as well as around Ontario's Golden Horseshoe, we were famous for the largest dance floor in North America, the most terrifying roller coaster, allegedly, in the world. Sunbathing on white-sand beaches. Picnics on perfect lawns. Crystal Beach was where workers from the Lackawanna Steel Plant or Welland Wabasso Cotton Mill would take their staff retreats. People who didn't have to live here loved this place. I could be a tour guide, except we haven't hosted any tours for a long, long time.

The grass is parched, not gaily kept like on the Crystal Beach of yesterday's postcards. Crab grass and dandelion claim each yard. Oaks are topped with billowing caterpillar nests. Vinyl-sided bungalows hunker low to the flat earth.

The first billboard off the highway shows a collage of fraternal group emblems: the Kinsmen, the Lions, Knights of Columbus, Order of Eagles, Odd Fellows, Masonic Hall Palmers Lodge 372, and their matriarchal counterparts: the Kinnettes, the Rebekahs, and on. Just a quick glimpse of the perfectly symmetrical maple leaf wreath logo of the Kinsmen conjures the taste of hot dogs. Today, I cannot name a single fellow from the kin of beer lodge good-doers who hosted potato-sack races and Easter-egg hunts in my childhood. The brothers are a single oversimplified archetype in my mind. Only moustaches. Polo shirts. Fishing caps.

I do remember posing for photos at their Christmas food hamper giveaway. Snap. Adorable fatherless brat accepts hand-out.

The second billboard displays a similarly crowded arrangement of religious banners. Saint George's—where I was baptized Roman Catholic and prayed for god only knows how many Sundays—displayed on the top left of the sign. I always thought the exterior of our church looked like a flying saucer: short and round, a low conical roof topped with an otherworldly spherical crown of polished steel. It was an ongoing disappointment to enter and see the queue of wooden pews, like in any other church.

The stained glass was something. Or at least it was something significant to my child's sense of wonder. As a girl, I insisted on sitting next to the stained-glass window that portrayed the sixth station of the cross: Veronica wipes Jesus's face with her veil. I imagined myself as Veronica. She was there at the right moment. From out of the crowd of bystanders Veronica was chosen to receive the Holy Face, the miraculous swatch of cloth said to quench thirst, cure blindness, possibly raise the dead. One opportune moment, and Veronica became legend.

I've since learned from an Early Christianity Studies course that Veronica was not a historical figure. Why are most of the women in the Bible mostly myth? Were they always fiction, or did time fictionalize once living, breathing women?

Years before university wrecked everything, Veronica's rose-coloured lips were truly holy. On the right kind of Sunday morning, the sunshine would send a slice of pink light through the glass window and down to the marble floor. If I reached my hand out, pink light would make my fingers glow.

St. George's congregation, like the Kinsmen, has also become in my memory a lump sum of Sunday-best-dressed. Besides my own mother, I can't remember a one. Even the priest's name is consigned to oblivion.

These lapses in memory mean I am returning to the village a stranger. I am returning as a failed Torontonian and a university dropout. For four years, seven months, and twenty-eight days, I managed to live as far away from here as I could. Only a two-hour drive, really, but another fucking world.

Now I am the only passenger in the back seat of the Niagara Car Service with all my belongings audibly bouncing around in the trunk behind me. My thighs are smeared grey by the unread pages of *The Globe and Mail* that I've allowed to wilt on my lap. The early appearance of cottonwood seeds dot the humid air and make me sneeze. I am returning on the hottest day of, not only the year, but, according to 91.1 HTZ FM, the hottest spring day in the last sixty-two years. April 28, 1990.

"Air con is on the blink," the driver says. "Boss wasn't planning on fixing it until June, but this sure feels like June to me. Like July." What appears to be a gnat has drowned in the sweat on the back of his neck. I stare at the pin-sized blot, then scold myself for looking so closely at him. For looking at any of it.

This is temporary, I tell myself. A blip. I will write a novel. I'll find a sugar daddy—not a dock foreman or a plumber, but an art dealer or entertainment lawyer. I'll become a one-hit-wonder pop star. I will set myself on fire and film it. I'll do something. I'll be someone. I will.

A third billboard once welcomed countless tourists. "You Can't Beat the Beach! Crystal Beach Amusement Park, since 1889." Now there is something I remember: a sign that's no longer standing. A small mound of overturned dirt—like the grave of a beloved pet—marks where it was torn from the ground.

# 3 Painted Lady

Nine Loomis Crescent is coated in at least six layers of Lunar Eclipse—a purple shade of paint that my mother chose for its name—and to set her home apart from the neighbouring cottages. The colour absolutely realized its full potential. Too brazen for the white panorama, the neighbours viewed the house as a painted lady, a tramp. The house may as well have taught itself to say, "Hey, sailor." Purple wasn't entirely to blame.

My mother—Barbara Enrica Martin—has always been too much for Crystal Beach. Way too much woman for the local hard-bitten bachelors. Luckily for her, the beach once brought in a steady flow of single American men each summer. Barbara adopted a strict cross-border dating policy. On-and-off, her personal ad ran in *The Buffalo News* from the early '70s to the mid-'80s. She always alerted me when strange men might start calling again. Her instructions on message taking were precise: Repeat the man's name twice, spell it once. And do not sound like a nervous kid at a spelling bee. Speak clearly, like a grownup. Once and only once did juvenile curiosity get to me, and I searched the paper for her ad.

> Pleasantly Plump and Entirely Experienced. SWF 5'8" brunette. Independent, liberated, educated and sexy (double D!) Not looking for a husband, just good company. Reply if you are a kind, adventurous man under 50. Unmarried only, please.

Oh, the teenage humiliation of discovering that your mother has made public her bra size. I will never un-see it. Show me anything written in Century Condensed serif, and it's burned into my mind.

Her suitors were often men with names that Barbara had to practice to pronounce. While she sifted through her sale-rack frippery for the perfect dress, Barbara would recite the newest man's name, painstakingly, as if she could learn a new velar, an alveopalatal, a new way for her tongue to curl. "Ar-na-ud," Barbara would say again and again to her sequined mini-dress. Watching this routine, I assumed that my mother was giving her dresses male nicknames. Barbara's closet soon housed a crowd of slinky polyester *Ishmaels,* long gauzy *José Luises,* and black lace *Rémis.*

In turn, these men were all inclined to exclaim all three syllables of Barbara's name. "Bar! Bar! Ra!" Some called her from the front yard. Some hollered as they pulled up in their cars. And on hot summer nights, "Bar! Bar! Ra!" burst from the open windows of her room. Gentleman callers rarely lasted more than a few months. A well-practiced and picturesque weeper, my mother (I swear) trained her tears to weave down her cheeks like the ric-rac trim on her polyester lingerie. Each man earned a day's worth, maybe two, of grief, then she was on to the next.

I never considered that by dating umpteen men from different cities, other countries, and various other cultures and religions, she had spared me the tired enactment of nuclear family role play. I was not dragged to dinner with the sad-faced divorcé down the street. At no time did I catch her flirting with my male teachers at PTA meetings. I didn't witness her having a poorly concealed affair with the father of one of my classmates. I wasn't asked to accept new brothers or sisters into our home. I never had to share holidays or birthdays. This is what she always told me anyway, "You'll never have to share a birthday. You are my one and only baby."

I also never considered that each brief love affair was a way for her to get lost. Passed from mess to morass of passionate hands, Barbara was constantly spun in unknown directions, a dizzy course that pointed away from her gaudy beach bungalow at Nine Loomis Crescent. No, children do not recognize their parent's need to escape. Instead, I grew up believing what the locals believed, that we lived in a whorehouse.

Coincidentally, the apartment number of my recently relinquished Toronto address was also nine. Apartment number 99. Double nine. Although few people knew I occupied number 99 because I had pried the peel-and-stick numbers from my door. And when the tenants across the hall moved out, I pried the number 98 from the vacant apartment door. When 96 and 92 moved, I did the same. To further confuse visitors, I singed the elevator buttons for floors eight through twelve with a lit cigarette. The stink of burning plastic failed to set off the fire alarm. Dumpy building.

One embittered one-night-stand—who returned unannounced in the middle of the night—incited these precautions. I was awakened at 2:30 a.m., just after last call at the bars. It wasn't knocking I heard but pawing. Feeble pawing that continued for more than fifteen minutes; I watched the time pass on my digital clock. A wounded animal was on the other side of my apartment door. I refused to let it in, but after awhile I crept out of bed and crouched down on my bamboo doormat to listen to the delicate and asinine pleadings of this drunken fuck. "I don't understand why you're avoiding me," and, "You can't tell me there wasn't a connection," and, "Am I nothing to you then?" The volume rose with each question, until one question was repeatedly shouted: "Am I nothing?" I sat perfectly still on the other side of the door. It was like overhearing a domestic dispute in the adjoining apartment. Listening in, vigilant, trying to assess at what point to call the cops. Except this wasn't the next apartment over, it was mine.

The question "Am I nothing?" tormented me for weeks afterward. Why should I have to endorse someone else's existence? Most days, I barely know what's holding me to this earth. Do I go around demanding others to validate my worth? No. I do not.

I removed the numbers so that my steady rotation of no-strings lovers couldn't find their way back to me. There was no longer a tangible place for them to lodge their complaints. I figured if they got past the patchy security door at the building's entrance, they would be unable find my un-numbered apartment.

Sometimes I still imagine them—raging punk girls from The Dance Cave, melodramatic theatre geeks from school, married men who would leave their business cards on my bedside table, all of them—wandering around the hallways of my massive apartment complex. All wanting to ask me the same troubling question.

Standing on my mother's porch, I am demoted back to single nine. Barbara's brass number isn't the cheap peel-and-stick type I had pried from my old apartment, at least. Barbara's nine is oversized and art-deco-like and fixed above the door with real brass screws. The deadbolt is brass too, and there is only one, and it's not even locked. No one outside of Toronto double bolts their doors. Songbird, a Yorkshire terrier, barks as I haul my largest suitcase inside.

"Songbird. Sit. Quiet," I command. Songbird isn't the terrier I grew up with. This is Songbird II. I don't allow this Songbird to lick my face as I bend down to pet her. The terrier dances in figure eights around my hands, nervously eyeing me as if I'm going to smack her. Then, as soon as I stand upright again, she rolls over to show her belly. "You missed your chance for a belly rub, buddy." I step over her, kicking my flip-flops across the floor. The ceiling fan that whirls above me is new.

I get earfuls about Barbara's latest home renovations in each of our telephone conversations. Now I stand agog, seeing the changes with my own eyes. This is not my mother's kitchen. This is the kitchen of a sane person with sane tastes. Where is the avocado-coloured oven? Where is the smiling sun-faced clock? The refrigerator magnets made of walnuts with googley eyes? I fling open a cupboard to find rows of aluminum canisters lined up and labelled: BROWN RICE, OATS, CORNMEAL. I open each cupboard and drawer in this imposter kitchen, run my finger along the inside of drawers to find that there is no dust, no spilled salt or crummy garlic powder. Clean. Even the empty wine bottles in the recycling bin are washed and sorted by colour.

This isn't the kind of makeover that happens overnight. How long has it been since I visited? I count months in my head as I shuffle undented, not-yet-expired canned goods around in the pantry closet. Finally, I discover something familiar: my mother's canning. "You're so stupid," I self-admonish as I wrestle with the lid from a can of peaches. The jar makes a rewarding hiss under my sweaty palm. Jabbing at the slippery fruit with my fingers, I slide an entire half peach past my lips, letting the syrup leak down my chin. Mouth full, I have the fortitude to tour the rest of the house.

The Martin home is a one-storey, winterized cottage bungalow just like every other house on the block. Standard six rooms: two bedrooms, living room, kitchen, dining, bath. Count the screened-in back porch and you've got seven. For a mere 1,400 square feet, I am lost. I find that the bathroom has been wiped completely white. White linoleum floor, white acrylic tub, white dressing room light bulbs around the mirror—a bathroom from a Howard Johnson hotel.

In the living room, an overstuffed pastel tropical print sectional sofa ties up two walls. A glass-topped rattan coffee table dominates the floor space. The twenty-seven-inch television set doesn't have rabbit ears like our old one, but it's not quite a new model either. The room screams liquidation warehouse. Clearance tags all around.

On the wall, a portrait of pregnant Barbara still hangs. She stands as proud and expectant as ever in the sepia-orange cast of the summer of '68. The sun haloes her long, centre-parted hair, and a macramé belt is slung below her pregnant belly.

"Macramé," I exclaim. Songbird runs to my side with her ears raised. "She finally got rid of the macramé," I tell the terrier. There's not a single plant hanger, lampshade, or owl. I inhale deeply, expecting the earthy stink of macramé jute—the odour of my upbringing. All I can smell is peach syrup on my chin.

Then, not a minute later, the awful sentimental aroma meets me as I enter my old bedroom. Jesus fucking Christ, literally, Jesus of macramé. The wall hanging is half as tall as I am. Wooden beads for eyes. A row of seashells make a mouth. Unlike the Jesus depicted in the stained-glass windows of Saint George's Church, macramé wall-hanging Jesus is completely naked. A flaccid rope of a penis dangles between his knotted legs. I doubt we had this gem when I was a kid. She acquired new macramé? Suddenly the original motion picture soundtrack from *Jesus Christ Superstar* rips through me, Yvonne Elliman singing, "I Don't Know How to Love Him." My teeth clench, as if tightening my jaw might keep me from remembering this unfortunate torch ballad. For five years, I've avoided John Lennon, Cat Stevens, Carole King, Buffy Sainte-Marie, Jefferson Airplane and Starship, *Hair, Gypsy, Godspell, The Wiz*, and at all costs, *Jesus Christ Superstar*. The soundtracks of my mother's nefarious moods.

I hop onto the bed and swiftly knock macramé Jesus from his nail. He slides down the wall behind the wicker headboard and onto the floor. Songbird darts under the bed after him. Without Jesus, my old bedroom walls are completely bare but for filmy outlines of absent posters that I adored as a teen, rectangle-shaped fades on the floral wallpaper. I wonder where my Siouxsie and the Banshees "Kiss in the Dreamhouse" tour poster is? It better not have ended up in the trash. It's got to be a collectible now.

Tiny terrier sneezes sound from under the bed. "If you're chewing on that Jesus, so help me," I bang on the wall. How many days before my mother notices Jesus is gone? How long before we fight over it?

Our first fight could be as little as four hours away. Barbara will pull into the driveway just as the sun is setting, gunning her Ford Fiesta a little faster than usual. *My baby*, she'll call. *You're home.* A minute later she'll be pacing the house, chattering, *I bought you fish sticks and canned tuna for your lunches. You still eat fish, right? Fish are vegetarian, right? You know where the towels are? Do you like the new sofa? I love Santa Fe décor. I'm thinking of returning these blinds. Wrong shade of pink. Is this your stuff in the hall? My god, so many suitcases. They're taking up the whole entrance way. Why don't we bring all of this into your room?* That's when it will happen. *Star*, she'll say gravely. *How long have you been here? A few hours, tops, and you think you can just tear down my handicrafts?* She'll tap her size-nine foot, and I will shrink a little each time the comfortable rubber sole meets the floor. *You think you can just waltz right in and ...*

"Get out from under there." I dangle my head over the side of the bed and whistle. Songbird looks up with a dust bunny stuck to her nose. The macramé corpse lies crumpled against the baseboard.

I had thought about being back in my old bedroom. Or at least I thought I'd thought about it when Barbara first suggested I come home. I thought, I lived here until I was eighteen, what's another year? I thought, small town quiet will do me good. "Without great solitude, no serious work is possible." Who said that? Picasso? Van Gogh? One of those post-impressionist dudes. I thought, there is literally nowhere else I could live rent-free. I thought, I'm making a reasonable choice.

I didn't imagine the furious thud of my body suddenly rolling onto my bedroom floor. Nor the sharp crane of my neck as I edged my head under the bed. I urged my eyes to swiftly adjust to the shadow, frantically scanning the wall just above the skirting board. Inches away from fallen Jesus I spot the first small squiggly "x" drawn on the wallpaper in Jiffy Marker. Half a dozen more "x"s sprawl upward, some in black or blue permanent marker, others in faded number two pencil. For a moment, I want to yank my bed away from the wall to count how many "x"s there are. Instead I press my forehead to the parquet floor. The dust itches my nostrils. The sugar from the canned peaches tingles a small cold sore inside my mouth. Impulsively I bite down on it, hard, and tongue that first lick of blood. Why did I come back here?

Songbird is still after something. The terrier butts her cold nose against my cheek a couple times, then resumes scratching at the corner of a flat, rectangular crate wrapped in plastic.

"What is it? What's under there, Songbird?"

The crate must weigh more than a sack of potatoes. I yank at the heavy plastic packaging, stirring up more dust. Songbird sneezes again. She emerges filthy. I pat the terrier off before ripping into the plastic. AUCTIONS AND APPRAISALS SOLD is stamped across the chipboard crate cover. What mysterious thing did my mother buy? She never buys mysterious things. The crate is as long as a coffin. I use my set of keys to pry the lid open.

Inside is a painted wooden signboard of two fat cartoon sailors standing in comic fear. Their lips are perfect red Cheerios. Evil yellow eyes glare at them through thick indigo paint. "Are you afraid of the dark?" written in bubble letters floats above the sailors' heads. The auctioneer's paperwork reads, "Circa 1960s Approximate Item Size in Inches: 92" Height, 49" Length, 1" Depth. Approximate item weight: 50 Lbs. Condition: Good overall, colours. Used as a stunt in the Laugh in the Dark ride at Crystal Beach, Ontario, for many years. Sold for $90."

"Look at that," I marvel. "It's the ugliest thing I've ever seen. I love it so much it hurts my eyes." I turn back to the now bare wall space above the bed. Just what this room needs—something new and utterly appalling.

# 4 Weak

Awake?

Put me back in the dark nothing. I don't wanna be woke again.

Or do I?

Or am I dreaming?

What have I got to dream about anyway?

A vineyard? Gypsy jazz? Chiffon stockings and Russian red lipstick? Saturday matinees at the picture house? Boardwalk strolls? Midnight boom in the ballroom? I could dance my way to heaven. Men's fat billfolds? Girls' French knickers? Eating hot nuts on the deck of a grand steamer ship? Fun-house mirrors? Ferris wheel? Flying bobs? Roller coaster?

Roller coaster.

My scream could be heard all the way to heaven.

Can the dead dream? Or only remember?

And what use are dreams or memories to me? I'm no master of either. I'm right confused—where, when, why, what, who, and how now? And worse than confused, I'm weak.

I need bebop keys and a warm body.

# 5 Bitch

"Down by the bay where the watermelons grow. Back to my home, I dare not go ..."

My bed rests in the exact same place it did when I was a child. Head in the west, toes in the east, and flush against a south-facing window. And in the same childlike way, I wriggle my feet from under the sheets and press my toes to the delicate aluminum mesh that separates me from the morning heat. My chipped glitter toenail polish twinkles in the sun. A collection of dead ladybugs lines the windowsill. One red shell sticks to a small tear in the screen window. She almost got out of here, I think. In Southern Ontario, ladybugs infest houses in late October to hibernate in our basements or attics, and again in April when they wake up. The heat wave must have cooked them on the wrong side of the window before they made it back to the tall grass. I crush one under my big toe. Its beetle body pops like bubble wrap.

Last night I left my worldly belongings packed inside their boxes and cases and instead turned my undivided attention to mounting the fun-house stunt above my bed. It was a trick to be seen, with the electric drill clumsy in one hand, while the other hand worked together with the top of my head or my knee or whatever body part I could employ to help hold the heavy stunt in place. The metallic taste of drywall screws are still in my mouth. I neglected to even unpack my toothbrush last night.

When hung, the stunt dominated the room with its hideousness.

"You're not very scary," I told it. "You have an amateur disregard for physical proportion and your brushstrokes are muddy. You're not a scary stunt."

I dozed off fast, then woke up routinely throughout the night. I thought I heard knocking. Once I rolled out of bed to make my way to the peephole, only to discover that I no longer had a peephole or a door or an apartment. No street lamps or headlights leaked through the bedroom window. No cars zoomed up and down the street. It was so pitch-black, a man could have been standing in the corner of my bedroom and I wouldn't have seen him. Once this thought was in my head, my mind spun with it. Then I lay awake trying to unspin. There's no man in here. There's no man. No man. Man. You're imagining things. You're hysterical. I know you are, but what am I? Pogonophobia is spelled P-O-G-O ... Go back to sleep. Infinity.

Now, at 8:27 a.m., Barbara is awake in the next room, singing one from her repertoire. "For if I do, my mother would say. Did you ever see a fox inside a box? Down by the bay."

Barbara is a Fauvist painting in her orange kaftan, standing in her tidy periwinkle blue kitchen. Yesterday's violet eye shadow flakes down her cheeks. Like me, she must have gone to bed without so much as washing her face. I am a pencil stroke of a woman next to her, pale legs planted in a pair of deerskin slippers.

She puts a mug of coffee in my hands and sings, "Down by the bay bay bay. My baby. My baby Star," she trills, then says, "I didn't have the heart to wake you last night when I got home. I just watched you sleeping through the bedroom door, like I used to do." And then—without a breath in between—says, "It was bad, when they tore the park apart. Auctioneers showed up to sell off the rides, everything. Some suits from across the border bought the old

40

wooden roller coaster. Awful. Then they said it was too expensive to ship, so it sat there like a trash heap with keep away signs tacked all over it." Barbara gestures air finger quotes around "keep away" as if she is using the word disparagingly, but she's not—she means literal "keep away" signs.

"Then there was this fire. The funhouse was burned to ash, the abandoned roller coaster too. Everybody says it was arson. Half the town came out to watch the blaze. Ash all over the park grounds. Did you know that Tommy Tu is still a firefighter? He looks good for his late forties. I mean, he looks really good. I almost asked him out on a date once."

"Ma," I bark. I need more coffee before Barbara starts talking about men. "Are you telling me all this because you saw that I opened the auctioneer's crate?"

"I can't believe I bought that old stunt," Barbara muses. "You sure loved that ride. I used to have to hold you in the trolley car seat so you wouldn't leap out onto the track. I'd say, 'Look at the lion' or 'There's a ghost!' You never cried like the other children. 'How does it work, Mama?' you wanted to know. 'Who's making those ghosts dance?' You drove me nuts with your questions. You were always too smart for your own good."

"Thanks, Ma."

"So one day I took you to the park before they opened, remember that? And we had Ralphie Finberg give us a tour, remember him? Ralphie showed us around with the lights on so you could finally see the mechanics. Not every mother takes their kid on a backstage tour like that. Remember?"

I shake my head "no," wishing I did remember. This amnesia is beginning to unnerve me. As if I've stepped into an imposter's life. I remember the ride, but not the ride operator. Just like I remember my old church, but not the priest. My high school, but not the name of the principal.

"Well, anyway, you weren't so impressed. Metal wires and duct tape on the ceiling and the floor. Pay no attention to the man behind the curtain," Barbara sighs. "Oz. I'm quoting *The Wizard of Oz*. If ever a wonderful wiz there was, the Wizard of Oz is one because because because because—"

"Ma!" I interrupt again. If she starts singing musicals we'll be stuck in a soundtrack loop for hours. "So you bought the stunt for me?" It makes sense that she wouldn't buy something so impractical for herself. Costly knee-jerk emotional purchases are commonplace for me, but not for Barbara. I reach my pointer finger—just my pointer finger—out and cautiously hook it around her plump thumb.

"I don't know what I was thinking," she turns away from me to refill her coffee mug. I have spoiled her surprise and stolen the moment when she—the good mother—presents me with a genuine artifact from my foggy, happy childhood memories.

"I love it," I offer (the ugly thing). "I hung it over my bed last night." (She already knows this. She's been in my room while I was sleeping.)

"That prop weighs a ton, Starla. It's not meant to hang on the wall."

Why can't she just say she got me a gift? Say something normal, like *I'm glad you like it.* "There's six drywall screws in it," I tell her.

Barbara snaps her lips at me. Each snap is surely meant to announce the argument she wants to have with me.

"You think I never learned how to put up a shelf or hang a picture in the time I lived alone?"

Silence. Lip smack. Silence.

"You just said you bought it for me. Well, I hung it up where I can appreciate it."

"Every hole you make is one I'm going to have to fix later when I turn your bedroom into a den."

"A den? What do you need a den for?"

"What? I can't have a den? You think I only like books when I'm at work?"

"Last week on the phone you said my room was always waiting. You never said anything about a fucking den."

"Ooph, the bitch is back," Barbara says, saccharine sweet. "Try not to be defensive, honey. Don't bite the hand that feeds you."

# 6 I Am Dead

What's this? Auctioneers. Trash heap. When fire? Who fire? Figures my life was burned to ash. Why must I learn of this new tragedy? I already have yesterday's grief for all eternity.

Why must I feel or need or be?

Darling girl threw her weight into that drill. Her, I certainly felt—the frustration of her elbow grease, her sad, sad exertion. I woke up as she drove the screws clean through.

I woke up mute and paralyzed, if I can be paralyzed without a breathing body. Bit by bit, the scene came into being. First thing I noticed is she must be about my age, and pretty, even with that awful bobbed hairstyle. By the time she was finished and settled in to sleep, I could manage to knock. What a cheat. I can't be back here just for knocking. I ought to be able to dance and wail again.

I ought to mention that I am dead, though not home and dry. If you ask me, heaven is hogwash. Least I haven't seen any pearly gates.

Laugh in the Dark. Now there's a place I sure have seen with my own two eyes. That ride was the mother of the amusement park. A mixed-up mother, part fun house, part haunted house, and part trolley ride. For fifty-three years, she took in an assortment of very odd children: the stunts. She gave each stunt equal affection. Each had their three seconds in which a dedicated light would buzz on as the trolley car approached, and each sprang up to frighten and delight her squealing patrons.

The first-born stunts were wartime cartoon characters: Maggie and Jiggs, Wimpy, Popeye shaking his bulbous Yankee fist—*I yam what I yam*. Hand painted on chipboard, like the stunt that now hangs on this young lady's wall. Stunts were proxy for our great generation by their colour palette alone. Hopeful and heroic colours. Fantasia blue. Casablanca yellow.

During the 1950s, Laugh in the Dark prosperously adopted an ark's worth of animal stunts: the dragon, the lion, mules, dogs, cats, swamp rats, the crocodile, and several unidentifiable critters that did more than simply spring up. They roared. They growled.

After the animals did it, every stunt had to make a racket of its own. Coffin lids creaked. Sirens rang. The skeletons danced to ragtime rhythm. The one true voice, the grandstand, was Laffing Sal, the *papier maché* mechanical lady clown who cackled through her oversized set of gap-teeth at grown men and girl children alike. We all thought Sal would die laughing. Guffaw herself into oblivion. She went cold even before the ride's last run. I remember now. She was a sign of the end, like a stopped clock. I bet poor Sal never saw it coming.

No, Laugh in the Dark kept her children, her stunts, innocent. She held them all in her great labyrinthine arms of wires and ropes and pulleys, letting go just long enough for them to perform their perpetual spectacle. It was not for them to know about war or bank crises or moral panic. Without a clue or a care for the changes outside their black-painted walls, they shrieked and roared and sprang up and sprang up and sprang up.

Is that what I am now? A stunt, springing up from my dark hiding place, again and again like someone's pulling my strings?

Now, if I say that Laugh in the Dark was the mother, then I likewise say The Cyclone coaster was the father. Vicious coaster. Cruel daddy.

I ought to mention that I am dead.

Not that anyone hears a word I say.

# 7 Freeloader

We enter the local pharmacy and Barbara says, "If you need to buy condoms, don't buy them here. They like to gossip." Her voice carries from the neon "open" sign at the entrance all the way to the locked medical shelves at the back. This will surely be one of many attempts to humiliate me throughout the day. My homecoming must be marked by some disgrace. The heavy-chinned woman behind the counter greets us with a sideways smile.

"Starla Martin, I haven't seen you since your high school graduation. I'm Tamara Matveev's mother." She eyes our purchases before shoving them into a plastic bag.

"You remember Tamara Matveev," says Barbara. "She's still here, too."

"Yup. Still here," tsks Tamara Matveev's mother. "For now, anyway."

Barbara perches her elbow on my shoulder, tugs a lock of my hair playfully. The two mothers grin at one another—a parental understanding passes between them. Somehow this is even more uncomfortable than when she forbade me to buy condoms. "Still here," was Barbara's wording, as if I've been sponging off her this whole time. Still here. I haven't even been home twenty-four hours.

"I'm going to get this one a job at the Fort Erie library. Then we'll live together and work together," says Barbara. A sour taste percolates in the back of my throat. When did I agree to take a job at the library? "Maybe we can find a handsome, wealthy father and son to go on double dates with."

The two mothers laugh. Theirs is a joke that can only be laughed at—the comedy of adult children still living with their parents, and the crack about the wealthy prince who will one day ride up on his steed.

My guts churn as she leads me back to the car, aches as I fasten the seatbelt. Can anyone feel fully grown when sitting in the passenger seat while a parent drives?

"I don't expect you to pay rent," Barbara tells me as we speed down Garrison Road into Fort Erie. Fort Erie, parent town of Crescent Park, Ridgeway, Stevensville, and Crystal Beach. The houses grow a little taller the further east we go (some a whole three storeys high), the lawns slightly more manicured. Fort Erie has a strip mall and strip clubs, a horse racing track and a golf course, a few Chinese restaurants and greasy-spoon diners, one barber shop with an old-fashioned red and white pole and one hair salon with a sun-blanched poster of Debbie Harry in the window, and a library—where my mother has worked for the last sixteen years. "Just get your debts under control," Barbara tells me. "How the hell did you ..."

Barbara's greatest, and perhaps only, asset is her lack of debt. Buying her washer and dryer through Sears layaway is the closest she's gotten to a loan.

"I mean, that amount of debt is horrendous ..."

Her house was bought by Raymond Brock, my estranged father. Brock got our then-unwinterized beach bungalow for the dirt-cheap price of $18,000, cash up front, in 1969. A draft dodger, dropout, and "Richie Rich"—as Barbara calls him—my father installed a furnace, had some insulation blown in between the walls, laid hardwood parquet flooring, planted a lilac bush in the back yard. Barbara has toured me through Raymond's handiwork many times, pointing out, "This was him," and, "that was him." Raymond moved back to the USA a couple years before President Jimmy Carter promised to pardon draft dodgers. I was barely walking then, so everything from the herringbone pattern of our parquet floor to Carter's electoral campaign promises are nothing but Barbara's say-so. I must have inherited my small hands and feet from the Brock bloodline. Barbara wears a size-nine shoe. I have her big nose, though, and the trademark Martin gap between my front teeth.

"And that's why I never pay with credit. Never."

I might bear a grudge or suffer lost-daddy issues, but instead I think of him as a donor, twice, literally. Before leaving, Raymond signed the house over to my mother. The house is in Barbara's name and only her name. Likewise, my birth certificate lists no father. Occasionally Barbara claims she'll go after him for child support, that she was owed a big paycheque from a rich family like his. "But who needs 'em, the fatheads" is her credo of independence. Instead, Barbara applied for the Ontario Mother's Allowance program and lived welfare cheque to welfare cheque. When I was in grade school, she took a part-time job as a book shelver, then a library assistant, and eventually—with a few night school courses under her belt—a small-town librarian. Barbara struck waste-not, want-not balance. She maintained the house and raised a kid without a lick of help—not even a nearby grandparent to babysit. Her financial life, like her romantic one, was always made known to me.

"Money troubles will ruin your life ..."

For this reason, when the ATM sucked up and refused to spit out my first Visa card, I kept it a secret. When the manager at my bank told me my account was frozen until I paid my minimum, another secret. I didn't tell her my student loan defaulted because I dropped one course and failed another. I concealed my ever-mounting money troubles until I owed a total of $48,290. I'm a fairly skilled liar, and even better at keeping secrets, but $48,290 is my confession price. When I confessed to Barbara, I imagined I would expire. The light in my Toronto apartment grew darker, the air more heavy and humid. I hoped I would implode over the shame of being a bad daughter. But here I am, standing before the brick, boxy, one-storey town library.

So now, what is left to do but hold my chin up as I hold the heavy glass door open for my mother and march in behind her? What is left to do but smile as she introduces me to her co-workers? To shake hands with a solid grip.

"Take your time with the application," Barbara instructs me as she hands me a clipboard and pen. "I'm not the only one making the hiring decisions. And don't be too clever. Got it?"

The beanbag chair in the nearby kids' story pit looks like a cozy and ironically appropriate seat, but I sit at the grownup work desks. The application asks standard questions: education, former employers, acquired skills. I write: University of Toronto Bookstore, file clerk and cashier, September 1986 to January 1989. The phone number I remember off by heart. My old boss should give me a glowing reference since I slept with him four times—about once for each year of employment. Plus, I never argued when I was stationed at the widely despised returns desk. If anything, I found solace in the scores of other students who were dropping classes and returning textbooks within the first few weeks of each term.

Then there are the qualitative questions: Why do you want to work at Fort Erie Public Library? And: Summarize one of your favourite books in fifty words or less.

I write: I love books! At University of Toronto, I studied a breadth of history, anthropology, and literature—from Greco-Roman mythology to Victorian novels to art history to science fiction. (I failed to declare a major.) I am familiar with Dewey Decimal

Classification. I have worked with microfiche and aperture cards and enjoy helping others with research or school projects.

I write: One of my favourite books is *Life Before Man* by acclaimed Canadian author Margaret Atwood. The three characters, Elizabeth, Nate, and Lesje, are each trapped in their own way by societal expectation and unhappiness. Like many of Atwood's novels, the connections between past and present, gender roles, and death are the main themes.

I do not write: I never understood why Elizabeth and Lesje didn't get it on. Or: I own a signed Canadian first edition. I paid fifty dollars for it at a rare book auction.

"Give it at least a week," Barbara says as she takes my application. She's wearing her nametag now: ASK ME. I'M A LIBRARIAN. I bite back the urge to tell her that, actually, a librarian is someone with a degree in library studies. "You'll have to start with weekend shifts. The one to nine p.m., Fridays and Saturdays. Bookshelvers start at five dollars an hour, so you might want to look for something else too. There's a help-wanted section on the bulletin board by the magazine rack." I stare just past her shoulder to a display of bestsellers. Library visitors can add their names to the wait list for copies of *The Stand* by Steven King. My stomach gurgles again. I spot a copy of *Medicine River* by Thomas King, which I had started to read in a Literary Anthropology class before I dropped out. I also snap up a copy of *The Complete Poems: 1927–1979* of Elizabeth Bishop.

"Can you check these out for me?" I ask Barbara.

"You just got here, but don't go burying your head in books. You get so reclusive. You have to get out there, get work lined up now before the high school kids are out for the summer. Check the Fort Erie Race Track, maybe. I bet the beer girls at the golf course make decent tips. You get the regular paycheque coming in, and I'll show you how a payback plan works. Deal?"

"Yes, I'll keep looking," I choke out my words. "I'll be working in no time."

# 8 Inside this Picture

Go.

In.

Sit beside.

Your mother.

Perform actions of attachment.

Act tender and maybe real tenderness will follow.

Here sits Barbara cross-legged on my bed. I am dripping wet in a small towel—shower steam still thick behind me. At a standstill in my bedroom door, I try to call off the many memories of her materializing everywhereallthetime, of growing up overwhelmed by her pervasive presence, her disregard for privacy. Or her flip side, her talent for ignoring me for weeks on end—usually timed with new romances or with break-ups. Always one extreme or the other, like having two different mothers, neither of them family-sitcom nurturing.

She's always at her apex in the morning before she begins her routine. Jovially caffeinated, sing-song bright, still robed in her chiffon nightgown. Her huge breasts beached on top of her belly make her look like some sort of a magnificent mermaid. Maybe she came from the lake? And I am a human child she stole? Will she devour me one day, like Lamia? Don't demonize her, you terrible daughter, I scold myself. My familial bonds are defective.

The right thing is to say, "Good morning," and, "Did you sleep well?" What stops me is the sight of one of my suitcases unzipped on the floor. In her hand is my red and white framed lenticular print by Barbara Kruger, number three in a series of only six. "Help I'm locked inside this picture," the caption declares in Kruger's signature Futura Bold Oblique font. Barbara's fingers better not be greased up with her bogus Avon Pearls and Lace hand lotion.

"I bought that in New York," I take a deep breath and say. "At the Annina Nosei Gallery." My mother shifts over on my bed, making room for me. I pull the bath towel tightly around my chest and sit beside her. "Four years ago, I guess, five? I took the Greyhound bus. I was so nervous to go to SoHo my first time. Before that, I'd never ventured from Museum Mile, you know, Fifth Avenue. SoHo was branching out, big time. I dressed for the occasion. Well, my dress was a cut-up, oversized black T-shirt from Zellers. But my shoes were Vivienne Westwood stilettos, late '70s, black leather, and those heavy metal details that tell-tale Westwood. Anyone who knows shoes would recognize those Westwoods, you know? I found them at the Good fucking Will in Newmarket. Twenty-five dollars! Twenty-five dollars to feel like I could march on into the Barbara Kruger show."

Barbara stares at me blankly.

"It's almost as good as that time we saw the identical rocking chair to Nonno's selling for eight hundred dollars at that antique store," I explain. "Eight hundred dollars, but Nonno got his for ten." Barbara half-smiles in recognition, nods her head. We can have a conversation, I encourage myself. She's listening.

"I remember the gallery being ridiculously quiet—a mid-afternoon on a weekday," I continue. "The silence made the Krugers seem so amped up. She, um, works with all these consumer messages, you see? Like, she says stuff like, 'Money can buy you love' and 'Buy me I'll change your life' and 'When I hear the word culture I take out my check book.' That piece really got me. The photo was of a ventriloquist's dummy. Not the body, just the strange grinning face, with the blown up text, 'When I hear the word culture I take out my check book.' Like the art itself is making fun of the buyer who can afford the art."

"Like you?" asks Barbara.

"I guess so." I pause. "Sure, like the joke is totally on me, on all of us."

Barbara's facial expression appears to be neutral as I recount the story, so I keep going. My mother knows capitalism is bullshit, right? She was a hippie. She's a single mother. And so I admit to her, "I wish I would have thought of that first. Standing in that gallery, I felt like Kruger and I are alike, or, like, we all think alike. We're all in this rat race, right?" I ask, using one of her hippie expressions, rat race. "We're all force-fed the same dumbed-down ideology. I understood then how clearly the tyranny and the irony of life are totally interchangeable, you know? In another time or place I could be Barbara Kruger, showing at the Whitney, at the Met. If I just was braver. More ambitious. If I just turned these brainwashed messages into art at exactly the right time. I could be a Barbara Kruger or somebody. We all could. It's timing, really. Timing and the will to just go for it."

My mother hands the print to me. The bath towel starts to inch down my bare torso as I hold it in my hands.

"You think I don't know who Barbara Kruger is?" asks my mother. "You think only snot-nosed college flunkies like you read *Art in America*."

"Ma?"

"You think the town library is a joke. How many times did I have to hear that bullshit? Well, Miss La Fucking Da, we carry *Art in*

*America* and *Fuse Magazine* and another one ... I can't remember it's name because you're pissing me off right now."

"Great." I'm sure I sound sarcastic. "Congratulations."

"You think you're so much smarter than your hick mother?"

"No. I never said that." She gets up from my bed; her throat flushes pink. What is happening? I replay the conversation to pinpoint when exactly I pissed her off. Barbara drops the Kruger onto the bed beside me. I raise my voice as she stands over me, "Come on, we're going to fight over art?"

"We're going to fight over art," she mocks me in an odd attempt at a British accent.

"You're the one who went snooping in my suitcase." My pulse chimes in my temples with anger. "How about we fight over, I dunno, the fact that you're a relentless busybody who always goes through my stuff?"

"I was looking for your address book. You should call a friend. You get strange when you don't have anyone to talk to."

"No, Ma, I get strange when I'm forced into these ludicrous conversations with you."

"How much money did you spend to prove you're better than your hick mother? Never mind. I don't want to know about *your stuff*. I don't give a goddamn." She slams my bedroom door behind her.

The Kruger only cost $300. It was a lesser piece in 1985 when I purchased it. It's gone up in value since. More then double. But I'll never let it go. "Help I'm locked inside this picture" is mine mine mine.

# 9 Sad Rubble

Lana Turner tears, what do you know? The girl puts on a real show. Like she knows I'm watching. No joke. She keeps looking right at me. It almost gives me the creeps. That's rich! The living giving the dead the creeps.

I haven't a clue why I'm back, why I must watch over Crystal Beach, especially now that the park's torn down. Loop de loop.

Maybe I'm back to bop with this crybaby.

Maybe she'll be more fun than the last dead hoofer.

It takes everything I got to hitch a lift on her shoulder as she rides her funny rusted bike. How she wobbles on those nearly flat tires! Put a hopping mad beauty like her on a child's bike and you got a clown act.

*Take me to the park. Let's see something to cry about*, I whisper to her, and, surprise, baby hears me. She rides right up to the jagged wire fence, and I boil over. Is that gutted shore really my home, my playground? No boardwalk anymore. No Ferris wheel or gondola. No jazz, I bet. No good-time cottages. No hotels. Nothing but burnt-out boondocks for as far as my phantom eyes can see. But still, I want to see more. I want to see where the roller coaster once stood. The girl spins one-eighty at the "no trespassing" sign. To hell if I'm turning back now.

*Enter*, I hiss, and she slips through the jagged split in the chain-link fence. I'm stronger here. This sad rubble still gives me strength. Or is it the girl? She hears me. Shall I pretend to care what has brought her to me? What brought about those tears to her lovely, sulking eyes? Nah, nah, she can be flipping her wig over any old thing, just as long as she carries me. A first-prize kewpie doll is what she is, except one with a woman's boiling blood. I know what it is to be hot. This corpse can still feel heat.

Oh, I'll say it again—this corpse can feel the heat. Rage or libido, give me both in turns. Right now, there's only rage. Not a single track from my beloved, wretched roller coaster. Ashes, ashes, it all burned down.

This place ain't nothing without the siren sound of my screaming.

I'm not through with screaming yet.

I'll regain my voice. Better believe it.

# 10 Slut

The last time I was here I was young and carefree.

Isn't that how childhood should be observed? Care. Free. What a concept. This cracked slab of concrete is where I would have boarded the sky ride. I'm certain that I stood exactly here, waiting for the turquoise-blue gondola to coast down. This sky ride was one of the few that Barbara would go on. She'd squeeze my hand in strong pulses as we floated above Lake Erie. It didn't matter how old I got, her hand was always bigger than mine.

She thinks Laugh in the Dark was my favourite, and she probably remembers what I liked better than I do. But as soon as I was tall enough, I was a Gravitron girl. I liked the '80s rides. I liked spinning. And Gravitron was the only ride without seat belts or safety bars! I would struggle to reach my arm out in front of me, only to have gravity slap it back down against the vinyl padding. But the best was riding beside Lynn Upper so we could pretend the centrifugal force was pushing our bodies together. We kissed one summer, inside the mirrored room at the Magic Carpet fun house. After that, she got a boyfriend right away.

I search but can't figure out where the Gravitron stood. Barbara was right, the park is completely torn up. A double tornado would have been kinder. Exposed iron cables try to hook my ankles. Ripped asphalt. Oily ash. Charred grass. Cremated scrap. It smells like I'm about to have a seizure.

I stumble farther into the abandoned ruin. Why did I feel compelled to come here? This place is the last stop before oblivion.

The thought spreads itself across the ruined landscape: I. Want. To. Die.

Suicidal thinking is a paralysis in my body. It begins with a tingle in my fingers and toes, then my knees grow so numb I can't stand anymore. Why can't it be as simple as burying my head in the rubble? I can actually remember the first time I willed myself to suffocate to death. I was face down in the sand dune at Sandbanks Provincial Park, begging god to make me stop breathing.

Mr Rossi, our science teacher, pulled me up by my arm to lead me back to the school bus. "Why is it always you who holds up the rest of the class?" he said—the entire field trip waiting for my antics to be over. None of the other students were scolded for throwing sand at my face or pushing me or calling me a "slut." It's less trouble to wrist-slap a runt, I suppose. Only eight years old and dubbed a slut. I doubt those kids even knew what they were saying. But I knew. I knew the meaning of slut at an early age.

The first time I heard that word, "slut," it was spoken by one of my mother's boyfriends; the one whose beard smelled like a Christmas tree. Awful synchronism: his name was Noël. Pine-scented beard oil and a name like that made a permanent association in my mind. I hate Christmas still. Or, worse than hate, a few times—when I've found myself at a shopping mall with a stinking real tree on display—I've become miserably turned on. This particular lascivious reflex makes me hate myself, which is much harder than hating Christmas.

The free counsellor at U of T's student services told me, "Lucky for you this self-hatred, as you call it, doesn't interfere with your studies. You've got a 4.1." I was a no-show at my fourth or fifth counselling appointment, not exactly sure how many appointments I made it to, and my grades bombed the following semester. After that, being a fuck-up became very regular.

I no longer need to rely on olfactory memory alone to trigger self-hatred. I have proof of Noël right beside me at night. After the first time he visited my room, I drew a little red "x" on the wall, low down beside my bed where the floral comforter meets the floral wallpaper, out of sight. And isn't this what survivors of childhood sexual abuse want? Proof? Some concrete evidence that confirms we didn't make this shit up. I've read *Kiss Daddy Goodnight*. I should consider myself fortunate that I have the validation of an x. And another x. Another xxxxxxxxxxxxxxxxxxxxxxxxxxxxxx.

At a glance (because I will never actually count them), the x's that still remain on my wall remind me that Noël lasted an unusually long time as one of my mother's dates. More than two years. Long enough for me to remember the holes in the upholstery in the back seat of his red Datsun. I remember him barbequing hamburgers on our patio. I even remember his corduroy slippers padding around the kitchen in the morning. But once he enters my bedroom, in my memory, he becomes a negative space. I was violated by a silhouette. A silhouette that smelled like pine and had an itchy beard.

I still wonder why Barbara kept a child molester around the longest. Was he extra charming with her, extra patient and tender and fun for her, so he could have ongoing access to me?

Barbara was always drawn to vulture-like men who came on strong and overpowering and insatiable. Men who watched me enter and exit the bathroom. Men who found reasons to sit next to me on the sofa. Men who said, "Are you sure you're only thirteen?" and "Pretty girls are supposed to smile," and "I'll teach you how to mow the lawn/drive a car/mix a drink/iron a shirt/tie a tie," and "Your future husband will thank me," and "It's just a joke, right, Barbara? Tell her it's just a joke." And Barbara laughed along, always advising me to "Enjoy it while you can. There will come a day when you'll be insulted when men don't pay attention to you."

I loathe men's jokes. That's not a phobia, more of an everyday annoyance. But pogonophobia is the fear of beards. Christougenniatiko dentrophobia is the fear of Christmas trees. I found these phobias in a medical textbook that I bought at the Toronto Library annual book sale. Whenever I think I might actually hurt myself, I spell out these words, like a chant, like right now. P-O-G-O-N-O ...

I hate myself for feeling like this, again. I hate being back in my old room. I might hate my own mother. "Losers live in the past. Losers live in the past. Losers live in the past." I don't know who I'm quoting, but this motivational-speak too has become a chant.

Except, when I look around, the present is a torn-up amusement park. Every sharp edge and gouged hole shows me a once sure-bet place of joy that is no longer available. All that remains are hundreds of chances to trip and bash my head around this sorry wreckage.

And there is something else. Something that tugs my stomach and weights my head, not unlike how suicidal urges pull and push. But this is a new feeling. Something is watching me.

Or am I making that up? Do I want someone to see me that fucking badly?

# II Bossy

The rattling rectangular bus window is the ultimate frame for the view. Fort Erie Public Transit has a fleet of two blue school buses that travel in tandem along a single route from the Peace Bridge (bordering Buffalo, N.Y.) to Crystal Beach between the hours of 6:30 a.m. to 7:30 p.m. No surprise, Barbara has refused to let me borrow the car. "You think I have forgiveness coverage on my insurance? You know how much the deductible is if you get into an accident? No, you don't know. You've never had to know about these things," she lectured me.

Where would I drive anyway? On the bus, I don't have to know. I can simply board and ride, all day if I want, for only a dollar.

The bus is a hideout. An escape of sorts. Each time we roll past the demolished amusement park, I mouth, "I'm so sorry." Passing the library I vehemently think, "Don't call me." Every so often I see a goldfinch flash by and can't help but sigh out a tiny appreciation. I'm still able to name all the local beauties: killdeer, kinglet, cardinal, mourning dove, rock wren, robin, swallow, sapsucker, lark. Maybe I carried a pocket-sized birding book as a kid.

This morning, a girl no more than four years old stands alone at the bus stop in front of the Avondale corner store eating a blue jumbo Mr. Freezie. What kind of parent gives their kid a Mr. Freezie at nine in the morning? Fifty feet away, I spot the dad with a rainbow kids' backpack slung over his shoulder, passing a joint back and forth with another man. The marijuana smoke doesn't rise, but sinks under the humid air, swirling around the men's feet.

"What's your name?" I ask the girl.

She pops the Mr. Freezie out of her mouth long enough to shrug at me. Her tongue is blue. Smart kid. She doesn't talk to strangers.

"Do you want to see a magic trick?" I take a loonie out of my pocket and her blue upper lip curls. This disappearing coin trick calls for sweaty hands. I coat the coin in perspiration from my palm through a series of showy gestures. Sweat then sticks the loonie to the back of my hand as I wave my empty palm in the air.

"How you do it?" she asks.

I refrain from telling her that you hang out at the bar kitty-corner to your apartment with drunks who have nothing better to do than to teach their tricks to anyone who will listen. She'll learn her own fool's magic soon enough. Her wake-n-bake father dry hacks as he strides up beside her. He steals a bite of her Mr. Freezie and she silently hands the whole thing to him, as if he's contaminated it. I stare off in the direction of the oncoming bus.

The driver is a woman in jean shorts and pink high-top running shoes. A sweat-shaped "v" marks her Glass Tiger T-shirt. A few similarly glistening passengers dot the vinyl seats. I've already gotten used to the rank and sweet smell of the bus.

I grab today's copy of *The Fort Erie Times* from the messy pile of newspapers scattered on the first seat. "Zebra Mussel Infestation Could Cost Millions" the front-page headline warns. A previous passenger has drawn a pair of devil's horns over each of the mussels, shown clustered along the bottom of a tugboat. The same passenger, presumably, also scribbled a series of lightning bolts over the text of a shorter article—"Fort Erie Native Friendship Centre Spear-heads Alternative School Program." Why is the media so dismally predictable? Out of all the synonyms of "to start," the paper had to pick "spearhead" for a headline about the Native Friendship Centre. Karla Moses. I remember my high school friend Karla Moses had a baby before I left for Toronto. That baby would be kindergarten age now. Or first grade. Do I call her to tell her I'm back? Or call the Hill twins? And say what—that I've turned into a wannabe nouveau riche college flunky who doesn't have kids or a boyfriend? That once I did cocaine with some of the cast members of *Three Men and a Baby* after they finished shooting in the Royal Alexandra Theatre location on King Street West? That I took an Aboriginal Studies course in university, and it was taught by a woman who appeared to be whiter than I am, who boasted her curriculum was "groundbreaking"? Would Karla or the Hill twins still consider me a friend? Years ago, we were simply kids with single moms and without lunch money, joining forces.

I flip through the paper with finer interest. I might recognize the name of one of my old friends-not-really-friends. Someone from my homeroom must have formed a Rush Tribute Band that plays shows at the Palmwood Hotel. On the half-page sports section, an enormous erect penis has been drawn on Dance Smartly, a local racehorse and the first filly in line to capture the Canadian Triple.

"You draw that?" A lanky boy of maybe sixteen years slides himself next to me.

"No. I cannot take credit for this masterpiece," I say, tapping the cartoonish penis with my finger to show that I will not be embarrassed by him.

He blushes at this, recovers, and says, "I can show you a big dick."

"Aren't you supposed to be in school?" I chuff. "Getting rejected by girls your own age?" Out the window there are cattails growing in the ditches, some already beginning to seed into cottony tuffs.

"I'm going to get a job," says Sweet Sixteen. He pushes his blond skateboarder haircut out of his face for a moment, looking confident, then lets it sweep back over his eyes.

"Oh yeah, what job?"

He pulls *The Fort Erie Times* help wanted section from his back pocket. Below a half-dozen ads for seasonal fruit pickers there is one that reads "Graveyard Shift" circled twice in red pen. I flip to the back of my own paper and find the ad:

> THE POINT! Campground and RV Park. Seeking to fill a Overnight Manager position to facilitate the nightly operations of a 60-space RV and tent camping park. This is an immediate hire for an on-site motivated person. Light grounds keeping and maintenance. A patient demeanor is essential. Weekly salary is dependent on level of experience.

"After I land this job, I'll take you out for a drink," he tries again. "I got love for older ladies."

"As a matter of fact," I say, "I think I'll apply for this job too." I'm already sleeping poorly at nights anyway. I've already emptied one-third of Barbara's Sonata from the bottle, which she'll soon discover and be pissed about. A graveyard shift would put me on a different clock from Barbara. From everyone.

"A girl? The only ladies who work nights are nurses and strippers," he tells me.

"We'll see." I turn away from him again. The stink of the algae blooms that dot the lakeshore wafts through the window. Smells no worse than Toronto's smog.

"So, nah, what," stammers Sweet Sixteen. "You're going to The Point right now to apply for the same job as me? You can't do that."

I will do exactly that if only to taunt him. I pull the compact from my purse and powder the perspiration from my nose and forehead. The boy watches me put on lip gloss and smooth out my hair. Both his attraction and his annoyance are palpable. This is the first time since I've been home that I've felt powerful. I'm sick, I think, to let this adolescent fluff my ego, but I unbutton the top button of my polka-dot baby-doll dress to bait him closer.

When we get off the bus, he sprints forward as if I'm going to race him, then slows to a march a few paces in front of me. His oversized Levis hide how skinny he is through the hips. Even walking behind him, I can see youthful uncertainty in his lurching gait. It's contagious. I anxiously shake the fabric of my dress away from my hot skin as we reach the driveway. I've never been to The Point before. Although most local kids have recklessly trampled this campground and the adjacent nature reserve—Marcy's Woods, home to the last old-growth black maple in North America. Both are local drinking and bottle-smashing spots.

The scenery behind The Point's perimeter of sumac and poplars is exactly what I expected—an absurdly blue spring-fed quarry rimmed with yellow paddle boats. A loose pool noodle hugs the rocky shoreline. Picnic tables with termite holes tucked under shady tress. No tents yet, though a few early campers have set up their aluminum-sided holiday RVs. A couple of permanent residents have custom mobile homes, each marked by its own small lawn punctured with excessive pinwheels and pink flamingos. I expected more mobile homes, actually, since even though the Park's shut down, there are still miles upon miles of working farms. Once upon a time, every guy around could get summer work berry picking. Not to mention the many who work corn and hay. It was something local boys looked forward too, seasonal farm labour followed by months of collecting unemployment insurance. But it seems that even trailer parks—home to farm workers—have turned into ghost towns.

Still, the residents who have stayed have a nice spread. We pass a trailer with a satellite dish mounted on its roof. Another is strung with patio lanterns and wind chimes and Canadian flags. Briefly, I imagine that I could live a simple life here, before a pair of middle-aged men in swim trunks catcalls me from their lawn chairs. One raises his beer bottle in the air and hollers a second time.

"New boyfriends?" Sweet Sixteen teases.

"What?" I say. "You're telling me those are your new boyfriends? Good going on accepting your homosexuality. Come out of that closet! Boy George and Elton John did it, you can too."

"What the fuck?" The boy punches my arm. I trip him. We tussle like siblings, stirring up the dusty path to the manager's house. A "Help Wanted" sign is taped above the doorbell. The door is propped open by a frog-shaped ceramic doorstop. To the left of the welcome mat, three pairs of flip-flops are lined up in a perfect row. Farther inside, talk radio chatters. I ring the doorbell. The boy hikes his jeans back up around his waist. I re-button the top button of my dress.

"Come on in. Take a seat at the kitchen table. I'll be a minute," a woman's voice calls.

Sweet Sixteen rushes to beat me to the Formica table and snaps up a chair. He doesn't know the lady of the house is peeking in at us. This is a set-up Barbara taught me, to watch guests who don't know you're looking, see how they interact with your living space. Do they admire the photos hung on the wall or stare at their feet? Do their hands stray in between the sofa cushions? Barbara tested her new dates in this manner. Another test was to eagle-eye the latest fellow's interactions with her peculiar daughter. If my mom was unsure about a guy, she'd sit me in the living room with them for about ten minutes and watch how they fared. "Ask him questions," she'd urge me. "Any question you can think of."

I remove my sandals and place them neatly beside the row of flip-flops. Sweet Sixteen shuffles his sneakers under his chair. I choose the chair with its back facing the door, guessing that the lady of the house never turns her back to the door. Hers must be the chair closest to the refrigerator.

A perfect pear-shaped matriarch enters the kitchen wearing a country-rose-print cotton housedress that I bet she made herself. Somewhere there's got to be a granddaughter wearing a tiny version of the same dress. She sinks herself into in the chair nearest the refrigerator. Her fingernails are rough and thick, but she wears multiple gold rings. A coral rose. A cameo. A pink pearl. No diamonds. *Che lei classica!* "I haven't got an application to fill out," she says dryly. "Never needed an application because I've never hired nobody before. Even our lawn boy is family, my nephew Vincent."

"I can mow," offers Sweet Sixteen. "Clip hedges, trim trees, mend fences." He enthusiastically mimes operating an electric hedge clipper, then glances at me as if I'm going to try to one-up him. The women's knuckles are swollen on her slightly trembling hands. She holds an almost empty tumbler; one last sip of watery brown liquid remains.

"Starla Mia Martin," I rise slowly. "Before I make someone a drink, I like them to know my name." Gently, I take the glass from her hand. As I expected, I smell coffee and amaretto. The glass is dewy, so I guess she's drinking her hair of the dog on ice.

"Rose Esposito."

"Esposito," I repeat. Half-and-half is in the fridge, and ice is in the freezer; those ingredients are easy to find. I move quickly, not wanting her to think I'm scrutinizing her boxes of Lean Cuisine.

"Italian name," she says.

"We used to be Martinis, but my Nonno wanted to change it to something more American sounding. He was also Nino, but became Nick. Nick Martin. You know, *dopoguerra*, lots of name changes," I venture, knowing I could get myself into trouble here. I risk insulting her if she doesn't speak *la lingua*, and on the other hand, I risk shaming myself. My broken Italian isn't anything worth showing off.

"My Pops had a heck of a time too. He was a World War II vet, you know, probably the same age as your grandpop. Not a good time to be a Guido," says Rose. The Moka Pot on her stovetop is still slightly warm. I empty the espresso into the glass of ice. Where she keeps the amaretto is the real test. One cupboard, I tell myself. I must find the booze right away or else she'll shoo me out of her kitchen.

"Mrs Esposito," I say. "You don't really need someone to mow the lawn in the middle of the night." My hand reaches for the cupboard handle with the gummy fingerprints. Inside there is a row of bottles, set tidily like the flip-flops at the door. Limoncello, Zucca, Frangelico, Amaretto, and an unopened bottle of Canadian Crown.

"What you need is someone who knows that if a campfire is burning green it only means some fool is tossing tin cans into the fire." I set her fresh drink down in front of her. "You need someone who knows that the hose alone won't wash away vomit from a concrete walkway. You have to use baking soda if you don't want a stain. That's what this job is about, right? Making sure the *festa* stays *calma*? I will do this for you. I may look like a *piccolina*, but I can be a boss when I need to be."

Sweet Sixteen audibly kicks the chrome table leg. He knows he's been beat. Rose reaches her weary hand toward me, places her palm over mine. Her smile is cautious as she says "Please don't make me drink alone."

# 12 Lesbo

guess I'll be taking you out, kid," I offer Sweet Sixteen—a consolation prize. He shuffles up dust at the bus stop, grumbles under his breath.

"'If someone's going to buy me a drink, I like them to know my name,'" he mocks.

"Don't blame me if you lack the good sense to introduce yourself." I stop him in his angry tracks, thrust my right hand at him. His handshake is slack, lazy-like. He tells me his name is Wendel. The name suits his Nordic looks—white-blond, icy eyes. "Wendel, tell me, which local joints don't check ID these days? Is Hot Diggity's still open?"

"Uh, that place closed like two years ago."

I shrug, and Wendel and I stare silently into the direction the bus should be coming. I don't bother suggesting another pub—it's like playing bankruptcy roulette around here.

"Let's go to Pure Platinum," says Wendel.

"The strip club!" I balk. He's still trying to win some immature battle between us. I recover with, "I doubt they're open this early."

"Two-for-one Caesar brunch, you in?"

I've got no other place to be, and it's not as if I have a problem with strippers. Two of my U of T classmates were strippers, or at least that's what they said they did to pay tuition. Is being seen at Pure Platinum a risk for a girl like me? Small-town gossip. A sore sliver of my youth digs in. This memory sounds like the syncopated clang clang clang of combination locks against lockers. This memory shows me the word "pervert" written across my own locker, not penned in black marker, but scratched permanently into the metal. In my freshman year, I made a habit of arriving either well before the first bell rang or late for class, hoping not to be seen at my locker. Although it hardly mattered how well I perfected invisibility, day after day I had no choice but to return to "pervert." Sure, I wore my jeans ripped in the butt, like every other teenager. Yes, I had made it to third base. At thirteen that was only slightly earlier than other girls, and at the time, I was dropping my pants for boys. Pussy came later. Nonetheless, my peers had already determined that I was that fledgling deviant, a queer, queer girl. I was the one who firmly faced the changing room wall for fear of being accused of gawking at other girls. The one who received prank telephone calls at dinnertime. Whose childhood friends would, one by one, turn on her as pubescent anxieties ballooned up in our collective teenage minds. I can't pinpoint a specific occasion that started it all—no crushes on English teachers or sleep-over party indiscretions. I only know small-town women aren't supposed to look at other women in that way, weren't allowed to touch their female friends in that way. No matter how many handjobs I performed on quasi-popular jocks, I never jerked away my reputation as the village queer. Maybe getting it on with boys never redeemed my credit because even in high school I liked my sex no-strings. I lied to and cheated on my only real boyfriend. Self-sabotage. This drove Barbara nuts. I can still picture her waving the phone receiver at me, "No, I won't tell him you're not home. Don't be rude. This is the third time he's called."

To piss off numerous boys, it turns out, creates collective teenage concern. I was marked to serve as a "what not to be" message. I believe this normalizes the rest of the group.

Now, at twenty-three years old, I ought to be safe from pack mentality. "Why not?" I say. "You're an under-aged kid playing hooky and I'm the adult daughter of the town librarian. Why shouldn't we watch naked ladies and get drunk on a Tuesday morning?"

As we ride the bus, I hope Wendel will chicken out. When we stand in Pure Platinum's parking lot, I am ready for him to excuse himself and go back to school—there is still plenty of time for him to catch his afternoon classes. Instead, he heaves the black-painted door open for me. Entering is like walking into a fun house, a dark place that my eyes could never adjust to, and so many reflective surfaces that there is no denying I'm here. Automatically, I fix my hair. My teeth glow ghoulish white under the black fluorescent bulbs. Wendel places his hand on my back to lead me inside. He might be showing off, except that there is hardly anyone to show off for. Three men in brown UPS uniforms sit in the front row. The blonde perched at the edge of the stage collects their US dollar bills between her breasts. One holds a bill between his teeth, and the blonde presses her tits into his face for a second before snatching the bill in her cleavage. The other two men eagerly copycat—filling their own mouths with money to be taken. There's a messy pile of cash onstage beside the blonde's discarded bikini. My heartbeat quickens, faster than the tempo of Aerosmith's "Sweet Emotion" that plays loud enough to ensure that real conversation cannot be made between any of the patrons.

Wendel pulls me over to a table in the shadows but still close enough to the stage to see the tiny red rose tattooed on the blonde's left ankle.

"She kissed me once. I swear to god," he punches my arm, nodding toward the stage. "I smoked a joint with her and she made out with me. True story. Her mouth tasted like baby powder."

Wendel waves for the waitress, and an hourglass silhouette takes shape in the burlesque light. She sways over. Her unreasonably green eyes don't settle on us. Her gaze drifts slightly above our heads. Her eyes remind me of the painted ones on my Laugh in the Dark stunt. Cartoon eyes—probably contact lenses.

"Welcome to Pure Platinum. We have two-for-one Caesars, Irish coffee, and lap dances before noon," she recites. "What can I get you?"

Wendel rapidly changes his mind back and forth before ordering us a round of Irish coffee. "With whipped cream," he adds, as the waitress makes her way back to the bar. "She's the best pole dancer you'll ever see. We nicknamed her The Flying Fish."

I roll my eyes.

"Ah, come on, it's a joke. She don't care. She's been working here forever," the boy huffs. "She hardly ever gets on stage anymore, so who cares."

"Forever?" I snap. "You start coming here when you were still in your diapers?"

"My dad's one of the owners," admits Wendel. For a moment I'm tempted to ask if he can get me a job here, my breasts would also like to collect piles of American money. I'll dance, get that stripper money, then write a memoir and get more money. Unfortunately, my breasts aren't anything like the set on the blonde. Barbara's big-boob gene was not passed on to me, and besides, I already have a job at The Point starting in less than a week, I remind myself. A job that the kid nags me about as we drink our boozy coffees topped with globs of glowing whipped cream. I barely listen to him whine about how I stole that graveyard shift as I sip the sugary, lukewarm drink. By the next round, he's complaining about his old man, who apparently is the type of asshole who believes a boy should buy his first car with his own hard-earned money. By the third round,

Wendel's grievances have grown sloppy and sentimental and the tale of his ex-girlfriend, Sarah, starts to dribble from his loose lips. What am I, his new school counsellor? I nod along with him in feigned agreement. Yes, they are still totally in love. Yes, she will come crawling back. Yes, I one-hundred-percent agree, Sarah's new boyfriend can bite it. It occurs to me that perhaps this kid has known something closer to love than I have—how he moons and carries on.

When the aroma of burgers and fries wafts from the kitchen, my stomach rumbles. I wish we were drinking Caesars so I at least had a stick of celery to munch on. The room spins when I stand. Where did all these men come from? Suddenly they are lining the bar and sitting alone with sandwich platters and whole pitchers of beer at their solitary tables. Men wave their dollars at the stage. All of them clearly see I am the only woman in the audience. Crooked grins—so many black-lit teeth I have to squint as I stumble to the women's washroom.

I fling my bag onto the counter and rifle through it for change. I have thirty dollars in my wallet, but I'm saving it. It is my last thirty dollars until whenever I get a first paycheque. Maybe I can scrape together enough loonies and quarters to order some chicken wings.

"Wanna make some quick cash?" I look up to see the waitress's reflection in the mirror. She stands so close behind me I don't dare turn around. Her green eyes have turned turquoise in the florescent bathroom lighting—definitely coloured contacts. Her bubblegum, talon-long nails have to be press-ons. Her bottle-black hair is starting to grow out light brown at the roots like a trashy halo. "I got a couple of regulars who want a duo act. They pay $100 for three songs, that's fifteen minutes. Problem is the only other girl who bothered to show up for the lunch shift is Tiffany, and every time I introduce her to my regulars, she steals them."

"What ... steals them ... um ..." I clutch my loose change in my hand like a stooge.

"Whatcha gotta do?" The waitress finishes my question. "Seriously, you can sit on your ass the whole time. Topless. Keep your bottoms on if you want. What are you wearing for panties?" She flips my dress up. My white cotton briefs glare at me in the mirror. I flinch away from her, but there's no space to recoil. My stomach is already pressed against the counter. "Oh, geez. You're for sure not a dancer."

"They're comfortable," I explain. "It's hot outside."

"Wear a pair of mine."

The waitress takes off a patent leather high heel; a tiny key hangs from the ankle strap. She opens a padlocked bathroom stall. "Voilà," she shows me. "My personal closet." Spandex costumes hang across a wire line. A Rubbermaid bin full of shoes and boots sits on the toilet seat. "All the girls smoke in the dressing room upstairs. I keep my stuff down here or else I end up smelling like an ashtray." She hands me neon green underwear with a yellow lightning bolt down the centre. "Put these on."

"R-really?" I stammer.

"Really," she confirms. "And if your bra is as ugly as your panties, take it off and leave it here."

Wearing the waitress's lightning panties makes everything speed up. She hurries me across the club toward a row of numbered doors. Two men leap from their table and tail behind us. Out of the corner of my eye, I notice Wendel and a middle-aged blond man gesturing apishly at one another at the back of the room. Father and son argument? Doesn't matter to me as long as the kid doesn't see where I'm headed.

In the cubicle-sized room, the waitress sits me down on a red velvet chaise. The two men sit side by side on bench seating, their backs rigid against the wall. The pair's faces barely take shape. I—like them—am too focused on the waitress. "Fellas, this is Jessica," she says. "Jessica and I just met in the ladies room, didn't we, Jessica?"

"Uh-huh," I agree. I could never make my voice squeak like hers.

"This is Jessica's very first time here, isn't that right?" The waitress strokes my hair like I'm her pet. I think she's the same age as me. I wonder.

"I have no idea what to expect," I play along. In unison, both men pull out billfolds. Each frees a red fifty, which the waitress scoops up and tucks into some hidden pocket in her skimpy costume. The billfolds remain displayed on the tiny ashtray table between them. I'm a natural at playing dumb, but any fool would get this hint. These men are willing to pay more. I'm not exactly sure what they'll pay more for—but four drinks in, I'm feeling pretty willing to go with any flow.

The waitress rolls out of her spandex tube dress. Of course her nipples point upward. Of course they are valentine pink. Maybe she stains them with rouge? She leans over one of the men, paddles him gently in the face with both breasts. The other lets his mouth hang open, waiting for his turn like a baby bird. I hear the breathing in the room slow as their pulses quicken.

"Jessica wants to show off her titties too, but she's shy," says the waitress. "A round of shooters will loosen her up." On cue, a tray of tequila shots arrives. A lemon wedge is popped in my mouth. Salt sprinkled on the back of my hand. The waitress coos as she licks my fingers. She is familiar, I think. She unbuttons all five buttons of my baby-doll dress. I'd forgotten about being braless until she scoops up my small breasts with her hands. She bounces them in her palms for the men to see. I hear myself sigh, then promptly follow it with a coquettish giggle—attempting to imitate the put-on girlish sounds the waitress makes. This routine is not so hard. I could totally work here.

The waitress returns her attention to the men, takes turns grinding her ass between their legs. "Line up another couple of shooters for us, Jessica." She winks. Sticks out her tongue a little when the men can't see. My dress falls around my waist as I reach for our drinks. I'm sloppy drunk, but these guys don't care. I rub a lemon wedge on my right nipple, salt my left. The waitress takes her time lapping up the juice, the salt. She tilts her head back as she empties the shot glass. She spits tequila into my mouth. "You're nasty, Jessica," she says as she passes me to the men. I imitate her movements—slow, slow motion, mashing my torso into their faces, bouncing between their splayed legs. The song "Stop Me If You've Heard This One Before" plays and I'm so taken aback to hear Morrissey's voice in a small-town strip club that I barely notice that one man is gingerly tracing his finger especially close to my ass crack.

"Do you want to see my pussy, Jessica?" the waitress tugs me away from him. I stumble into her, then try to cover my clumsiness by dropping to my knees to remove the waitress's panties. An egg timer rings from an unseen hiding spot. "You want to extend?" she asks the men, her voice steady and certain again. This time she tucks their crisp fifties inside the lightning bolt panties I'm wearing before laying me down on the chaise lounge.

What I think about as she is on top of me:

There is a cigarette burn in the red velvet of this chaise. Where can I touch her? This red velvet chaise smells like feet. Where can't I touch her? She's so familiar. She's so beautiful, it must be a burden. I've always considered the female body to be sacred. Smells like feet stink and mothballs. The men totally have boners. If I had a cock, would I have a chub right now? I have one hundred fucking dollars between my legs. I hope that spoiled brat Wendel thinks I left the club. Are my hips grinding involuntarily? Keep your hips still. Breathe through your nose. Arch your back. Am I a failed female? What's wrong with my body? I wonder what Radclyffe and Una did in bed. Only touch her on the places she touches you. Hair. Cheeks. Lips. I bet we went to school together. Amaretto. Irish Coffee. Tequila shooters. Do I have the word "lesbo" written on my forehead or something? How much have I had to drink today? The word "pervert." There go her panties flying through the air. Men yip like backwoods coyotes. The word "sodomite." Her pussy is only a slit, an innie. Don't stare at it even if it's perfect. If I had a cock, I'd skewer her right now, one upward thrust. Only touch her shoulders. Neck. Breasts. June absolutely must have penetrated Anaïs—muses hit the G-spot, right? Muse means wet mess. She can be my muse. What time is it anyway? I wonder if I'll ever go back to university. I bet I could pay for an MFA in Creative Writing with stripper money. One man is wearing her panties on his head. Those coyotes. Her thighs. We were in the same grade together, the same homeroom. Her thighs. What is wrong with my body? Wait a second, I know her.

"For another fifty bucks, I'll pretend to not see what you're doing," she says. The men have undone their pants. Tentatively they wax the heads of their cocks in uncanny unison. "We'll just close our eyes, won't we, Jessica?" Tamara Matveev closes her eyes and kisses me.

Afterwards, the buttons on my baby doll dress are done up crooked. Tamara tells me I can keep the money that's between my legs—my cut. "Maybe I can call you if I ever get private shows? Bachelor parties, easy gigs." I'm working up the courage to interrupt her, to tell her I know who she is. "Oh, and can I have my panties back, Starla?"

My name stops me like a swift kick. I feel the sticky dried lemon and saliva itch my chest. Another Aerosmith hit from the *Toys in the Attic* album thumps at the back of my head. Tamara's unnatural green eyes widen. "Unless you've gotten them all wet?" She motions toward me like she's going to grab my crotch. I run.

I push through the heavy door and run directionless in the dazzling sunlight. Tamara Matveev's panties are indeed wet between my legs. The two fifty-dollar bills scratch me with each humiliated stride. None of this was anonymous. I know her. She knows me.

# 13 Sucker

May 1st brings cold weather. Or average temperatures, though compared to our late-April heat wave, it's cold. Barbara inspects the fisherman's knit cardigan and fingerless suede gloves I've selected to wear for my inaugural graveyard shift. I wait for her comment, "Suede, really? For outdoor work?" But the way she estimates the precise warmth of the wool with her meticulous hands is her own form of protest. As expected, she took the news of my new job at The Point as a betrayal—another unconventional move of mine that sets me poles apart from her. Night and day, literally.

She packs me a snack. The tomato and cheese sandwich in a Ziploc bag means *I still love you, dummy.* The apple juice box, *be safe tonight.*

The bus stops running at seven p.m., which is when my shift begins. Seven p.m. to seven a.m.—dusk to dawn. I guess it's about a forty-minute walk, so I give myself an hour. The nearly set sun stretches my shadow out long behind me. Street lamps blink on as I pass. Their fluorescent shrill is the only sound as I zigzag through the side streets. I am painfully reminded as I walk that I am lucky to have employment. Particle board to my left. Papered-up windows to my right. What used to be called Hotdog Alley has become a ghost town stroll. The bus doesn't turn down this street. It is the first time I'm truly seeing the once cute pastel-painted storefronts now time-beaten and completely abandoned. Of course I understood, conceptually, there wouldn't still be bustling fish fry shacks or souvenir shops. Even when I was a teenager, Hotdog Alley was already in decline, with fewer and fewer tourists coming each year. Some blamed Canada's Wonderland and Fantasy Island—newer and much bigger amusement parks a couple hours to our north and south. Some blamed the rise of heroin and hashish smuggled up from Buffalo. Some blamed Prime Minister Brian Mulroney and President Ronald Reagan. That's apt—blame conservatism. We've always been a party town, after all. We blamed the exchange rate, which put the Canadian dollar at only seventy cents to the US dollar. Some blamed factory closures on both sides of the border. Some of the more superstitious locals—a fair few—blamed Lemmy, the local legendary Lake Erie Monster, for making too many appearances within the pages of small-town tabloids and scaring away tourists.

Blame, too, is a concept.

Smashed windows are tangible.

Ripped-up awnings are tangible. The faded "For Rent" signs are about the same as a painted x on each door. Sickness lives here—not the Black Death, but Black Monday. This credit crunch couldn't be quarantined. It looks like, when the Park was dissolved by creditors, the community was more than bit by the recession bug—it was chewed bare.

The last storefront on Derby Road is the former home of the Hall's Candy Company. No one should see a favourite childhood sanctuary swollen with failure. The white wood siding is warped from being empty and unheated for the winter, though the rot is more than one season old—the candy company must have struggled to its end. The door has buckled out from its frame and hangs askew. The street lamps aren't really bright enough to allow a proper peek, but I pry the door open anyway and am surprised at the sugary stillness inside. The aroma is almost how I remember it. How can neglect smell so sweet? I could lick the humid, dark air. I take a step farther, right up to the candy counter, and run my fingers along the dusty countertop. Unidentifiable debris crunches beneath my feet. I lean in. "One cinnamon sucker," I say to sentimentality. If you grow nostalgic for this place—I warn myself—then it will have you. It will be that much harder to move away a second time.

Something scampers across my foot. I'm not yet finished screaming before more somethings dart past my face. Mice don't leap—I manage this single, rational thought before I bolt for the door. A succession of small, unknown objects skip off my back. House sparrows maybe? Has to be birds, has to. Swallows nest in abandoned buildings. And bats, fucking bats, do too. Right? Bats?

Back out on the street my voice is choked, as if stretched thin by the expansive vacancy of Derby Road. The Hall's Candy Company storefront is dead quiet. I wait for the sound of swallows whistling a warning from inside. Nothing. I cross the street, quickly. No one witnesses my outburst, which for some reason makes my screaming seem more foolish. The flash of fear quickly rendered unreal. Just like no one witnessed me launch myself down Niagara Boulevard, fleeing Tamara Matveev. All my embarrassing moments go unseen now that I've left the city. I'm not going to be that girl who cried on the subway while other commuters tried to look away. I'll just be that girl who cries. Period. How many times have I wished I could turn invisible? Careful what you wish for. Ironic self-fulfilling prophecy is something to be nervous about. An abandoned candy store is a creepy metaphor, but it's not real. "It's not real," I say aloud as if saying it will break the spell. But my heart pulses tediously at my temples as I speed along the stretch of closed-up cottages off Derby. Their busted shutters and screen doors seem to clack at me as I pass. Overgrown grass rustles. Leave me alone. It's not my fault no one wants to vacation here anymore. I curse under my breath.

Mostly middle-class Americans own these summer properties. Barbara always made it her business to introduce herself to any single men staying long enough for her to "befriend." There are certainly no more David Hasselhoff types to be found. The cottages look more slasher film and less *Baywatch*. Where are the Americans with money now? I'm relieved when the last deserted holiday home is well behind me and I walk the unlit gravel road. Whatever could go wrong for a young woman walking alone along a rural road at night? Besides, there's the occasional banjo twang of frogs in the ditch to keep me company.

Rose waits for me in a lawn chair set squarely on her front step so she can hear her television through her screen door. I hear a muffled Buffalo Channel 7 Eyewitness News with Irv Weinstein signing off as I approach. "You came." She sounds despondent as she stands and wraps her arms around me in warm greeting. I hug her back, guessing that I set the standard of familiarity at my interview. "What the heck you got stuck to the back of your sweater?" She spins me around. "Sweet God in Heaven!"

I can't help myself, a yelp bangs past my teeth when I see it. My toes curl in my sneakers as if I might run yet again. Rose shoots me a sharp look before her gaze returns to the improbable object in her hands. We both marvel at it. Except my wonderment is laced with a heavy measure of dread. One cinnamon-flavoured Hall's Original Sucker, perfectly intact inside the cellophane wrapper. "They don't make these anymore," Rose says, handing it back to me. "Where did you get it?"

# 14 Treats for the Ladies

**W**ho says the age of chivalry is dead? James Cagney in *Blonde Crazy* said it, that's who. Well, Cagney never met me. There's two kinda people in this world. Those who pitch woo and those who catch it. Me, I pitch. My soft curls and stockings may have fooled 'em. But I've always been a winer and diner.

It's coming back to me. She's giving me my life again. I used to buy treats for the ladies. I'd take moolah from the men, my generous gents, and spend it on girls. A real dyke Robin Hood, if you will. Welcome to Sherwood, my lady! Go figure my first clear memories to return to me are queer. A loganberry drink or Coca Cola never hurt nobody, not even the ones straighter than a bobby pin. The secret is to buy only one. Put two straws in a single soda glass and see what happens.

If I was pretty sure a gal was in the life, I'd buy a sucker. The Hall family made cinnamon, peanut, butterscotch, lemon, and coconut. A flavour for everybody. Cinnamon was always my pick because I sure liked a spicy-mouth kiss when I could get it. A girl who lets you have a lick of her sucker is lavender, for sure.

If I woulda returned home to Horseheads, New York ... that's where I was born and raised, wasn't it? When's the last time I thought about old Horseheads? Much less going back? If they woulda let me return home to Horseheads, New York, more like, I'd be matched up with a fella straight away. No sooner than I'd stepped through the door of my father's house, I'd be marched down the aisle, better believe it. Only redemption for a trapeze artist like me woulda been a husband

and children. And by redemption I mean back in the Finger Lakes bourgeoisie fold. And by redemption I ain't talking about god. If my muddled tick-tock is right, I've been dead for an age, about half a century, that is, and the closest thing I seen of heaven is this girl.

There's something special about her. She made me move something, something from the living world. Those suckers were buried in dusty boxes. About as forgotten as I am. And I resurrected them. I brought them back to life. What else from the good Park might spring up again, I wonder? Talk about redemption.

# 15 Ugly

Strange begets strange. Rose stops short at the threshold of the small log cabin that will serve as my new office. Does she distrust me now—me and my inexplicable cinnamon sucker? Just as I start gushing about the charming link-log construction, she pinches the bridge of her nose as if the sound of my voice has given her a headache. She hands over the keys and mumbles the most minimal workplace training instructions: "Walk the grounds about every hour. You'd be surprised how eventful the nighttime hours can be around here. When you're in the cabin, keep the door open. Never shut yourself in here alone."

"I won't sleep on duty, Rose. I leave that for data-entry nerds and policemen," I quip. I want to lighten her sober instructions. Turn her ominous into humorous. Her frown upside-down.

"I doubt you'll get a chance to fall asleep." Rose yawns, as if she has grown tired just by the idea of sleep. "Leave the door open because soon enough someone will come looking for you. Someone always needs something. Medical supplies, light bulbs, household cleaners, bleach and stuff, it's all in that trunk or under the cot. There is only one hard-and-fast rule: never call 9-1-1. Drag me out of bed if you have to, just never ever call 9-1-1. *Capisce?*"

"*Capisce*," I nod.

Rose's flip-flops sound like a metronome as she marches away.

"Night," I call after her. And it is night, like someone-just-switched-off-the-lights night. A night-blindness kind of night. No blue television light pulsing in trailer windows. No campfires. Certainly no campfire songs. The nearby tree line is pitch black, and again I think, there could be a man standing out there, several men, all lined up at the campground's perimeter, and I wouldn't be able to see them coming.

I decide within seconds of my shift that the cabin is a womb. Snug and warm. I shake the dust from the burlap lampshade, appreciating the lopsided speckled orange ceramic base. A beginner's pottery project, I suspect, along with the similarly slanted mug beside it. The desk is a live-edge slab on rusted sawhorse legs. I run my finger inside a lacquered termite groove. Am I inside someone's back-to-the-land art project? Could this link-log cabin be by the same maker? I see axe marks on the timber. Hand hewn—not cut in the hardware store parking lot. I squat down to inspect the rag rug under my feet—woven old flannel and blue jeans. The supplies chest looks to be made from reclaimed barn wood. And the single cot along the wall must have a real straw mattress (it crunches delightfully under my weight), topped with a simple square quilt made of worn denim and flannel that matches the rug. A room of my own, I muse. Much more butch than if I designed it myself, yet this is just the type of room in which I could write a manifesto, a collection of letters, a future banned book. I could be just like Simone de Beauvoir retreating to Kate Millett's folksy feminist farm in Poughkeepsie. I bet the final draft of *When Things of the Spirit Come First* was penned in a room just like this.

This cabin is a kazillion times better than a university classroom, I decide. I curtsy to the straw broom in the corner before beginning to sweep. The broom can't waltz and neither can I. I whisper, "One, two, three. One, two, three," anyway, as I rid the ceiling of cobwebs. I sweep a fine coat of dust from under the cot and stop.

I am certain that it's a painting from the amusement park before I kneel down to check. A peculiar pause trips the seconds. Here and now sort of falls forward—feels like coming up on LSD. You're fine, I tell myself as I kneel down beside the cot, everything is fine. Dust bunnies rim the frame, the same way they gathered around the Laugh in the Dark stunt under my own bed. "Come on!" I exclaim at the bare nail I spot above the cot. "Is my calling to re-hang all the ugly Crystal Beach art around here?"

Mustiness punctuates the air as I lift the wooden board off the floor. It's almost as heavy as my stunt. It reads, "Hold on to Your Hats" and "Not Responsible for Lost Articles." I can almost hear the Comet roller coaster in my head. That tick tick tick as the chain heaved the train cars up to the first drop. I remember that this was one of the many signs at the front of the line, along with "You Must Be This Tall to Ride" and "Keep Your Arms Inside the Car at All Times"—which no one obeyed. Who could resist the thrill of raising both arms in the air as the coaster dropped eighty-some feet?

I turn the sign around to look for a nail hole or framing wire and discover the flip side is, as I suspected, a painting. Ugly art. Or ugly is way off. What is more than ugly?

I hold a strange libido before me. A utopia of Id. Tits of all sizes ascending to heaven. "Pervert," I spit, not considering whether the jab is at the painter or at myself for feeling so giddy looking at it.

I force my eyes down to the bottom of the canvas where the heavy, rippling brush strokes imitate Van Gogh. Painterly, but disharmonized. This landscape brings together The Point's turquoise blue quarry and the harried tree line beyond the grounds. I can spot where a fan brush was brought in—wispy little spruce trees. Bob Ross's *The Joy of Painting* kind of trees. At the midline, the view begins to change. Peeping out above the treetops is an odd half moon rising—it's the tallest peak and drop of the roller coaster, oddly, the very peak I was just imagining. Except the coaster isn't painted. It's pieced together in a kind of decoupage of faded photos and newspaper clippings of the Comet. The edges of each cutout are ragged and lifting from the canvas. Perhaps the artist used ripped-up photographs and painstakingly doctored them back together? I trace my finger along the scrapbooked track. That coaster was quite the tooth chipper. I was always afraid to holler like the other kids because I didn't want my open jaw to slam shut at the bottom of the first drop.

Above the coaster, the painting's skyline takes a deviant twist. Instead of stars or sunset colours, there are glossy porno magazine images. Vaginas and puckered lips layered over more vaginas and puckered lips. A galaxy of ass. Dissected breasts are low-hung planets. All heavily glazed with so much glitter glue it needles my eyes. I can't decide if this expressionist-esqe landscape meets celestial jerk-off is trash or brilliant. "R. Esposito," I read the autograph. "Is that Robert or Rino? Rocco?"

Without fail, there's a nail above the head of the cot where I hang Rocco's painting. The wooden board rattles slightly against the log wall, and I flinch as if it might fall. I have to right it on the nail a few times before stepping back to appreciate the mounted view before me. My head buzzes just looking at it. I blink hard and head out the cabin door. Better get to work. Rose isn't paying me to gawk in bewilderment at ugly art.

Everything seems very ordinary after experiencing Rocco's artistic rendition of The Point. My flashlight illuminates a slim path of ordinary gravel bordered by ordinary grass. At the dock, I find a canoe resting right side up in the rack, collecting dew, and manage to turn it without making much noise. I collect a trail of bottle caps along the shore. The pay phone receiver is dangling on its hook. I pick it up to check for the dial tone, then hang it back up again. Along what I just now dub Resident Row—a long paved walkway—are only three trailer homes. The first is a giant orange, blue, and white Winnebago set slightly back in the trees, with a red Volkswagen Rabbit parked beside it. This resident loves colour. There are bumper stickers covering the entire right side of the trailer. I let my flashlight briefly rest upon the collection of gnome ornaments on the lawn. One of the gnomes has dropped his pants, and his little ceramic butt moons anyone who might approach the Winnebago's door. A flagpole mounted at the end of the tiny driveway flies black and purple flags. I watch the flags sag, then slightly sway in the night breeze for a long time before I figure out what they are. The black: a pirate flag. The purple: a Haudenosaunee flag. I recognize the Great Tree of Peace symbol, the Eastern White Pine. The white squares represent the Cayuga, Onondaga, Seneca, Mohawk, and Oneida. C.O.S.M.O. Cosmo, like the cocktail or the magazine. A mnemonic I created in high school to help me remember the Haudenosaunee Confederacy.

We had one teacher, Mrs Paul, in high school who taught Aboriginal studies, and she was a substitute teacher. She was Mi'kmaq and Acadian from Dartmouth, Nova Scotia—she told us that on her first day. Sometimes she'd say, "Pens down and just listen," and she'd talk for an entire hour. I guess that's why I created a mnemonic to remember Cayuga, Onondaga, Seneca, Mohawk, and Oneida. We took so few notes in Mrs Paul's class that I started inventing mnemonics and songs to try and remember her lessons. Maybe I knew she wouldn't last long at our school.

I remember Barbara complained that there weren't enough books in our library for our class of twenty-five students to all be doing school projects on Native peoples. I think there were a lot of reports on arrowheads and knives made of chert that year. Mrs Paul never smiled, but somehow I felt like she cared about us more than any other teacher. Most teachers took us out of town to a museum, but for our field trip Mrs Paul brought us to Shagbark Park and had us pick up garbage. Afterwards, she took us to the beer store to collect money for all of the empty beer bottles we picked up.

It was on this field trip that Chris Sakokete asked me out, for the second time, and I said "yes." We liked to listen to The Clash and smoke hash from a dented Coca-Cola can and fuck awkwardly under the train bridge. Normal teen dating stuff. But we also did real stuff. We'd go fishing for walleyes in Black Creek or babysit his nephews or drive up to Niagara Falls just to go to Ripley's Believe It Or Not museum.

I liked the guy, and I never liked anyone in high school. I liked him so much I became a genius at concocting stories about how he was cheating on me. I retaliated by wearing frosty pink lipstick and partying overzealously with all his friends. Normal teen drama. Fear-drinking with boys isn't the best revenge, it turns out. Nowadays, when I see teenage girls riding the subway or wherever, with their depressed bitch faces, I think, Hey, I know that face. That's the face of having your tits and ass groped by hands you were too wasted or too trained up in the ways of feminine passivity to ward off. That's the face that wears next-day shame, the face that appears blank when being next-day shamed by your bogus friends. And then the whole miserable scenario happens all over again the following weekend. Girls earn their depressed bitch faces. Anyway, I did my history report for Mrs Paul on the Haudenosaunee flag, created in the 1980s to honour the Haudenosaunee Confederacy, probably the oldest participatory democracy in the whole world, if I remember what Mrs Paul told us during one of her "pens-down" talks. I lost my so-called virginity to Chris Sakokete the year she was a substitute teacher. Way to make it all about me. I'm such a narcissist.

When Mrs Vandemere came back from maternity leave, Aboriginal studies was no longer a part of History. Chris Sakokete started dating some girl from Fort Erie High School. I only saw her once at a bush party, and I'm pretty sure her face was just as depressed and bitchy as mine.

I back away from the Winnebago before I can attach any more of my crybaby teenage memories to it.

A few paces further, the next trailer is one of those vinyl-sided shotgun homes. My flashlight beam wanders close to the front door before suddenly noticing the man sitting in a lawn chair in the dark under a corrugated aluminum awning. He flicks a lighter to let me know he's seen me. How long has he been sitting there watching me? "Sorry," I mumble, and swiftly slink away.

"Management entering," I call out at the washroom door before venturing into the campground washroom. I call out twice before entering the men's. Apart from a thin lip of mildew, the showers are empty and so clean I almost feel let down. There's not even Magic Marker graffiti for me to scrub off the washroom stalls. I suppose this will change once camping season starts. "There's literally nothing for me to do around here," I complain aloud.

"Help my boy," a man bellows nearby. "Girl, come help him."

Okay, I spoke too soon. There is the sound of late-night chaos. I rush, almost crashing into him a few paces outside the washroom. My flashlight falls into the freshly cut grass. Bending down to retrieve it, I see the man's bare feet peel off ahead of me. "Come with me."

"I'm the new night manager," I say, catching up to him. "Starla ..."

"Welp, we brought our son to you, but you ain't there."

"To me?" I realize he's hurrying us to my cabin. "What's wrong with your son?"

"Rabbit fever," he tells me. Slapping his hands down on each of my shoulders he halts me in my tracks. His breath is malt liquor.

"What am I supposed to do?" I ask, quickening my pace.

"Are ya th' new girl or are ya useless?"

The cabin door is open. Inside a woman kneels beside the cot. "I already got the first aid kit," she says, the contents of the trunk spilled out around her.

I rush inside to find her kneeling beside an awfully small and fragile child. He can't be more than four or five, while his parents must be headed toward fifty. I was expecting a teenager, not this last-call baby. An unexpected-pregnancy little nip. His mother delicately holds his head like it's a helium party balloon that might float away.

"If you didn't gobble up all our aspirin by the bottle his fever woulda never got this high," the woman hisses. The boy has a weeping rash around his mouth. His PAC-MAN pajamas are sweat-soaked.

"I swear I'll bust both your knees with your own damn hammer if he get's any hotter. I'll soak that old goat beard of yours in kerosene and set you on fire."

I scramble through the scattered contents of the chest. The woman has already popped open a bottle of Tylenol. "What do you know about this rabbit fever? Anything," my voice is angry too, rivaling the woman's. Stay calm, I tell myself. "How'd your son catch it? " I grab Bactine, Solcoseryl ointment, and a few bottles and packets I don't recognize. The mother and I begin to clean his broken skin. The boy's sweat smells like a cheese platter at the end of a party. The soft skin around his lips moves under my finger. He whines, and the mother nudges me away. Her hands are quick and gentle. Her wedding ring is a thin gold snake eating its tail.

"If you wanna do something, dampen his socks in cold water and get 'em back on his feet," she says to me, and then to her husband, "Make yourself useful and fetch your big wool socks. You know where your own socks are?"

"My rabbits are clean," he says.

"That ain't news, Hal."

"Clean," he repeats.

"Hal keeps rabbits," the woman explains to me. "Clean rabbits, like he says, for the meat. We eat more rabbit than we do hamburger."

" 'Cept a wild rabbit comes around the pens. Young buck wantin' to mate. I runned the pest over with the lawn mower."

"And left him, guts and all, on the lawn." The woman gulps on her words. I don't want to see her cry. "Lucky is a sensitive boy. If he found the dead rabbit, he wouldn't let it lay on the wrong side of the grass like that. Boy's got respect. Not like his stupid father. I figure he gave it a proper burial."

"Boy ought to know better. Rabbit fever's contagious even after the animal's dead. I bet he stuck his fingers in his mouth afterwards."

"He's a kid. I told you a hundred times, kids put every darn thing in their mouths."

"What about this?" I ask the mom, showing her a sticky bottle of cherry-flavoured penicillin V syrup. I take a closer look at the label. "Probably expired."

"Better than a kick in the head, I 'spose," she says.

"He'll never touch another rabbit again, that's for sure," grunts the father. He crowds behind us, rubbing his palms together frantically.

"Only a dimwit leaves a dead rabbit on the lawn! You think you own this whole place? Do us a favour and go for a long walk, would you?"

To my horror, the man shoves his wife in the back. She topples onto her son as the rag rug buckles under her husband's feet, and he comes tumbling down to the floor, cursing and slinging insults.

"I'll go to sleep in this bed, thank you. I like it here," little Lucky says. His throat must be swollen for his voice to sound so slight. "The lady likes it here," the boy tells me. "She makes the windows glow."

Fuck no. This can't turn into some kind of rock 'n' roll Keith Richards near-death drama. My hands shake and he shakes with them. I realize I'm holding him by both shoulders. I can't bring myself to tell him he'll be all right. But that's what a normal, compassionate person does—says that everything is going to be fine. I'm the worst caregiver ever. I'm such a bad caregiver that I'm indulging my insecurities about being the worst caregiver rather than just giving the fucking care. My shaking's no more than a tremble, but his sweaty little head bobs around on his neck.

His mother pushes me away again. "What lady, Lucky?" she asks.

"She says you got a treat for me."

"Yes! I do have a treat. A special, special treat," my own words startle me as I pull the cinnamon sucker from my sweater pocket. "So special that there is only this one left in the whole world." Something in the air shifts as I hold the sucker up for the boy to see. His mother lets out an awful gasp and curls her body closer to her son. His father becomes quiet and still on the floor. Rocco's painting clacks against the wall again. And just as Lucky said, the window seems to grow a bit brighter, like the moon's pointed directly down on us. I get the urge to rush away, like I rushed out of the abandoned candy store and run all the way back to Barbara's house. I hold the sucker out of his reach, my hand trembling more than ever. "I can only give you this treat if you promise me you're going to be a very brave boy and get better."

Lucky's puffy eyes widen as he makes his promise. To my surprise,

I find myself crawling into the cot beside him and his mother. The three of us lie together, side by side, listening vigilantly as the rhythm of his sucking and swallowing grows steadier. She hears what I hear, I can tell by the slight smile on her lips. The smell of cinnamon fills the cabin. This must be the strongest, strangest cinnamon Hall's sucker ever to be made. Truly the last of its kind. Stuck to my sweater so that I could bring it here to this boy. *Ammazza!* Weirder than what's what.

"I'm Bobby."

"Starla," I tell her.

"Next time we meet, we'll drink some tea together, and you can tell me a bit about yourself." She closes her eyes, presses her lips to her boy's flushed cheek.

Hours later, I wake up on the rag rug beside the cot. The cabin is whirling, and I'm weak-kneed. Lucky is still tucked under his mother's arm, sleeping. Bobby's half awake. "Check his socks, eh?" she whispers.

His fever still hasn't broken. The dampened socks are warmer than room temperature. There's a halo of sweet cinnamon heat around his entire body. "Should we give him another Tylenol?" Bobby wriggles her arm free and gently rolls him up to sitting. Lucky seems to swallow the pill without waking up.

His father is gone. We must have fallen asleep long enough for him to wander away. I step outside, expecting to find him passed out in the grass. He's not outside either. He's not on the campground payphone calling the health hotline. He didn't go to their neighbours' to ask for help. Nope. My guess is he merely crawled back to his own bed.

The first of the mourning doves coos, and I decide that all there is left to do before the sun comes up is pray, except I am a lapsed

Catholic and therefore conflicted about exactly to whom I should pray. Boobs of heaven, I think, picturing images from Rocco's painting in the sky above me. Boobs and Vivienne Westwood shoes and lightning bolt panties. Sacred objects, no doubt, but can they answer prayers?

"Dear Saint Veronica," I try again, as if I am dictating a carefully worded letter to a completely mythical woman. "Children in this half of the twentieth century should neither suffer nor die from rabbit fever. We're both aware that Lucky deserves better than an over-the-hill alcoholic for a dad. The mom's solid enough, but there's only so much one woman can do, eh." I realize I'm quoting Barbara. She always used to say *There's only so much one woman can do*. It was her single mother's catch phrase. "Anywho, I'm not here to ask for the world. I only want the tiny scruff to get well. If you save him tonight ... "

A light goes on in Rose's home. It's all I can do to finish my prayer before making for her front door. "If you save him and watch over him, then I promise to look out for him too. I'll personally make it my duty to ensure he stays healthy, at least through the summer, and that he has something besides a rabbit carcass to play with, and I'll read him Maurice Sendak bedtime stories just like my mom read to me," I break into a run. "You have my word. Sincerely, Starla Mia Martin."

All I have to say to Rose is "Lucky" and she yanks her housecoat on. She pauses again at the log cabin door, and I whiz past her to the cot where the boy is sitting up, sipping water. "Do you have juice?" he asks. All three of us exhale audibly in relief—Rose, Bobby, and I. Bobby scoops Lucky up. For a moment, I wonder if she'll head back to her trailer, but she marches directly to Rose's house.

"Should we call the hospital?" I ask Rose, as we trail behind.

"Lucky's already been to the hospital once this year for 'falling off his bike.' Another emergency room trip and the hospital will get suspicious."

"Yeah, and they should be suspicious."

"No, they shouldn't. You ever see the way child welfare treats poor mothers around here? No way."

"Lucky's a little kid."

"Yeah, and Bobby was a little kid when foster care scooped her up. What did that do for her? Listen, I shouldn't have to be telling you everyone's business. You're making me gossip. Just trust me and don't argue."

Rose darts ahead to hold the door open for Bobby and Lucky. Sets them up in the living room in front of morning cartoons—Bugs Bunny waving a carrot in the air. I watch her shoot around her kitchen turning on stove elements and pitching food from the fridge into pots and pans. She won't look at me. Did I offend her? Or is she just one of these hyper-focused kitchen matriarchs? Within minutes eggs are scrambled and toast is popped.

The three of us exhale another audible sigh as Lucky digs into his breakfast.

Rose picks up our conversation again as we're drinking coffee at the kitchen table. She leans in closer, makes eye contact. "*Ascolta me!* Bobby is hard to get to know. For the longest time I thought she was just an old hippie with a suntan. She's Native, now you know, and she's got no blood family around her, no aunties like she ought to, and the hospitals in Fort Erie and in Welland already have crossed her real bad, and her husband has been on a wicked bender pretty much since their son started walking, you understand?"

"I'm sorry. How was I supposed to know?"

"You don't have to know everyone's p's and q's to know better. No hospital. No police. No 9-1-1. You've been in the city way too long, Starla. You forgot how things are round here."

I nod, sincerely. It clicks—I'm definitely back in Crystal Beach. The land of bootlegged off-sales, under-the-table employment, and unspoken rules.

"I don't mean to be hard on you, *cara*. You couldn't have come along at a better time. It's been a tough year." There's a considerable pause between Rose's words "tough" and "year." She pats my hand, her gold rings cold on my skin.

My walk home feels like a distorted déjà vu. The sumac branches leaning low with dew along the back road. The vacant beach cottages backlit by pink morning clouds. Hall's Candy Company Store—I cross the street to avoid it, then cross back again and defiantly stare at it until the world turns sideways. I am so fucking tired. Into Barbara's kitchen I float, toward her singing to her bowl of cereal. When she hugs me I go limp.

"Thank you for reading me Maurice Sendak at bedtime," I say.

Barbara recites what sounds like the first couple pages of *Where the Wild Things Are*. She has a magnificent memory for story, and she likely reads this very book to children at the library. I let myself be soothed, listening to her soft, storytelling voice.

# 16 Women 'n' Fuckin' Children

Lucky wears nothing but a Mario Brothers sweatshirt. Not twenty-four hours after his fever broke, his bare bum hangs out in the chill of the night air. He plays ball all by himself under the log cabin's porch light. Tosses the ball up, claps his hands, and catches. Tosses, claps twice, catches. Tosses the ball way up, claps three times, catches.

"How you feeling, Lucky Star?" I try out a new nickname for him as I approach. "Did you take your medicine? The cherry syrup?"

"Yes, thank you," he says. "Mama gave it to me before bed."

I unlock the cabin door. "Come inside. Let's have a look at you."

He hops on the cot and I angle the desk lamp toward his tiny face. Crusty sores rim his lips. No doubt he's been rubbing the rash. Kid still needs a doctor. "You know what helps you get all the way better? Rest and more rest. How come you aren't asleep in your bed?"

"I like it here. I want to see the lady light up."

"You do have a bed, right?" I promised Saint Veronica I'd ask these kinds of caretaking questions.

"It's bang bang o'clock at my house." He bangs his hands up and down on the straw mattress, and his unassuming genitals skip with the motion. He notices me looking and cups his hands between his legs, suddenly embarrassed. Unconsciously my own arms fold tight across my chest. For a heartbeat, we are both kids with nothing but our kid bodies between us and the complex and sharp-edged world.

"You curl up here, Lucky Star. I'll go see what's happening at your place." Saint Veronica give me courage, what in the name of sin is going on with Lucky's parents? I tuck Lucky under the flannel and denim quilt.

"Mama sings me a song," he says.

"Well, I'll go ask her to come out and sing it to you." People lie to children all the time, right? Watch him, I nod at Rocco's painting, as if perverse art is any kind of babysitter. The composition of tits and slits seems to nod back at me.

I only need to follow the sound of a blundering domestic row to find the right trailer. A small group of shadowy figures is a sure sign, too. I hear one bystander hiss, "This is the worst they've ever been."

"You said that last time," says the other. He points at me and shouts, "Here comes the new girl. Hey, girl, you ain't thinkin' 'bout goin' in there, is ya?"

A sturdy woman with a mullet gets in my path. She's the type who, if she lived in the city, I'd say she was a bull dyke, but in Crystal Beach she's small-town tomboyish. "Bobby never invited you in," she says.

I push past her, past all of them. Maybe I ought to stop and take a deep breath or something, except I'm kind of high being as mad as hell. Anger is a great motivator because it never operates alone. The anger of this moment has already joined forces with past angers. I'm always pent up—not-so-secretly waiting for any chance to unleash. I feel a familiar prickly heat radiate through my body as I stand outside their trailer. There's a raised rabbit hutch to my left, twenty-four empty James Ready 5.5 bottles to my right. My whole body is vibrating. I storm in with such fervor, the welcome mat goes skittering under my step.

"Do you know where your kid is?" The question flares from my lips before I even take in the spectacle. Hal squirms on the linoleum floor; Bobby holds a forty-ounce bottle high, ready to bring it down on Hal's grizzly white head. Brutal, aside from the bottle being plastic, and still half full. She's fixing to crack him with a useless plastic bottle. Stinking cheap Georgi vodka trickles the length of Bobby's arm, soaking into her blouse. She swings the bottle down and it bounces like a child's Nerf bat off Hal's head.

"Get on your feet, Hal." I kick the refrigerator beside his crumpled body. Outside, a flashlight beam swoops past the window. I hope it's not Rose. I want to spare her this uproar. "Where's your boy, eh? Where's Lucky?"

Bobby edges over to a vinyl accordion door, peeks inside a darkened room, and lets out a defeated sigh. She turns to Hal, shaking her head to tell him the room is empty. "I told you to put a screen on his window, Hal. Do I have to do everything around here?"

"Not even twenty-four hours after he comes down with a fever, and he's outside unsupervised and half-naked," I hiss.

"Who asked you?" Bobby spits back at me.

"Lucky did," I tell her. "He was waiting outside the cabin for me. Says it's too noisy at home to sleep."

I put a hand on her shoulder, cautiously. She looks like she might haul off and punch me. Instead she turns to Hal, voice booming. "You told me you'd dry out, you s of a b. You told me you were gonna start being a real father. You said you wouldn't do to your son what your Paps did to you. Those are your words, Hal. You said that, Hal. Ya fucking lying sack of manure."

Hal's brow screws up and, as he rises from the floor, his hulking chest pushes forward.

"I'll remove any booze you got around here. We can have this place cleaned up before Lucky wakes up," I say.

Hal looks from Bobby to me, back and forth. I can't tell if he's listening or just recouping before an attack. "You are not touchin' th' bottles tonight 'n' not tomorr'a either," he slurs, shaking his finger an inch from my nose.

"Have you ever even tried?" My edge has already been replaced by irritation. Hal hears it—the thin slip of weakness in my voice boosts his rage. In one swift, liquored moment, he catches hold of Bobby's hair and clamps his other meat hook of a hand around my arm. The plastic vodka bottle bounces and spills across the grimy linoleum floor, and both Bobby and I start slipping around in the drunk puddle. But not Hal, no. Hal stays firmly rooted. Firm enough to shake us.

"Women," he shouts. My hip hits the corner of the kitchenette counter, hard. The pain is blinding. I hear people gathered outside begin to speak louder. My mouth fills with bitter saliva. "Women 'n' fuckin' children," Hal shouts again. "Women 'n'—fuck!"

Behind us, the trailer door bangs open. The mullet-haired woman either kidney-punches Hal or kicks his knees out, and he goes crashing down to the wet floor beside us. Rose is in the doorway shouting, "*Basta! Basta!*"

Then Hal's cursing gets caught in slow motion, even slower than the dreadful crawl of drunken violence. We all feel it—the suspended pause of astonishment. From out of Lucky's room the unthinkable floats, baby blue and nearly three feet tall. It points a fuzzy arm at us and freezes. A terrible feeling rips into me. Hal lets go of me, and the feeling grows worse. I lean into his bulky body, not wanting to be alone before this vision. My eyes search the air for fishing line or any kind of string holding this stuffed thing in the air.

"Make a wish," babbles Bobby. "Make a wish, make a wish, make a wish ..."

"I wish that Lucky would always be safe," I say, desperate to answer her. The awful weight of inconceivability slightly lifts as I say it aloud. Something deep inside me almost accepts that what haunts us is a hovering jumbo Care Bear. I freeze, waiting for the ridiculousness of it all to counteract my terror. It's too funny to be scary, isn't it? My chin trembles uncontrollably.

"I wish Hal would stop drinking," Bobby cries.

Hal hollers, "Yes, anything, yes."

"I surrender to a higher power," Mullet shuffles herself down beside us. Rose, too, hunkers low in the doorway.

"Cold turkey, Hal?" asks Bobby.

"Alright! Alright, almighty."

The stuffed Care Bear falls to the floor, lifeless.

The five of us breathlessly rise and robot around the trailer, our movements detached from reason or emotion. We solemnly assist Bobby as she fills a hockey bag with bottles. We right tipped kitchen chairs and straighten furniture. A bottle of Windex and a rag subconsciously make their way into my hands, and I find myself cleaning surfaces. Mullet beats and beats sofa cushions, releasing clouds of dust.

None of us touch the Care Bear. Bobby gets brave and emphatically steps over it to get into Lucky's bedroom. Then she emphatically steps over it again to rejoin us in the kitchen. "Hal won that bear at the duck shoot. He won it for Lucky the last day the Park was open. He was a sure shot then, practically a whole different man," Bobby tells us. "It's called Make-a-Wish Bear. See the shooting star on his tummy?"

I don't dare look. I'll take Bobby's word for it.

A few onlookers murmur as we exit with a clinking hockey bag full of bottles. I hear one whisper, "Hal quits for one whole week, and that girl's a miracle worker."

"I'll bet you twenty dollars he don't last a ..." says another.

I run my tongue across my front teeth, swallow back a bit of blood. I've never been in a brawl before, if you can call that a brawl. I survived whatever that was that just happened.

Back in the cabin, Lucky's tiny head on the pillow is my touchstone. When Bobby scoops him up he sings a line from "Twinkle Twinkle Little Star" with his eyes closed. Is he dreaming?

"It's his favourite song," Bobby whispers to me. "He can sing it in his sleep."

After they leave, I stand alone in the dark cabin wondering if I had a favourite song as a child, a song I could sing in my little girl sleep before P-O-G-O-N-O-P-H-O-B-I-A began creeping into my bed.

Can people really change? Can Hal? Can I? Dear Saint Veronica, I don't know if I want to live or die. Tell me what to do.

I lie on the cot and try it. I cup my hands over my mouth so my voice won't carry. "Twinkle, twinkle, Lucky Star. How I wonder what you are …" Above me the perverse painting seems to light up.

# 17 The Grit I Am

Fight and pain and kindness. What a trio. Each time I witness this gal in action, I wanna get closer. Get in her skin. She makes me remember the grit I am. The fists I've swung. I want to love her up with all ten of my lady bruiser fingers. We just might have a fine romance. Only the scrappiest of mamas could love me. And she would make a fine mother, come to think of.

I wasn't built for bringing up children, myself. I've always maintained that.

I have just about got my life sorted in my mind again, and as far as I can remember I had plenty of chances to get knocked up. I used to sport for a ringer house in Buffalo, and I'm not ashamed one bit. If Betty Grable's legs were worth a million dollars, than mine would go for a million and a half. Sporting legs, dancing legs, too sexy to be getting all flat-footed and swaybacked working eight hours a day as a soda jerker or drive-in waitress. Besides, my health certificate always came up clean, and besides, the house madam reminded me of my own Mama Famke. Madam Fannie—almost sounds like Mama Famke. Made me a little homesick every time I said her name. But only a little. A lady in my profession can't pine too much for her childhood home, can she?

On my days off, I could go anywhere and be anyone. I did a fine job blending in with the well-to-do housewives who paraded around Adam, Meldrum & Anderson fingering the imported damask linen and writing paper. Only difference between them and me is I had my very own bankroll for shopping.

But my money was better spent at Ann Montgomery's Little Harlem Club on Michigan Avenue. Ladies never paid a cover and didn't need to bother with a male escort, neither. Women ruled that roost. Smart women. Business women carrying even fatter purses than mine. Women with sensational magic hands—mixing drinks, shuffling cards, entertaining gentlemen, and even leading the orchestra. And the floorshow girls, hot damn! You can't put a woman in stockings and French knickers in front of me. Call me queer, why don't ya?

Cecilia Rhythm was the name of the fast stepper I took up with. You better believe she was a sweet stroll in the moonlight. I remember her well for her clever tap revue and more so because it was her who bought us tickets to board the *SS Canadiana*—a round-trip ferry ride to Crystal Beach. Three stories tall that ferry was! And there was a dance floor. I'd never heard of a dance floor on a boat before. Cecilia couldn't be bothered to dance on the *SS Canadiana*, though. She was saving her legs for the Crystal Ballroom.

"This ballroom is more colour-blind than those in the city," she told me when we arrived, meaning it was just colour-blind enough for her and me to be seen walking or sitting together. But there's no such place as a bull dagger-blind dance hall, so we started looking for fellas to dance with quick. There were plenty of partners to choose from—with Brylcreemed hair and fresh flowers in their lapels—thousands it seemed. All come to jolly up at the largest dance floor in America.

"Smell the bacon. There's money here," I said to Cecilia, and off I went.

You bet I found sugar daddies on the Crystal Ballroom dance floor. Soon enough, I left the ringer house in Buffalo to become a dime-a-dance girl in Crystal Beach. If there is one thing I'm good at it's dancing.

If there is one thing I'm better at, it's screaming. I could scream continuously the whole length of the Cyclone roller coaster. It wasn't about being frightened, it was about making the gentlemen believe I was scared. Men love a scared female!

I perfected three screams. Which one I used depended on the fellow I rode with. Most often, I did the Fay Wray scream-for-your-life because by 1940, even Ontario farm boys had seen *King Kong* a couple of times and were dizzy for that siren. For the skittish—the ones who looked like they might spew before the ride was done—I did the laughing-gas scream, a delirious treble that I threw my whole body into. I got my elbows pumping and my head rolling and my legs all tangled up in theirs. Sure enough by the third drop, the most edgy man had forgotten about his "coasterphobia" and was cracking up right along with me. Finally, there was the cat in heat—my golden scream. The cat in heat is only for the megabucks misters who kept my room in roses and my wrists fastened with jewels. Riding the roller coaster was foreplay to them. They wanted to hear what type of whoop I'd make if they were lucky enough to lead me to the bedroom.

Funny, I thought I'd make my living dancing. Turns out, what these men really wanted was a scream queen to share a car on the Cyclone. Like the radio jingle said, it's the thrill of a lifetime!

So how did a little gal like me get herself a reputation as a scream queen? Practice and nerve. I rode that coaster nineteen times in a row—once for every year of my life—before I could grin and bear it. The Cyclone was the most terrifying of the infamous Terrifying Trio, the three meanest roller coasters in the world. I ought to have thanked the madcap engineer Harry Guy Traver for his twisted layout. Amen to Traver's two hundred tons of steel and four miles of track—and not just any wooden track, but Douglas fir shipped all the way from British Columbia. (A gal must know her facts so she doesn't come across as a dud.) At night, a thousand incandescent lamps lit up like Broadway. Perfect for my performance.

The one flaw was the reek of the loading and unloading platform where smelling salts and upchuck stung the nostrils. The only woman more popular than me was the nurse stationed to care for the fainters and the spewers. Luckily, she was an old broad, and married too. She kept the sick ones. I didn't want 'em. It was for the fellas with nerve that I kept my hair perfumed with Chantilly. I cuddled up as we waited in line, positioning my hair right under their noses. The boys on military leave were particularly sentimental when it came to scent. They didn't have Chantilly Houbigant in the barracks.

Once we were loaded in and the safety bar clicked across our laps there was no turning back. The chain lift heaved us up ninety feet in the air, which made the Cyclone the tallest standing structure north of the Ellicott Square building in Buffalo.

The first drop was so steep we plunged ninety miles per hour, pointed right at Lake Erie. The twists and turns that followed were real knockouts too. This was right when limbs started mingling unwittingly. A jazz track, it's called. Imagine the jazz pizzicato of an upright bass. Or better yet, Leroy Anderson and his entire orchestra. "Fiddle Faddle" performed live at the Boston Pops. Now that's the kind of snaps and hops the Cyclone put us through. Jazz tracks were Traver's signature. That roller coaster man was a real pain in the neck.

But the real screamer was the final drop, which sent us into a figure eight. The mind surrendered at one end of the loop and the heart quit at the other. And what's left of a person without a head or a heart? A frightened lump of wildly firing nerves is all. The Marquis de Sade said, "It is always by way of pain one arrives at pleasure." (A gal must know her French revolutionaries so she comes across as sophisticated.) That coaster was painful enough to make many a big spender feel like they loved me. Damn fools.

Harry Guy Traver got stinking rich off his coasters and his electric

Tumble Bugs, his Flying Bobs, and his fun houses. And I suppose his terrible creations helped keep me from working myself flat-footed and swaybacked. Or worse still, becoming a wife and mother.

# 18 Creep

T he silence depressed me. It wasn't the silence of silence. It was my own silence."

Quoting Sylvia Plath never lightens the mood.

There is nothing to do. Rose warned me that The Point is quiet until May two-four weekend. I suspect she hired me on early for her own comfort. "Consider these three weeks your warm-up," she told me. Tonight, without the maelstrom of Lucky's illness, Hal's booze blowout, and the terror of jumbo Care Bear, The Point has returned to the tense stillness I sensed on my first shift.

I should be working on that book that will be a future bestseller. I manage to write a few pages about the first woman I fucked in Toronto before I give up the pen. Helenka was a dance theatre dropout who vehemently hated men and had an affinity for amphetamines. We understood one another. We understood one another tremendously for seventy-two hours, after which time she disclosed that she was engaged to a guy named Dougie who lived in Moncton, New Brunswick, where she would be moving immediately. I've tried to write about her a few times now. Each time, I write about her feet. They were so wonderfully warped. Bunions and hammer toes. The kind of feet that, if I had a cock I'd want to foot-fuck. The memory of this desire is so much better in my head. The words I use to render it, contrived. I re-read my pretty handwriting, the fastidious cursive far more impressive than the prose itself. Embarrassed, I tear out the pages and feed them in small strips to the candle's flame.

12:40 a.m. I survey the property with a flashlight, picking up an occasional cigarette butt or bottle cap. Only one window is lit throughout the entire campground, and in that window I spy a man watching me. I bet he's the catcaller from the day I applied for the job. His moustache gives him away. I shine the flashlight at his window and wave. He shuts his blinds and retreats from his trailer window.

1:10 a.m. I open the boathouse and inflate a dozen or so lake toys. Toddler-safe pink starfish and smiling turtles. Blow-up lounge chairs. Inner tubes. I patch invisible holes with duct tape, then deflate the entire lot and pack them away again. It will be a few weeks before the quarry is warm enough for swimmers.

1:40 a.m. I find the pay phone receiver hanging from its cord. There's the beep beeeep beeeeeeep of the dial tone as the receiver swings ever so slightly in the non-existent breeze.

2:10 a.m. I find the pay phone receiver hanging from its cord again. After I just righted it. I dial zero. "Can you tell me if a call was made from this pay phone in the last twenty minutes?"

"No, ma'am. I can't give you that information," the operator says. An uneasiness hits me as I hang up. Quit acting like you're in a spy movie, I scold myself.

2:45 a.m. I glove up to sift through the dumpster for empty Coca Cola cans. Maybe I make a little extra noise, hoping that one of the residents will emerge from their trailer to keep me company. I mean, I did help save a child from rabbit fever and stage an intervention with the local drunk and witnessed a super-fucking-natural phenomenon. Doesn't that warrant me a fan or two? In the city, a young woman doesn't have to perform any awesome acts to find company. She simply needs to go outside, ride the train, or sit alone at a coffee shop. No one comes for me in Crystal Beach, but I do pile up an overwhelming tower of aluminum cans. Mental note: sign The Point up for the blue box program.

Pity there isn't a local community college I could attend just to do homework at night. There must be somewhere I could enroll, excel for the first few weeks, then plummet into a practice of missing classes and handing in incorrectly completed yet defiantly clever assignments before dropping out. Maybe there's a practical skill I could learn during the wee hours? I could crochet toques and scarves for the Rebekah's auxiliary. I could take late-night private guitar lessons from one of the old hippies who live at The Point. I could practice conversational Italian with one of Rose's relatives. I might buy a metal detector and comb the grounds for buried treasure. I'd make a great pen pal for an isolated kid in up in Minaki, Ontario. I am sort of writing a book. There are so many gosh darn prospects for me to gradually fail at. Wow.

3:10 a.m. I just heard an owl hoot three times. The crook is on the cabin roof. I strain to hear the rake of its talons directly above me. Barn owls are bad luck on wings. Moony-eyed death omens. In Romania, owls are said to be the only creature that can live with ghosts. In Spain, the onomatopoeia associated with an owl's call is "cruz, cruz"—translated "cross, cross"—perpetually reminding all the sinful people of the earth that Jesus was crucified for us. Why in the name of fuck did I have to study Classics? Pair that with my useless course credits in Religion, Literature, and Women's Studies, and I may as have well enrolled in a Bachelors of Dissolution and Betrayal. My mother once warned me that too much education and not enough practical experience would leave me jaded. But I too have lots of what Barbara would call "experience."

I open the wooden chest, remembering that I spotted some books under the first-aid boxes and assorted spray cans of cleaners. There's nothing but a modest pile of what looks like personal journals and four high school yearbooks: '81 through '85. I graduated in '86, so I seize the '85 to find my junior class photo.

I was a pretty girl. (How many women say that about their teenage selves?) At the time, I didn't know what it meant to be pretty. Looking now at the stamp-sized black-and-white photo, it seems I was trying to hide the pretty. Typical teen angst hair, not backcombed into a jaunty arch over my forehead like my classmates, but crimped forward to blanket my eyes. Black lipstick just like my favourite punk divas of the day: Siouxsie Sioux, Cosey Fanni Tutti, Paloma Romero, Poly Styrene, Lydia Lunch, and Poison Ivy Rorschach. Obscure divas. So obscure in Crystal Beach, I felt like they were mine, all mine. My first loves. I couldn't yet copy their pointy wide swag lips. I doubt I owned a lip pencil. My teen mouth was a smear, like someone had taken an eraser to the photo and failed to rub out my lips. More profound existential thoughts may be had when looking back at yourself as a teenager. Nuts if I know what those thoughts are. I'm just grateful I learned how to do my makeup. I wonder if I'll lose that art by working graveyard shifts and sleeping all day. Will my careful pout once again become a naïve smear?

Ridgeway Crystal Beach High School, home of the Blue Devils. *Per ardua ad astra* is the motto written on the school's emblem. Through adversity to the stars, it means. Solid words, if they weren't borrowed from the Royal Air Force. The school's emblem is the Masonic lamp of knowledge, identical to the one painted across the front of the Masonic Lodge. When I was a freshman, I mistook our emblem for a genie's lamp. A year later, I mortified my grade ten history teacher with an oral report on our school's shady military and Masonic roots. When I veered into conspiracy theory, the school called Barbara in for a parent–teacher meeting.

116

Perhaps this is when my mother began to believe that book smarts would make me jaded. Really, what did my mother or my teachers expect? You can't swing a cat in Southern Ontario without hitting a conspiracy theory or a fabled sea monster or tales of ghosts from the underground railroad or the great fire or a UFO sighting. Do rural places have stranger tales than cities? Is it because we're bored? Do we make up shit to shock and entertain ourselves with?

Flipping through my year, I read surnames: Armstrongs and Doxtators, Labontes and Murdochs and Hills, Trembleys and Trentinis, the lone Zang. I think about capture-the-flag football. Red floods and strobe lights at Halloween dances. A noisy ring of onlookers around two boys fighting. Smoking poorly hand-rolled cigarettes on the beach. And field trips to the Park just before school let out—queuing for the flume ride or waterslides. And I remember hiding from my classmates, too. A talent for avoidance that allowed me and other outliers to slip through high school mostly unscathed. Amongst the graduating class I find my perverted painter. Not Rocco, but Ricky Esposito. He certainly is Rose's son. Same square jaw and Roman nose. Tell-tale gap between the front teeth. The grad photos are bigger and in colour. I can make out the gold stud in his right earlobe. Gay? Or merely a touch of glam rock?

"Where are you, Ricky?" I say. "You blow this popsicle stand just like I did?" Maybe Ricky's living in Montréal, speaking a crap mix of French and Italian as he orders a smoked meat sandwich. Or all the way in Vancouver, playing bongo drums beside the Pacific Ocean, eating marijuana brownies, kissing braless women or possibly bearded men. Is Ricky embracing every darn identity that Crystal Beach is not? Great, now I'm jealous of a photo in a yearbook. Doesn't take much, I suppose. Jealouser still when I find Tamara Matveev's signature at the back: *Ric, Thanks for being the big brother I never had. xo T. Matveev. P.S. I'm keeping your shirt. Ha Ha!*

I flip pages to find Tamara's perfect junior photo. Ricky, or maybe Tamara herself, drew a heart around it. Were they sweethearts? Lovers? What if he brought her to this very cabin? There's a question. As I lie back on the straw, the show takes shape in my mind. She wears a cheerleading outfit, which is pure fantasy because our high school was too rinky-dink for a squad. Ricky slowly removes his pink button-down Oxford—the prep costume that boys wore to blend in. This is the shirt he'll never get back from Tamara. She straddles him, toying with the burgeoning black hair trailing down the centre of his chest. A week ago, she straddled me just the same way. For money, sure. I can recall her tequila breath on my neck all the same. How her thigh muscles relaxed and flexed. I should push down this arousal. I knew that, in leaving Toronto, I'd also leave behind bars and house parties and any familiar place where casual sex could be found. I've lost more than fish in the metropolitan sea. I've recently been made sexless. More than sexless. I have a sex shortfall. Sex in the red. Like my money debt, I'll have to work my way back up to zero. I can't masturbate in my childhood bed, not without fixating on the x's penned on the wall beside me. Without fixating on how Barbara's probably had sex with a hundred men in the room right next to mine. If I reached orgasm I'd be sick. Sicker. I'd die. Barbara could deal with my fucking corpse. Poetic justice.

If I jerk off at work, then I'm a creep, right, I'm the bad guy? I've been called worse than a creep. Tamara Matveev has been called worse than a creep. What an awkwardly choice moment for a memory to surface. I remember Tamara's tailspin into small-town scandal.

Only a few saw her in the football field that June day, and I was not one of them. I was writing a final exam in a cafeteria along with a hundred or so other juniors. The only reason I remember the incident at all is because some kid flung open the cafeteria door and hollered, "Tamara Matveev bare naked," then sped along the hallway shouting other indelicacies. By the time the teacher called "pencils down" the gossip had already spanned the school. Allegedly, Tamara had drifted out of the examination and into the girls' change room, then emerged again without any clothing and continued to drift across the football field. She was spotted by a couple of stragglers from senior class who were about to begin their "everybody wins awards ceremony"—a tradition marked by phony certificates for the "Sunniest Disposition" and "The Honest Abe Award." I bet Ricky was one of those stragglers. This would be a perfect moment to be the "big brother" Tamara wrote about in her yearbook autograph. He must have sped out to her with his big, strapping boy-sized shirt spread open like a blanket. It's possible. Any number of scenarios are possible. I still couldn't say why she put herself on display. The only clear detail I remember is that after our exam, a fleet of teachers rushed us past the guidance room and out the front doors. Through the slits in the counsellor's blinds I thought I could see Tamara's silhouette. She was folded into herself on a chair. I thought I could hear her sobbing. A tall man or boy stood against the counsellor's door, his back blocking the square frosted-glass window.

Did this truly happen? Or am I imposing some other teen girl's humility onto Tamara? I flip to her photo in the yearbook. She's got a pageant smile—Miss Teen Ontario. This is the girl who returned to her senior year to become our school's femme fatale. Inciting catcalls was her daily routine. It was impossible not to notice her, not to know her face, her name.

This stain in her history makes me want her more. I want to take her back to our high school football field and make a fresh memory of our own. I press my eyes shut. I dare my fingertips into my underwear, telling myself that I only want to find out if I can still feel sensation or not. When I open my eyes, there's a glowing sphere on Ricky's painting. A hot spot of white light. I leap to my feet to see who has pointed their flashlight through the window. Nothing. Quiet and dark outside.

Something? Sparkles in the distance. Small flame? My job is to check it out, right? To go calmly into the iris-coloured predawn and see what's making the woods glow, but the air suddenly feels at a strange standstill again. I should be brave after the last two days, I tell myself. I should accept that the barrier between reality and the unknown is porous, right? I shiver from my feet to my head as I disrupt the dewy grass. My flashlight beam catches the green bodies of grasshoppers as they skip out of my path. The path toward the curious light turns to shrubland before the tree line. I press on through what I'm sure is moonseed or poison ivy or another vine that gives me a rash. This is what I get for not walking the full grounds on my last couple of shifts; I haven't learned the paths through the campsites. But there is definitely a flickering light in the woods.

"You can't start a campfire. Campsites aren't open yet," I call ahead, hoping I can avoid getting any closer. It's an unnatural fire. I hear the snaps and pops, like young branches. Palest yellow glow. Then nauseating fluorescent white. A shadow puppet of a figure stirs nearby—its torso is long and twisted. "You can register to camp. Early bird special. Just let me take your name down. Okay?"

The figure appears to be a woman. The outline of her legs is uninterrupted, toes to hips. The contour of her back, perfectly smooth. Is she nude?

I laugh, stunned at first, then nervously, caught in some appalling delirium. This moment is not human. I'm in the wrong place, witnessing what is unseeable. I don't feel myself fall, but gradually become aware of my hands in the cold earth. My flashlight has landed several feet away from me. I laugh harder, manically, dry heaving. The shadow is Tamara Matveev naked in our school football field. No. No. My mind is still intact enough to understand that it can't be Tamara. No. This woman has come to repay me for lusting over Tamara. The small rock I suddenly tongue in my mouth tells me I deserve it. I am shameful. Dirt in my hair, clothes tearing on the thorny scrub as I crawl and skid. I am a slut. My left hand tries to claw its way past the zipper of my jeans. Uncontrollable. Possessed. I will rough myself up. The forest floor will eat me. I will get what I deserve.

I'm so close to the fire now, I can smell ash. The woman remains a faceless shadow. "Who ...?" I struggle to my knees, then cast myself toward her.

And all of it is gone.

The sun has risen over the horizon line, and beams of first light wriggle through the trees. Carved on a nearby stump is the number nine. I lie in the fetal position in the centre of an empty circle of hard-stamped soil. This is campsite number nine. I am alone here.

# 19 Calm Down

Barbara brushes my hair away from my face. A cord of snot trails from my nose along my cheek.

Apparently, I woke up talking in my sleep. "Hollering," claims Barbara. "Loud enough to wake the whole neighbourhood." Now I can barely speak. She suggests I make myself bacon and eggs at two in the afternoon—a proper breakfast. She suggests I draw an Avon Skin So Soft bubble bath. Songbird hops up on the bed to lick my ear, making little dog sympathy whimpering sounds. A second later, Songbird is growling feverishly at the stunt. Growling and turning in small doggie circles. Barbara picks her up.

"See! Something bad is going to happen to me. Even Songbird knows it."

"What? Honey, you're being dramatic. It's a bad dream," says Barbara, and, "You always had nightmares, ever since you were a little girl."

"I can't get any sleep in this bedroom." I thrust the blankets away, then, realizing my night gown is see-through in the afternoon light, I yank them back up to my chin. "It's not a nightmare." Stop talking. Keep it in. Barbara is the last person to act hysterical around.

"I told you that graveyard shift would be too much. You better calm down and get a few more hours sleep before you have to go back to work again."

# 20 We Become a Duo

I weave through the streets named after trees: Rosewood, Elm-wood, Birchwood, Lakewood, Beachwood, Westwood, Ashwood, Oakwood, Cherry. None are more than a few blocks long. All of them populated with one-storey cottages not much bigger than the mobile homes at The Point. The same ornaments hang in their front porches: novelty flags and beer-cap wind chimes. Ordinary homes.

I'm taking this new route to work, and I've armed myself with offerings. *Poems and Prayers for the Very Young* by Martha Alexander, a book I retrieved from a box in the basement marked "Starla, Age 0 – 5."

"Part of your job is babysitting?" Barbara asked skeptically. "You're not really ... the patient type, Star. Can't someone else watch the kid?"

"If I tell you to go fuck yourself, will you still make peanut butter cookies?" I asked.

Barbara made the peanut butter cookies.

Hal will need to recover the calories he's used to getting from drinking, otherwise he'll lose weight as well as his mind during this cold turkey stretch. I don't know how much of a drinker Bobby is, but who doesn't want cookies, right?

The small gifts are offerings. Maybe if I'm a good employee, committed to Lucky, kind to Hal and Bobby, and if I come bearing gifts, maybe tonight will be normal. A normal person would quit. Find a normal job. But no, not me. I'm the idiot in a horror film who heads on down to the basement.

Freud would have said horror films allow us to explore feelings that are repressed by the ego—that's what my psych professor told the class, many times. The expressionists loved Freud's psychoanalysis. The same expressionists moved to America between WWI and WWII. They got jobs in Hollywood. Early horror films are all-Freud, all-the-time. Sex and childhood trauma, bad dreams and the subconscious. I've seen *Nosferatu* three times, same with *Dr Jekyll and Mr Hyde*.

During my own era of horror, sex, childhood trauma, dreams, and the subconscious struck again in *A Nightmare on Elm Street*. Basically, Freud would have been a Wes Craven fan. He would have owned a red-and-green striped sweater.

But that's the movies. Curses! Revenge! Bloodlust! But what happened on The Point's forty-nine acres? Not just what happened to Rose, but what shitty secrets do the grounds themselves hold? Does the property sit on an ancient gravesite? Or am I thinking of Poltergeist or Amityville Horror? Horror movies on the brain. The ancient burial ground is a horror movie cliché, but for real, archeologists did find those human sculls down by the Niagara Boulevard a few years back. Shipped the remains to Ottawa, if I recall.

Who thinks of human skulls as they're headed to work? Who thinks of buried secrets? Of repressed memory?

"If you must subscribe to this *The Courage to Heal* fad, repressed-memory nonsense that it is, you must first learn Freud's sexually symmetrical memory." The same psych professor said that too. I never asked about trauma and recovered-memory therapy in class ever again. Instead, I wore my "What Are You Looking At, Dicknose?" T-shirt (shout out to *Teen Wolf*) to his class as often as possible. I could wear that T-shirt all I wanted to. I still have every word of his fucking lectures practically memorized.

My stride quickens the closer I get, my heart rate too. I conjure a series of things that could go awry as soon as I arrive. Worst-case scenarios, most of which involve something bad happening to Lucky. Please, Saint Veronica, don't let anything happen to Lucky.

I smell burning. More like melting plastic than campfire. There's a searing glare in the woods. The light skips and leaps a few feet at a time. Will-o-the wisp. Foolish fire: *Ignis fatuus*. Knowing the Latin doesn't save me from following it. Go back to the road, I order myself with each involuntary step. But I press forward because this is a pretty pretty pretty dream. The tree branches crackle like a PA system switching on, and suddenly a soundtrack trails my steps. Gentle tenor guitar, finely picked, not strummed. Slow-tempo, slow and sickly sweet like my breathing, like the night air around me. I feel humiliated, not afraid. Something bad is going to happen to me. I asked for this. Go back to the road. A remote voice croons, "I don't want to set the world on fire ..." She is here too, my shadow woman. My woman. My? I'm desperate to see her face, but each time I spot her in my peripheral vision, she dissolves. My head snaps in all directions on my drunken neck.

"Who—" I try to ask. My voice hiccups in the back of my throat. Acid reflux.

"I just want to start a flame in your heart."

The woods are dark, and the road is far behind me. I'm on my knees again, as if I've been bounced out of a bar. I cup my hand on the inseam of my jeans. It feels like I took a kick to the groin. The cold ground reaches my forehead. I allow my cheek to rest in the dirt. I try to recall the first time I decided life was unlivable. If I could locate the exact moment, recover that precise memory, maybe I could call off the curse. *Dura è la stella mia.* My harsh fate. *Lasciami brutta fattura.* Leave me alone, bad hex. Am I remembering more of my mother tongue because my crotch hurts? Is that the true centre where language lives?

Trailer lights are a few paces away. Lucky's darling giggle in the distance brings me to my feet again. There's nothing to do but lumber onward. I find my tote hanging from a tree branch. "Thanks a lot," I mumble, retrieving the bag.

Hal, Bobby, Lucky, and Rose all gleefully greet me. To them, it's not odd that I arrive through a thicket of shrub. Rose reaches me first, whispering, "They woke this morning after sleeping all night and a day. Now they're full of piss and vinegar. Keep them quiet, if you can." She kisses Lucky on the top of his head and blows past Hal and Bobby.

"I said I was sorry," Hal calls after her. "Rose, don't be like that." Rose waves her hand in the air, doesn't look back. Hal turns to me with his mouth wagging open, but I don't care to know what he and Rose are fighting about.

"I brought cookies," I chirp, my voice more scratchy than happy.

I invite Hal and Bobby into the cabin because their own place is haunted by a Care Bear, and Lucky has already tucked himself under the quilt.

Hal and Bobby set themselves up in lawn chairs and sleeping bags. Hal chews with an open mouth, while Bobby takes small bites as if she's suspicious of the cookie. Peanut butter cookie crumbs collect on Hal's lap, while Bobby tucks her long grey-and-black locks behind her ears to make sure no crumbs get in her hair. The four of us settle in for *Poems and Prayers for the Very Young*. Bobby and I take turns reading lines of poetry.

"Mama, aren't you going to sing?"

"I sing to him before bed," she explains to me, then turns the rhyming couplets into song, "White sheep, white sheep/On a blue hill," she sings. Lucky squeezes his eyes shut—a few notes are all it takes to settle him in. The poem-turned-song is "Clouds" by Christina Rossetti. "When the wind stops/You all stand still."

As Bobby sings, I start simultaneously running lines from Rossetti's famous "Goblin Market" in my head. "She cried, 'Did you miss me?/ Come and kiss me./Never mind my bruises,/Hug me, kiss me, suck my juices.'" Rossetti, that Victorian lesbo. Is that what my problem is? I accidentally ate fruit from a strange orchard, goblin fruit? I'm enchanted now, or cursed, more likely.

Lucky is asleep before Bobby finishes. She says, "You keep reading. I like to be read to too. And you've got a pretty good reading voice. Doesn't she sound like that woman on the radio, Hal? Who's that famous woman on the radio?"

"Rush Limbaugh," Hal spits. Bobby feigns agreement, echoing Rush Limbaugh's name, while shaking her head "no" and rolling her eyes. They're certainly a pair. They squirm alike. Hal scratches his beard, and Bobby rakes her fingers through her long salt-and-pepper hair. I miss long hair. Maybe Bobby will let me French braid her hair for her. I'm not bad with scissors, and she would look kind of chic with curtain bangs, like 1960s Cher. This newfound nurturing side surprises me. It's nice. It puts a tender wedge between this moment and my maenad frenzy in the forest.

"Read another one," Bobby requests when the poems are done. She speaks softly, both of us peeking at Lucky to make sure he stays asleep.

"There is no other one," I tell her. "I'll bring more books next week, after I have a couple nights off. I've got lots of books I can lend you."

"What d'ya mean 'nights off'? Who's gonna help look after Lucky?" Hal scolds.

"How about you help look after Lucky? He's your son," I scold right back.

"How about in the trunk? There any books in there?" Bobby points emphatically, trying to catch Hal's attention.

"Ya shows up here, Miss high 'n' mighty. Don't have kids of your own, so don't act like ya know shit." Hal stamps his foot, making him teeter in his lawn chair.

"A minute ago you were upset I wasn't going to babysit non-stop, now I don't know shit about kids." I shouldn't antagonize him, but as usual, I can't seem to back down.

"Say, that hockey bag is under that cot, ain't it? You stupid enough to keep our bottles anymore?"

I am stupid enough. I never even thought to dump the booze. Hal rises up so quickly the lawn chair sticks to his butt for a second before it comes crashing down. "You shoulda got rid of it," he says to me. His throat reddens.

"You should sit back down," I counter.

"He's not too good to hit a girl," Bobby warns. The back of Hal's meaty palm connects with my cheek. A bell of heat rings in my head. And that was only a warning blow, I'm sure. I'd flee if I could, but he is too big and this cabin is too small to slip past him. I eye the open exit, and the iron latch twitches.

It's her—the shadow in the woods, the moonlight lady, my goblin fruit—with her unseen hand on the door. It's been her all along. The miracle cinnamon sucker. The Wish Bear. This mad ache in my body.

Her invisible hand slams the door then swiftly opens it again to thump into Hal's towering frame. My own hand lifts like a magic trick. I wave my fingers and the door swings closed again. Instinctively we become a duo, goblin fruit and me. She is smoke, and I am mirrors. *Whoosh*, I wave my hand, and the door flies open and hits Hal a second time. He is too stunned to move, so I whack him with the door a third and a fourth. My chest pleasurably warms, like I just downed a single-malt scotch neat.

"Sit down, Hal. Before she turns you into a goddamn toad."

Hal retrieves his collapsed lawn chair and lowers himself. He sets his hand on Bobby's knee, and she takes her own out from underneath her sleeping bag. Holding hands, they both begin to weep. I'm afraid I'll have to pay for goblin fruit's favour later. For now I silently accept Hal and Bobby's trembling awe. Nearly half an hour passes before Hal and Bobby's breathing finally slows to a normal rhythm and my jaw stops tingling from Hal's backhanded wallop.

I retrieve one of Ricky's journals from the wooden chest and begin to read. It's an intrusion, reading a private journal, but it's all I have to get us through. The first dozen pages are merely a handyman's logbook written in impossibly neat longhand. The opening page alone confirms Ricky as the cabin's builder with the illustration of an axe labeled "Fig. 1." Ricky writes, "The best axe is John Neeman Netherlands Felling Axe, 813 mm in length with an axe head of 175 mm. Weighs 2.2 kg. Can cut through small diameter timber, i.e. birch or young aspen, in ten firm swings. Costs $400."

"Four hundred flippin' dollars!" says Hal. "Gimme forty bucks right now, and I'll get an axe for ya." At least he's speaking to me again.

The prices and uses of a Husqvarna Wood Splitting Hatchet, a DMT Diamond Sharpener, a General Tools Moisture Meter, and Polytarp plastic wrap are also listed with elaborate drawings. If Ricky did what he drew, then this cabin was made from trees he cut down, de-barked, split into logs and planks, stacked, and dried himself. "Damn," I remark. "All I did in high school was listen to punk records and mope."

"All I did in high school was ..." says Bobby. I wait a second or two for her to finish her sentence. "Never mind," she says.

Several pages in, Fig. 11 shows an Eastern White Pine, with a closeup of a circular log sliced to show the age rings. "Grown in the forests of Ontario, the Eastern White Pine is a slow-growth soft wood that should be winter-cut and air-dried for at least 150 days (build with dried lumber in June). Hew away the newest annual rings and the sapwood; these are the living parts of the tree. The heartwood is dead and hard and dark. Only build with the heartwood."

"You making that shit up?" says Bobby. She too catches the bleak metaphor.

"Nope. This author has quite the way with words," I tell her. "A real Renaissance man. He's written some poetry, it looks like." I flip to the centre pages. "In my heart I have but one desire," I recite the poem in my best romantic voice to entertain Bobby. "I don't want to set the world on fire./I just want to start a flame in your heart."

Wait. Ricky's poem—is the song from the woods, word for word.

"Keep reading."

I swallow, hard. "I've lost all ambition. I don't have any aim./I love you like you want to be loved./And all I ask is that you do the same./I don't want to set the world on fire./I just want to start a flame in your heart."

## 21 Faker

**B**arbara is entertaining. "Starla, this is Dr Rahn Johnson," she introduces the man with a greying moustache who sits so casually on the sofa that I can tell this is not a first date. Second clue: he's wearing shoes in the house. Nobody wears shoes in the house on a first date. His leather loafers are Gucci, though—the classic kind with the red-and-green stripe and a miniature horse bit. "Rahn is a pediatric surgeon at Women & Children's Hospital in Buffalo." Translation: this man is a hot ticket so make yourself scarce.

I hightail it to my room as Dr Rahn Johnson says, "She inherited your good looks." Barbara whoops theatrically. She would have to entertain on my night off.

I pop Bongwater's ninety-minute *Double Bummer* album into my Sony Discman. I also have the *Love and Rockets, Vol 5: House of the Raging Women*, a 125-page comic book with which to occupy myself. My favourite comic book characters of all time are Maggie and Hopey. If only they'd make out more. My sex life is down to reading comics, so here's hoping for some graphic action. The problem is that *Love and Rockets* is still inside the brown bag from Dragon Lady Comics on Queen Street West. If I pull the comic out of the bag then another one of my belongings will be unpacked. Bag by bag and box by box, it's happening. I live here, in Crystal Beach.

My room is cluttered and confused by half-unpacked items from Toronto and the two dusty boxes I hauled up from the basement, the first labelled Starla Age 15 & 16, and the second Starla Age

17. My senior yearbook rests on top of the second box. Terribly happy-go-lucky for age seventeen, I find "DIE" scrawled across the photos of several of my classmates, and "STRAIGHT TO HELL" over a few others. Senior year was tough—I haven't forgotten—tough enough for bitter death wishes, apparently. I flip to Tamara Matveev's senior photo. To my surprise the very page is bookmarked with a felt Crystal Beach Amusement Park flag pendant on a yellow yarn string necklace. Five plus years ago, why had I marked Tamara's page? Coincidence? Her senior superlative reads "Most Likely to Be Famous." I put the pendant on, tuck the little flag into my T-shirt. It seems to thud against my sternum, like a locket or key might. I pull the pendant back out to look at it. Our logo wasn't much to look at. A smiling sun with the "C" and "B" (for Crystal Beach) awkwardly forming the sun's eyes and nose. It's cheap, but instantly I am attached to it. Nostalgia, I suppose. Maybe I'll wear it every day, just like I always wore my blue scapular of the Immaculate Conception under my clothes. Back when I was into church.

Sprawling out on my bed, my gaze seesaws between Tamara's yearbook photo and the Are You Afraid of the Dark painting that looms over me. I've grown fond of the sailors' oversized red lips. Drag queen lips—at any minute they might start lip-syncing Carol Channing. Hello, Dolly.

I slip my headphones over my ears and Ann Magnuson scream-sings about wrist slitting. I wish I could poach the song "Frank." Bongwater is exactly the type of post-psychedelic hardcore noise band that I would form if I formed bands. I'd do a speed-metal cover of the *Jesus Christ Superstar* soundtrack. Sort of Judas Priest meets rock opera à la Andrew Lloyd Webber. The live stage show would feature fake-blood stigmata and homoeroticism between the guitar-playing apostles. I've got so many ideas and pretty much no capacity. I'll hit my stride. I bet I'm on the brink of a big creative bang.

According to some, I can cure rabbit fever, maybe alcoholism too. Not that I really did those things. I wonder what other ersatz stuff goblin fruit might pull? I wonder what is happening at The Point without me. Does Lucky miss me?

No more than three tracks elapse before I grow stir crazy. I press pause on my Discman only to hear Barbara's sound bite from the living room, "I have no filter. I say every darn thing that pops into my head ..." Literally, that's what she's saying to her date, as if her endless prattle hasn't already demonstrated her point. Quick! Press the play button again.

I roll off the bed and open my closet door. All these gorgeous clothes I may never wear again, or at least not around here. Many are second-hand, found during meticulous searches through Kensington Market. As much as I detest shopping malls, I admit that Lime Rickey's Restaurant in the Eaton Centre beckoned to me. An embarrassing number of dresses in my collection came from that mall—purchased directly after I devoured a cheeseburger and root beer float. I grab a black Bill Blass silk chiffon bustier dress and swing it on its hanger, admiring the weightlessness of the fabric. I never wore this number in Toronto either. It's what I'll wear to my funeral—at least that was my intention when I bought it. Live fast, die young, leave a beautiful corpse.

Macramé Jesus hangs in the closet with the rest of my clothes. I take him off his hanger and hold him in front of my torso like a dress. The reflection in my vanity mirror cracks me up. Jesus's head droops around my breasts. His legs dangle above my knees. When I kick my legs, his floppy legs kick too. Like a puppeteer, I make him wave "hello" and salute the sky. Here's exactly what I grew up doing—entertaining myself in my room while Barbara entertained men in every other room in the house. Maybe I should call a friend in Toronto, like she suggested, reach out or something? Gloria Orr referred to herself as my best friend once. She might miss me? Josie Cruz and her fiancé Zed always liked me, even if they did set me up on that terrible blind date, so I guess they only liked me enough to have a threesome with me. Therese from the campus bookstore was a generous listener, or at least generous with her feedback. Always so ready and willing to offer odd advice that I would never actually heed. What comments would she offer me now? See a doctor, a priest?

My crotch is still sore from the phantom kick I am not entirely certain I took yesterday. I shut down the associated thoughts that seem to link my sore crotch and having been molested in this very room by turning the volume way up on my Discman. Ann Magnuson sings a Johnny Cash cover while some musical instrument that sounds like an overplayed jack-in-the-box knells in the background. I love this song.

Tentatively, I grab hold of macramé Jesus's knotted penis, positioned just over my own pubic bone. It scratches my hand as I stroke it. I pause my CD. "Hey, Tamara, it's me, the big JC. How about I turn your water into wine?" I coax. "Come here, and I'll heal your sick."

Call me a sodomite.

Why must I torment myself?

What if I want this ghost thing to be real?

What if I want it to be all about me? Like unexplainable shit is actually happening because of me. I know, I know! *Amour de soi* is my high; it's the swing side of depression. Toronto is over, I'm so sure. The Twilight Zone has closed, and besides, they hadn't booked a good band since the Beastie Boys. Mayor Eggleton will never proclaim the Pride Parade or commission an AIDS Memorial because he hates gays. And everyone under thirty with their arts degree is vying for the few crappy jobs left in the city. I can't think of a single true friend I had in Toronto. But there is fucking magic in Crystal Beach. Like, on par with David fucking Copperfield walking through the Great Wall of China kind of magic.

A guitar ballad lulls outside my window. At first, I think the din is coming through my headphones, but the CD inside my Discman is perfectly still. With a horrified yet giddy keenness, I listen closer. "I don't want to set the world on fire ..."

"Maybe I want this to be real." It's titillating, *those* words in *my* mouth.

"I want this to be real," I say louder. Outside, the sumac and maple trees feel fucking alive in the breeze. My heart pounds right up to my throat as I scan the darkness. She heard me. She's out there waiting for me. I pop the rusty screen out of my window. Only thing in this house my mother didn't replace, the screen windows. I've got one foot out, dangling. For a second, the night seems to pull back the velvet curtain of a vaudeville stage. She's not quite vaudeville, but another age. She flickers before me like old film, her beauty dimpled by light burns and flashes, like a leading lady for Bela Lugosi.

Then only her tiny fire glows ahead. I race to catch it, past the neighbours' vinyl-sided bungalows, past dogs barking behind chain-link fences, past the last street lamp, past the bumpy rim where the asphalt turns to gravel road. I run and run until she is standing smack in front of me. "I can see you," I say.

And as if saying it makes it all the more real, she reacts, steps back. Startled, I step back too. I hardly expected a ghost to have facial expressions. She seems rattled. "Can you speak?" I ask.

"I have been talking this whole time, ever since you woke me up. I was having a little snooze in that stunt of yours," she says as clear as the living. "The real question is, can you hear me? Please, say you can." I suddenly find myself barefoot. Did I lose my slippers? Was I wearing slippers when I left my room? The bottoms of my feet throb against the dirt and gravel path we stand on.

"I can hear you," I whisper. I'm not sure where I am. The neighbours' homes seem very far away. Did I run toward the lake or away from it? I can't smell the algae anymore. I don't know where I'd run, in which direction I would flee.

"How 'bout that. Word for word, or do I sound like gibberish to you?"

"Word for word."

"And touch? It's been an age since I touched somebody."

I flinch as she reaches for me. She makes time skip like a scratch in a vinyl record. We stand together as she takes form. She is tiny, like me, and my knees meet her knees, my hipbones meet her hipbones, my breasts meet her breasts. My breathing becomes stronger than my body, like my lungs might burst, like I'll balloon up and float away. Her arms circle my waist. She looks me in the eye, and I am so worthless. I am invincible. We are goddesses together. I'm her dog. I'll do anything for her. My brain is leaking out my ears.

"You want this?" She touches her cheek to mine.

"Yes," I tell her. But it's not the real me talking. There is no real me. Not anymore. Her kiss is the extinction of everything. All thoughts halt. I will no longer ask myself if this is happening or if this is about me. All creation vacuums out around us, leaving our bodies the last two burning stars. Her tongue on my skin, and I'm burning. I am breaking. She can break me. I am willing to explode. Supernova. I will get what I have coming. Then I hear myself screaming, "Stop, it's too scary. It's too scary." She raises a cross eyebrow.

"Frankenstein's monster is scary. Me, I'm hot stuff, don't ya know."

She turns her back to me as she fades away.

Am I standing upright? After her, I can't make sense of my physical relationship to the world. I rake my fingers through the air. Air? Yes, air. I am not on my hands and knees, like the last two times. My body thinly undulates on two leaden feet. A very small dance. The air is maliciously cold. Why did I tell her to go?

The sound of each footstep startles me.

I find my way to a long gravel path that seems unreal. Trees are plastic, and as I make my way back toward the houses again, they are also two-dimensional. Everything is trying to trick me. But now I understand so much more than this artificial place. I can't help but laugh at every fake thing around me. A man walking his pitbull stops to stare. I laugh harder when he asks me if I'm all right. He walks away shaking his robot head. I swallow back the urge to call after him, ask him if he is real or not. Ask him if he's out to get me.

Ask him if he knows I'm the most powerful bitch he'll ever meet.

# 22 Weird

A tumbler of rye and ginger and I'm gutted. I suspect graveyard shifts shrink organs. That's why I have to pee all the time—my stomach and liver have atrophied. After only a week of overnights, I'm no longer a match for a single highball. I order a second drink anyway—liquid courage to ready me.

Pure Platinum undulates to the synth-strings of INXS's "Never Tear Us Apart." I imagine what music I would choose if I were a stripper. Midnight Oil's *Diesel and Dust* is a better Aussie-rock album than INXS's *Kick*—but is "Beds Are Burning" a proper panty-remover song? There's got to be some science to pairing naked women and Billboard hits.

Tamara Matveev materializes during the saxophone solo. I bite my lip, a little too hard. She waves at me and says my name. I can't hear her over the music, but her lips form the words "Hi, Star."

"Hi, Star" she says again, in my ear.

"When do you get a break?" I ask. She's about to tease me—I can tell by her pert facial expression. And she can tell by my face that I'm not fooling. I need to ask someone, besides Rose, about how I can find Ricky Esposito.

"Sure, okay. Soon as I settle the bill with that table of six," she nods toward a group of young Mormon men. "We'll get a bite to eat, okay? Not here."

Late lunch at the Ming Teh Chinese Restaurant. I presume Tamara choses the restaurant because of the windowless front façade—no passerby will see us together. Then the aroma of sesame and five spice greets us. "I haven't been here in forever," I say. "I love this place."

"I know. I could totally eat their moo shu soup every day," she says. Ming Teh is *her* place. She's brought me to *her* place. I'm flattered enough that I impulsively reach for her elbow; my hand briefly loops through her arm as we pick a table like a married couple. I notice a small white owl tattooed on her inner bicep.

"Wisdom or death—the owl symbol," I say while reading the menu.

Tamara palms her tattoo. "Both are bound to happen. I'll get wise and then I'll die." She winks at me. What is such a confident woman doing in our home town? The few other customers are elderly couples, all slowly working their way through fried rice dishes. They slump in the very same chairs I remember from eating here as a child. Cracking red vinyl. The red patterned carpet is also the same. The Ming family sits at the round table at the back, also taking a late lunch. The young mother passes her toddler to a grandparent and gets up to wait on our table. "Hiya, Tamara," she says. "How's business today? Slow? So slow here. You want the usual?"

Between courses of spring rolls and chicken and pineapple fried rice she volunteers more about her life, as if she sensed my curiosity. "I tried Toronto, like you. The music scene, eh? I never knew there was music outside of Casey Kasem's Top 40 until Toronto. Skinny Puppy, Butthole Surfers, Teenage Head, Bad Brains, Chris & Cosey—I saw them all."

"I'm surprised we didn't run into each other. We like all the same bands." I wish she had run into me in Toronto—I was far more interesting when I was there. Or was I?

"I saw the Cramps at Concert Hall on their A Date With Elvis tour. Remember that show?"

I nod "yes" even though I wasn't there.

"Yeah, well, then you saw how some guy jumped from the balcony while the Cramps were playing 'Human Fly'? I was wearing these platform Mary Janes, and I got knocked over as everyone rushed the stage. Twisted my ankle so badly. Doctors put a metal screw in me to hold my fibula to my tibia. I thought I wasn't going to be able to dance ever again. But ankle fractures heal, apparently. Plus I mostly do floor work now, low-impact moves. Anyway, I had a lot of fun in Toronto. Yeah, pity we didn't run into each other. Did you ever go to Chez Moi? When did you come out?"

Tamara lets me stare wide-eyed and wordlessly back at her for a moment before she changes the subject. "Yeah, so, I moved to Vancouver for awhile. All the circuit girls kept talking about this club called The Penthouse, like it was some sort of stripper heaven where every girl would land her own high-rolling celebrity patron. All I did was small-bills shifts. Oh, and once I did a table dance for Christopher Plummer. That's a story I can tell my grandkids.

"I caught the tail end of midtown Manhattan clubs. The Harmony Theatre, Adam and Eve, The Living Room, Baby Doll Lounge—geez, these places don't mean anything to you, I'm totally blathering." She sifts through the plate of fried rice with her chopsticks.

"You can't stop now! I know exactly where you're talking about. Near Grand Central Station, eh? I've been there. I've seen, you know, the neon signs—Girls Girls Girls."

"I'm sure you've seen those signs, Starla," Tamara wisecracks.

"Altria is around there. One of the Whitney's buildings. On 42nd and Park. It's where I saw Joan Jonas's *Volcanic Saga*, this art house film. Yeah, um, it's about Iceland and dreams, like, feminist surrealism. Tilda Swinton's in it. She's that actress in the Derek Jarman movie, *Caravaggio*. *Caravaggio* is really good. You should watch it with me sometime. I have it on VHS. Now I'm babbling."

"You'd fit right in, in New York," she says, her gaze still preoccupied with the rice.

"Naw, I felt like an poser," I admit. "I've only been a few times. Last time I took a walk down Lexington to check out the girly clubs. I was just window shopping. Is it rude to call it that? I remember there were literally women hanging out in the windows. I was too chicken to go inside the clubs. You're the first ... stripper ... I've actually seen ... do a ... private dance. Is that what you call it?"

Tamara makes eye contact again. "You sound so embarrassed."

"I'm not," I lie. "Tell me what happened next, in New York. I want to know."

"In New York we were called hostesses, usually twenty-five of us worked at one time. Plus most of these clubs played pornos in the back room. It was like titty overload. I never worked so hard, dancing two floor shows, and I can't even say how many private dances a night. I lasted four months.

"After Manhattan, there's only two places for a dancer to go: Vegas or Japan. I went to Japan to work in the hostess clubs. That's a really long story."

"I bet. I want to go to Japan one day," I say, gobsmacked by her experiences, but still not close to knowing what she's doing waitressing in a shoddy club on the Niagara Parkway. "Now you're back where you started."

"I got really homesick in Tokyo. Had these coughing fits all the time. Or I'd hyperventilate. I'd sleep all day. I signed up for as many shifts as the agency would give me—too many shifts. The only reason I went out sightseeing was to buy presents for my mom and aunties. I sent them a buttload of souvenirs–lacquered boxes and rolls of cute *washi* paper. Half the stuff is back in my room at home now. I'll show you. I keep it around to remind myself that I get depressed if

I leave home for too long. I'm just happy here. Or, like, not happy, exactly. More like not overwhelmed. I don't feel like the world is going to swallow me up here. Small-town girl, eh? Oh, and I got my owl in Japan." She palms her tattoo again; rotates her arm around for me to see it better. "My last week in Tokyo I saw these owl and cherry blossom woodcuts. There, see! I've been to art galleries too! Japanese art galleries. Yeah, the owls. I got so homesick looking at the fucking owls. Made me miss the screech owls you hear around here. It feels good to tell someone all this," says Tamara. "It's not like a lot of us leave and come back, you know? Anyway, I got this tattoo, and I got on the next plane."

Our hands are almost touching on the table. Sweet and sour sauce bleeds into the white tablecloth. I think about her six years ago, trailing naked across our high school football field. All the small-town gossip that followed. No wonder she travelled half way around the world.

"I got a job at The Point," I tell her.

"Oh?" She removes her hand from the tabletop.

"That's what I wanted to ask you. I need to talk to Ricky Esposito. Do you know how to get in touch with him?"

"You're not serious, are you?" She leans back in her chair, folds her arms in front of her chest. "Starla, he died four months ago. No one told you? It was suicide."

"I'm sorry, no." *I just want to start a flame in your heart* plays in my head. Fatigue sweeps me sideways for a moment. I fight the urge to lay my forehead on the tabletop. "I work in his cabin. I lay in his straw bed. I hug his mother. Shit, poor Rose."

"Shit is right, Star." Tamara shimmies her chair around the corner of the table. She pats my shoulder. "We all took it pretty hard. Sorry you're just finding out now."

"It's just that ... things have been happening." I want to run again. I wish I was anywhere besides the Ming Teh with Tamara Matveev about to unload. "At The Point and in that cabin, and other places too. I can't even tell if I'm making it up or not."

"I doubt you're making it up. It *is* weird around here."

"What do you mean?"

"You know. Just weird. Like *Weekly World News* UFOs, two-headed squirrels, haunted barns weird. Great. Now I sound weird. You know, a bunch of us really freaked when Ricky died. Thought he was haunting us and stuff. I lost so much weight that after the funeral my ribs started to show. Customers started asking me if I had a drug problem. Grief is like a drug problem. It's like being possessed."

"Yes! That's it. Like being possessed," I say. The thrill I experienced last night feels tender and tainted now. A waking up on a Sunday morning with bruises on your thighs kind of feeling. "Definitely, possessed."

"It won't always feel this way, I promise. Time heals."

It's not grief, but I don't say that to Tamara. I feel like puking. She looks so determined to comfort, and pulls me in for a hug. I let my head roll into her and slump against her torso. She smells like a suntan and cigarettes.

"Gosh, Starla, this is not what I thought you were going to ask me. I was hoping you were going to ask me out on a date."

# 23 No One Touches Me

Rahn is spending the night," Barbara tells me. "Try to be quiet when you come home from your shift." She covers a cream-coloured mixing bowl with a tea towel.

"Pizza dough?" I ask, nodding at the bowl. The kitchen smells like fresh minced garlic. Songbird is licking the floor along the stove.

"He claims he can eat pizza and wings every meal. Good for him, he's tall and thin." White flour rings her fingernails. Her hands are aging. She's slowly becoming a *nonna*, a *nonna* without grandkids. "Wait 'til he tastes my pizza. Want to know the secret? Whole cloves of garlic baked right into the dough. That's how Pops taught me."

"You like him? Rahn? It's been, what, a couple months?"

"Oh, he's kind of an odd duck. Did you hear his laugh? He's good in bed, though, if your old mom can say that," she says.

"Say whatever. It's not like I can stop you."

"Who knows if I actually like him, or if he just keeps me entertained enough to not drive my car into the lake."

"Mom! Don't talk like that."

"You're too young to understand, Bay. A year from now, you'll be on your way again. I've been here most of my life. I'll die here. I doubt I'll even get to pass the house down to you. You don't want it." She hugs me close, rubs my back like I'm the one saying the depressing shit.

Outside, it's raining for the first time since I've been home. Rainwater gushes from the eaves. I tell myself I'd better get the

147

ladder out soon to clean out Barbara's gutters. I ought to prune the lilac bush too, to save her the trouble. What else can I do to be a good daughter?

She's packed me another lunch: Nutella and Fluffernutter on white bread, and a Ziploc bag of crackers and cheese slices. "Take my car. It's a real summer storm out there," she offers. "If we go anywhere late tonight, we'll go in Rahn's Beamer. 'Bey Em Vay Means Get Out of the Way!'"

The last time I drove these roads in the dark I was a drunk teenager coming home from a tailgate party. About one young driver per year crashes their car around here. Not only from driving under the influence, but from doing risky stunts on risky roads. Skateboarders who bumper surf. Jocks playing chicken. The first black ice of each winter is deadly. Same goes for the last of the muddy slush in early spring.

The wipers squeak across the windshield of Barbara's Ford Fiesta. My hands are tight on the wheel at ten and two. Through the rain, I spot the glowing eyes of a couple of little critters as they scamper across the road. My heart speeds up as I swerve around the opossums.

My fingers turn cold on the steering wheel, then hot as frostbite. Driving's made no difference. She's here, she's caught me.

Her chorus girl legs appear ahead. The kind of womanly legs that would dance in time with a towering kaleidoscope of other womanly legs. An American musical darling. As if she's going to step brush ball change, right on the hood of this Ford. I hit the brakes. She stands fiendishly still. I flash the high beams but still can't make out more than her legs in the rain. She is waiting for me to get out of the car. What choice do I have? I step into the storm before she forces me out. Her curls are dripping wet. She has discernible clothes now. I can pinch the worsted cotton of her red, white, and blue swing skirt.

"You're a ghost." Speaking to her seems to make her clearer. I see her eye colour for the first time. Sepia brown. Like sundown in an old movie, like Kansas sky in *The Wizard of Oz*. She shrugs her slender shoulders. Does she not know she's a ghost? Is she one of these spirits who doesn't understand she's dead? I doubt it. I think she understands too much about living and dying. I'm afraid of what she knows. But looking the other way is no longer possible. Ignorance is no longer something to plead.

"Did you have a name?"

She scowls at the question. I brace, expecting to topple to the ground and black out only to wake up a minute later alone in the wet road.

"Etta Zinn. Still is my name, as far as I know. But you can call me Goblin Fruit. Suits me fine."

"I am so sorry ..." She can read my mind? "Please, I didn't mean to insult you."

"It's all the same to me." She steps toward me and I cower. The falling rain grows more icy the closer she gets. I have to say something. People in movies and books don't just stand around speechless.

"Is there something you want from me? Is there something you need from the living world?" I ask the question *Poltergeist* taught me to ask. Steven Spielberg's ghosts were gruesome, ghosts you should run from at full speed. But Etta Zinn's skin is as soft as a living woman's. I find myself leaning toward her. She presses her palm to my face. Her giggles in my ear sound tinny, like a sitcom laugh track.

"Ah, nuts. What am I, the ghost of Jacob Marley? 'Boooooo. I am dooooomed tooo waaaander without rest or peeeeeace.' That makes you Scrooge, thank you very much."

All at once, she has me pinned against the car.

"Say my name. A girl likes to hear her name called out by the one she loves."

My jaw wrenches open. She kisses the corners of my gaping mouth, pokes mockingly at my lower lip with her finger. My tongue swells. I can't swallow my saliva. My nostrils burn like I might vomit through my nose. "E. E. Et" She forces her name in my mouth. "Et-ta."

I push back. My body bucks against hers. She stumbles backward on her beautiful feet. "You touched me? No one touches me," Etta shrieks. "Not since ... Not since ..." She flashes her teeth, her irate eyes, and disappears.

# 24 Sore

ucky, think back to the night you were sick with rabbit fever."
I pause my bedtime reading of Dr Seuss's *The Lorax*. I've been
impatient to get Lucky alone, to reach the right moment to ask him
about Etta. "You said a lady told you I had something for you?"
Lucky nods, squeezes his eyes tighter shut, and pulls the patchwork
quilt up to his chin. "What did she sound like?"

Lucky shrugs. "Like a lady."

"An older lady, like Bobby, or a younger lady, like me?"

Lucky giggles, he cracks open one eye. "I dunno. She talks funny.
Like, faraway talk. Like the TV at nighttime. Heeeerree's Johnny.
Da bap da da bah ..."

"Can you think of something she said?"

He shakes his head "no."

"How often does she talk to you?" Lucky can probably hear the
urgency in my voice. I take a breath. "Does she speak to you every
night? Once a week? Lucky, try to remember when was the last
time you heard her. Please—"

"I dunno. She comes when I sick or when I havin' bad dreams,"
he says. "Finish the story, please ... I said 'please.'"

Lucky screws his sleepy eyes up at the orange and pink pages of
*The Lorax*. I read the book cover-to-cover, twice, before kissing his
forehead and tiptoeing out for my rounds.

I look for Etta at campsite number nine. Several times I trick
myself into thinking I hear the opening hooks of the rhythm and

blues ballad that announces her arrival. I flinch and flinch, but the anticipation is my own making. The campsite is empty. I then search all seventy-five other seasonal campsites. Each site is almost identical: a clearing of stamped dirt rimmed by large quarry rocks. More quarry rocks ring the fire pits. Picnic tables usually on the left, tent space on the right. Premium sites with electrical hookups, regular sites without. Trees for privacy. I kick fallen pine cones and branches away out of the sites. It's too early to do this chore. I'll have to redo it before the May long weekend. No one likes to set up their tent on scraggy ground.

I hover near Hal and Bobby's darkened trailer, but hear only Hal's phlegmy snoring faintly through the door.

In between my rounds I scan short passages from Ricky Esposito's handyman's notebook, hoping to find further evidence that he had been contacted by Etta. One page is marked with a strip of Crystal Beach ride tickets. Here, his step-by-step instructions turn from how to sand and finish a live-edge tabletop or braid a rag rug to a catalogue of wild mushrooms and berries. He had identified and illustrated more poisonous kinds than edible. Is that how he killed himself? Is this an unaskable question?

The strip of tickets twitches on the page. It's her. I knew she wouldn't leave me alone for the entire night. "Again," I whisper, and the tickets twitch. "Again." I wait, willing them to move a third time. A discouraging amount of time passes before I fold the tickets into my jeans pocket and move on.

Before the sun begins to rise, I sit at the east side of the quarry and turn off my flashlight. The water makes paddling sounds that grow louder the longer I sit in the dark. Sheepshead and catfish are nocturnal feeders. Same goes for the whip-poor-will chanting in the distance. This time in May, he's calling for a mate. Roosting season is coming soon. Behold the natural world I forgot about in Toronto. There were chickadees in the hedgerows outside my old building; their onomatopoeic calls, I thought, sounded more like "cheese-bur-ger" than "chick-a-dee-dee." But a whip-poor-will is unmistakable. I'm becoming a rural girl again with each whip-poor-will call. I belong to this stamped flat earth, to the stinky lake. I belong to every cricket and bullfrog and coyote and whip-poor-will. And I suspect I'll belong to Etta. I'll hand myself over, if she'll have me.

"I know you can hear me," I whisper into the pitch. Ghosts always listen, right?

"And you can hear me." She is beside me. I don't have to turn to look. The entire left side of my body is numb. "And you can touch me," she says.

I extend my arm toward her, slowly, as if reaching into a lion's mouth. Only my middle and pointer finger tap her skin, and my body changes. I salivate, almost spit. The fine muscles of my eyelids spasm.

She says, "no" and skims away. I briefly panic, my outstretched arm left dangling in the night air, as if I can't remember how to retract it. She says, "Just lay back, darling." Her voice in my ear pops like a pocket of air, like the air pressure around me is changing.

The sand is covered in cool dew. Her weight is on top of me, but she doesn't show herself. Again, I try to reach for her, and she warns me. "Tuck your hands behind your back."

Don't fight her this time, I tell myself. Give up, I tell myself. My hands burrow in my back pockets. My left hand clutches the strip of ride tickets. "I got good stuff, if you let me. You gonna let me? You gonna be mine?"

She pushes down on me. I can't see anything. Not her. Not the darkened tree line. Not the moon. The quarry is silent. Birds, mute. I can't hear if I'm crying or if I'm moaning. I only know that my throat feels hoarse. My chest feels like I'm coughing. She is so heavy. I will be sore in the morning. Is that true? Can she bruise me? I'd like a bruise. Proof. I am sure this is real. Everything from this moment onward is impossible. And real.

# 25 Delirious

I tumble in through the front door. Barbara and Dr Rahn Johnson are not sleeping in.

"Starla, did you walk home?"

"Your car! Fuck. I left it." I slap my hand over my mouth before I swear again. If I swear, she'll swear louder and meaner. Barbara begins to ream me out. Each time the word "fuck" comes out of her mouth it's more muffled. She never cares about swearing, except when a date is over. Dr Rahn Johnson dashes into the kitchen, smiling and waving.

"I'll drive you to your car, dear," says Rahn.

*Dear*, I think. Play it cool, Rahn, or she'll show you the exit so fast ... Barbara notices the "dear" too. She leans away from him as she accepts the ride, her round hip resting on the counter top.

"When I was a new doctor," he continues, "I worked the overnights, like new doctors do. And I'd leave the hospital so tired, I probably would have left my own head behind if it wasn't attached to my shoulders."

Barbara is faux composed. She's not listening to Rahn, I can tell. She's mitigating her pending blow-up at me.

"Shoulder bone connected to the neck bone. Neck bone connected to the head bone," Rahn sings, tapping the kitchen counter top. This gets Barbara's attention.

"Fats Waller, 'Dem Dry Bones,'" Barbara says, snapping her fingers.

"Impressive," says Rahn. "Try this: 'Dinah, is there anyone finer, in the state of Carolina.'"

"'Every night, why do I shake and fright ... right!'" squeals Barbara. "The Delta Rhythm Boys? The Mills Brothers? Am I right? Whose song is it? Tell me."

"The Mills Brothers."

"I knew it!"

"I don't want to set the world on fire." Rahn takes up my mother's hand. His croon is sweet, like he's sung his way into women's hearts before. She allows him to pull her close. The two of them bleed through their amorous silhouettes. Barbara's frosted blonde hair fuzzes into a halo. The whole room seems to be floating, actually.

"I just want to set a flame in your heart," I say. "I just want to set a flame in your heart. I just want to set a flame ..."

"Your daughter knows The Ink Spots!" Rahn shakes his head in disbelief. "What teenager knows early doo-wop bands?"

"Ha! Starla knows too much," Barbara gloats. "She hears something once and she'll remember it for the rest of her life. Real brainiac, my daughter. She thinks herself crazy."

"I'm not a teenager."

"They might have played right here in Crystal Beach," Rahn says.

"Probably. Along with Jelly Roll Morton. Cecil Gant. Roy 'Little Jazz' Eldridge. You name it."

"I didn't know you were such a jazz aficionado, Barbara."

"Not bad for a white lady, huh?"

"Not bad for your age," Rahn corrects her. "Those bands are more than a bit before your time."

"Local librarian, here. I can name every big band that played Crystal Beach. You should see the record collection we've got. Original twelve-inch vinyl just sitting in the stacks. It's up to me to play them. No one bothers to sign them out anymore."

"We'll sign them out." Rahn kisses her cheek. "We'll have an old-fashioned date night listening to records."

"I just want to start a flame in your heart. I just want to start a flame," I echo. Barbara and Rahn glance at me with identical "get lost" looks.

"Give me the keys, Starla. And go to bed. You're delirious."

# 26 Dirty Wine

This is how Tamara Matveev asks me out on a date: Barbara Enrica Martin, 9 Loomis Street, is listed in the phone book. Tamara calls on Tuesday evening at 7:30 p.m.—courteously avoiding the dinner hour.

My mother's cordless phone chimes out Beethoven's Fifth.

"Starla?"

"Yes." I take the phone outside. "Tamara?"

"You got so many callers that you can guess it's me first try, eh?"

"Just wishful thinking," I say, easing myself into a yellow plastic Adirondack chair. Smooth one. I pick at the frayed edges of my jean shorts, grinning. Tamara makes a breathy noise into the phone—not quite a snort or a sigh.

"You wear old lady underwear and too much eye makeup in the daytime, but otherwise you are totally a babe." She sounds like she's reading from a script. "I don't get a psychopath vibe from you. You're not normal either, and I think that's kinda cute. Weird and cute is my type. I've been thinking about you—a lot," says Tamara. "It's a pretty big deal that I'm calling you up even after you ran away from me.

"The movie theatre at the County Fair Mall went bankrupt. *Top Gun* was the last movie that showed there before it closed. I remember because it was the last time I was out with a guy. Do you catch my meaning? There's no cinema in town. And no boyfriends on my dance card. So maybe you have some art film we can watch.

Together. At my place. Like, on a date?"

I haven't been asked out on very many dates. Most of my sexual encounters, especially with women, have transpired spontaneously, often drunkenly. Tamara's is a quality proposition for all I know. I wrap a loose frayed string from my shorts around my index finger until the tip turns purple.

"Sure," I say. "I have Radley Metzger's grindhouse adaptation of *Therese and Isabelle*. Or, better yet, we'll watch some Cassavetes." Worst lesbian line of all time. I have no idea what I'm doing.

The house where Tamara Matveev was born and raised is an old brick two-storey on Emerick Avenue, where all of the homes are old two-storeys, each set back in a deep front yard, each yard marked by a stately old oak or maple tree. I could live in this neighbourhood, I think. But single women never live in a neighbourhood like this. Not even grandmas who moved in as brides and outlived their husbands; they go to retirement apartments. This is a neighbourhood where men are perpetually seen mowing lawns, shovelling snow, or washing four-door cars.

Tamara appears in her doorway before I reach the end of her drive. "Yum," she says taking the bottle of wine still wrapped in brown paper from my hand. "You gonna get me drunk and take advantage of me?"

My eyes dart, making sure no neighbours are within earshot. "Good idea. Thanks for suggesting it."

Her mother's kitchen is bluebell blue with a country cottage geese motif wallpaper border. Tamara tosses a cup of popcorn into a large saucepan waiting on the stove. "You really do wanna get me drunk," she jokes as she uncorks the bottle of Ontario Malbec. "Fourteen percent!" She pours and smells a sip. "Leathery. I like a dirty wine."

"I wasn't sure if you'd find it too acidic." Stop talking, I warn myself, she totally knows more about wine than you do. "I brought a couple of films, too"

"Cassa ...?"

"Cassavetes, yeah. *A Woman Under the Influence*. You may not like it." The first kernels begin to pop.

"What do you like about it?" Tamara looks intently at me. She is no longer wearing the strange artificial aqua-blue contacts she wore at the strip club. It will be a lot easier to make out with her and her natural brown eyes, I think.

"I guess I like the idea that I could lose control, rant and yell, like the leading lady ..." Stop talking. "And someone would still love me." Fuck a duck, I wrote a paper on the film's aesthetic significance. I have a hundred other things I could say, but no, I have to sound like a needy nutcase. Tamara clamps her lips with her teeth but says nothing. What does that facial expression mean? The kitchen is loud with popping corn. She turns away to shake the pot on the stove. Little sparks shoot from the gas element. I watch her breasts jiggle with the motion and imagine myself running from her house. How long have I been on this date? Ten, twelve minutes, and already I'm choking.

She leads me unceremoniously into her bedroom, bumping her bedroom door open with her hip as she holds the bowl of popcorn in one hand and her wine glass in the other. A Butthole Surfers poster—the one with the three-legged Betty Page—is tacked to Tamara's bedroom ceiling. "You still hang posters above your bed," I smirk.

"Old habit."

"Old? That tour was, like, last year."

"New poster, old habit." Tamara shrugs. Her entire room is unapologetically teenage. A beat-up shop mannequin wearing a leather jacket stands in the corner. Blue string lights serve as mood lighting. I prop a pillow behind me and am oddly comforted by the PAC-MAN print pillow cases. She doesn't live in a crystal palace; she's human, like me. Tamara sets the huge bowl of popcorn between us on the bed. She cocks her head a little at the film's unrefined, almost vulgar opening piano track. I've heard this soundtrack a hundred times—so I listen, as best as I can, to the sound of her chewing popcorn and sipping wine. Our fingers touch in the popcorn bowl, just like fingers are supposed to during a movie date. Gradually, Tamara's lovely bare feet edge along the bed toward mine. She tucks her hair behind her ear, and her bare neck beckons. I finish the wine in my glass. On the TV set, Peter Falk says, "I don't mind you being a lunatic." He blows a kiss at Gena Rowlands from across their dinner table. This scene I've memorized, every word. Rowlands says, "Tell me what you want me to be, how you want me to be, I can be that." Tamara's eyes widen at that line. A great moment in cinema just got even better. I run my hand along her thigh.

"C'mere," she says, patting her lap. I suddenly notice the flush of wine on my skin. The room leans forward as we kiss. I hesitate for a second, wonder if I should tell her about Etta. What would I say? You should know I'm not totally single, I'm kind of seeing this ghost? A second later I grab at her T-shirt in a clumsy handful. We're both eager for it; our mouths are butter and tannins. Her hips buck up. I grind back into her, and the white metal headboard clacks against the wall. "No one's home," she assures me, and we carry on pulling and tugging at one another's clothes. I yank at loopholes in her jean shorts. She tears at the buttons in my blouse. I run my palm along her sternum. "I like your pretty freckles," I tell her, tapping the small diamond-like constellation under her collarbone. Her back arches for me to take off her T-shirt, maybe shimmy her shorts off. A hot, fearless part of myself returns each time she coos at my touch. Fuck, I've missed this feeling. I unhook her bra with one hand and she whispers, "I'm not going to let you fuck me, not on the first date."

"Three date rule?" I ask. Her left nipple crests over her lace bra.

"I suspect you're the type who will fuck on the first date, then won't return my phone calls." Tamara's accusation is stunning, though accurate for my track record. "I just don't want you to do that to me," she says.

I close my eyes. I no longer want to see the half-moons of her nearly undressed nipples, the mess of her dyed black hair on her PAC-MAN pillow. She rubs my back. "It's okay. We don't need to rush, right?" We've officially left sexy and defaulted into soothing—killing our first date. I lie next to her like a child and let her hug me. A zippy kazoo has joined the banging piano as the final credits roll on the film. How have I never before noticed that *A Woman Under the Influence* has the worst soundtrack? Tamara exhales in a long strange sigh before sitting up to straighten her clothes.

She makes the same sigh as she catches me looking around nervously after we kiss goodnight on her driveway. "Who's going to see us?" she asks. "If you're embarrassed about what people will think, then you probably shouldn't date the town stripper."

Her street is small-town quiet as I walk away. All the neighbours have switched off their porch lights.

# 27 Bipolar

D r Rahn Johnson, Barbara, and I eat plates of baked ziti and garlicky green beans set atop TV trays. We watch the six o'clock news.

"Rahn, honey, can you pass me the thing?" Barbara raises her left foot under the TV tray and points with her toes at the coffee table.

"What thing?" asks Rahn, already shifting and reaching forward to accommodate her vague request. "More wine, dear?"

"No, the thing." Barbara's purple-painted toenails point again.

"She wants the remote control. She wants to mute the commercials," I tell him.

Rahn chuckles. "You two! You can read each other's minds."

Dear. God. No. I can think of a million minds I'd rather read than Barbara's.

"No thank you," says Barbara as she hits the mute button. "Starla's been a sourpuss since she was seven years old. I'd rather not read all the dark thoughts she keeps to herself." She gazes casually at the silent screen, as if she's merely mumbled something trivial about the dinner we're eating. The "It's on Fox 29 Buffalo" logo flashes between a montage of clips from their evening programming: *Alf*, *Married with Children*, *Star Trek: The Next Generation*, and *The Arsenio Hall Show*.

We've had this conversation before. Maybe once, maybe several times, maybe I'm too "sour" to be sure how many times I've asserted the boundary where I tell Barbara she has no right to comment on my mood as a child or teenager. That she lost that parental privilege when she brought a predator into the house years ago. Or, if she can't help herself, which it seems she can't, she can talk about what a moody child I was, if she also owns up to being a shitty mother within the same conversation.

I bitterly consider a comeback. Something sharp yet coded that I can say in front of Rahn. "*Vai a quel paese.*" Get lost, or fuck off, really.

"*Vaffanculo.*"

"How come the only Italian we speak are insults and swears?" I ask. Rahn honks out a few of his loud laughs that Barbara has complained about, slaps his long-fingered hand against his well-pressed trousers. He is an odd duck, but a very likeable duck. I suppose he'd have to be to date my mother.

Barbara turns the sound back on. A newscaster with feathered blonde bangs slightly purses her lips together before announcing, "You've never seen a parade like this before. Some call it diversity, but others call it shocking, as members of a group called the Buffalo Gay & Lesbian Community Network prepares for the city's first Pride Parade and Festival. Governor Mario Cuomo had this to say ..."

"I marched on Washington in '87," Rahn cuts in. Barbara turns down but doesn't mute the news. Her lips part and she exhales with a slight "phhh" sound. I pat my fingers against my own lips to make sure I'm not wearing the same slack mouth expression as her. "I may be a children's doctor, but I believe in funding for AIDS research and patient care. Vehemently believe, in fact. Money for AIDS, not war! That's what we were chanting. Plus, I saw Jesse Jackson and Whoopi Goldberg. A thrilling day."

"My hairdresser is gay. Frankie," says Barbara. I already want to leave the room. "He goes to this bar in Buffalo. What did he say it was called? Buddies! Yeah, Buddies. Good name for a gay bar, eh? He says the DJ booth is the cab of a real fire engine and there are brass poles on the dance floor. I'd go there. Whew! Can women go there? It's a terrible thing, being gay and Italian. His family has nothing to do with him. Gosh, I hope he doesn't have AIDS." I grab my empty plate and excuse myself. "Rahn, do you know where he can get an AIDS test? Star, don't you want ice cream for dessert? Spumoni, no?"

In my bedroom, I kick the box marked Starla Age 17. Frantically I reach into my leather art portfolio and scoop up the framed lenticular print by Barbara Kruger and press it to my chest, then place it carefully back into the portfolio. I'm too agitated to handle art. Or at least not a Kruger. Hopping onto my bed, I lean my forehead against the funhouse stunt. I want it to smell of decrepitude, of dirt—like a lost Rembrandt found in some great-grandma's basement. Fuck, why can't I find a Rembrandt in a basement? Cash in.

Too soon there's a knock on my bedroom door. It is an unfamiliar sound. I turn, expecting Barbara has come to scold me for my rude exit. But Barbara never knocks.

Rahn knocks, then gingerly cracks my door open a sliver with a warm and silly smile on his face. "May I come in?" he asks. His question strikes me as phony. Who actually asks to be invited in? Rahn looks around my small room for a place to sit, and decides to simply lean his lanky body against my dresser. He begins with, "Your mother ran to the corner store for some chocolate sauce, so I'm taking this opportunity to talk to you about something private ..." and the room fogs.

"This has to be our secret ..." I hear Rahn say before his voice mutes altogether. One part of my mind tries to rationally calm myself: He's harmless. Look at his polite hands neatly folded one on top of the other. If I act weird, he'll think I'm afraid of black men. He marched on Washington. Smile, but not maniacally. Maybe he knows I'm queer. He's offering me this moment to come out. Shut up, shut up, stupid, noisy brain. Another less rational and very loud part of my brain begins to spell. P-O-G-O-N-O—

"Starla, are you all right?" Rahn takes a step toward me and I recoil. Immediately he steps back, almost pressing himself against the dresser. We share a quiet moment, a moment where I should apologize or say something to put him at ease. Instead I let the quiet moment stretch out awkwardly.

"You know, Starla, I have a daughter," says Rahn. "Brilliant girl, smart like you, well, not a girl anymore, it's been a long while since she was a girl. When she was just about your age, mind you, she suffered terrible anxiety. I sent her to see a psychologist colleague of mine." Rahn closes his eyes, as if he's closely considering what to say next. I imagine running past him and out the door. "Bipolar disorder, she was diagnosed with."

Ah, he doesn't want me to come out as queer, he wants me to come out as crazy. "And you think I'm bipolar too? Is that it?"

"No, no!" His eyes pop back open. "I mean, there'd be nothing to be embarrassed about if you were. But I'm not that kind of doctor. Anyway, if you ever want to talk to someone, for any reason, I know several counsellors—"

"Rahn," I interrupt as politely as I can. It's too late, though. I'm already visibly flustered and sharp. "Please, tell me why you knocked on my door in the first place. I'm all ears."

"Oh, certainly," says Rahn. "Your mother's birthday is coming up in a few weeks. I thought you could suggest a surprise gift for her. I was thinking of a weekend getaway. Is there anywhere you think she'd want to go?"

I hope Rahn lasts another few weeks. He's nice. More than nice. If my mother was smart, she'd at least wait until after her birthday to carry out her knee-jerk pattern break-up. "She's always talked about going to the Smithsonian, and it sounds like you've visited Washington before," I offer. "She reads a lot, historical fiction and stuff like that, but she's hardly been to any museums. She'd never spring for airfare and a hotel room."

"The Smithsonian, yes!" Rahn straightens from his meek stance. "Why didn't I think of that?" He turns toward me, coming in for what looks like a hug, then stops himself. "Thank you, Starla," he says as he backs out my bedroom door. "She loves you, you know that, right? She worries about you."

# 28 Needy

Y ou work under the table?" Barbara asks.

"No. I signed an employee contract," I lie.

"This is a personal cheque."

"I'm her only employee. Me and her nephew Vincent. Hardly worth the trouble of getting official paycheques printed up." We stare down at the pastel butterfly design on the cheque for $600. I do the math—$600 every other week (actually a fraction of that during the winter months) and I should be out of debt in ... oh, eight years, give or take. I'll be thirty years old before I've paid back defaulted student loans from an undergrad I never finished. Could I admit that hopeless calculation aloud? I imagine forming the words, "I'll be thirty years old," and my tongue curls back in my mouth.

"At least you're not paid in cash," says Barbara. "We both know cash goes right through your fingers."

Again I wonder about the tips Tamara takes home after each shift. How long could I keep stripping a secret from Barbara? Maybe if I dyed my hair flaming red and called myself Carmine no one would figure out that I was her daughter. The kitchen radio is tuned into WBEN; on low volume, the radio host chants something about Buffalo having a record forty-four percent unemployment rate. The front page of the rolled up *The Fort Erie Times* lying on the doormat announces that Lake Erie sturgeon has become an endangered species. If Barbara subscribed to a decent paper, like *The Globe and Mail,* we could find out how spectacularly the Canadian government is flailing on its promise to end national child poverty. If I turned on the morning FOX news, statistics about the ten million cases of HIV worldwide would probably be scrolling across the bottom of the screen. Why does anyone bother to get out of debt? It's not like there are debtors' prisons in this century. And we'll all be dead before the next century. Millennial doom.

Barbara passes me a pen, and I sign the back of my paycheque. "I'll go to the bank on my way to work," she says. "You get some sleep."

"Wait! I want some cash back."

Barbara eyes me like I'm a dog that peed on the carpet. She swings her stupid ugly quilted pleather purse over her shoulder and turns toward the font door.

"I can't live on nothing."

"Last time I checked, you were living off of me." She doesn't turn around to speak to me, but she stops in her tracks. Her shoulders brace. The fight is too familiar and tempting to walk away from.

"My Toronto pocket money ran out days ago."

"I pay rent. I buy groceries. *Something something* ... hydro bill ... *something something* ... phone company ..." Barbara drones. When I was a kid, I would actually cup my palms over my ears to let her know I wasn't listening.

I only want a dollar to ride the bus into Fort Erie. Then sixty cents for a can of Crush Cream Soda at Kar-Mel Variety & Bus. Then $12.50 for a round-trip Greyhound ticket to Niagara Falls. Then roughly thirty dollars to go to Poptones Records because I have to have Diamanda Galàs's *You Must Be Certain of the Devil*, on cassette or CD, I'll take either. And I want to buy Ween's *GodWeenSatan* as a gift for Tamara because she listens to the Butthole Surfers and so I should be the first one to introduce her to Ween before every wannabe starts listening to them. And I want to flirt with whoever is working at Poptones. I'm so starved for attention, I'm about ready to give a handjob between the record stacks to the first punk to look me up and down. Then six dollars for some maple nut fudge at the Fudge Factory for Bobby, Hal, and Lucky. Then another six dollars to treat myself to a root beer float and fish and chips at Simon's Diner before I return home on the Greyhound because if I don't eat something deep fried soon I'll lose all reason. Then, finally, another dollar to ride the local bus back to Crystal Beach.

"Are you even listening to me, Star?"

"Are you even listening to *me*?" I snap. "I need cash."

"Tell me you're not doing drugs. I bet there's a nothing but bunch of crack heads living at The Point."

"You don't know shit about them or me. You have no clue what's going on with me." That was the wrong comeback. Now she'll really suspect I'm up to something.

"What now? What big ordeal do you have going on this time?"

"I've already told you all my 'big ordeals.' Not that you care."

Barbara heads for the door again, this time backing away from me in shuffling steps. "When are you going to forgive and forget, Starla?" she asks.

"Forgive and forget what, Ma?" Barbara appears confused by this question. Her lips meet in a pucker of what will too soon become a row of fine wrinkles. The house feels like it's shrinking around me. Somewhere in this claustrophobic bungalow is that letter I wrote to Barbara, during my campus women's centre revelations, about how she failed to protect me from sexual abuse. Most likely I wrote the words "sexual abuse" in that letter. I was so damn empowered to break the silence or whatever the fuck. I can't imagine writing those words now, actually putting it down on paper or speaking it aloud. Apparently, I've lost my voice. And not only can't I imagine being acknowledged by Barbara (who never wrote me back), it occurs to me that I no longer care about her acknowledgement. What could she possibly say to remedy the venom between us? The angry flush of her throat tells me it's too late. The anxious breath caught in my chest confirms that I lack the will, and perhaps the communication skills, to carry forward this conversation between us.

It's a pity that pain isn't a narrative arc. It's not some Freytag's fucking Pyramid when a man's pointer finger tearing a grossly under-aged girl's hymen is the inciting incident. The climax is not the ultimate pass or fail test of speaking the truth—to a mother or a campus women's group, to a free counsellor, a lover, a friend, or anyone. There is no falling action. Never a denouement. No one writes "the end" when the pain is over. We only find ourselves more or less able to stand on two steady feet in the house we grew up in, look our antagonist of a mother in the eye, and say, "If you can't even say what exactly I should forgive and forget, then I suggest you don't ask me to do so."

I bound for my bedroom fast enough to be the one to get the last word in. Good old sympathetic nervous system; it waited to hear Barbara slam the front door before letting loose the tears.

"Etta," I call to the Are You Afraid of The Dark stunt. The stunt, I now believe, was fated to make its way to me. I didn't come home to make nice with my mother or repay my debts. I came for her. She came for me. "Etta, I want more." I look around at my single bed, at the timeworn cardboard boxes at the foot of it with my faded name written on them. The last unpacked backpack of my Toronto possessions. The clothes in my closet I paid too much for. The towering stacks of books. Somewhere in one of the piles of books is a $500 first edition of Ayn Rand's *Atlas Shrugged* that I splashed a few drops of red wine on. In that closet I have a $3,000

Jean Paul Gaultier Rock Stars Collection leather jacket that I may never wear again. When I'm upset, I calculate the value of my shit. "I want more than this. I want to be more than this." Even though I'm shouting, Etta is the only who will hear me.

She pours out of the stunt, spills into the room like sunlight. "Yes, let's make us some more, why don't we?"

# 29 Choice Bit of Calico

Jeepers, where'd she get them weepy peepers? Gosh, oh, get up. How'd they get so bawled up? What can I say, I got a weakness for the wounded. After all, I was born in the wake of one war and died in the middle of another. Life was nothing but "darkest hour" this and "Hoover shoes" that.

When I was alive, the fellas barely asked me a thing about myself. I suppose they saved their questions for gals they fixed to marry. And I doubt wifeys get asked all that much either. All the same to me. The less questions the better. An unwed woman making her own way had to be careful. Heaven forbid I earned more than an able man with a family to support. Funny thing, no one barely had nothing, but still all types had prosty money to spend. Heck, men collecting welfare cheques somehow still found extra for a choice bit of calico. Where there's a war, there's a whore, as the saying goes. My guys may have been bent outta shape parting with a dollar or two, but still, they parted. You bet I tucked their money away faster than they could say "peach tree." Best a woman like me not flaunt her bankroll.

I had it far better than the dykes at the factories. I took up with one or two, so I heard all about the woes of working the line with macho men terrified their jobs were being stolen by women. Lucky me, men never worried I was taking their place. My job was to wail and whoopee them into feeling right again. No man wanted my place, ha!

On the prosty clock, I was always faking a giggle, like a good-time girl ought to do. When I was spending nights with a lover girl, there were always tears. Her tears or mine; sometimes both were one and the same.

Sister of the road or homemaker on the sly, summer romance or one-night-stand—didn't matter. An hour on the mattress is all it takes to break the dam. Women hold sadness beneath their knickers. It's true. Why do they call us bent? Most honest, tender thing a woman can do is make her love come down with another woman. I fell in love with that honesty. I fell in love with saltwater.

For all the love of salt, we still hardly asked each other anything either. All questions lead to the one unanswerable question, "Why can't we really be together?"

And death. Even worse. Forget questions. No one hears a word. Not a peep. Years come and go like pretty faces. Nothing much happens.

Until now.

This girl here is my Venus in a clamshell, my kewpie doll. My naked angel singing on a cloud of our shared melancholy. Hot damn, I'm a poet and I didn't know it. Starla, she calls herself. That's poetry too. I'll still call her Dollface.

I hear Dollface, and Dollface can hear me.

I have touched her, and she has touched me.

As long as I have to remain here, I say, she stays with me. She's game to stay. Not even a week ago, she was a headless chicken running from me. Now she calls my name. Now she moves over in her bed like I am flesh and blood on the sheets beside her. Now she speaks to me.

"What else do you like, besides that Ink Spots song?" Her eyes are glassy and black from crying. My stars, the messy kohl she wears. In my day, you'd never see kohl run like that.

"Oh, I liked all the jazz bands that played the Crystal Ballroom. The bigger the better. Glenn Miller had a twenty-piece band," I say, my mouth moving like my teeth are still sharp, like it's possible for me to chew the fat as we are.

"Etta. Tell me something else that you used to like."

I have to think about it, as unaccustomed to questions as I am. "Rocky road ice cream. Two scoops on a waffle cone. And cinnamon suckers."

"What else? One more thing." She stirs, and the cheap Crystal Beach flag pendant coils close to her throat. She wears it for me—only reason to wear something so ugly. Clever doll. I bet she knows I'm stronger under the stunt or the painted park sign when she holds a strip of ride tickets or when she wears that pendant.

"I liked the pictures," I tell her. "Scary ones. *Werewolf of London* and *39 Steps* and *The Black Cat*. I've seen *The Black Cat* half a dozen times."

"I know that one," says Dollface. "*The Black Cat*. Béla Lugosi, right? 'Come, Vitus ... Are we not both the living dead?'"

Oh, little enchantress. What memories, what comfort she gives me reciting lines from Universal pictures. Makes me wanna grab that pendant close to her throat. Squeeze her for more tears. I wonder if I might taste her tears, if she'll make me that whole again? Whole enough to taste.

"If you could wish for something ..." She places a finger on the middle groove of my upper lip. A single finger, but the touch is too much. I can't make out who recoils first. Her eyes widen. Her hands tuck back into her sides. "I mean, like right now," she stammers. "If you could ... wish for something right now, what would it be?"

She yowls like a stepped-upon cat. I must be riled by the question, as I grab her too hard. "Dollface? Where are you?" Light fails. Her voice is too far away to hear. And much too far for me to answer her.

# 30 Evil

I read Ricky's journal, impatient to find mentions of Etta beyond the Ink Spots song. Did she speak to him too? Could he hear her garbled, like Lucky hears her, or word for word, like I can? But Ricky remains a writer of lists and instructions.

What I guess is that, about six months before he killed himself, Ricky kept a detailed record of everything he ate and drank. I scold myself for my own death wishes. How did Ricky do it? Surely not by starving himself.

July 6, 1989—nearly a year ago—there's a self-portrait of Ricky, scarecrow thin with a flame across his chest. In block letters, he'd written, "The smaller I am, the less heat she'll need to set me on fire. I'll become kindling thin."

It's happening again. Sickness swells in my stomach. I kissed her. I let her in my bed. Am I cursed now? I slam Ricky's journal shut, but immediately regret it. I want to know, don't I? Knowledge is power, isn't it?

She reappears now as a scorch-marked silhouette on Ricky's painting. A candle-flame-sized version of her. "I just want to start a flame in your heart." Her calling card melody is deeper than an echo in my head this time. It stabs.

"Tell me what you want from me," I shout. She buckles my knees and down I go to the floor.

"I never asked for nothin'." Hal is roughly three steps behind me. I can hear him wiping his boots on the cabin's doormat, but I can't turn around to greet him. I'm paralyzed as he comes muttering up, "Whatcha mean 'What do you want from me'? You work here, don't ya?" He waves his swollen hand in front of my face to get my attention, then follows my fixed gaze to the painting. He sees her too. "Mother of God." Hal drops to his knees beside me.

Hal confesses: "Virgin Mother. Blessed Lady in Heaven. I'm a humble a servant. Th' dog under your holy feet. It's Harvey Varin from Grey County. That's written on my birth certificate. Born in the cinder block house at the mouth of Potawatomi River. Do you know me?

"I ain't lived no good life, but, here 'n' now, I vow ta serve ya best I can. Praise be for givin' me another chance. I been prayin' for another chance. I never thought you'da come. God sure play'd a joke, havin' me born in the last damn dry city in all of Canada. Curse'd Evangelicals. They never drink, they never pray to Mary neither, pardon me sayin' so. Owen Sound is rum-runners land. If you were watchin' over me at all, then you saw I was runnin' back 'n' forth from Barrie or Toronto since I were pretty young and drinkin' younger still. I s'pose god warned me when Paps got the drunk's hepatitis. His eyes turned yellow and his stomach made him look like a pregnant gal.

"Fifteen, sixteen years old, and what did I have to say 'cept he couldn'da died fast 'nough. Paps lungs got bad, and he'da choke when he lied down. I had'da make our armchair up like a bed, and that's where he'd sleep, if he ever did sleep. Sometimes he'da piss in that chair, sometimes bleed out.

"It was me and only me that heard him cough his last. It was me and only me who had to burn the bloody bed linens out back. Worst smell—your own father's blood burnin'. God coulda spared me that, but who am I to question? God coulda spared me all th' old man's beatin's too.

"So I spit on my own father's grave. Figured he was going ta hell, and I'da follow. Now I confess the evil in my heart. That's why you've come, right—to hear my confession? Nothin' more I'da like to tell you than I straight'n right out after Paps died, but we both knows that ain't true. Took six years in a cage ta change me. Kingston Penitentiary. And lord knows, the place let me out worst than when I'da gone in. But you sends me them priests and their half-way house in Welland to bring me 'round to peace.

"God bless them hippie priests—Father Neil and Father Juan Carlos—with their guitars and their vegetable gardens and the chickens they'da named after the Saints." Hal chuckles at himself. I exhale; it seems like the first breath I've taken since he began his monologue. "Eight months to the year, I stayed with them. Dry too. Ah, welp, mostly dry. Can't lie to you anymore, can I?

"The steel foundry use'ta hire ex-convicts, so that's where I went. Workin' steel, same as ever'body else, 'til the foundry closed in '83. Manufacturers were handin' out lay-off papers like advertisement flyers back then. Lotsa guys left Welland to go work the Artic Pipeline.

"I left too, 'cept I left for love. I ain't a chaste man, but Bobby was the first gal I loved. I use'ta tell her that every single day. Didn't matter we weren't no spring chickens—still felt like young sweethearts do. She got knocked up, so I asked her ta marry me, no doubts 'bout it. What else is there besides love?"

Hal couldn't have delivered a better redemption soliloquy if he'd pre-written it. I want to turn around, reach out to him, perhaps even hug him. But Etta had us both locked in place like inanimate scenery props.

"I figured it woulda been like a storybook. We'd buy this mobile home, live humble and happy. Raise our son right. Nothin' like the childhood she or I had. I can't say I know why, 'xactly, it turn backwards again. Maybe I should'a found another job? I for sure shouldn't never have start to drink like I have.

"If I gonna be true, Blessed Virgin, real 'n' true so I might earn your forgiveness, I say it's Lucky. Since he got born, I got angry. It's like all my anger at my own Paps is back again. I never knew it was lingerin' so deep, but it's back. It's a curse that'sa been waitin' all this time. It nags me. 'You're a bad father. You're a bad father. Your son hates you. Your own son gonna hate you.' Virgin Mary, this is my real 'n' true confession. I confess there be anger in my heart that stops me from lovin' my son.

"I swear I'll trade all the anger for your blessin'. Thank you. Thank you for savin' me Mother Mary. Thank you for showin' your holy light. Tell me what ta do. Please, Mother, tell me what ta do."

"The rotgut is a Catholic," Etta's voice worms in my ear. Her voice feels like it's right in my scull, scratching, scratching.

*You said only I could see you.*

*Listen to you,* Etta exclaims sharply. *How quickly you learned to speak with that pretty little head. Special girl. Don't be jealous. He can't see much of me, not like you. And he can't hear me like you can. You can hear my every word still, can't you?*

"I can hear you," I call out. If I yell aloud, maybe she'll get out of my head.

"Oh blessed be. What do she say?" Hal latches on to my shoulder.

*You know, I always thought I could play the role of Mary. Just like Dorothy Cumming in* The King of Kings. *My Mama took me to see that show when I was a sprout. I'll never forget the eye-popper ending when the screen turned Technicolor. Technicolor in a silent film! I figured anything was possible when I saw heaven in colour that day.*

*Guess what? I thought anything was possible again last night when you asked me what I wished for. Remember that? Well, I do have a wish, thanks for asking. I want the Park back. The ballroom and the steamship and the roller coaster. I want them all back.* Her voice is hot liquid in my ear. *Tell the old man I want to ride the roller coaster again.*

I try to speak and my jaw locks. I squeeze my hands against my head. "Hal, it's not Mary," I manage to say.

"She ain't Mary?" Hal asks. "Who then? Not the devil comin' for me? I need one more chance, is all. Tell her I need one more chance."

*Clip the man's hope, why don't ya?* says Etta. My mind splits with her words. I lower my forehead to the floor. *He'll really hit the bottle, now. Better tell him I'm an angel. I've been called that enough times, it's as good as true.*

"She's an angel." I can't believe I say it, but I do. "She's an angel," I exclaim again as if in ecstasy. I'm drooling onto the cabin floor. Maybe Etta is right. Hal needs this chance, and I need this searing pain in my head to stop. Already he thinks his kid's stuffed animals are possessed, and I'm a witch. What's the harm in adding an angel to the mix? "An angel that goes between Earth and Heaven," I tell him. My jaw loosens a little. "To save our sorry souls. To give you the chance you asked for."

"I can't hear her. What she sayin'?"

"She says you're on the right path, Hal. Stay sober." Is this a step too far? Too manipulative? I'll grapple with ethics later. "Now is the time to be a good father and husband."

"Yes, Lucky will straighten me out. I promise. The boy's one of your children, for sure. Lamb of god, not like me."

*Nice performance. Looks like we'll be co-stars after all. So while he's being so agreeable, tell him to build me a shrine. A huge shrine. More of a large gazebo or a dance pavilion, really. And tell him to build it with salvaged wood from the* SS Canadiana. *I miss that ferry boat. And from the wooden roller coaster. And the ballroom. Bring the Park back to me bit by bit.*

I silently tell Etta, *You hear his whole pitiful story and what do you come up with? He doesn't need anything else put on him. How's he going to build you a gazebo?* Forming the words in my head is easy. It's Etta's answers that scrape through me.

*You listen to me, this geezer needs a calling, I know men, and this one needs something bigger than his thirst and anger. He'll stay dry, and I'll get a shrine. Win-win, Dollface.*

"Hal," I say gravely. "She says there is something you must do as penance ..."

Hal's eyes grow wide and glassy. A broken blood vessel blooms around his left iris. Flash hemorrhage. He is already gesturing widely in eager agreement before I can tell him what he must do.

# 31 Filth

After Hal receives his divine calling, he seeks help from the one person whom he deems an authority: Rose. If he's to build a sacred gazebo, he at least needs Rose's permission, for starters. He also needs the tools from the locked shed. "Your boy had more tools than most grown men," Hal reasons with her.

This strikes a nerve with Rose. I watch her lips thin in a taut line across her face. Rose says, "Hal, look into my eyes and tell me you're not planning on pawning the tools. Are you drinking again?" Now both react. Both warp their mouths and eyebrows as if their faces are warming up for a literal face-off.

Hal says, "Damn it."

Rose says, "Don't!" And the one person who really shouldn't be within earshot of this adult ugliness comes tiptoeing up: Lucky.

"Damn don't damn don't damn don't damn ..." Being three years old, Lucky is a parrot. Louder and louder with each "damn" and "don't." Bobby comes racing out of their trailer, calling Lucky's name, which he loops into his parrot call. "Damn don't Lucky damn don't Lucky ..."

The five of us stand off on the lawn between the bocce ball courts and the family barbecue pits, each of us competing to be heard, none of us listening.

"Camping season starts next week. If you can't pull it together, Hal, so help me I'll ..." says Rose.

Bobby yells, "Christ on a crutch, he's ten days sober, what else do you expect—"

Lucky yells, "I don't feel so good ..."

I yell, "Stop! We're making Lucky fucking cry ..."

Rose yells, "Lucky, not now."

Bobby yells, "Don't you dare raise your voice at my son."

Lucky yells, "Damn damn damn damn damn damn and fuck."

Bobby yells, "I told you not to teach him swears."

And then Hal yells, "Don't point no finger me. Only Our Lady of the Painting can judge me now."

At this Rose cocks her head in one direction and her hip the other. The uneasy moment I was too stupid to consider has arrived. We each have different information. Lucky can hear Etta but only in his dreams or when he's sick. Hal's sort of seen Etta, his angel, but can't hear her. Bobby has witnessed the ghostly Care Bear. Rose knows nothing. I know way too much. Since these conflicts always seem to happen over an uneven sharing of information, Rose and I are in direct opposition. I can feel the fight coming on. The tension changes the temperature of my skin.

"What did you say, Hal? About a painting?" She asks Hal, but she's looking squarely at me. Without waiting for an answer, Rose lumbers toward the cabin. We all chase her. She halts at the door, just like she always does. We freeze a polite distance behind, except for Lucky, who sneaks around her legs and into the cabin. Rose does not turn to look at me, but I can tell by the sound of her voice that she is speaking through clenched teeth. "You take that ... filthy painting and go. I don't want to see you or it on my property again."

*Please, Etta, work your goblin fruit magic. Make things right.* Listening for Etta to respond is like an ice cream headache between my eyes. I concentrate through the ache.

"Hello, lady," Lucky points to the painting.

Hal edges closer. With an uncharacteristic grace, he places his hand on Rose's back. "She's come for you, Rose. Go talk to her."

Rose literally launches herself away from Hal's touch. He and Bobby both gasp. A second lunge puts Rose right on top of the cabin's cot. She dances and yells, as if the mattress is hot coal under her feet. Lucky points at Etta's flame. We can all see her burning contour in the left corner of the painting. Etta's light brightens the cabin to a glare. Hal drops to his knees again, pulling Bobby down beside him. The alarm in Rose's eyes is indescribable as she looks at us and back at the painting. Rose passes her hand in front of the glow, as if to disrupt a projector's beam. She touches the light, then recoils. She tilts the painting away from the wall and peeks behind it. "It ain't a trick, Rose," says Hal.

Rose gently lifts the painting from its nail. Hal eases toward her, his hands tentatively stretched before him like he's approaching a growling dog. He begins to say her name, and Rose hurls the painting at him. The wood hits the floor with an uncomfortable crack. "Trick! My son is gone. Is that a trick? *Porco dio!*"

"Now, slow down. Slow down and see the miracle." Hal holds up the painting, turns in a circle with it, flips it over and over again. Ricky's painting on one side and the Crystal Beach Amusement Park sign on the back. "You Must Be This Tall to Ride." Etta's little illuminated figure remains a constant in the lower left corner of the painting no matter which way Hal turns it.

She slips into my ear. *Tell her Ricky says "Hi, Mom."*

*I'm not telling her that.*

*Tell her Ricky is with Zio Eugenio, and they're up in heaven turning wood bowls.*

*You don't know what you're talking about!*

*I have been around a lot longer than you, Dollface. You'll be surprised what I know. I got the boy's whole life story, and then some.* Could she read his mind, like she reads mine? *Put his memory to some use, tell his mama what she wants to hear.*

"Uncle Ugo," Lucky sings out. "Uncle Uggie."

*Stay out of his head. He's just a little kid.*

I hope Rose is not the type of Italian who thinks it's bad luck to call the dead by name after the mourning period. If so, I'm about to screw up this divine moment, big time. "Uncle Eugene. The angel is in contact with Eugene, and with your son, Rose."

"What?! You came into my house? You went through my things?" There's little anger left, mostly exhaustion in her voice.

"No, Rose. I'd never do that."

*Sing her a verse from "Fa la Ninna."*

*You think I know village lullabies?*

*You don't need to know. I'm the brains, you're the brawn. Now repeat after me.* When Etta sings, it sounds like the hiss of an old radio being switched on. A dial garbles across a frequency until the lyrics become almost clear. The song is in a dialect very distant from my own bastardized third-generation Italo-Canadian. Maybe Sardinian or Corsican? I only recognize the words "baby," "sleep," "death," "darkness," and "mother." Otherwise, I sing what I hear, trying to make meaning out of sound, to follow phonetically. It's mondegreen and faux-harmony, but I keep singing.

Each nonsensical word that bursts from me is a pact I am making with Etta. I am agreeing to conspire with her. To comply. To serve that which I do not understand. To use this strange power and to let it use me. There is no turning back from this moment.

Rose's hand clasp her chest. "Why, Ricky? Why?" she finally speaks in bewildered awe. She turns to me, grabs me by both arms as she collapses forward. "Why, him? My son."

"Ricky has joined your brother, Eugene. That's the message I'm getting," I tell her. I place a benevolent hand on her shoulder, then wrap my arms around the flimsy seersucker fabric of her homemade housedress. Rose trembles in my embrace.

"Don't cry, Rose. I can see into the spirit world where your son and your brother are woodworkers, Rose. Fine walnut bowls and goblets and boxes, like the set of goblets Eugene gave you for your wedding gift, or the box you keep Ricky's baby ring in. An angel watches over them. She wants us to build something with wood too. Ricky would have wanted it. A shrine." Everyone gasps at my awesome necromantic message.

*You really ran those lines. Lay it on thicker, why don't ya?*

Rose's crying is the true show-stopper. Rose's crying is unlike anything I've seen in my twenty-three years of living. Sorrow that outdoes any angel or apparition. Sorrow that becomes its own might and magic. Sorrow that silences and bows each of us—even Etta, who becomes utterly silent, not even white noise. Each of us lays a tender hand on Rose's slumped body. We are in awe at the otherworldly sorrow of her crying.

The majesty of uncensored grief lasts only a few minutes before Etta is back in my ear. *Tell her we want a big shrine. Big, like a dance gazebo. How 'bout I let her name it after Ricky? So sentimental. That oughta get things started.*

# 32 Grabbing the Gusset

Who would have thought I'd turn them into fast friends. Me? They're bonding like blood. Here I am bringing everybody close, and after all the times I've been called a homewrecker. Even managed to tear up my own family. Tore 'em up and ran away. Now here I am with this lot, bonding. I guess an old ghost can learn new tricks.

My Papi was a determined tower of a man. His colossal arms weren't made for loving. Like "The Young Giant" in *Grimm's Fairy Tales*, he worked as if every day was a chance to prove how hard a man can work. He hit all sixes like his boss might drop him any day. But Mr Champlain—the wine boss—would never fire Papi. Papi was the best vintner in the U S of A. He kept the wine flowing—coulda been blindfolded, hands tied behind his back. Even if the Anti-Saloon League and the Salvation Army and the Klu Klux Klan picketed our vineyards, even if god himself came to seize the wine, Papi woulda kept on.

Papi was Pleasant Valley Wine Company and the Pleasant Valley Wine Company was Papi. Bees and flowers. He came from Beeranuslese and Eiswein vineyardists. He knew the Riesling grape, the Scheurebe, the Ortega, and the Finger Lakes good stuff, the Chardonnay. The grapes were his children, cradled in harvest baskets with care. He would turn the screw lid of the basket press with such piety. Each morning he touched the oak barrels in the same sequence for good luck—finger tap, finger tap, full palm, thumb stroke, finger tap—et cetera.

Next in line for his neat affection was Kaiser, man's best friend, the

German Shepherd. Kaiser learned Papi's language of whistles and ticks, for which he was awarded with even-thrummed pats to his head.

But on New Year's Eve, Mama Famke made Papi kiss her for ten continuous seconds as I banged a wooden spoon against a saucepan at midnight. One night a year, I witnessed a real cash kiss, a silver-screen kiss, and I savoured the image the rest of the 364 days. I believed that all men were like Papi and women like Mama Famke.

I was sprout small, but plenty old enough to recall when Mama Famke came to Horseheads with nothing but a sap's grasp of English and a violin. She came from Holland, but she looked nothing like a little Dutch girl, more like a little Egyptian queen, which the neighbours never hesitated to snicker about.

She came for American Ragtime. She came with the notion that every point on the map was just like New York City or New Orleans, and that soon enough she'd meet Joe Venuti or Eddie South or some other jazz man who would take her on. Mama Famke was no canary; she wanted to be in the ensemble. A lady in a band! I bet she coulda done it too. Her fiddling was killer.

Instead she met Papi, a widower with a daughter only eight years her junior. Papi coolly, but very steadily, rewarded Mama Famke for dashing her musical hopes to become the head of our house. She drank from Papi's secret champagne cellar. She picked out a new phonograph record for every birthday, anniversary, and for Christmas. When Amelia Earhart appeared in a Lucky Strike advertisement, Mama Famke asked Papi to buy her cigarettes and light them for her whenever he was within reach. She learned English at the State Theatre in Ithaca, where she and I could both see a show for just a Liberty quarter. When entertaining Papi's friends, she imitated Katharine Hepburn's ingénue charms in *Morning Glory*. When she was cross, she sounded more like a wicked Leila Hyams during the wedding scene in *Freaks*:

"Holy Christmas! What must I do? Must I play games with you?"

A great dame through and through, she never had a stovepipe silhouette. All the same, when the winery wives started dressing like flappers, Mama Famke had Papi order her the latest Fifth Avenue styles from the Sears catalogue. And if anyone dared call her a gyppo, she'd calmly snap her fingers and Papi would silently loom over the offender until they excused themselves. When a gentleman asked Mama Famke to dance—and one or two did at every dinner dance—Papi obligingly loomed at the edge of the dance floor until she was done hoofing and then gingerly returned her to their table.

I grew up a dreamer, a flirt, and a ducky dancer. Education in stockings and lipstick outranked learning to can pickles or bake sugar cookies. "Chiffon now; we used to wear silk. But these are only seventy-nine cents, so who's complaining," Mama Famke told me. When we couldn't afford new stockings, she hand-drew the seams up the back of my calves in kohl. Sure, we were frugal, we dined on rabbit stew and Ritz Crackers like everybody else. Still, we painted our lips darker and darker red. "See the woman your little *mausi* becomes," said Mama Famke, and Papi would lower his aloof head and turn away.

I turned sweet sixteen in 1936, after we'd all been singing and singing "Happy Days Are Here Again." President Roosevelt heralded that America had risen "together, rallied our energies together ... and together survived." The Pleasant Valley Wine Company survived, I'll say. It was the last vineyard standing in New York State after Prohibition, and it had a monopoly all along the East Coast. The Champlain family was fixing to open a second winery at Cayuga Lake. My sweet sixteen party was as grand as the Champlain daughters' debuts, with candles and bubbly and a jazz quintet.

Mama Famke—who hadn't yet seen twenty-five years herself—was the real belle of the ball. I didn't mind sharing the limelight one bit.

She surprised us all by joining the band to play "Marcheta." She was made for fiddling Eddie South. Her fiddle said, nuts to you modernists; behold my older-than-old soul. She really honeyed it thick. We were fried to the hat from her fiddling.

During my shoe ceremony, I kicked off my Oxfords to reveal toenails polished as red as my lipstick. Mama Famke had painted them for me. Papi knelt at my feet with my first pair of heels. Sandals! I was becoming a woman in sandals that revealed my bare toes. The whole ballroom held its breath while Papi's beefy fingers bested the little brass buckles, then exhaled with a smitten sigh as we danced our first dance.

The first and only time we danced as father and daughter.

Young fellas asked to cut in, and this time it was for me that Papi loomed like a ghoul at the edge of the dance floor. But he couldn't loom nonstop. Thinking back, my debut meant double duty for Papi—watching over his Sheba of a wife and his ingénue daughter. After a dozen or so dances, it was college frosh Robert Ahlers who led me through the French doors and out into the garden. He'd had tons of practice sneaking off with girls, I'm sure. He said, "Young lady, I'm going be your first. You're lucky because I'm a guy that knows how," and I immediately pictured New Years Eve's silver-screen kiss.

Robert perched me on the arm of an oversized Adirondack chair, fed me a single line about my good looks, and started heavy petting, home run, hit on.

"Lift your gown," he told me.

"Says you!"

I heard the sound of rayon tearing. White dresses are a pain to mend, I thought. I was such a dumbbell. I didn't know yet that anything could be worse than a ripped dress.

"Don't be stingy. This is what turning sixteen is all about." Robert's hand was in my jersey skivvies, grabbing the gusset in his fist. I felt his fraternity ring down there—I swear it. I suppose my coming out as a scream queen happened that night. I hollered so that the whole vineyard could hear me.

Robert never knew what hit him, but he had good enough sense to run. Papi's head eclipsed the moon. The night air around him turned darker. For a split second I could hear the crickets chirping before he took me by both shoulders and shook until I heard nothing. Shook until everything to my left turned black, everything to my right, haze. "*Scham*," he said before pulling me down from the oversized Adirondack chair. Shame.

I wish I woulda skipped out that very night. Slunk away like a bandit along the exit tracks Robert had laid.

I stuck around for another year, waiting for Papi to come around, but his austerity only became increasingly austere, his distance, decidedly more distant. I can't recall a single word he has said to me since my debut. It's possible that he never spoke to me after that night.

In his silence, a new part of me opened up like a secret door. I stepped through it the night Rebekka Kruken, who debuted a month before me, and I went to the picture show together and I stole too many glances at her face instead of watching the movie. I stepped in further when I pretended I couldn't find a partner at our annual Foxtrot social and danced with a girl. Secret step by step, in and in, and farther away from my father. He never saw me leave, and I never turned around to look over my shoulder.

The trouble with *scham* is it follows you forever. *Scham* undoes a family. I ought to know. Even death didn't relieve me of Papi's *scham*.

# 33 Nobody

'm headed to the library in an hour or so. I thought, since I'll be in your neighbourhood, maybe you'd like to go to the Robo Mart for ice cream before your shift?"

"I might," says Tamara. She sounds sleepy. Is eleven a.m. too early to call a stripper? I do the math. Last call is at two a.m., so she must get off work at least four hours earlier than I do, and I'm already awake. I hardly sleep more than a few hours a night anymore. Exhaustion may be the reason I so breezily dialled Tamara's number to ask her out on something as wholesome as an ice cream date. Anyway, I had to call sometime. It's definitely my move. "Will you buy me a soft serve with sprinkles?" she asks. "Will you hold my hand?"

"I could do that. Well—"

"Well?"

"Well, if, say, the graduating class of '86 happens to be having a reunion in the Robo parking lot, then I'd rather those assholes didn't see us. Or, like, if there is a big rig truck fuelling up, and it's covered in Trucking for Jesus stickers, then maybe not." This is my attempt at humour—though I'm not actually joking.

"If I worried about what assholes think, I'd never leave my house." Tamara doesn't find me funny. "Never mind. Scratch what I just said. No public affection in front of assholes. That's reasonable. And Star, I'll meet you at the library. I got to return a couple VHS tapes. You ever watch that American Masters series? I'm totally addicted. I have overdues on Lillian Gish and James Baldwin."

My cheek accidentally mashes into the number buttons. The phone beeps in our ears. I almost blurt out, "I studied him in my Race and Sexuality course," but I stop myself. Embarrassing. She's so perfect she watches James Baldwin documentaries when she's not working as a stripper, and meanwhile I'm a U of T dropout who can barely operate a telephone.

I do my makeup on the bus. I need to buy myself time alone at the library before Tamara arrives. The driver addresses me in the rear view mirror. "You got lipstick on your teeth. I can see it from here," she says. She's right. I tilt my pressed-powder compact to see an eggplant-coloured smear across my incisors. Today the bus driver's wearing a Rush Power Windows tour T-shirt. "You're the gal who works nights at The Point, aren't you?"

My first thought: She knows I'm queer and on my way to meet a girl. What did I do to give myself away? Lesbo written on my forehead.

"My friend Bobby lives there. Bobby says I ought to come talk to you."

"Oh?"

"I don't usually tell people this, but Bobby, she was saying how things are getting better between her and her old man since you helped them out. So, I was wondering if maybe you could help me out too." She slides her aviator sunglasses down her nose, winks at me with a swollen black eye, tilts her head to show an inch-long laceration held together by two bits of blue tape. She pushes her shades up again. I roll my eyes up so I don't start to cry. Crystal Beach bitches don't need my pity.

But I have nothing else to give her, nothing real, nothing I can control. And yet I find myself asking her name in a low soothing voice, moving up to the seat directly behind her. She says it again, twice—"I don't usually tell people this"—before spilling. Her story unfolds between bus stops. By the time I reach the library I've told her which nights I work at The Point and a description of the cabin so she can easily find me. There has to be something I can do for her. She needs me—needs something. What the hell am I thinking?

At the library, my fingers drift across public records. I'm distracted. Barbara is working. I hear her babbling near the literature section, then by the periodicals—getting closer. She patters up to me, her navy blue pumps squeaking. I hate her shoes. I think about saying something callous and true about how U of T's library was ten times bigger than this two-bit book room.

"I've hardly seen you for days, Star." What she means is we've been avoiding each other since we fought over my paycheque. Barbara wraps me in an awkward hug that I reciprocate after a second or two. "What a nice surprise you came to visit me."

Talk. To. Your. Mother. Normal. Right? I coach myself: Leaving yesterday's quarrels in yesterday is what it means to be family. Today is a new day. "Ma, I need to find a boat. Can you help me track down the *SS Canadiana*?"

"The Crystal Beach boat? Did those 'float the boat' guys ask you for money too? Why they want to get the boat running again is beyond me. Sure, it's our history. What part of our history hasn't gone to shit? Oops, I'm not supposed to say 'shit' at work. But out of all the lost causes to take up. How about these guys raise money for daycare or something? You know how many single moms live around here? Do you know that boat ran on coal? Coal! Even if they managed to restore it, who's going to pay to ride that thing? I told those guys, I said—"

"Ma!" I interrupt. "Will you just listen?" Barbara's body language shifts from stiff annoyance to bowed empathy as I explain my mission to help Rose build a memorial gazebo in Ricky's honour using salvaged wood from the park. "We don't need the boat to sail again, we just need the wood." I leave out any mention of an angel—Rose, Hal, Bobby, and I agreed to keep that strange little phenomenon a secret.

From out of her smock dress pocket comes a tiny flip notepad. She writes "*SS Canadiana*" across the top. "No mother should have to bury her child. If you died, I'd build you a whole grotto. How'd he die?" she asks me, then, "No, don't tell me. Drunk driving? Awful, too awful. Cancer? Teenagers can get cancer too, you know. I read this article—"

"Let's just find the boat, Ma."

She clutches her hand to her chest and lets out a sigh, then races off to the phone desk.

With Barbara occupied, I hastily search and fail to find Zinn, Etta or any other Zinn in the public records. Jane Does, however, are numerous. I whoosh, like I've left my body for a moment, seeing the lengthy list of Does. How can there be so many unknown deceased women in a town so small? I stamp my feet, ground into the present time and place, then proceed in narrowing my search to Does who died between 1925 and 1945, Etta's era, as far as I can tell. As I read, the *whap whap whap* of the date stamp hitting library cards at the checkout counter sounds freakishly close, while my own movements are mute as I scroll through the newspaper index. I rap my knuckles on the desk. Silence. I can't hear myself. Again, I rap with both hands. Silence. Then I read, "Deadly Fall from Cyclone Roller Coaster" and the Ink Spots begin to play in a remote reach of my mind. Can she follow me anywhere?

*Are you here, Etta?*

*So it seems I am. Seems I got no choice.*

*Tell me how you died. I'd rather hear it from you than read about it.*

*Or we both look away. I got a gift for forgetting. I'll teach you.* She tries to steer me away, but I root down again, firm. Her ghostly hand gives up.

*I've already read the headline, Etta. I can't un-read it.*

*Well, the headline says it all, don't it? I went for a ride and I never got off.* Etta's laugh is an echoey studio laugh track from *I Love Lucy. How did I die? Ask me how I lived, why don't you?*

She is hurting. Her discomfort is deadweight in my body. A lump in my throat. My tongue starts to swell. Before now, I've only felt two sensations with her: fear and desire. The heft of her hurt is almost enough for me to stop reading. *You said we're partners. Bonded together. I have to know.*

Between blurry lines of tiny-font microfiche is a composite drawing. Etta's mouth is overdrawn and cartoonish—like the sailors in my ugly painted stunt on the wall. *They could have sketched a better likeness. This makes you look like a clown.* She doesn't answer. There are quite a few articles about Etta, a.k.a., the Erie County Jane Doe.

August 17, 1941: " A witness says the young woman reportedly stood up to adjust her stockings while the ride was in progress and was thrown from the train after the first drop. She fell to her death after being hit seconds later by the same train she had been riding. A failed lap bar is deemed to be the cause ..."

August 22, 1941: "The body of a woman remains unidentified days after her death after falling from the Crystal Beach Cyclone Coaster. The woman is believed to be between nineteen and twenty-four years of age, although she may be as young as seventeen. Her hair and eyes are dark in colour and she was approximately five feet two inches tall. An Erie County Fair pin-back button was found in her purse, along with a Fred Koch Brewery brand wire bottle opener, and a matchbook from Shea's Buffalo. Jewellery found on the body included a pearl and rhinestone necklace and matching earrings that are believed to have been purchased at AM&As in Buffalo ..."

September 28, 1941: "No one has come forward to identify the body of the Erie County Jane Doe. The medical examiner shall furnish the Niagara Regional Police with copies of fingerprints and other identifying effects for ongoing inquiry. Jane Doe is scheduled to be buried in an unmarked grave in Ridgeway Memorial Cemetery by the end of the month. May God rest her soul ..."

I don't believe it. She was left unnamed. Like a nobody. Like a nothing. *Adjusting your stockings? What really happened? Tell me.*

Static fills my skull, like multiple distorted Ettas speaking all at once. It grows from a whisper to a squall in the time it takes to cup my hands over my ears. Shadow images of wooden track and steel unfurl before me. The jangle and bang of chain dogs lifting a roller coaster car. Thick sugared air. Sick. Dizzy. Dizzy. Sick. Something grabs my thigh. Rough hand. Bitter grip. My cunt grows warm. My bladder gives up a little of my morning's coffee. Fuck. Sick. For a breath, I see myself like a tableau, still and quiet in the library. Nothing is touching me. There's no reason to be afraid. Breathe. Be here, I tell myself. But my next breath catches, and everything is incomprehensible again. Somewhere amongst the bedlam I hear a single scream ring out. High and clear. Operatic. The kind of scream that brings down the red curtains.

To my left, Barbara is waving her hands in the air. To my right, I think I see Tamara drop a handful of books to run toward me. The fluorescent lights on the ceiling close in. The olive green-carpeted floor warps as I collide into it.

# 34 It Was Magical

mmediately recognizing their matching Roman noses and wide hips, Barbara and Rose breeze into a cheek kiss. Until this moment, I've only seen Barbara perform this ritual greeting as a way to flirt with men. The two women pause in their embrace, their right hands patting each other's left shoulder, until a sad tremor ripples up Rose's back. She pulls away as she starts to cry. Barbara, always ready to escalate emotions, says, "*Ora faccia a faccia con dio.*"

"Christ, Mom," I hiss, "Rose isn't religious." Not to mention Ricky killed himself.

Rose tosses her hand skyward, either in exasperation or devotion, I can't tell. "Face to face with God," she repeats, practically spitting the words. Jeez, this meeting is off to a great start.

Bobby, Lucky, and Hal wait in an awkward receiving line. Bobby reluctantly receives Barbara's double cheek kiss, then quickly releases herself from Barbara's embrace and turns to pet the dog. Lucky gets Barbara's baby voice and hair tousle. Hal receives a handshake.

Barbara guides us to her dining room table, which is only a four-piece set, so she's brought in a few pollen-speckled lawn chairs from the back patio. The anise and almond cookies, however, Barbara made herself. And there's coffee in her purple enamel Moka Pot. Lucky scrambles into Bobby's lap. He swipes two cookies, fast, as if the plate is about to be taken away.

"Hal's the man who'll build the gazebo," I tell Barbara. I notice a flash of skepticism as she eyes Hal. I doubt Hal notices, though.

He has one and only one thing on his mind.

"Did you find my boat?" he asks.

Barbara puts on her reading glasses, which I'm still not used to seeing her wear. "So, the SS Canadiana, 'travelled between Buffalo and Crystal Beach. In its heyday, it featured a live band and swing dancing.' I wish I was around to have seen it. I came later, when all the college kids rented out the cottages to party. We partied like it was the last summer of our lives. I met Starla's father at a cottage party. Crystal Beach in the '60s was magical. Anyway, the SS Canadiana stopped running in 1956."

"Same year I was born. I've been celebrating my thirty-fifth birthday for years now," chuckles Bobby. Hal elbows her in the side. Maybe Barbara is making her self-conscious. They're not too far apart in age, but Bobby is holding a three-year old in her lap.

Barbara continues with cumbersome facts and dates. Her voice speeds up as she gets to the good part: "In the late sixties, the SS Canadiana was moved from Buffalo to Cleveland for restoration. Sadly, instead of restoring her, Cleveland sank her."

"Fuckin' Cleveland!" Hal pounds my mother's kitchen table. The cookie tray bounces under his fist.

"But she was saved," Barbara exclaims. She's enjoying her story time. I bet it's like reading to kids at the library. I begin to regret involving her and think about how I used to come to her for help with my homework or when I was sick or upset or scared. I either got dismissive Barbara or domineering Barbara.

She speaks in her extra-loud voice, her speech meandering. Hal looks as if the top of his head is going to blow off. The search for the SS Canadiana has brought out domineering Barbara. "In 1983," she reads to us, "she was rescued by a local non-profit preservation society who got her home with the intention of turning her into a historical site. But! ..." Barbara pauses on the "but" and Hal readies his fist for another table pounding. "After years of fundraising and red tape, the society wasn't able to reach its goal and she was lost again."

"Lost?" asks Bobby. "Like at the bottom of the lake?"

"Lost," Lucky parrots her.

"Oh no," says Barbara. "Now she's dry docked in Port Colborne where they've already started cutting her up for scrap."

"Fuckin' Port Colborne."

"So we're too late?"

"Do you really think I'd make almond cookies if we were too late?" Barbara squeezes my hand under the table. "We're right on time. I took the liberty of calling the dockyard manager myself." She happily waves a flip notepad before my eyes, then reads a list of ship-breaking salvage for sale. Wooden passenger benches, forty dollars each. Interior floorboards, ten dollars per four-by-four. Beams from the hull, two dollars per inch. Wooden hatch covers, twenty dollars. Mahogany doors with brass fittings, one hundred dollars. The wheelhouse is intact and for sale, too. "The guy said if we bought a lot of wood he'd give us a deal. Nice guy. O'Regan I think he said his name was. He had a bit of a Newfie accent. He kept saying 'wah' instead of 'what'—"

"Ma!" I interrupt. "Focus."

"Let's go get the damn boat," growls Hal. He pours the coffee down his throat like a shot of whiskey. "What are we waiting for?"

Rose looks to be a few seconds away from tearing up again. I wonder if I could slip some Amaretto into her mug without Hal and Bobby noticing. "I may as well spend some of Ricky's college savings. He can't study forestry—or whatever it was he said he was going to school for—from the grave." She riffles through her brown leather purse for her chequebook. "How about I just give Starla a cheque, and you bring home as much of that boat as you can get?"

I watch Rose write out a cheque for $1,464. I recognize this number. It's the same amount as a year's tuition fees. *Etta,* I call. *Looks like you're going to get your shrine.* No reply. Or a fuzzy reply, more static. I am dizzy again. No more fainting, I warn myself. I press my fingers into the goose egg on the back of my skull.

"No, no." Barbara waves her hands. "Don't make the cheque out to Starla. I'll take it."

"Ma!"

"Honey, you may not believe me, but I'm doing this for you." Barbara makes meaningful eye contact with each of her guests. "Starla's got money trouble. Whole reason she moved home was to get her debts and spending under control. It's a real problem. Like an addiction, you know? Let's not tempt her by putting such a large cheque in her hands."

"Fuck. Ma!"

Bobby shushes me for cussing in front of Lucky. Hal shakes his head, but I can't tell if he's judging me or Barbara for being such a blabbermouth. Rose points her pen at Barbara. "I write her a paycheque every other week," she says. "What's the difference?"

My legs feel numb as I rise from the table. My hearing gaps and rings. I can't listen to Barbara tell them that she now oversees my bank account, credit card bills, overdrawn line of credit, and defaulted student loans. I can't watch Rose's shifting facial expressions or Hal's frustrated body language. Under my shirt, the Park flag pendant twitches. *You are here, Etta.*

*Let's best this disagreeable scene,* she says.

The lamp overhead flickers on and off again. Then the bulb over the nearby kitchen stove burns out with a loud pop. Songbird turns

210

on her doggie barking alarm. Barbara yips in shock, then yells at Songbird for barking. Lucky claps his hands. Bobby wraps her arm around him tightly. Hal makes the sign of the cross. Rose calls out Ricky's name three times.

I say, "We will gather wood from the Park and build a shrine. The end."

# 35 Pitiful

Barbara complains, "It's always a production with her. If I got upset every time she found herself screwed up in the middle of something, I'd have died from worrying by now."

She's racing around the house, cordless phone wedged between her shoulder and ear, getting ready for work. Etta blew the light bulbs, and Barbara calls it a production. I could fly around the damn dining room and she'd still find a way of not believing it happened. We nearly collide in the hallway. Both of us keep going without as much as a nod. From the other side of the bathroom door, I still hear her muffled voice. "*Hush hush hush* ... crazy *hush hush hush* Starla ...*" Should have peed in an empty mug in my bedroom. I pick up a three-year-old *National Geographic* from the magazine rack beside the toilet and speed-read an entire article on how the Great Lakes are toxic and shrinking waters. Barbara is by the front door now, probably jamming her feet into her comfortable work shoes.

My urine is dark in the toilet bowl. I press my hands into my distended stomach. What did I eat besides one of Barbara's almond cookies yesterday? I step onto the scale Barbara keeps hidden under the laundry bin. 101 pounds. I'm smaller.

Ricky lost weight too. According to his journal, lots of weight.

I'm scared of my body. I bet I'm a size four now.

Wait a second, the Bill Blass silk chiffon bustier dress in my closet is a size four. I spring the Bill Blass from the line of hanging dresses and lay it gently on the bed.

*That's what I call a get-up*, says Etta. *Put it on, we'll stroll along the pier.*

"I was hoping you would notice," I say.

We walk together for several blocks. It's unlike walking with the living. She's more static and cold electricity beside me, but she is walking. One graceful foot in front of the other. We sashay as far as Queen's Circle before I feel alone again. *Etta*, I call to her. Why did I choose my Vivienne Westwood shoes? Walking in stilettos over busted-up asphalt is a sore march—left, ouch, right, ouch. At least leg pain is something. *Are you still with me, Etta?* I ask and ask again as I stomp forward. *We're supposed to be walking together.*

When I was a kid, I thought Queen's Circle was it. Our very own traffic roundabout. May as well have been Columbus Circle in New York City. A scene out of *Taxi Driver*: "You talkin' to me?" Jodi Foster should have won an Oscar for that film. For the love of sin, she was fourteen years old. What a babe she grew up to be.

This is not Manhattan, and our Queen's Circle is dust and scrags of Dutch clover. More grass grows between cracks in the sidewalk than in Circle Park. The trees are thirsty.

Outside the Crystal Mart, a woman wearing a pink terrycloth bathrobe fans herself with a set of scratch-and-win tickets. I wait for her to look at me like I'm a movie star in my dress. She pays me no mind. Maybe I'm a ghost now too?

Our post office flies a clean Canadian flag, always. Every local picks up their mail. Post doesn't come door-to-door. The house beside the post office is for sale. The house beside that is boarded up—I'd like to say boarded up for the winter, but it is summer. At least the boards are painted the same army green as the vinyl siding. That's more than I can say for the rest of the clapboard patch jobs along the way.

A tiny cement plaster building is our Sears, and it's closed on a Thursday afternoon. Not actually a Sears, but the place where items ordered from the Sears catalogue are sent for pickup. Barbara's washer and dryer came through here. That was a proud day, I remember. No more village laundromat for us.

A little boy whistles at me from across an empty parking lot. His littler sister punches him. I think of all the ways I know to say "girl." *Ragazza. Puella. Niña. Fille. Menina. Mädchen. Neska.* This is my new thing now. I translate "girl" when I'm upset. Am I upset? What have I got to be upset about? Just a little paranormal possession is all. Translating "girl" is better than spelling the names of phobias. I'll call it progress. *Etta, where are you? Please!*

A tar snake in the middle of the intersection grabs my stiletto. I could recover, but instead I allow myself to fall, receiving the summer-hot asphalt with indifference. A man pops his head out of the nearby Auction House to ask if I'm okay. My bustier dress bloopers down past my nipples as I pick myself off the ground. Two-handed, I emphatically correct my outfit fail. I'm so inappropriate. The man looks away, retreats.

I spot him again through the Auction House storefront window. He won't make eye contact with me. Our Auction House is a shabby stucco castle. Weather-beaten red turrets represent a time when every local business appeared to be an extension of the amusement park. The windowsills are grimed with dead sand flies. Through the milky glass I ogle rows of English cups and saucers, pink and green Depression glass, brass candle sticks, Christmas nativities and a motley crew of Royal Doulton figurines. So much white ceramic. White ceramic peasant girl holding flowers. White ceramic Georgian lady reading a book. White ceramic elder carrying apples. White ceramic girl child in pajamas praying beside her bed. I tear up again. Fucked if I feel empathy for the ceramic child. Her ceramic prayers. She wants me to buy her, to rescue her from her dusty display shelf of sadness.

I push myself along to the next window. A showcase of knives and books. Whoever dressed this window is a genius. Boning knife. Boning knife. *The Complete Works of William Blake.* Carving knife. Cleaver. *Ulysses.* Gut hook. Gut hook. Gut hook. Gut hook. Gut hook. *Anne of Green Gables.* I have read *Anne of Green Gables* four times—three of those readings were from the one summer I had mono. The number of times I watched the CBC miniseries is uncountable. I could easily recite lines from both novel and film. "Tomorrow is always fresh, with no mistakes in it," I say aloud. Is that so, Lucy Maud Montgomery, because I'm not sure you know what you're saying. I never did get to see the ocean. Not Lucy Maud Montgomery's Atlantic. Not Joy Kogawa's Pacific.

Me, I'm headed for a dead lake.

*Etta, I want to go back. I'm tired. The lake stink is making me nauseous.*

She doesn't answer. I touch my hair and chest and stomach and hips. My body is mine. I'm the boss of me. I turn back toward Queen's Circle and her hand becomes palpable. A firm push at my back. A panicked tightening of my throat. I could fight her, but why resist? Deep down, I want her to push me.

The chain-link fence around the gutted Park now has a few breaks in it to choose from. The opening to the left is wider; less chance I'll tear my dress. Lake Erie smells like a phosphorus bathtub, a toxic-algae spa in this heat. Plus the smell of ash and beer. Amateur taggers have spray-painted every vertical surface since the last time I was here. I count one, two, three expired bonfire rings, step over broken beer glass confetti, register the mandatory dumpster sofa.

It seems this is the summer party spot for local teens. How long would I have to wait around before some young gun arrives and offers me hash? Bottle tokes in an abandoned lot are my birthright. So is unwanted pregnancy. So is diabetes. So is dropping out of school. So is depression. So is date rape. Fate rhymes with date rape.

I halt. Am I afraid of my hometown or of myself? Sure, I was afraid of men in Toronto. What woman isn't? Still, I was brave enough to go to the bars by myself. Now I'm alone in an empty lot and I can't stop catastrophizing. Am I manifesting danger? Maybe Barbara is right about me—I'm always making a production out of nothing. Am I nothing? Am I nothing? Oof, there's the very same question that embittered one-night-stand asked me: Am I nothing?

What's scarier, Etta or nothing? Mother of all fears.

*You brought me here for a reason, Etta. I hope you got something to show me.*

She doesn't answer. The only sound is a cacophony of bird chirps—I guess they're chimney swifts—as I walk closer to the water. Crystal Beach pier is roofed in concrete and corrugated steel—an echo chamber for birds, and chimney swifts are the worst birds in the history of avis. They look like flying cigars and have feather mites. I clap my hands and whistle as my eyes adjust to the pier's dim canopy. They're birds, not bears. Swifts don't give a flying fuck that I'm alerting them to my presence. Dozens-strong, the flock twists and sweeps overhead. Together, they could pick me up and carry me to Buffalo. "Damn you and your helpless naked babies!" I shout. It's good to shout at something. I stomp in my Vivienne Westwood shoes, and my clacking tread echoes above me, weirdly harmonizing with the stirred-up swifts.

Once the sun hits my skin and I'm far enough from their nests, the swifts settle again. Lake Erie is so still that hundreds of brine flies have settled on the floating algae. The remainder of the pier ahead if me is cracked, with large slabs of the walkway collapsing into the water. Wire rope juts out from the gaps. I hear my silk chiffon dress tear as I squat to unbuckle my ankle straps. My pinkie toes are bleeding. Both big toes are swollen with fluid bubble blisters. Is this my self-harm? Impossible shoes? How long has it been since I told myself I hate myself? Autophobia. *Mi sei mancato.* I've missed you.

*Etta, are you watching? I'm scrambling around barefoot for you. Do you see me?*

I pause at a body-sized hole in the concrete to watch the still water below. An empty plastic Coke bottle and dead fish bob side by side. One of my shoes slips from my hand and drops in the lake. A sacrifice to Lemmy.

Or Lem for short. L-E-M—Lake Erie Monster. Tamara was right, our hometown is bizarre. Myths, monsters and meagreness. Home sweet home. I'm going in after my shoe. Damn if the dead lake is stealing my Vivienne Westwood.

My fifth-grade school speech about Lemmy won a regional public speaking competition. I bet Barbara kept the trophy in my Starla boxes. I try to remember words as I lower myself down the jagged, slippery pier. "Paranormal historians will tell you," I recite the opening sentence aloud—I must have felt very grown up using the word "paranormal"—"Paranormal historians will tell you that the first people to report Lemmy to the authorities were the Dusseau brothers, two French settlers who, in eighteen … Eighteen-something something. The Dusseau brothers claimed to see a huge monster writhing and struggling near the shore. Afraid for their lives, the brothers fled and returned hours later to find scales the size of silver dollars washed up on the beach. One of the brothers claimed she had vicious sparkling eyes and a head that looked like a dog." The dog-headed image stuck; tacky Lemmy collectables often look like a German Shepherd with a snake tale.

I tread the water until I reach the very edge of the pier. Another fire pit was burned at the very last concrete slap that's half-sunk into the lake, leaving an oily black ring behind. The bonfire was extinguished by urination. Stinks more than the algae. It's a cloudless sunny day. My dress floats around me like a black puddle. I'm a floating target. Lemmy's going to come for me, for sure.

As teenagers, we used to say "a sacrifice for Lemmy" when we'd drunkenly toss our empty beer bottles into the lake. In the early '80s, Lemmy allegedly sank a sailboat. Coast guard rescued five survivors. It was an American sailboat, so we kids made a joke out of it. We used to sing Lemmy Is Gonna Get You to the tune of Gloria Estefan's "Rhythm Is Gonna Get You."

A wealthy boater from South Bay posted a $100,000 reward to anyone who could capture the Lake Erie Monster, dead or alive. Money does strange things to folklore. Money turns folklore into "broke-lore." "Broke-lore." I should write that down. Suddenly, our beloved inside-joke of a monster was all over the Niagara Peninsula and Buffalo news. People wanted photos of it. People wanted to claim they saw it on public record.

I push my head under the surface, but the water is too mucky to see the bottom. I hope Lemmy likes fashion. I hope this sacrifice appeases her. I push off from the pier, swimming deeper to where the algae clears away.

Cryptozoologists. That was another, grown-up fancy word I used in my award-winning speech. Cryptozoologists search for animals whose existence has not been proven. After that award was announced, cryptozoology hobbyists toured our shores. Monster hunters, not Lemmy, then became our local folklore. "Did you see the one in the

funny diving suit? Right outta *20,000 Leagues Under The Sea*, eh?"
Or "The guy with the Indiana Jones hat was at the Tim Hortons this
morning. He showed everyone the scar on his leg. Claims the monster
bit him, eh. Been tracking him for years."

The pier is a good hundred metres behind me, though I've never
been good at judging distances in water. I float on my back. My Bill
Blass silk chiffon dress weighs me down. I feel a tug, then another.

Karla Moses's aunt Candy told me that long before monster-hunting
wannabes got carried away about the monster, her aunties said
dragons lived in the lake and would travel the skies above their lands
as shooting stars. I didn't mention that in my speech. Despite being
a dumb kid, I knew not to repeat what Candy told me. I read a little
about Six Nation's Pantheon at university. Folklore was a longer unit
than the first contact unit in the Aboriginal Studies class. I'm an even
dumber adult. Thanks again, university education.

*Etta*, I call and call. I scan my body. Can I feel Etta on my chest? Can
I feel Etta between my legs? Tugging at my limbs? Holding my back?
I feel nothing. Curling into a cannonball, I sink. It takes a second or
two before I open my eyes. I've lost my water-baby instincts. When I
do look, everything is as soupy green as I expected. A septic Emerald
City. Lake Erie is not that deep; it's wide but not deep. I used to be able
to touch bottom once. I swim downward. Junk is everywhere. Below
me are slime-blanketed manmade objects I can't identify. I'm pleased
my dress is so flowing. Dark mermaid. Lemmy's new wife. Live fast,
die young, leave a beautiful corpse. Live downcast, die wrung, leave
a pitiful corpse. Live outcast, die unsung, leave an invisible corpse.
Live unchaste, wry tongue, receive a devil's pitchfork. Give trash, buy
dung, leave this world worse. Live vast, die strong, leave collected
works. Can I see in the murky dark? Can I breathe water? Do I want
to die? How many times am I going to feel like this?

I surface and am winded by chest pain. The water's grown choppy. Seagulls *keow*. I tread frantically, gasping for air, then allow my head to sink again, mouth and nose below water level. I used to think I had no control over my life. Shit just kept happening. I could die drowning in Lake Erie, and it would be nothing but another accident. Now people believe in angels because I made them believe. Hal is convinced he's part of some sort of miracle. Rose is spending her money—her dead son's college fund at that. I can't do this to them. I can't spin these lies. Besides, I've ruined my Bill Blass dress. Now I need to find a new dress to wear to my future funeral, an even more fabulous dress.

"Tomorrow is always fresh, with no mistakes in it." Damn you, Lucy Maud Montgomery. Damn and bless you, in turns. I swim toward shore again.

The sun begins to set as I reach the pier. Was I in the Bermuda Triangle? Twilight Zone? The day is gone. My arms and legs feel like stretched-out rubber as I flop myself half-way up a slab of slouching concrete. Plastic bottles and dead fish bob beside me, along with a mess of yellow planks. Yellow? I recognize that yellow. Gooseflesh rips up my torso.

*Etta?*

*Who else, Dollface. Grab ahold of that, will ya?*

*Etta, I can't do this!*

*You're just tired. Having a living body will do that. Why'd you swim so far away? I've been waiting here, with our wood.* She forces my hand, and I cut my thumb on a rusted spike as I yank up the first plank. *It's from the roller coaster. It wasn't all burnt, you see. I ought to know, I've traced every inch of this disaster. Anything that didn't burn or sink is floating right under this pier. I want it for my shrine. Here they come. Tell them to use it in my shrine.*

I lift my head just enough to see a trample of feet running toward me. Someone calls my name. I gulp a mouthful of air and both ears pop. I hear my dress rip on exposed wire rope as I try to scramble up the broken pier. Zebra mussels crust the foundation columns; shells break under my fingers. A hazy voice says "stand back" and "give her some room." I cough up metallic-tasting water.

When my eyes crack open again, I'm in the back seat of Rose's station wagon. My head rests on Hal's lap. In the front passenger seat, the woman with black mullet hair from The Point asks Rose if I'm on drugs.

"You did the right thing, coming to get me, Dolores," says Rose. "Thank God you spotted her." The motion of the car makes me feel like I'm still underwater. I roll my head to look down at Hal's shoes. I retch, but nothing comes up.

Rose makes a shushing sound and slows the car to a halt. Hal pats my back. "Did you have another vision?" he asks me. "What did the Angel say?"

I sit up. The sun through the windshield is blinding. I tell them about the yellow wood washed under the pier. "The amusement park is sacred," I say. "We have to save it." I'm babbling. Rose reaches over the seat to check my forehead with the back of her hand.

Dolores laughs as this. She unrolls her passenger-side window and lights up a hand-rolled cigarette. She has a stick-and-poke tattoo of a tiny wolf on her wrist. Rose starts the car again.

# 36 Making Declarations

Rose spoons up homemade chicken and rice soup. I get the bowl with the bay leaf floating in the broth, lucky me. She's bundled me up in a quilted polyester housecoat and plopped what I think is a crochet tea cozy on my head. She warns, "I'll kill you if you die on me. *Capisce?*" If anyone can shake a pointer finger at me, it's Rose. Her gold rings streak before my bleary eyes. "Should we call your mother?" She picks the phone receiver up from the cradle.

"No," I say. "My ma is like 9-1-1." (Meaning, we never call her.)

After dark, I add slinking around Rose's bedroom window to try and determine if she's sleeping soundly to my nightly chores. I don't want her to stay up worrying. She doesn't need more grief. None of us need more grief. *Hey Etta, How about everything becomes easier from here on in?*

It is Thursday, May 17, and I've worked eleven shifts total and all of reality has collapsed. Days of the week don't make sense anymore. Hours of the night, less so. I still plunge toilets. I still rake the bocce ball courts, collect empty bottles, chores, chores, more chores. And I talk to the dead. I lie about angels. I constantly remind myself that I should be terrified. I had a chance to tell the truth today at the lake, and instead I proclaimed the amusement park to be sacred. Way to be a hero.

Dolores and Hal, my rescuers, sit together at a picnic table in the dark, passing a cigarette back and forth. Dolores, I've learned, lives in the Winnebago set back in the trees. This is the first time I've seen her at night. I edge up to them and overhear Dolores speaking softly. "You can quit drinking, sure, don't let another drop pass your lips. But until you deal with whatever it was that made you drink in the first place, you'll still be stuck in your rut." As I ease back from their conversation I hear her say something about "program" and "meetings." Hal nods and nods.

"You swam the lake all day, now you'll walk the grounds all night," Dolores calls out to me as I'm U-turning away. "You know what they say about people who don't sleep?"

I exhale an "mmmmh" sound in reply because what else is there to say? Is she asking me how I'm doing it? How I'm staying awake and moving for hours on end? And what do they say about people who don't sleep? Where am I getting this maniacal energy from? Adrenaline rushes don't last for ten hours, plus.

I've finished one of Ricky's journals, cover to cover, and could now wire a lamp or fillet a rainbow trout, thanks to his exhaustive instructions. The second journal I currently pore over chronicles the last three months he was alive. There were no fishing trips to write about. No rabbit pens to build. I become more conflicted with each page and repeatedly pause and begin re-reading one of Ricky's lists titled "Choice Ways to Naturally Dispose of the Body." "The Body," not "My Body," I note. Ricky weighs the pros and cons of different methods of suicide from an environmental perspective. Except he never uses the term suicide. Rather, he talks of *progetto scomparsa*: roughly, project go missing, or disappear. Besides a couple of *stronzi* in reference to the Beta Tool Company, this is the only time Ricky writes in Italian. Was it less violent, or more, to switch into a second language? Was he unable to put the word "suicide" in writing?

I can barely say the word aloud. For how often I've thought about it, I never disclosed suicidal thoughts to a counsellor, not even to a friend. I doubt I could discuss decomposition of my own body either, whereas Ricky had written pages on the subject, as if it were as plain as building a bed frame. Methane and carbon dioxide and hydrogen sulfide released after death, it seems, upset Ricky. He wrote about the hole in the ozone. He included several newspaper and magazine clippings of the British Antarctica Survey of the hole, along with his own list of CFC products to avoid, with hairspray listed thrice. Ricky did not want his rotting corpse to widen that hole. There are a few scribbled then scratched-out equations that contain variables like Ricky's body weight to the average time it takes a body to decompose. Now would be a good time to put this journal away, back in the very bottom of the trunk, bury it under bleach bottles and Band-Aid boxes. Surely somewhere, outside in the crisp night air, there's loose garbage I should pick up. I keep reading.

Ricky stopped eating meat and dairy on January 6, 1990, a week or so before his death. He writes about vegans having a quicker "bowel transit time." This would help render him into what he deemed "better compost." Like a good only son, he did enjoy his mother's Christmas and Epiphany meals. He writes four sentimental pages about his last midnight Christmas Eve fish feast, and the next day, his last tortellini in *brodo* after opening presents, and his last Epiphany dinner of anchovies in green sauce, braised veal, and panettone pudding. His meticulous way with details strongly translates into food writing, and I find myself nostalgic for home cooking.

Barbara can make most of these dishes, though I remember very few holidays when *Nonni* or *Zii* came to visit. There was tension. Even as a child I recognized it. I was born out of wedlock. Bastard baby and *putana* mother. And Barbara never bothered to find a husband after I was born. Now she's too old for marriage. *Putana zitella* (spinster slut)! Most of our holidays, we ate our meals while sitting on the sofa watching *The Sound of Music* or *The Charlie Brown Christmas*. On an ambitious year, we'd drive over to Buffalo for Chinese food.

Rose must go to Florida next Christmas, I think. Or Hawaii. The first holiday alone is bound to hurt. I haven't noticed any family checking in on Rose. Maybe it's because I work at night? Maybe family members visit in the day? Or maybe they don't come at all because Ricky committed suicide?

"Can you vermicompost flesh?" The question is followed by a lengthy passage on red wriggler worms and what types of bacteria they eat. Ricky wrote, "Flies and maggots are the key." After putrefaction, flies and maggots can eat up to sixty percent of the body within a week. I read the phrases "mouth hooks" and "tissue-eating larva" and again I recognize that now is an appropriate time to stop reading. I feel small. The cabin, cavernous. I feel ill. The cabin—revolving in a gross nauseous circle.

No one should read Ricky's journals. I might burn them, if only to make sure Rose never sees them. Does Rose need to consider whether dying near still, shallow water makes the decomposition process faster? No. Rose never, ever needs to know about her son's final macabre thoughts.

Only one more page, I promise myself. January 7, 1990: Ricky had drawn a rather accomplished illustration of a ghost with Etta's eyes and mouth. This is the closest thing I've seen in his journal that confirms his contact with her. "Kiss of Death" is written above her head in sharp heavy-metal block letters. I slam the journal closed.

*You know exactly how he died, Etta. Tell me you didn't have something to do with it.* I direct my question at the painting. She hasn't spoken to me all night. *If you drove him to death, I'll find out.* My threat is merely an attempt to get her attention.

Outside, the darkness needles me. I hug my cardigan across my chest. Hal and Dolores have gone to bed, but I see Moustache Man's light on in his trailer again. His face cranes to see me in the dark, then he shuts his blinds. I think my ears are ringing, then realize it's the off-the-hook tone of the payphone. The receiver is dangling from its cord again. As soon as I hang it up, it rings. "Hello, hello," I repeat, panicked. Nothing but dial tone.

I find a quarter in my pocket. Did I leave the cabin intending to make a call? I rub the coin between my thumb and forefinger before pushing it through the slot. I make a mental note to clean the dead flies off the illuminated "Telephone" sign as I wait on hold for the bartender to find Tamara.

"How you feeling, Star?" she asks with the boom of rock music behind her. "Everything all right?"

I didn't prepare for her question—everything all right? I lean my forehead against the phone booth's scuffed Plexiglass wall. She's asking because she saw me faint. Because she knows I'm afraid. Because I am a freak. Because I'm about to flip my shit. "I was just thinking about you, Tamara," I say, cool as a cucumber.

Hours later, I am tending the flowers growing in tractor tire planters in front of Rose's house when Tamara Matveev arrives. No garden gloves, my filthy hands sunk into the soil beneath the marigolds. I wanted her to come, but as she pulls up in a ridiculously cool mint-green classic Ford Galaxy 500, I realize I have no idea what to say. I am paralyzed, squatting between the flower beds. Lucky greets her before I can even cobble together a "hello."

"Rise and shine," Lucky says, as if he knows her, as if they see each other every morning. Tamara walks hesitantly up the walkway, eyeing me as Lucky skips up and takes her hand. Her hair is up in a messy bun that she surely styled without bothering to look in a mirror. Her dress is shiny electric blue, a work dress, but she's swapped her heels for a pair of Converse and mismatched socks. It's the socks—one plain white tennis sock and the other with a pink pom pom sewn on the ankle—that rouse me from my numbness. "I'm sorry I dragged you all the way out here this early," I apologize. "Looks like you've been up all night too. You didn't have to come."

"I wanted to see how you were doing. You sounded a bit … on the phone." A bit what, I wonder. What adjective best describes how I sound right now? Tamara notices my discomposure. "Let's just go for coffee and talk. Easy, right?" she says. "I'll take you to Tim Hortons."

At the mention of Tim Hortons, Lucky bounces into Rose's house, singing, "Donuts. Dough. Nuts." We both laugh, the mood lightened just enough for me to accept that she is here, that she showed up despite my ongoing fumbling. I hug her with my grubby hands. My anxiety-sweaty body meets her cigarette smoke-scented hair; my work jeans and old cotton T-shirt meet her cheap spandex dress.

I see Rose and Lucky peeking through the screen door and wave; motion them to come out and meet Tamara. I may be off my rocker right now, but maybe she will be my girlfriend, the love of my strange fucking life. I'd better learn how to introduce her to people. "We knew each other in high school," I explain.

Rose smiles and shakes Tamara's hand, though she does not extend an invitation to come in for a cup of coffee. She keeps smiling and nodding strangely as we get into Tamara's car. There's a tautness in her voice as she calls after us, "You girls get some breakfast, now."

"Mrs Esposito's met me a handful of times. Last time was Ricky's funeral," Tamara tells me. And here I thought Rose's tone was because

228

she suspects we're queer. Reality check, it's not all about me.

Dawn hasn't crested the tree line, and patches of light hit the windshield intermittently through the trees. I pull the sun visor down to find a perfect pink lipstick print on the tiny vanity mirror, and I wonder who else has sat here. The crank handle is stiff as I attempt to roll down the passenger-side window. The classic rock radio station plays "Fast Car." I sing along for a few lines.

"Tracy Chapman fan?" Tamara nudges me from across the long bench seat. Her other hand is draped effortlessly over the big steering wheel. She sings a few lines in a voice that is both terrible and charming. I undo my seat belt so I can wriggle closer to her. My shoulder rubs against her shoulder, and I catch myself thinking of Etta. Not really a thought as in contemplation, more like a sensation. Like Etta has left a tactile residue on my skin. I feel touch and there she is. I tip my nose into Tamara's hair, as if the hairspray and cigarette smell can trounce Etta's existence.

Then, without warning, as if she knows there is a moment to spoil, she stands in the centre of the road. So bright and lucid, I'm sure Tamara can see her too. We careen into her only for a blink, long enough for me to cry out as something thumps the car's bumper. Another blink and Tamara is swerving sharply. I lurch, my shoulder slams the passenger side door. The car swerves a half circle.

"Shit." Tamara slams on the brakes. "Are you okay?" She's got her right arm stretched out across my chest, as if to hold me in place as she braked. "I think I hit a bunny." Behind us a young rabbit lies in the spot where Etta just stood, the rabbit's tawny fur crushed into the pavement. "Did it just move its back leg?"

"It's gotta be dead, Tamara. I think it went under the back tire."

"What if it's not dead? I should check. Put it out of its misery."

"Don't," I clamp my hand down on Tamara's bare thigh. "Rabbits around here got diseases. Rabbit fever."

"Rabbit fever," she repeats dubiously before our lips crash. We both know we are about to have disaster sex. Without coy check-ins or permissive flirtations, our bodies draw together. Bobbypins ping out of her hair as I rake both my hands through it. The neck of my T-shirt complains as it rips. Without pause, she slides two of my dirt-stained fingers in her mouth, then guides them down between her legs. "This is a messed-up way to start a relationship," she says.

"I promise I'll call you tomorrow." I let myself be hypnotized by the even bluer panties under Tamara's electric blue dress. The colour is obscene next to her tan skin. I watch my fingers disappear inside this blue like a sleight-of-hand magic trick. I trace my pointer finger up and down her slit, that flawless innie I was awed by at the strip club. Bikini stubble rubs the back of my palm. "I promise I'll call you. I promise you," I coo in her ear. Etta darts in and out of my peripheral vision as I touch Tamara Matveev. Each time she does, my eagerness surges. I see the muscles in my arm twitch. I hardly know if I'm making declarations to Tamara or to Etta. Tamara's raspy moans goad me further. How hard is too hard for the first time? She kicks at the car window. Etta's reflection appears on the glass. A fist beats against my chest and I want it to be Etta's. I want Etta's unnatural weight to bear down on me. "Fuck," Tamara says. "Fuckin' there there right there."

An hour later, we are sticky hot and severely sleep-deprived in the back seat of her Ford Galaxy 500, which sits only a few feet from the morning's road kill. "I still want to know how you're doing, Starla," she asks. "We were going to talk, remember?"

A series of impressive lies flip through my head. Then, "I'm being haunted," I admit. I figure my soon-to-be new girlfriend (and, knowing me, soon-to-be ex-girlfriend) deserves my honesty. "By the ghost of a woman who died on the Cyclone roller coaster. I'm pretty sure Ricky was haunted by her too."

I worry Tamara is too exhausted to react. She calmly rubs my back in slow, comforting strokes, and says nothing. What is there to say? This truly is a messed-up way to start a relationship.

# 37 Messed Up

After Tamara drops me at home, I walk from room to room trying to calculate how many consecutive hours I've been awake. Thirty-one maybe. In the kitchen there is a "remember to eat" note for me placed beside a plate of raspberry scones.

An empty popcorn bowl has been left on the coffee table in the living room. Barbara's buttery fingerprints smear the inside and I wonder when we last watched TV together. I place the bowl on the ground for Songbird to lick.

The shower in the white-on-white-on-white bathroom never gets hot enough. The cheap Irish Spring soap smells sickly strong. I rinse quickly and turn the water off. Lightheaded, I creep into Barbara's room and lie in her bed. Her sheets are dusty rose-coloured cotton. Three blown-glass hearts hang over her bed, like an adult mobile. Maybe a different bed will allow me to sleep.

Minutes later, I'm frantically sifting clothes from my closet. Etta is in my room. I knock on the stunt above my bed to draw her nearer. She's attracted to anything from the Park. *Right, Etta? That's what binds you to the living world?* I knock on the stunt again. *The Park is sacred.* No answer. She isn't speaking today. Instead she nudges my thigh. Tugs my hair. Sweeps behind me, feather-light. Her touch feels alarming and heightened on my body, like I've been blindfolded by a lover. Like I'm about to sex cry. Like the endorphin high that is particular to bringing a lit cigarette close to one's own skin. Amygdala ammunition. Fire. I reach my arms at random, grasping. Etta chooses to remain dark and void while I go mad.

I pretend I'm not going to do what I'm about to do. That's part of it, the pretending. Pretending facilitates many of my fuck-ups. I pretend not to notice my white T-shirt is see-through, or that the bra underneath is red lace. I pack Djuna Barnes's *Nightwood* (the twenty-third edition in paperback—a worthless printing) and a hot-pink bottle of pepper spray in my purse.

On the bus, I bow into my book to avoid eye contact with the driver, reading, "She wanted to be the reason for everything and so was the cause of nothing." Oh, Djuna Barnes, in 1937 I would have been your lover, your puppy dog, your boot licker.

I get off at the stop closest to the Peace Bridge. Here is my hitchhiking origin story. Karla Moses and I donned head-to-toe black, including black lipstick, bound for Toronto for an all-ages Love and Rockets concert. We were smart girls. It's safer to hustle a ride from truckers on this side of the bridge than to thumb it on a highway on-ramp. With on-ramps, you've got to jump into just about any car that stops. At the bridge, a girl can chitchat for a minute, watch where the driver lays his eyes when he speaks.

I pick the trucker with a handshake that is the right amount of shakes: three. No revolting finger lingering. He states his first and last name, "Neil Thompson," then heads straight to the driver's side, not bothering to open the passenger door or offer me a boost into the cab. As I pull myself up, I notice my right wrist is cramped from fucking Tamara. Can I be in a relationship? Fall in love like a normal idiot? Like brushfire, the crick in my wrist spreads. I yank the truck door shut as pain shoots up my arm. My chest tightens as I fasten my seatbelt. Why am I doing this? I can see the very tip of Pure Platinum's neon sign from the bridge parking lot as we pull out. It's not too late to bail. Drink boozy coffee and run a tab at the strip club instead.

Neil Thompson is hauling frozen goods, and that's why I chose him. I figured a man with a temperature-controlled transport would be especially high-strung and on the clock. I'm surprised his cab isn't littered with empty cans of Jolt Cola. Neil Thompson says he's going directly to Marshall's Truck and Trailer in Hamilton for a fuel-up and that's as far as he'll take me. I trust he won't boot me out half-naked along the outer reaches of Rural Route 107. A driver with a temperature-controlled transport wouldn't do that. But now I can't quit thinking about meat. I imagine large cubes of ground beef boxed in cardboard. Meat boxes packed like bricks. A wall of meat. A fortress. Or whole hanging cow carcasses. Rump up, neck down, swaying on icy metal chains as we merge lanes on the highway. Aged beef twice the size of me. White with fat on the outside. Cut down the middle so their ribs jut out like crooked red ladders.

"Quit scratching," Neil says.

My thighs are pink with nail marks. Crawling hot skin. Fever leaching through my pores. Where's Etta? Why didn't I wear my pendant? Did I tuck a strip of ride tickets in my back pocket?

"You worried about something? Because if you're worried about me, quit worrying. I said I'd take you to Hamilton. I'm not looking for anything in return."

"What if I want to give you something in return?" I ask. This gentle man with two-day stubble on his chin could distract me. My mind has already placed us in the back of his rig. I have to cool down. Breathe chilled Freonic air. Press my bare back against a frozen cow. Fuck atop a gutted carcass big enough to feed a family for months. I want a cock in my mouth. I want to close my eyes and listen to the rattle of meat hooks and become nothing.

Maybe Neil is crying. His tears are the kind that could be mistaken for perspiration. Glistening. He wipes his forearm across his face, but he's wearing short sleeves and his bare skin only spreads his damp tears around. He cranes his head into his hunched shoulder to dab eyes on the yoke of his work shirt. The movement is strangely macho. Dominate those tears, Neil Thompson. Don't let them fall. Or what if he's a sex crier, like me? We could drain our tainted fluids together. We could ugly cry. "There isn't a proper rest stop with a pay phone until the Husky station in Saint Catharines. I won't take you that far north. I'm gonna pull off Exit 5 and let you out. You can call a cab from the Border Town Grill nearby. I'll give you a few bucks to go back in the direction you came from."

"You're kidding me," I say.

"You're a working girl. How old are you?"

"I'm not. Did I ask for money?"

"I have too many friends, if you can call them friends, who go out looking for a fight. They say they're going out for a beer or to watch a band play. Truth is they're out to fight. Doesn't matter if they win or lose, as long as fists meet cuffs. I'm going to tell you exactly what I tell them. If you got a fight in you, stay home. Stay home."

"Fighting wasn't exactly what I had in mind." I hitch my fingers around the crook of his elbow. This is my last chance.

"No way. A young girl like you, no thank you. What you have in mind is even more dangerous than a fist," says Neil Thompson. He flicks his turning blinker on and glides into the exit lane. "You got people you can talk to? Girlfriends or a mom?"

"It's okay. You don't need to get all paternal. I gotta work tonight anyway."

"Work tonight," Neil repeats, humming out the words.

"Not as an escort or stripper, if that's what you're thinking. I got a square job, just like you."

Neil's hum tells me our conversation is finished. I think about Tamara in her electric blue underpants. I really should have gone to Pure Platinum. An Irish Cream toothache would be a thousand times better than judgmental man humming.

·"Not that there's anything wrong with being a stripper," I say, mostly to myself.

Neil leaves me outside of Stevensville, about a two-hour walk from The Point, tops. I'm actually closer to home than when he picked me up. Is this Etta's doing? Can I not leave the area? The nearby on-ramp is a quiet one. Still, I'd be picked up within the hour in my wet dream outfit. White cut-off jean shorts say drive me to Toronto, don't they? In the midday sun my white T-shirt is more see-through. I ogle my own bra. Red lace. I think about meat again. Red meat under a layer of white fat. I'm a cow carcass. I'm a cow carcass hanging in the back of a truck driven by a man too stupid to receive a blowjob. What's wrong with my body?

I've always wished for one solid irrefutable reason to be as messed up as me. Somehow being molested by my needy-slut-of-a-single-mother's boyfriend doesn't measure up. I was poor, but never starving. I party, but was never an addict. Now I have a reason. Etta. I can't even wonder if I've made her up. Others have seen her.

And tomorrow, the May Two-Four Weekend will bring campers, many campers, and conceivably they'll see her too. Should I be comforted by these witnesses?

Can I be a witness to myself? I should write that down.

I walk Stevensville Road, leaving the slow rumble of the highway behind. My future book will be called *A Hitchhikers Guide to the Fallacy*. So long and thanks for all the bullshit. Too derivative? *Pity Parade: A Memoir*. Pity, from the Latin *pietas*, closer to devotion than sadness. I'm devout. Rapturous. I haven't slept in, like, thirty-four hours.

I use the lousy five dollars Neil Thompson gave me to buy a strawberry milkshake and a side order of hash browns at Mae's Place. The waitress is so rude I suspect she knows I'm only going to tip her seventy-five cents. I bet the old guy half-asleep at the table by the window only tips her seventy-five cents, too. No, the waitress rudely bangs down my milkshake so that strawberry goo spills down the side of the glass because I'm dressed like a tramp. This red bra is cursed. Everything is cursed except this milkshake. This milkshake is saving me. I don't feel a trace of Etta in my body, only milkshake. The photograph of James Lewis Kraft mounted above the cash register is not cursed either. He grew up here. A Crystal Beach boy, and he invented processed cheese. Velveeta. Miracle Whip. Kraft Dinner. Kool-Aid. Junk food billionaire. White trash to white cash. When there's only, like, six famous people from your hometown, you recognize every single one at a glance. "One day there will be a photo of me hanging right there," I say to the waitress, pointing at Kraft. "I'll be your poster girl."

"Get a life," says the waitress.

I have a life, I think. What now?

# 38 What Message

What are you wearing? What, you want to catch a cold?"

I should have gone home to change before coming to work. Rose wraps me in a terrible argyle cardigan. Not even a knit, but a sweatshirt with an argyle print. She buttons it up past my ridiculous red lace bra. At least it's not another polyester housecoat. "It still gets cold at night," she tells me, and, "Please, for the love of Christmas, don't dress like that tomorrow. The boys will be wild enough."

According to Rose, tomorrow will mark The Point's all-time-low opening weekend. When the park was in operation, she saw 100-percent occupancy. Twenty-nine out of fifty seasonal campsites reserved seems busy enough for me, considering most of the campers will be teenagers. Sixteen is the legal age to reserve a campsite in Ontario, a bylaw that clashes with the drinking age. I'm prepared for a shit show.

I visit each campsite, inspecting the handiwork of Rose's nephew, Vincent, who sands down old picnic tables, who trims tree branches. Vincent, whom I've never met, only heard Rose glow about, who shows up at The Point in the daytime. Vincent, who probably takes his shirt off in the midday sun to mow the lawn. While Ricky was hunched over his desk plotting his death into the wee hours of the morning. While I invite the dead to lie in bed with me. Lucky Vincent. Or not. Perspective. Who knows?

For now, Etta is absent. I circle campsite number nine again and again. Nothing but a couple of log benches and a tidy fire pit.

I haul my one part bleach, one part water, one part vodka all-purpose cleaner into the men's washroom. For some reason, I still haven't dumped the booze. Too wasteful. Thrift is in my bones. The fluorescent light closest to the door doesn't flicker on with the rest. Changing the fluorescent bulbs is supposed to be Vincent's job. "Shit," I grumble.

"You shit."

I laugh, almost reply, "No, you shit." But Bobby isn't joking. She's slumped between two urinals on the floor. I drop the mop bucket; cleaning solution splashes my feet. "What happened? Are you all right?" My question is answered as soon as I reach her side. Beer breath—on Bobby? I squat down beside her. No, not her breath. Her hair and clothes too, as if she soaked in Budweiser.

"Lucky's asleep. And Hal is drinking again. Mister Servant of God. Hal's drinking. If he wakes Lucky up, I swear ... " She dry gags as she speaks. Without thinking, I hug her into me. Her arms are incredibly strong as she pushes me away. I fall back onto my butt. I should have known better—Bobby's not a hugger.

"How drunk? Should we go in and check on him?" I ask.

She grabs my arm. Her fingertips are freezing. I slip off Rose's argyle cardigan and wrap it around her. "Bobby, we have to do something. We can't just sit here crying."

"Who's crying? Are you? What do you have to cry about? Hospital took my baby—cry about that, why don't you?" She pushes me away again.

"They took Lucky? You said he was sleeping."

"My first baby. A baby girl. Social worker from CFS came and took her. Nurses calling me a negligent mother. Poking at me with needles. Say I need a drug test. I was clean when I was pregnant. I was clean. They never listened to me. Grabbed my baby right out of my arms. You wouldn't understand. No one knows how much that hurts."

Her fists pound the tiled floor. I want to comfort her without touching her in any way she doesn't like. I pat her back tentatively. I think about reading Lee Maracle's *I Am Woman: A Native Perspective on Sociology and Feminism* in an Intro to Aboriginal Studies class. In her book, Maracle said Native women were an afterthought in the feminist movement.

"Stole my baby, same as how they stole me. CFS fuckers. What right do they got?"

Native kids and white trash—we could be allies. That's what growing up in Crystal Beach taught me. We did the same shit. Or did we? Roamed the golf course at night collecting golf balls to return to the caddy shack for five cents a ball. Or snagged empties from neighbours porches to cash in at the Beer Store. I remember the many times the Hill twins and I would push open the doors to Golden Nugget Bingo Hall to yell "Bingo" then run, laughing through the parking lot.

Then I went to university. I took out a student loan to enroll in an Aboriginal Studies class that I was told was groundbreaking. Has the world always been this fucked?

Okay, fucking focus, I scold myself. My white guilt wake-up isn't doing sweet fuck-all for Bobby.

"Were you drinking back then? Did they take your baby because you were Native?" Fuck my stupid mouth. Why ask one condescending question when you can ask two in a row? Why does she stink like beer, though? Did Hal dump it on her?

"If I lose Lucky, I have nobody. Nobody in the whole wide world. That Dolores told Hal he'd better start going to meetings. If that don't help, I don't know what I'll do. I'm so tired. I'm so tired I just want to give up. If it weren't for my boy ..."

"You're a good mother, Bobby," I say. "Seriously, you're, like, a thousand times better than my ma."

"Don't talk ill 'bout your mother, girl."

I want to bump heads with that advice. Why should she stick up for Barbara—she doesn't even know her. "My ma had dozens and dozens of men in and out of the house when I was I kid," I spit out. I can't help myself. "Some of those guys make Hal seem like a real gentleman. She didn't even protect me from being molested. I used to think it was just normal to feel sore down there. That's just what it meant to be a little girl." What am I doing? Trying to be the most hurt woman? Bobby doesn't need to hear this. Shut up. Shut up.

"Hmm, you're angry," says Bobby. "Hal's angry too. I used to be angry too. Still am sometimes. But now, I'm mostly tired." She pats my leg. "I 'spose we still need to have that tea. Get to know each other, especially if you're going to keep looking after Lucky."

"Or I could make you tea? I bake too, a little. Whatever help I can give you, it's yours," I say, too eager. I offer to help her again as we stand in the doorway of her trailer, listening to Hal vomit. And again as we fill Lucky's plastic Snoopy cup with lemon-flavoured electrolytes, delicately place the cup in Hal's hands, and slip back out of the trailer.

"He looks like a baby when he gets drunk sometimes," says Bobby. "I have two babies. He wasn't always like this, eh. There was a time when we were quite the match."

The blushing morning sun presses through the trees, and we pull lawn chairs into the grass to watch the sky change. "I never knew my father either. Only my mom."

She looks away from me, then a second later she reaches over and pinches my arm. "Your dad must have been the skinny one.

The one who gave you that bony butt." She tickles and pinches me some more, and I wriggle in my lawn chair. My giggles come out in relieved bursts. "It's been a long time since I seen the sunrise. I sure did go on fussing and complaining all night, eh?"

"You weren't fussing, Bobby!" I want to put my arm around her. Laughter and physical affection seem to be the only cards I have. My words don't say enough, but I try. "People care about you. Dolores and Rose. I even met one of your friends the other day, the bus driver, eh? We're going to stick by you, whether Hal quits drinking or not."

Bobby nods, slightly. She stares into the distance, her eyes tracking something. She's watching a set of high-beam headlights cut toward us. A red Ford Ranger bumps up the driveway. Bobby and I squint, waving at the driver to cut his light bar.

"Where do you want me to unload?" the driver asks, leaning out his window with a smoke hanging from the corner of his mouth. His flatbed is piled with salvaged wood; beams and doors and moldings almost glow in the early light. What Bobby and I marvel at, though, is the perfect shell of the *SS Canadiana* strapped down with bungee cords. The glass from its round windows is missing, and the weathered white paint is peeling off in large strips, but it's perfect otherwise.

"I never expected Rose's money to buy us all this."

"I should wake up Hal," says Bobby.

"I should get Rose," I say. Bobby and I make eye contact and wordlessly we agree that this moment is for us alone.

"Let me check that everything's accounted for before you unload," I tell the driver. "You got the inventory sheet handy?"

The driver snorts at me as he hands over a dog-eared, hand-written itemized list. He wanders toward the quarry, cigarette smoke trailing behind him. I notice Rose's bedroom light switch on. We don't have much time before she joins us in her slippers and robe. I boost Bobby onto the flatbed and scramble up behind her. "Smell it?" says Bobby. "It smells like the lake." We squat down, pressing our noses to the salvaged wood. Turpentine. Smoke. Mildew. Algae. Lake Erie, all right. Bobby rests her ear down, as if she might hear the water the boat once travelled. She smiles. "A little sanding. A stiff-bristle brush scrub and washing powder. It'll be as good as new. Hal better roll up his sleeves."

*Etta! Come to welcome* SS Canadiana, *have you?* I see her hazily standing in the wheelhouse. I think Bobby sees her too by the way she jolts backwards.

*Wouldn't miss if for the world, Dollface.*

"I see her," Bobby whispers to me. "There! There! There! Look at her!" She crawls on her hands and knees into the wheelhouse. The wood is rough with a few exposed rusted nails or screws. Bobby's kneecaps scrape up so quickly that faint dabs of her blood trail along the wood behind her. When I reach for her, she screams. She's in a trance that I don't dare shake her out of. Several times, she starts to speak, but the words gag in her throat. She looks so angry. Angrier than the night I found her bashing Hal over the head with a plastic vodka bottle. She reaches a trembling arm forward.

*Don't mess with her, Etta,* I warn. *She's been through enough tonight.*

"What kind of spirit are you?" Bobby spits out. She slaps an outstretched hand down on the wood. The entire truck vibrates. "What have you got to teach me? Show me! I ain't afraid."

The wheelhouse fills with an impossible light—brighter than the high beams of a thousand flatbed trucks. Instinctively, I cover my eyes, then cautiously lower my hand. Etta's light is not sharp or blinding. Etta's light has no temperature. It has a weight, though, or an anti-weight. It's buoyant. If I jumped, I would float up into the light. Bobby has risen to her feet again, her tiptoes. She looks like a high-contrast illustration on a white sheet of paper. Her laughing is mistimed with the movement of her mouth. A split second later she is shouting words I can't understand. I too feel swift rotations of happy delirium and terror. My own hand in front of my face is a faded photograph. A ghost image. Fingertips vanishing. Like Etta. We're disappearing.

*Stop it.*

*Stop now.*

The bright light swiftly cuts out.

The pale blue of morning is a farce. To my surprise, Bobby and I clutch onto one another. I can feel her heart pounding against my own chest. A layer of sweat is sandwiched between us, as if we've been standing skin to skin for a long while. Outside the missing wheelhouse windows Hal, Rose, Lucky, Dolores, and the driver all gawk at us.

"You saw the Angel, didn't you? What message did she bring this time?" shouts Hal.

Bobby doesn't let go of me. She hugs me closer. I smell beer in her hair. The stink of mildewed wood around us.

"She says ..." I take a deep breath. Etta did say something, but what was it? Some kind of premonition, a warning. "She says that tough times are coming, and we need to stick together."

# 39 Guappo

**M**other of mercy, she sleeps. After I lit things up, I thought she'd pace in circles forever, blinking and blinking her big eyes. Poor thing—I frightened her. Finally, she's put that dizzy head on a pillow. She's a beautiful dreamer too. Long eyelashes dancing their smallest dance. Must be the wop blood. Those long eyelashes and thick mess of hair she tries to tame into a flat bob. If I had that hair, I'd let the curls plunge like Isa Miranda in the bedroom scene in *Adventures in Diamonds*. All these years later, and I've still got Isa Miranda's crepe gown on the brain.

Turns out, olives were my type. What did it matter? Once I became a disgrace to the family name Zinn, I figured I could go out with whoever I liked. Tough brown-eyed broads—give 'em a shot of whiskey and line them up for me. I didn't mind the fellows either. Guappos had money they needed to spend quick. Easy come, easy go. Except it wasn't easy. Living never is.

Most Italians lived at Windmill Point. The old folks came across from Buffalo, same as I did, to work the quarries. Bunkhouse men. Back-broken men. No wonder Italians shrink four or five inches after they retire. The young guappos stayed clear away from the quarries. They owned cars and ran rum across the Peace Bridge. For a summer party town, we weren't wet. There was only one Brewer's Retail Store this side of the border, and it was three miles from the beach, only open until six o'clock nightly, and never open on a Sunday. When Prohibition was repealed, New Yorkers—from Buffalo to Albany—got used to buying liquor at any corner store, all hours of the night. You can't have thousands of Yankee tourists without booze. Like junior Al Capones, our local guappos made sure we had enough to drink.

Mostly, I did business with Dino Vee, as I always needed a few bottles on hand for entertaining. Dino used to say, "Call me *mafioso* if you must, but don't you dare call me a fascist." At night, he was overdressed and mean and wouldn't step a foot out of his white Chrysler Royal for anything less than twenty dollars. In the morning he reappeared in a coppola cap and a cotton vest (no jacket) to help out with school and church business for St. George's, driving parish schoolteachers and priests from place to place. Dino the do-gooder by day, we called him.

He was a prouder Catholic than he was a bootlegger. He'd be the first one to tell you stories about when St. George's used to congregate at the roller rink before their timber frame church was erected on Ridgeway Road. I always delighted in picturing it—women in their lace head coverings skating in circles as they recited the rosary. The same year the war began, Dino formed his Italo-Canadian Club. With this frat, he became Dino the damned. The lot of them would crowd around Dino's car, clinging to the radio. Their faces grew long and their voices stifled. Any conversation with Dino quickly led to death.

"How are you today, Dino?"

"Eh, I'm still on this side of the grass."

"You're looking handsome this evening, Dino."

"Men always look well when we're near death."

For all of Dino's dark moods, I only saw him raise his fist once, when Ed Ridley told him he was lucky to be in Crystal Beach. "Anywhere else in America, you'd be rightly treated as an alien national," said Ed. Then he cowered knowing what he had coming.

Everybody was always telling everybody else they were lucky to be in Crystal Beach. Sam Wong was lucky to own the laundry on Waverly.

Skippy Jung Kwong was really lucky to own the restaurant right off of Derby circle. Everyone said how lucky the men from Grand River reserve were to work alongside the women at the soda bottling plant. Luckiest of all were those who refused to cut their braids and still worked the line. Long hair was an occupational hazard, that's why every working girl went Rita Hayworth short. People said the Natives were lucky their hair didn't get caught in a cog. They were lucky the machinery didn't "scalp them." That's what folks would say with a snicker and a jeer.

Progressives delighted in saying how lucky we were that whites and blacks could stroll the Park together like we were in some future America. We shared fun house trolleys and sky ride gondolas. We drank and danced together. The grand Crystal Ballroom was non-segregated—same goes for Nick's Afterhours Rhythm Club. Most of the local hotels welcomed everybody for meetings or for lodging. Jesse Owens and Eulace Peacock trained for the '36 Olympics in Crystal Beach. I saw them racing the ashed path in front of our grandstand with my own eyes. Lightning fast, all right.

Oh yes, we loved to brag that Crystal Beach was better than Buffalo. Better than New York City. Really wealthy white folks who owned hotels or restaurants all had Harriet Beecher Stowe's *Uncle Tom's Cabin* and W.E.B. De Bois's *The Souls of Black Folks* visible on their bookshelves. They called Harriet Tubman Moses or North Star, as if they were personally acquainted. They could point out where the De Bois's first Niagara Movement meetings were held, or where Little Africa Cemetery was located on Curtis Road, or the exact locations of underground railroad terminuses along the lake.

But black people could not point out the exact locations of underground railroad terminuses because they weren't allowed on the beach. The beach—the glorious beach we were famous for—was the one segregated place, no ifs, ands, or buts. Land owners didn't post "Whites Only" signs. It's true, we weren't Buffalo. Black folks disembarking from the *SS Canadiana* were stopped by a hired attendant who warned them, no bathing and no bathing suits. That had to be most dreary way to make a buck. Telling people what they can and can't do with their bodies. The world spins on dread and money, I suppose.

The Jewish women of Crystal Beach openly agreed they were lucky too. They were lucky to own property or businesses. Lucky that droves of their friends summered in our cottage county. Lucky to see the sun rise in the East and set in the West, be it in the parlour of the Herbert Hotel or the lunch counter at Schwartz's. I could count on Leah or Sarah or Abby to say, "Call me by my first name, dear. I'm lucky my mother didn't name me Tzipporah." Like Dino and his frat, they gathered around the radio, often for hours at a time. If CBS World News was airing, everybody tiptoed round the room and slipped quietly up or down the stairs. But if Burns and Allen was on, it was an open invitation to sit with them and listen in. They were comedians in their own right, and they let me join in on the jokes, maybe because I had a Jewish last name. Abby, who owned Herbert Hotel, was especially fond of our comedic routine. And, as I remember, I was especially fond of her.

"Abby," I'd say, "I've lived here for how long, and yet I've never had a conversation with your husband."

"I'm lucky. I married a good Jewish man," Abby would reply. "He knows not to speak."

"Abby," I'd ask, "is it wrong to ride the roller coaster on Sabbath?"

"As long as you keep your seatbelt on," Abby would reply. "That way you are wearing the coaster car, not riding it." She would slap her thigh when she laughed, and the little coin bracelet she always wore would jingle at the end of her slender wrist. I would have loved her, in another lifetime. I would have been her husband. I would have unpinned her oiled brown hair and brushed out every tangle.

The men I sported with never failed to tell me that I was lucky to be in Crystal Beach. "You got a good life here, girly," they said, "away from the worries and war." What bull! Tell it to the first drop of the Cyclone. Tell it to gravity. Tell it to the force of impact. Tell it to my spilled blood.

Dollface rubs her eyes. "Are you here, Etta?" she asks sleepily. "I was having a bad dream. I was falling."

*You weren't dreaming. That was me slipping behind your eyes. I just showed you the last moment of my life.*

# 40 Too Happy

ay Two-Four!"
Not even a so-called angel of holy light could prevent the teenagers from all over the region, including Wendel and his pack of skater boys, from getting shitfaced drunk before sundown.

"As long as they're drinking 7 Up out of 7 Up cans," Rose says, with unnecessary emphasis on the 7 Up. "And they drink their 7 Up quietly after eleven p.m. And pray none of these kids has a vision. Lord help us."

Watchdogging sixty or so high school students may prove to be a welcome change. Let them hoot and holler. I bet group recklessness will make the supernatural feel very far away. Maybe base mentality upholds the wall between dimensions?

The first hours of my shift pass without incident. I clean up poor teenage attempts at cookouts. I scrape melted plastic wrap and charred hotdog buns from the family barbecue pits. Next I slowly rake cigarette butts from the quarry's rim and the surface of the water—this kills another hour. All around me the boom boxes battle as I work: heavy metal mashes against Madonna, MC Hammer bumps up against acid house. Just after one a.m. I hear the first sex noises, loud, shamelessly declaring victory. The carnal cacophony makes me muse over Etta, then Tamara, in turns.

Around 2:30, the first chunk blower lets loose in the woods. It's an admirable soundscape, as far as puke goes, with a solid build-up of gasps and spitting, a pleading whimper or two, a suspenseful, yet not alarmingly long prelude of suffocation before the stomach's contents come rolling out to a dramatic crescendo. I've always had an iron stomach, me, resilient to chain reaction vomiting. But a few youngsters with less fortitude dash for the washroom to hug the toilets.

By three a.m., a half dozen or so campers are crying, boys and girls both.

Hal joins the weepers. He holds a crushed can of Molson. "Found it right outside our door. There's one sip left. How low is it to be thinkin' 'bout the last sip outta a can some kid used as a goddamn ashtray?" He holds the can up and a short trickle of beer and ash pours onto the ground. "Ya seen the angel?"

"Total radio silence," I say. "It's like she's testing us."

Hal harrumphs. "Ya wanna come in? Everybody's awake."

"What's Bobby say?"

"'What's Bobby say? It's my house too," Hal snaps, then softens. "Sorry. May Two-Four is gettin' me." Hal sticks his head in the front door and I turn away as he mumbles something to Bobby inside. He pops his head back out, asks, "Got books?"

"A few, at the cabin. There's this book I took out from the library. *The Joy Luck Club* by Amy Tan. Everybody is talking about it. Amy Tan just won the National Book Award." Hal looks dubious. He further crushes the dented beer can under his foot, unimpressed. "I also brought my *Vampirella* comic collection. Scantily clad bloodthirsty lady vampires."

At this, he leans through the door, and after another few seconds of mumbling, out again. "Nothin' too scary, eh? Lucky gets nightmares."

"It's kind of like Wonder Woman, except she's wearing even less clothes as she fights evil."

We read Vampi Issue #101, *The Attack of the Star Beast*, aloud together. Bobby reads the part of Vampirella in a consistent husky voice—even her battle cries are low and guttural and pretty darn sexy. Hal reads the narrator, skipping a word every so often, though still doing a fine job of sounding like a redneck Vincent Price. I read all of the other parts—monsters mostly—doing the best I can to change my tone with each new dialogue bubble. Lucky crawls over all three of us, more interested in our funny voices than the comic book pictures.

Lucky falls asleep within the hour. I hold the urge to stroke his hair as he sleeps. I don't want Bobby to think I'm creepy. Is it creepy? Touching a child's hair while they sleep? I have no idea what's normal.

"Another sunrise—how about that? We'd better get a nap in today, Hal," Bobby whispers. "I'll put on the kettle."

We sit at the table together, bloodshot eyes, yawning. Bobby clangs her spoon on her Crystal Beach Amusement Park collectable mug four times. "Today the day, Hal?"

"'Spose today's as good as any."

I take this as my cue to page Tamara, then I wait eagerly by the pay phone for her to call back. "Everything all right?" she asks as a greeting.

"You up for an early morning good deed?"

Tamara arrives in her Galaxy 500, which still is way too cool for these backwoods roads. She's got her hair in a neon-pink scrunchie and one of her green hoop earrings is missing from her left earlobe. I'm crushing on her hard. Together, using our high-pitch baby voices (not unlike how Tamara speaks to customers at work) we cheer Hal on as he shuffles into the back seat of her car. Rose, Bobby, and Lucky wave to us as we drive off.

St. George's Catholic Church, the same church where I was baptized, holds rise-and-shine Alcoholics Anonymous meetings on

Saturdays. Dolores has been on Hal to try it out. We pull around the back of the church, park beside the row of other cars—a Volvo with its front bumper and hood busted up from what I guess to be a collision with a tree or street lamp, a triad of motorcycles, a soccer-mom van, a couple of rusty clunkers, and a newly washed and waxed Mercedes Benz.

"Don't just leave me here. Promise," Hal says before he gets out of the car.

"We'll be right here, waiting in the car in case you need a quick getaway, right, Tamara?" Tamara nods emphatically, then tilts her head toward the church, urging him on. Hal gingerly takes his baseball cap off before he enters through the large wooden doors.

"He's kinda cute," says Tamara. We watch the basement entrance for a few seconds before she's in my lap kissing me. "We can't fuck in a church parking lot," she warns.

"We won't fuck ..." I nip her breast through her tank top just to hear her yelp. "We'll just fool around a little."

"Just a little," she echoes. I unzip the fly of her jean shorts.

An hour later my T-shirt is on inside out. Tamara wears a crooked grin. Hal comes striding toward the car with Dolores and another man following. He looks elated, a kid on Christmas.

"She used to work the front door at Platinum," Tamara nods at Dolores. "She was boss. Always looking out for us. I've seen her bounce a few guys from the club. Not little guys either, grown men. Tipped them out on their ass."

"Really? Small world. She lives at The Point." I don't mention that she pulled my half-drowned ass out of the lake. I wipe my face in case any of Tamara's lip gloss is smeared on me before we get out of the car to shake hands.

"This is Joe Foster," says Hal. "And he's gonna be my sponsor.

Just like that! Joe's sober for ten years today! Had his ten-year cake to-fuckin'-day! Joe's a carpenter by trade, and he's gonna help me build that gazebo, starting to-fuckin'-day!"

I search Joe Foster's face for any sign of hesitation. He appears calm, smiling, and open toward Hal's proclamations. Dolores silently nods behind them—her strong chin bobbing, smiling toothily. I suspect she's helped facilitate Hal and Joe's fortuitous meeting.

Hal's spry animation continues all morning. He practically leaps over the toolshed as he and Joe begin hauling out what they'll need to get started. He whistles as he and Joe inspect the salvaged wood. A rough cluster of roller coaster wood sits upon two sawhorses, still drying in the sun. The SS Canadiana wood is arranged in neat piles around the wheelhouse. Hal hugs me and spins me around for bringing him graph paper and pencils from Ricky's desk drawer. Hums wildly while the two of them sketch out a plan. "We'll have this built in no time," Hal declares.

"That's what you call a dry drunk," Bobby whispers to me. "Dolores told me all about dry drunks. Magical thinkers, eh? Like, not all here in reality."

"Are any of us in reality?" I whisper back to Bobby. "Things around here haven't exactly been ... normal."

Bobby shrug-nods. "You seen her yet today?"

"Still no sign." I cross my fingers that Etta doesn't light up the wood while the men are working. It's all fun and miracles until someone gets a hammer in the eye.

Although, these funny fellows surprisingly aren't butterfingers types. While comically opposite in stature and belly girth, the two instantly fall into a kind of man dance, digging holes and driving decking posts into the ground. Quickly they develop a quippy communication that allows them to lightheartedly boss each other around with ease. They even know the same repertoire of jokes.

"What's the difference between an American and a Canadian?"

"A Canadian not only has a sense of humour but can spell it."

By the time Rose brings around the first pitcher of lemonade, they are singing: "We never eat fruitcake because it has rum. And one little bite turns a man like a bum ... Away, away with rum, by gum, the song of the Salvation Army."

By lunchtime, Howie Foster arrives. His face is sunburned—I'd say it's from sitting on the patio rather than from doing outdoor chores. The Foster brothers greet each other with an awkward handshake with one hand and rough shoulder tap with the other hand. Joe seems more comfortable with Hal, whom he's just met, than with his own brother. What is it about family?

Howie is less agile and handy than his older brother, and after a few rounds of hauling wood, he coolly gravitates away from the gazebo construction to keep company with Bobby, Tamara, Rose, and me. "Why dig holes with those jokers when I can be surrounded by beautiful women?" he repeats several times. I excuse myself to haul cinder blocks just to get away from him.

I'm pushing rocks down into postholes when Wendel creeps up beside me. "Can you get me a day's work or two? You owe me," he says. He smells like gym socks and smoke.

"I'll ask Rose, but you can't drink on this crew, got it? No pot either."

Within five minutes on the job, Wendel makes the mistake of referring to Hal and Joe as "old timers." After that, they accidentally clunk him with framing wood, spill gravel on his white skate shoes. "Oops, me old eyes didn't see ya there, lad," Hal chuckles. I figure Wendel is worth the five bucks an hour Rose offered him just to keep Hal entertained.

Mid-afternoon, Rose gets on the phone with Barbara. "She's right here," Rose intentionally speaks loud enough that I overhear her conversation. "No, she hasn't gone to bed yet. She's staying awake to watch the men lay the gazebo deck ... Yes. The boat wood arrived yesterday ... Well, I'm telling you now ... I was going to call, but you beat me to it ... How about you come on over and help me make these boys some lunch?"

Barbara is at The Point within minutes. She volunteers Rahn to help. He toils away with the measuring tape and decking wood, marking every sixteen inches exactly as Joe and Hal showed him. "Measure twice, cut once," Hal repeats, affirming Rahn's role in the labour. Rahn doesn't seem to mind being a lesser crew member. His eyes drift again and again to Barbara. He smiles adoringly at her. Even after Barbara and Rose apron up and excuse themselves to the kitchen to cook (surely enough to feed an army) Rahn's smitten grin does not cease. I hope Barbara reciprocates his love, if she's capable of love. Maybe there's hope for her yet?

Hal and Bobby steal a smooch as she's refreshing lemonade glasses. I've never seen them kiss before. After, Bobby girlishly finger-combs her long salt-and-pepper hair, tilts her head up to let the sunshine hit her face.

Lucky takes a shine to Wendel, and Wendel actually accepts the chance to play big brother. "Let's check the posts one more time, kiddo." He leads Lucky from post to post giving each a rowdy shake to ensure they're firmly in the ground. He seems like a completely different kid than the teenage brat being scolded at the back of a strip club by his sharp Nordic father.

In this cheerful synergetic moment, I lead Tamara to the quarry, and the two of us lay side by side on the warm wooden dock. It feels easy. Her and me, together. All around us campers paddle by in blow-up boats and chase each other along the shallow side and whoop those happy whoops that only happens in the summertime. The smell of barbecue hangs in the humid air. Tamara's tank top is coated in dirt and sand. People around us might be looking but I truly don't care. "I'm too happy," I tell her.

"Too happy? How can you be too happy?"

I let my lips graze her neck as I speak. "So happy I can hardly believe I get to feel like this." She threads her fingers through mine. We hold hands as postcard clouds hang in the perfect sky. I think about Etta and about death, like I always do, but instead of trying to push these thoughts away or mentally call Etta into existence, I simply let her be. Like any other thought. Like mentally reciting the words to a favourite poem or song.

Just before we set the picnic tables for dinner, Howie Foster brings out his camera. "You girls want a minute to freshen up? I know how women are when being photographed," he winks at us. I catch a whiff of beer on his breath. His nose is even more sunburned than when he arrived. He summons all of us to the freshly laid gazebo floor. Everyone squirrel-paws around, exploring the different pliability and squeakiness of the new lumber versus the boat wood. As soon as my foot touches the boat wood, I feel Etta tap me on the shoulder. *Decided to join the party, Etta? Seeing as we're doing all this for you.* I expect an answer, a flame or a bright light, a floating object, the sky to darken, any sign. Nothing. No booming show. Only a ghostly hand on my back.

"Good-looking bunch," says Howie Foster as he mounts his camera on the tripod. "Hell, I'll even make us the front page."

PART
TWO

# Prologue: Summer 1990

The most famous photograph of the angel of Crystal Beach was taken by a self-proclaimed shaman from Centre Island, Toronto, who specialized in spiritual energy anomalies and called himself Dr Jaguar Tongue. Tongue arrived in late July in a sports car with a lithe flower-child-like assistant in the passenger seat and a trunk that, like a magician's hat, contained far more specialized gear than seemingly could fit inside.

He wasn't the first apparition seeker to turn up at Crystal Beach over the summer. But he was the only visitor who showed me just how helplessly chaotic I had become. The two mediums from Lily Dale, New York, gave me a firm talking to. Likewise, Father Mario, the local priest, spoke to me in a particular foreboding tone. And the tremendous desperation of the daily masses overran us all. However, every one of those visitors came searching for their own interpretations of truth in order to gain something personal to them.

Dr Tongue was after a photo. A photo that would cement his fame within his niche communities of high-paid supernatural-hunting weirdos. In the photo, Tamara Matveev and I lie together on the log cabin's cot. I am unconscious, like a Sapphic sleeping beauty or something, Tamara's lovely dancers legs tangled with mine. Lips parted in a half smile, she looks to be whispering something warm and sapient in my left ear. On my right, Etta is more humanly formed than she appears in any other photograph. She is a half-draped nude carved in glowing marble or acrylic resin. Dovetailed next to me, her hips perfectly allied with my hips, our shoulders squared together. Her spectral hand firmly holds mine. A supernatural lesbian threesome? That's what the photo became famous for.

I've submitted to the idea that I will live the rest of my days knowing—no—feeling—no—re-experiencing her hands. Prickling my skin, yes. Curling my lips and tongue, without doubt. And deeper, of course. In my blood. Bone ache. Lead belly. My cunt, raked and bankrupt. Stone-broke desire. If I block out all the miracles and spectacle, if I reduce Etta to only what she's done to my cunt after being inside me, that's exactly what she is. Stone-broke desire.

If my body alone could have bore her, could have spared the others and kept her all for me me me me me and the famous suffering I so deserve, then I undoubtedly would have tried to hold her inside.

# 41 Venus

**H**oney, I'm home," Tamara announces as she bounds through the front door, then spots Barbara sitting on the sofa painting her toenails. "Last-minute pedicure before your trip to DC, Ms Martin?"

Barbara has packed two large suitcases for a week's getaway. Tamara steps around them and around Songbird prancing at her feet. We both thought Rahn and Barbara would have hit the road by now, leaving us with the place all to ourselves. Bungalow bunnies—borrowed from *Dirty Dancing*—that's how we've been referring to ourselves leading up to Barbara's trip. Tamara and I are going to pretend we're "bungalow bunnies" on vacation.

"Well, I don't think I have the right sandals," says Barbara. "I should have gone over to Buffalo to hit the Galeria yesterday. They have an L.L. Berger there. A big one." My mother waves her arms in an arch to emphasize big. The nail polish wand in her hand almost drips fuchsia onto the upholstery. "Like, way bigger than the L.L. Berger in McKinley Mall. Plus, I figured out that we can take Walden Avenue most of the way. Duh. All this time I've been taking Thruway. I don't know if you've driven the Niagara Thruway lately, but it's shit. Potholes as far as the eye can see ..." Tamara listens and nods graciously. I look out the front window, willing Rahn to get here faster. Like clockwork, his black BMW turns onto Loomis Crescent. Barbara hears him pull into the driveway and flusters, "Shoot, my polish isn't dry." She awkwardly eases on her wooden wedge sandals.

Rahn wisely does not comment on the two suitcases. He simply glides into the house and grabs both bags with his customary jubilant expression on his face.

"You're sure you'll be okay, Star?"

"I lived alone for years. I'm sure I can survive a few days without you."

"Tamara, you'll be checking in on her, right? It's good to have a gal pal. A bestie. Star, I think you look pale and thin. Rahn, does she look pale to you?"

"Actually, she has a nice tan," Rahn assures her. He has recently adopted Barbara's habit of speaking about me as if I'm not in the room, except he has the decency to make direct eye contact with me in acknowledgement. "I would never guess she works graveyard shifts. It looks like she spends her days in the olive grove." He wedges his foot in the front door, attempting to hold it open for Barbara.

"I spoke to Rose. She's going to feed you breakfasts from now on. You're spending all your time there anyway." I can't tell if Barbara sounds mildly resentful as she says this. "You are looking thin. Working those extended hours. You better be getting paid for your overtime. Rahn, do you think Starla looks thin? I swear she's lost twenty pounds since she moved home. How can I call myself a mother?"

"She's still an ideal body weight, medically speaking."

"Oh? And what am I? An un-ideal body weight, eh, Dr Johnson?"

"Mom! The man is taking you on a vacation for Christ's sake. I'm pretty sure he's into your body," I snap. I couldn't have said a more perfect thing if I thought it through before I opened my mouth. Barbara has always wanted me to speak to her as if we were friends, for me to gush like her. She giggles coquettishly as Rahn guides her to the car, and lets him hold the car door open for her. I hear jazz radio sounds from their open windows as they zoom off.

"So long, lovebirds," I yell after them. Tamara and I wave in the driveway. Songbird lets out a few pitiful barks.

"She hasn't a fucking clue," I say as Rahn's car turns the corner. Tamara pats my shoulder. "For real. I'm in the middle of a super-natural phenomenon, and she thinks I'm just working overtime. She thinks we're 'besties.'"

"Have you tried to tell her?"

"No way. I tell her as little as possible."

"She must know something. People are talking."

"About the angel or me being a lesbian? What have you heard?"

Tamara has some dish. I've learned that our small-town strip club is a hub for scandals. But she gives me one of her caretaking shoulder pats and says, "You promised. Just us this weekend. No drama."

We eat toast and drink coffee at the dining room table. I know Tamara drinks Coke as early as nine a.m. She eats Carnation Breakfast Bars and Pop Tarts. Sweet tooth. I offer her some of Barbara's homemade jam. She dips her pinkie into the jam jar for a sample taste before she spreads some on her toast.

I want to see Tamara cover every inch of this place. Sprawled on the sofa like Venus. Soaking in the tub. Barefoot in the backyard. Back at the dining room table each morning or whenever breakfast falls between her shifts and mine. We promised each other at least one night in. No The Point. No helping finish the Ricky Esposito Memorial Gazebo. No supernatural shenanigans of any kind. It's going to be a feat to block Etta from my mind, but I've got my stay-home date suggestions ready. I rented *The Color Purple* and *I've Heard the Mermaids Singing* from the video store.

After her last bite, Tamara suddenly pushes her plate away. She hops up onto the table, letting her legs hang and sway. She isn't wearing underwear under her zebra-striped dress. She flashes me, bangs her knees together, and flashes again. My ears pop—she's so fucking sexy, she makes the air pressure change. I already have Depeche Mode's *Violator* album cued up in the stereo. Sex music. By the time David Gahan reaches the chorus of "Personal Jesus," Tamara is curled into a fetal position on the table. My fingers remain inside her, feeling the pulse pulse pulse of her pushing out the tail end of her orgasm. The tabletop is a mess of spilled coffee and cum. What does it feel like to have a faultless body, to hold perfect pleasure like she does? Her thighs contracting against my wrist bait the words "I love you." But I clench my jaw, warning myself that it's too soon. Real couples, couples that last forever, wait, like, three months to say it, right? We're almost there. The eve of capital-L love.

Then, later on the sofa, we listen to The Sugarcubes' *Life's Too Good* album. Björk sings about birthdays and smoking cigars, and I have the forethought to lay a towel under Tamara's ass before burying my face between her legs. She twists my hair in her hands to keep me from eating my own hair to begin with, but soon she is guiding my head in small circles. Pulling me deeply, smotheringly into her, then easing the reins a little. My face, from nose to chin, is muzzled in her wet. I practice holding my breath until I am woozy. I've never let someone this close to me. For weeks, I've been taken aback by firsts again and again. I've never been as intimate, as unashamed, as sober, as clear, as ridiculously damn hopeful as I am with Tamara. But even as I think this, I know that we're having sex on the sofa because Etta never comes into the living room. I try not to even think about Etta too much, nervous that I might unwittingly beckon her. More nervous that I secretly want to beckon her.

Tamara's forehead and upper lip are sweaty when I lie down beside her. I should get up and turn the ceiling fans on, get us some water. I don't want to be away from her even for a minute. "Have you been with many women?" Ugh. I sound like I'm in a movie. Isn't that the question that celluloid lovers ask?

"Sure. I mean I work with a lot of beautiful women. I suppose it's, like, there's plenty of fish in my sea, or something."

Should this confession bother me? I make sure my voice sounds steady, open. "When did you come out?"

"You don't know?" Tamara props herself up on her elbow. "I thought my 'coming out' was broadcast across town? I was the laughing stock."

An uncomfortable pause lapses before I say, "You mean the thing about you naked in the football field?"

"Yeah. For starters, the naked thing." Tamara sits up. She makes no attempt to cover her body, just sits, unclothed, like she's watching TV. I poorly timed this conversation, post-coital, her sitting naked while bringing up "the naked thing." I sit up beside her. Resist the urge to cover myself with throw pillows.

"Do you want to tell me anything about it?" I ask.

"Fran DeRossi. Steph Dunn. David and Danny Gallo. Nancy Lew. Blake Munroe ..." Tamara recites a list of the popular kids. I would include her on this running list. Her crowd. "Steph started it, I guess. It was her that caught me making out with a girl at Fran's devil's night out party. There was a bunch of us running around Crescent Park, all dressed in black, you know, drinking shit mix and Coke, egging houses, tossing toilet paper rolls. We met up with this other bunch of kids from Fort Erie Secondary. They had fireworks and pot. There was maybe twelve, thirteen of us altogether, smoking doobies and setting off Roman Candles in the street. Then the twins got this idea to go into that abandoned house. You know, the one on Ferndale? It's still empty. Now there's a "no trespassing" sign out front, probably because of us. None of us had flashlights. Steph had her key chain penlight, and a couple of the guys had lighters. We groped our way around. It was disgusting. Right out of a horror show. Graffitied walls. Big holes in the ceiling. Loose floorboards. The whole bit. Great location to kiss my first girl. I don't remember her name; she was one of the F.E.S.S. kids. She kept hugging onto me, like she was all scared. She had whiskey in a flask. What high school girl carries whiskey in a flask? I doubt I'd even had whiskey before that night. I thought Malibu was sophisticated.

"When we kissed, we acted like it was an accident. Like our lips just bumped together in the dark. It was pretty hot in that teenage way, you know. Until Steph and her stupid keychain light caught us in the act.

"I told her I was drunk. Too drunk to know what happened. I told her not to tell anyone. Yeah, right. First it was little things, you know. Anonymous notes slipped in my locker that called me a lezzie. Guys making v's with their fingers and doing the pussy-licking gesture at me. If I kept my head down, I bet it would have stayed like that. But you know me, I had to run my big mouth. I can't remember what I said—something like, 'Yeah, and I liked it too.'

"After that, Steph and Fran totally turned on me. They said they'd only keep being my friend if I did stuff for them, like stealing bags of chips and cookies from the cafeteria. Dares like that. I went along with it at first. I guess I was worried about my reputation.

"When I refused and started standing up for myself, they threatened to out me to my parents. They prank-called my house. That was really bad because ... because my dad was fucking dying at the time. Lung cancer. Lung cancer is living hell. The nosebleeds and face swelling. Throwing up blood. And the phone was ringing at eleven o'clock, midnight."

Songbird runs into the living room to lie at Tamara's feet. Even the dumb dog can detect the sting in her voice. I wrap a chenille throw over our naked bodies. Find her hand to hold under the blanket. "I wasn't a smooth talker back then." Tamara tries to laugh. "The more I pleaded with them to stop, the worse it got. The naked thing happened right after Steph and I got into a fight. The guy she liked had just asked me to the end-of-year dance. Boy, she was pissed. So she dared me do it. 'The naked thing.' And the whole gang egged me on. If I didn't, she'd go to my house and personally tell my parents. By then, it was more than about how I had kissed a girl. There was all this other bullshit gossip, like that I was stealing girl's bras from the gym change room, and sleeping with the school counsellor. I was sick of it. So I let them win. I let all of them win. I stripped down and walked outside. They expected me to run, to streak the football field as fast as I could."

"You walked slowly," I say.

"I took my sweet-ass time. I'm surprised I wasn't suspended. My mom gave them some sob story. Said I was seeking attention because I was so upset over my dad. Principal LaPoint didn't even give me detention."

"I thought I had it bad. You were bullied way worse than I was."

"Maybe that's true. Or maybe I just hung out with different people. Meaner people."

"Yeah, the popular kids were assholes. It's such a cliché," I say. "I wish we had known each other back then. Like, *known* known each other."

"Are you kidding, I was intimidated by you." Tamara cuddles into me, teasing. "You were always wearing those Doc Martens steel-toed boots and tons of black makeup. Even after 'the naked thing,' I was still trying to fit in. I was a Polo shirt and Bass loafer girl right up until I moved away. I thought listening to that Violent Femmes song was totally rebellious."

Of course, I have the Violent Femmes' first album on vinyl. And I have a record player. Tamara is impressed when I pull out my transistor portable player from the '70s. We dance naked in the living room, yelling out the lyrics to "Add It Up." " ... why can't I get just one fuck ..."

It is only 11:45 in the morning. I watch Tamara close her eyes and thrash her black hair as she dances. We have four whole days together to play house, to be bungalow bunnies, to fall into the greatest love of all time.

# 42 Buckle into the Wall

Tamara and I take turns reading to each other from *Geek Love*. I had already cracked the novel's spine last week. For Tamara, I don't mind starting over.

The sun dipped below the rooftops about an hour ago. Songbird is busy chewing some unknown garbage she found in the backyard. Mosquitos buzz close despite the citronella candle I've lit. Barn swallows swoop through the dusky light for a mosquito feast. Barbecue smoke and algae stink hang in the humid air. Days only feel this long when they've been drawn out either by misery or by joy. Joy is something I'm learning to notice, to measure.

Tamara's voice is punctuated by little hiccups when she reads lines that she likes. "The nature of lies is to please. Truth has no concern [little hiccup] for anyone's comfort." She looks up from the book. "What are you staring at?"

"True beauty," I say.

She snuffs the citronella candle with the bottom of her shoe. "You got a bedroom to take me to, or what?"

The house feels different as we go back in, clenched narrower somehow. I switch on the bedroom light. Not the ugly frosted ceiling light, but the mid-century Murano glass lamp on my bedside table. I bought it for only $160. Total steal. My room is junk and money. Tamara stares at the stunt above my bed. For a moment I worry she'll be stuck there, locked in place by Etta. But no, Etta's powers of physical manipulation are saved for me. Tamara breaks from the stunt and makes her way around the tiny room.

Price tags flash in my mind with each object she passes by. Forty dollars for my chrome-trimmed record carrying case, which contains records I spent a total of $455 on (worth more now), arranged alphabetically according to the artist's surname, from Ethel Azama to Frank Zappa. Eighty dollars for my black leather-jacketed CD binder; approximately 1K of music is sandwiched inside those plastic pages, again alphabetically, from Adam and the Ants to ZELDA. Positively valuable books lie amongst the piles on my dresser, books I had to hunt for, including signed first editions of Marilynne Robinson's *Housekeeping* and Toni Morrison's *The Bluest Eye*. My leather art portfolio was only seventeen dollars at the flea market. Inside, my Barbara Kruger lenticular print is tucked safely away, along with a couple of pen-and-inks by Toronto's J.B. Jones and Fiona Smyth, all of which are surely rising in value. Gertrude Stein said, "You can either buy clothes or buy pictures." Of course, I bought plenty of clothes too. Thankfully, my closet door is closed. I've got to stop obsessing over value. When aroused or when anxious I think about capital, about worth. Maybe torment is recognizing exactly what is wrong with you, but not knowing how to right those wrongs.

Tamara pauses at the "Starla" boxes, all of which I've rescued from the basement and piled up gracelessly at the foot of my bed. She traces the worn cardboard edge of one box with her finger and looks expectantly at me. I nod in permission. I shouldn't be surprised when she finds my first childhood toy. I knew he was at the top, just under the lid. Mr Winky is a fully jointed, wool-stuffed teddy bear. Could be a Twyford. I should have him appraised. Barbara cut out his eyes—she was worried I'd swallow them as a baby. Being eyeless will depreciate him a fair bit, though his stitched nose is good as new.

"No," I blurt out.

Tamara quickly puts Winky back in the box.

"Sorry! That 'no' wasn't for you. I was telling myself 'no.'" Here goes. Time to reveal to your girlfriend that you are nuts. "I have this really bad habit of obsessing over the resale price of, well, like, every single thing. Just now, I was wondering what that teddy bear is worth. But I don't want to think about that."

"You're worried about money?"

I nod. Shrug my shoulders.

"Well, we aren't exactly living in boom times," says Tamara. She sits on the edge of my bed, pats the empty place beside her. She loops her arm around me as I join her. As we kiss, I tell myself quiet, quiet, quiet. I begin to spell P-O-G-O-N-O ...

Our bodies undulate together. She nips my bottom lip. Her earrings are cute little silver lightning bolt studs. I love how she jolts when I run my tongue behind her earlobe. I should have put music on. P-O-G-O-N-O ... O ... O. I should take it slower this time. I'm so greedy. I always want her to spread her legs right away. More foreplay, right? What do they suggest in that funny illustrated *The Joy of Lesbian Sex* book? Breast massage. Twirling your lover's pubic hair. I bought a copy of that book before it went out of print. *La plume de ma tante. Crème de la crème.* I hide it at the bottom of my underwear drawer because it's démodé, embarrassingly out-of-date. Tribadism. Mound of Venus. Honestly, I can't even look at the book because anything from the '70s reminds me of Barbara, and that's a problem. I already have my mother's macramé Jesus hanging in the nearby closet. If any more of Barbara ends up in my bedroom, I'll likely never have an orgasm again. Tamara tells me, "You feel so good," and undoes the button on my jean shorts.

"No," I say. It just comes out.

"No?"

"It's ..." Damn it. "It's hard for me. You know? Receiving."

"You did before."

Right. This is why I only fuck people once or twice and don't have relationships. To avoid convoluted explanations of what's wrong with my body. Why what was okay on date one or two becomes not okay on date five or six. You see, my carriage turns back into a pumpkin after midnight. My cunt is like a mayfly—its lifespan is only twenty-four hours. Ever notice that sex is like a setting sun? I'm pacing the length of my room. I wish Tamara was wearing her aqua-blue contact lenses to mask a bit of the uneasiness as she watches me stomp around. Excellent. I'm creating a new bad memory in this bedroom. Just when I thought it was impossible to hate myself more.

"Talk to me, Star." Tamara stands, reaches a hesitant arm out to me. "You gonna break up with me? Whatever you have to say, believe me, it can't be as bad as what I'm thinking right now."

Well, that almost sounds like a dare. I grab the wicker headboard and yank. My single bed moves almost effortlessly with the adrenaline of this moment. A few of the Starla boxes crash to the floor. Mr Winky rolls out, lands teddy-face-down on the floor.

"Right here." I point to the many x's penned on my wall. Seeing them scrawled in a huddled cluster, I realize I've wanted to pull my bed away for a long time to view the full panorama of it. The x's begin at about my knee level. The air feels sappy and thick as I squat down to get a closer look. Some of the marks are so small—grain of rice-sized scratches. Others aren't made with pen, but rather show where my six-year-old fingernails scored the wallpaper.

"I thought I'd be angry. I'm not. Just incredibly sad," I say, pointing again at the wall. Pointing alone offers no clarity for Tamara. Right,

I can tell her I'm faking angel apparitions with a ghost who fell off a roller coaster, but I can't tell her this. I push out the words, "Each x marks a time when I was molested."

One second is a second too long to wait for Tamara's response.

"I should have never brought you in here. I fucking hate it here." The air's gotten thicker, almost slippery. My head feels like it's skidding through this conversation.

"Then let's leave," says Tamara. She takes my hand, then my other hand, stands facing me without a hint of trepidation. "There's plenty of empty rentals around the beach. I've saved up some money. Let's move in together."

"Okay," I say without a beat. I mean it too. I want to move in together. Tamara won't have to pay for everything. I make a living. Why pay back what I owe? Seriously, fuck the savings and loans industry. Better to evade my debt. Let my loans slip completely into default, into paper trail. We'll pay for everything in stripper tips and under-the-table paycheques. I have a girlfriend, and we're starting a life together. As we float into a woozy kiss, I consider my answer again. What's the worst that can happen?

"Okay," I echo. This time I guide Tamara's hand back to the undone button of my jean shorts.

"Star?" She gives me a sharp look. "You don't have to."

"I want to," I tell her, shifting us a step closer to the wall. "I want to be stronger than all of this. I want to be free of it." I steer her forefinger into my underwear. She makes an appreciative hissing sound that tells me I am probably wet. I grab her wrist. "Maybe it'll be better if I turn around." I shimmy my jean shorts down my hips, down my thighs, turn my back, and move her hand between my legs again. I only buck into her once before she senses I need her to be rough. Rough enough to overtake me. Tamara hooks her left arm around my waist. Her forearm muscles, those pole-dancing muscles, flex against my stomach. Our breathing quickens. We lurch forward. My hands brace, knees buckle into the wall. I don't gauge the pain before swiftly kicking my knee up. I hoped the drywall would crack with my blow, the floral wallpaper tear. I'm not that strong. Tamara pauses. "Keep going?" she asks. Words sound strange, like we haven't spoken in days.

"Keep going," I say.

But we've lost our animal rhythm. I can feel her behind me, watching, monitoring my reactions. She is afraid for me, or of me. Same difference. My Laugh in the Dark stunt has been patient, quiet, but I know she's inside. The same as she is inside the reclaimed boat wood built into the gazebo, strips of ride tickets, or Lucky's prize Care Bear.

I promised Tamara no ghosts, no angels, just us.

To say that Etta makes me stronger is to underestimate her. Etta allows me to be ... bigger. Bigger than nausea and panic and failure and anger and all the things that make me hate myself. And I need to be bigger to be with Tamara, don't I? This is good for both of us, isn't it?

*Etta,* I call. *Etta. Etta.* She answers with ghost hands that surge through me, overrunning fear, overrunning everything.

# 43 Stronger than Ever

Tamara and I take turns pretending that she'll skip her evening shift. I hide the dress she picked out for work. She unplugs the kitchen clock. Even Songbird joins the game by disappearing somewhere beyond the backyard for a good hour.

"Well, you can't leave now with the dog missing," I say. We don't want to be separated. Or at least half of me doesn't want to be separated, and half of me wants her to go to work so I can slip back to The Point to see the gazebo. I notice Rose's number several times on the call display, but Tamara must have turned off the ringer to the phone.

She kisses me goodbye for a little too long. I bait her out the door with the promise that our next paycheques will be used for the first and last months' rent on our future apartment.

After she's gone, I go through the motions of a quiet night at home. I sit on the sofa, flipping TV channels. I open the refrigerator again and again. I read one poem from *quilting* by Lucille Clifton. Clifton is brilliant. Her poetry saved my life, but right now, even poems are not a worthy distraction. I press Play on the answering machine. The first message says, "Star. Rose. The men finished ahead of schedule. Men and women, I mean. Even the town bus driver came out to lay the shakes. Wooden shag shingles, just like Ricky would have wanted. No rubber or tar. The varnish is still drying. I'll tell you about it tomorrow."

The second message, "Star. Rose. I hope you're enjoying your night off. We're full. Every damn campsite. *Buona stella*. I got Vincent here helping me. But, huh, well, a few of campers say they came to see you. You catch my meaning?"

The third message, "Rose again. You better get down here."

I squint into the evening sun as I hurry to The Point. Tonight, the rows of cottages aren't creepy and empty. They've been transformed into potential rentals, cheap and abundant. I pass a dozen cottages with "For Rent" signs tacked to their dark doors. A few commercial buildings are also plastered with "For Rent" or "For Lease" signs. Tamara and I could live in Hotdog Alley. Our future home might even have a deep fryer in the kitchen.

The town's blue bus is parked on Cherry Street. I turn onto Rose's property and there's the completed gazebo. Rose is right, it looks exactly how Ricky would have wanted it. Folksy yet cleanly crafted. From a distance, I marvel at different-coloured planks of wood pieced together like a quilt. It's also exactly what I wanted—womb-like and weird. I asked for the roof to be stained red, and red it is. A dome of red and amber and mahogany crests the sky. Like walking into a Louise Bourgeois sculpture, like Ricky's perverted painting—a great floating vulva. Most of all, the gazebo is true to Etta's demands. It's big. Obscenely big. A dance floor indeed.

At least thirty people sit together inside. Men, women, and a few children. Several wave at me. Rose, Hal, and Bobby stand up, waving higher. There's Dolores. The bus driver. The Foster brothers, Joe and Howie. And Lucky jumping up and down in the dead centre of things. "The lady. The lady," he squeals. Etta thumps my chest. I cup my hands around the Crystal Beach flag pendant and brace for a second thumping. She stands beside me, flickers, vanishes. She's powerful enough to fully materialize, if she wanted to. I feel her heavy and weightless in my body at the same time. She's stronger than the ghost I just let fuck me in my bedroom. Stronger than ever.

*Come back. I'm not going in there alone,* I beg, and she complies. She's clearer than ever too. I can make out the row of tight curls along her forehead. Just how carefully thin-plucked her high arched eyebrows are. I touch the beauty mark penciled in on her chin. *Can any of them see you?*

*I'm nothing but razzle dazzle to them. Lights and sparks. No one sees me. No one touches me,* she says as I tap her pouty drawn-on mouth. She startles.

*No one touches you, except me,* I remind her. I put my hand on her chest only to see if I can. Maybe her new strength works both ways. Maybe the shrine will allow me to touch her more. I skim the V-neck of her dress. Etta kisses me. Her kiss feels like a pact. People hush as we approach. We're only just up the stairs and everyone claps.

*They're applauding? What do we do?*

*Say 'Philip Joseph.'*

"One of you is here because of Philip Joseph," I say, hesitantly. Thirty heads rubberneck around.

"Hell if I know how you figured that," says a man's voice. I recognize him as one of the few year-round residents, the loner with the *Magnum, P.I.* moustache I suspect is always checking me out through his trailer window. "I'm Philip Joseph's stepdad. Or least I was."

I stare incredulously at him. I'm supposed to spiritually advise him, this peeper with hockey hair and bad moustache? *What now, Etta?*

Hal rests his bear paw of a hand on Moustache's shoulder. Gives him a meaningful man nod. Were these men friends before, or is it the finished gazebo that's facilitated this camaraderie? Moustache begins, "Eighteen years I worked for Sherwin Williams. Yeah, the news has a lot to say about lead paint this and lead paint that.

Everybody knows Sherwin Williams quit making lead paint a long time ago. So if that's the bullcrap you heard, tell it to somebody else.

"Lead had nothing to do with it. Phil fell, was all. We were loading sixty-gallon paint vessels from a forklift. Moving fast, too, because it was a few minutes into our lunch break. 'Get 'er done,' I remember saying. When that lunch bell goes, I'm the first one you'll see eating.

"I was supposed to be looking out for Phil. He was the only son of this gal I married. Our marriage is done now, you betcha. She wants nothing to do with the likes of me. I got Phil the darn job at the plant. Had to pull for him too. I never knew if he was sissy, but he sure acted like one. Not exactly the first in line for a factory floor job.

"I saw him scramble up there, on top of the forklift. I could have said 'Careful, Phil' or 'Slow down, son,' but no, I wanted my lunch break. I wanted my lunch break, and goddamn it, if this is the part where I'm supposed to confess, I thought to myself, let that sissy swing around if he wants. He's obviously got something to prove. Next thing I know the pallet shifts and down comes the paint and down comes Phil.

"Hearing a young fella's neck snap like that is enough to drive you around the bend. The guilt, I tell you. Sherwin Williams did me decent and laid me off so I got Workers' Comp. Now all I do is sit around replaying the sound of Phil's neck breaking.

"So, uh, yeah," Moustache reaches for the pack of Du Maurier Lights that is rolled up the left sleeve of his white T-shirt. "You talk to an angel, is that right, girl? What I'm asking is ... for her to take care of Phil, you know, up in heaven. How about you do that for me?

"And if she has any ideas how I can be a better man ... Apparently, I'm a real son of a bitch, so my ex will tell you. Couldn't help but piss her off."

I've been away less then forty-eight hours and men are talking about feelings and admitting their mistakes. I'd better stick closer to The Point. Maybe Tamara and I can get a nice trailer and live here? Maybe we can be like Lucky's lesbian godmothers.

*Have him bring me more memorabilia from the Park.*

"The angel says the amusement park was sacred." The crowd doesn't even flinch as I charge them with bringing anything saved from the park to The Point. Moustache shrugs. He's getting off too easy. The words "girl" and "sissy" start to sting me, delayed provocation. "As penance, you can babysit," I say. "Any woman who wants her child minded when she comes to visit. You will babysit." Moustache spits out his smoke.

*Whoop! Good for you. I've never seen a fully dressed man's eyes pop like that.* Etta thumps a terrible drum roll across the floorboards under Moustache's seat. He jumps straight up to standing, eyes wider still. He stomps his boot on floor, livid.

"You can stomp all you want," I raise my voice to tell him. "But your penance is the same." Etta, lovely con artist that she is, waits for his kicking and fussing to end before cracking the wooden beam closest to where Moustache stands. His fist swings through the air at his invisible foe. "You will babysit children. You'll read to them. You'll sing songs with them. Hal will show you. He's becoming a role-model dad."

The women in the crowd cheer. Especially Bobby. I put on a good show. I think I'll start a women's circle. Like a feminist conscious-ness-raising group ... but haunted.

# 44 Enchanting

Phooey Superman. I am able to leap tall buildings in a single bound. Put the kibosh on Phantom. I'm quick like lightning. I got eyes and ears everywhere.

Everywhere is my dance floor. Named after Ricky, but I don't mind. It's my domain, no doubt about it. When I walk across the floorboards, the rhythmic click click click of my heels can be heard in the living world. Their mouths drop open like ventriloquist dummies. They press their ears to the floor for more. If they could hear my voice, I'd tell them, "You're sitting right on top of an old boat hull, and you there, you're on a weathered soda stand sign—magic wood, perfect wood."

She always situates herself on the roller coaster track. Same track she nearly drowned to find for me. My sweet girl. So sweet, too sweet.

With all the wood they salvaged, I've got space enough to Shag Down and Big Apple Stomp and Box Step. I can dance upside-down on the funny clamshell-shaped ceiling if I want to. Twirl around the perfect wooden columns. Slide down the bannister and run back up the three wide stairs. But the greatest feature, the one thing I would have never guessed in a million years, is I can see myself. Those swell fellas with their saws and hammers. Not only did they leave the *SS Canadiana* wheelhouse intact, they filled the three empty windows in with mirrors and glass. Black age marks dot the reflection, yet there I am still, twenty-three plus a summer. Not a hair out of place. Bumper bangs and finger waves that I kept long to set me apart from working women with their above-the-collar bobs. Rosy rouge and cat eyeliner, unsmudged. Swing shirtwaist dress with fabric-covered buttons. I never wore plastic buttons. And I never ever wore military brown or navy, despite the trend. Black and white and red for me. Florals, if there were floral patterns to be found.

I am forever twenty-three. Same age as her. 'Cept she will turn twenty-four and five and six and maybe see thirty and forty—if she can manage not to fall off her wobbly perch. I ought to be appreciative, or angry. Can a ghost feel both? I feel more now that my dance floor is built. I *am* more.

Directly in front of me, the men have fixed a funhouse mirror. I remember those long mirrors—your whole body warped up one way and twisted down the other. But this mirror is no bigger than a vanity, a perfect fit for the wheelhouse window. I can't look in this mirror for more than three seconds. I timed it—one Mississippi, two Mississippi, three. I got three seconds giggle at my ballooning forehead or banana-bent neck before I disappeared. And not just my reflection, I mean disappear, like I'm being pulled away. Like falling out of the picture. It's like I barely know where here or there or now or yesterday are anymore.

But her voice keeps me here. She has a few dozen or so folks coming 'round now—all women. A small house, but you gotta start somewhere. She's getting good at trembling and moaning, like a bonafide fun park fortune teller. I'd like to stretch out on any one of the built-in benches and watch the show, waiting for my cue. Bit by bit, we're perfecting our tricks. Rapping. Flashes of light. Spitting oracles and swapping divinations. They fall for it all. She merely says the name of someone's dead grandmother or runaway daughter and they swoon, enchanted. People just wanna see themselves. I've always known it. People just wanna be their own show.

But this production is missing something.

I can't put my finger on it quite yet.
Something's missing.

# 45 Divine Poetry

Leanne Knight-Kwong pulls up in the town's blue bus with a roaring horn honk.

"They just keep coming." Rose shakes her head at me as Leanne leads nearly fifty women up the gazebo path. Local women, all. Most have visited before, just not all at once like this. They know we have special guests tonight.

I only had to tell Leanne about the mediums' visit—leave it to her to inform the rest. Judging by how dolled up they are in snug-fitting stonewashed jeans and ruffled blouses or in flowing maxi dresses, I'd say Leanne's gossip was heard loud and clear. Not quite Easter Sunday dressed, though care was put into their earrings and bangle bracelets, their fresh coats of nail polish. Leanne still wears her customary sleeveless rock T-shirt, Steppenwolf this time, though even she has put on a feminine scallop-sleeved cardigan overtop.

Reverend Agnes Radin and Reverend Esther Lutz wait in easy cross-legged seats on the gazebo floor for the group to arrive. Around them Tamara helps Bobby light the candles and lay the altar—some crystals, fresh-cut vervain and chicory, a sacred-heart pendant. Mostly, our alter is decorated with offerings of Crystal Beach Amusement Park memorabilia; a strip of ride tickets, a few dog-eared postcards, and a blue felt flag with the Crystal Beach smiling sun logo embossed in gold. Everything the way Etta likes it. Tamara and Bobby aren't doing it for Etta, though. Tamara's here for me—at least that's what she told me. And it's Hal's devotion to the angel and to his still new sobriety that brings Bobby.

A wooden donation box—Hal's latest handyman creation—sits at the threshold of the gazebo. I agonized over where was the most non-intrusive yet highly visible place to put the donation box. I chew the inside of my mouth as the women drop their donations in. I mustn't stare. It's not about the money. Not. About. Money. Although these women aren't broke. Leanne drives the bus. Dolores and her co-workers Marge and Dolly are linen porters at Fort Erie Hospital. Union pay. A few more work over at the Bick's pickle factory in Dunnville. Etta snoops ID cards in their purses.

Nearby, Hal ushers in a few campers who curiously circle around. "Tonight's fer ladies only," he says audibly, "Not my rules, just doin' what I'm told." His burly silhouette lumbers around in a weak attempt to keep his distance. Bobby stiffens. She makes like she's going to scold him. Dolores pats her left shoulder and I pat her right. She turns her attention back to the women assembling around us.

Hal will stay twenty yards away as I have asked him too. He needs to be always within visual contact. Since the last coat of spar varnish was applied, Hal hasn't ventured more than a hundred feet from the gazebo. He's appointed himself the watcher. Tonight, however, he and Moustache will be the watchers of children. They brusquely herd Lucky and a trio of other toddlers to the cabin, where I've instructed them to read bedtime stories and make flashlight shadow puppets. I set *The Velveteen Rabbit* on the cabin's cot for them—any fool can make rabbit shadow puppets, right? On principle, I'm glad that Bobby and the other moms can join the circle without distraction. But it's the hot prickling across my skin that makes me grateful that the kids are tucked up in the cabin. Etta is antsy tonight. Fired up.

"Welcome," I say as the last couple of women lower themselves onto throw pillows. "Tonight we are joined by Reverend Agnes

Radin and Reverend Esther Lutz from Lily Dale, New York ..."

"I heard you were all a bunch of witches?" Leanne cuts in.

Reverend Agnes's smile is bright and toothy. Her hair is a white bubble perm wrapped with a pink glitter headscarf. She wears an eagle pendant, a fox's head ring, and butterfly earrings. "We are an assembly of Spiritualists, devoted to finding the truth and divinity in all things," she says.

"You talk to the dead?"

"We believe communication with discarnate humans is possible and natural. Spirits are capable of growth, emotion, and the desire to communicate, like any other being," says Reverend Agnes.

"Can you contact my ancestors?"

"Did the angel tell you to come here?"

"Are you here on a supernatural investigation? Like in that movie? Are we going to get our picture taken?"

"Do you think the angel is real? Or is she a mischievous spirit of some kind?" Bobby asks. Good instincts again. But why do smart women even bother with that which they can't completely trust? Pot. Kettle. Black. Truth is, I can't claim to know why Bobby or anyone else comes to the circle. Maybe they just find me more entertaining than *The Love Boat* and *M\*A\*S\*H* reruns that air all summer long. It's more than that, though—there's no making light of personal desires. Aching desires too. Desires that needle my skin like frosty air. Even the mediums want something—I feel it.

"Our guests have come to observe," I announce. Which sums up what Reverend Agnes told me on the phone prior to their visit. To "observe." How they found us and what they want was never made clear. I wonder how word of our little operation crossed the border and travelled down the I-90. Certainly they are all loose-lipped, but which one's gossip could have possibly reached two mediums from

Lily Dale? It makes me nervous. Etta and I could use more time to pull our act together. And am I supposed to perform miracles now?

*Who's here, Etta?*

*It's hard to hear in this hen party. They're all clucking at once. Calm 'em down so I can pick up something.*

"Women," I say. "Put your questions aside. Quiet your minds. Meditate on the reasons you've come here. Imagine yourselves speaking directly to the angel. Ask her for what you need."

A minute passes. Another and another. I make meaningful eye contact with each apprehensive woman. I close my eyes and hum like a low-C on a pipe organ. Okay, maybe I don't hit a low C, but I've been practicing a guttural trance, and tossing my head, rolling my eyes. Etta plays her part much better than I do. She raps on floorboards. I rap back three times. Etta echoes. Most of the women titter in awe, except the Reverends, who exchange wary looks.

*They suspect we're a smoke and mirrors show, Etta. Let's show them.*

Every inch of the gazebo creaks, as if the entire structure draws in a deep breath. The floor beneath us seems to swell for a second, then relax. Leanne scrambles to her feet, panicked. Then, noticing she's the only one about to make a run for it, she awkwardly lowers herself back down.

Etta has information for me. I'm ready. "It's okay to be afraid. It's not our fault that we instinctively want to flee, want to hide, want to survive any way we can." I eye Leanne. The shiner she had when I met her is long gone, but the inch-long scar above her left eye will last. A swipe of her eyebrow is missing where the hair likely won't regrow. "We all have our reasons for being scared. Tonight, June 21, summer solstice, the longest day of the year, I cast a circle of strength around us." This speech, too, I've practiced. Pretty darn good, if I say so myself.

I turn to the Reverend Esther Lutz. Unlike Agnes's bright, gaudy style and lively face, Esther is the epitome of neutral. Hair in a bun. Beige button-down shirt and pressed khaki pants. No makeup, not even pierced ears. "You carry the Eye of Horus in your left pocket and a chunk of garnet in your right. There is no need for protection charms here. This circle is about undoing harm, not causing it." I studied the Bronze Age for two weeks total. Booyah! Reverend Esther's face remains cool, though Etta tells me she's curled her toes into *little feet fists.*

*The teenage ginger to your left is in the family way. About six weeks ripe.*

*You looked inside her body?*

*I see what I see. Jeez. I don't tell you how to do your job. And she's carrying a book of poetry in her purse. Is that better? You're a bookworm, aren't you, Dollface? This one's called* The Gold Cell. *She's marked a page.*

"'The Premonition' by Sharon Olds," I say aloud. The women lean in, confused, expecting. Except the ginger, she tilts away as if I've just given her a little push. Etta slips her name to me. "I too know this book, Becky McPhee. I have a copy myself. Good for you for reading it." Did that sound patronizing? She's so young. I didn't discover Sharon Olds until university. Etta feeds me lines to recite; my vocal intonation, I believe, is perfect for reading poetry, "... the condom/ripped and the seed tore into me like a/flame ...

"It's your choice," I say, cryptic to all but Becky.

"The angel says that? That it's my choice?" Becky cries the kind of cry where her voice and facial expression remain controlled while tears stream out of both eyes. I'm about to keenly reassure her, but pause. Damn Catholic upbringing. Would a so-called angel of so-called god approve of abortion? Am I going to burn in so-called hell for this? Ah, fuck a coat hanger, who knows what god thinks? This young woman is reading *The Gold Cell*, for Christ's sake. You can't get that book at the town library. She's obviously got a thing or two figured out.

"All that any of us have during uncertain times is the ability to make the best possible choices with the options we have. Do you know what you want to do?"

"I don't want to be a mom," she says with more assurance than I could have mustered at her age. "Not now."

"You're pregnant," blurts Dolores. "Who's the father? Please tell me you got knocked up by a guy your own age."

Becky hugs herself. She looks like a crying statue, utterly still and wet-faced. "Who are any of our fathers?" I ask. I'm hardly prepared for it to get all Sally Jessy Raphael around here. I should instate some sort of confidentiality agreement. I'd prefer to pose pro-choice arguments to the group, like a classroom discussion, but I'm supposed to sound holy, not sociopolitical. Are race, class, and sex separate from spiritual life? I mean, obviously not. Good Friday is a statutory holiday and Yom Kippur isn't. White Jesus is pictured in the church I grew up in. All of this would be so much easier if we'd never claimed an angel apparition. Why couldn't Etta appear as a unicorn? Or some faerie queene or she-goblin or whatnot?

*Etta, help. I'm not making any sense. What do I say now?*

*They'll buy whatever you say*, Etta insists. *Who are our fathers, really? Keep going.*

"Who are our fathers? Who are the men that show up for us? Who are the men that know us, our hearts and minds? The men who are never suspicious or critical of us? The men who nurture us without expecting something in return? The men who trust us? Who support us in being the women we truly are? Who, I ask you, are the men in our lives that know that we are gathered here right now?

"How many of you had to tell a man a lie about where you were going tonight?" Etta grandly raps on the floor. A few women jump, startled, but soon each of them, with the exception of Reverend Esther, raps back, beating their knuckles on the floor.

"Why should we name the men that fail us?" I ask. "No, Becky. You do not have to name the father. There is no father. There is only the choice that you alone get to make."

Now Becky is leaning on Tamara, allowing herself to be comforted. A few other women sitting closest take Tamara's lead and reach their hands out in support. Fingers crossed that Becky is at least sixteen and has an OHIP card. It's not like Brian Mulroney has made it any easier to get an abortion in this country.

"The angel says one of you must volunteer to drive Becky to the clinic in Hamilton. And a few others must volunteer to care for her after her doctor's visit. Form a group of caring."

*Is that what I said, did I? Cut. Print it. What happens in the next reel?* Like a puppeteer, Etta forces my hands up. I am a puppet. When she moves me, my bones become light. Wooden popsicle sticks. Toothpicks. Limbs so flimsy a child could snap them in two. I feel no pain, only insignificance. Everyone suddenly turns back toward me as if I'm about to make a proclamation

*Etta, let go. Focus on getting me more info.*

I shift my seat closer to Leanne as my tingling arms float back down. Tonight is her fifth or sixth meeting and still Etta and I haven't been able to work with her. She's got walls, Leanne.

"I know what I said before. I'm fine now," she tells the group, though she ever so slightly shifts her body toward mine.

"Your husband is Anton Knight."

"I thought we weren't naming men." Leanne's face grows mean.

She turns away from me. "Besides, you don't have to be psychic. Everyone knows the bastard."

Etta hangs over her. I see her first as a clear figure, a beauty who winks a daring eye at me. Then I see her as the rest must see her, as a shining axis of light above Leanne's head. Some bow right to the floor. A few cry out ecstatically. Reverend Agnes scrambles to her feet, breathy. "What reason have you come?"

*No way bad-perm lady is stealing the show. Get me more, Etta. More.*

Etta lifts me to my feet, leads me to the wheelhouse nook on the north side of the gazebo. The women trail me, keeping near. In the funhouse mirror only I can see our misshapen faces, mine and Etta's. She cups her hands over my eyes and what I see then is fast-moving water. What I feel is freezing night air.

"Your wedding ring lies at the bottom of the Niagara River. In the river near the foot of Bowen Road where you threw it." My voice trances, and not in the low-C I've rehearsed, but popping and staticky—Etta's voice writhes through mine. We sound like distortion-feed on a two-way radio. Everyone hears our strange harmony. I have eyes and ears everywhere. Behind me, Rose is abruptly stricken with worry. Bobby's teeth begin to clack. Tamara motions toward me, waving her hands near the back of my head. Leanne tugs her to settle back down.

"It is early March," we continue. "You notice crocuses peeking out of the melting snow as you walk down Bowen Road. Those little purple flowers, so encouraging. See how they bloomed early for you. The sun hasn't quite risen yet. You wear flannel pajamas and winter boots, but no jacket, you were in such a hurry to leave the house.

"You almost stumble when you jump the guardrail. The snow-covered rocks are slippery as you scramble down to the riverbank. He didn't follow you. The truth is, he never follows you. Always it is you going to him. If he is in a loving mood, you go. If he's cruel, you also go. Now you are completely alone. No one to tell you if what you are about to do is right or wrong. The long, linked floating ice boom crackles in the river. The wind is still cold enough to hurt your ears. Your ring doesn't travel as far through the air as you imagined it would. You listen, but don't hear it hit the surface. The sound of river ice is too loud. You don't see where it hits. There are still too many ice circles for the water to ripple. It's as if you never threw the ring at all. As if it never existed.

"You were free in that moment. One self-determined and free moment. You didn't stay free, did you, Leanne?" My own voice returns. I turn to face them again. Etta is perched a few feet away on the gazebo railing. I suspect Reverend Esther sees her too—her head suddenly swivels toward Etta's sitting spot.

"You made it work between Bobby and Hal," says Leanne. "The angel got them patched up. Why can't she do that for me?"

"Hal has changed," Bobby says. "Sure, he prays, he prays a lot, but it's more on account of he was ready to change. The old coot, sometimes I think it's too little to late, but he is trying his darn hardest. He's doing the work of a good father and a pretty good husband. He's doing the work. You understand? I doubt ..." Bobby hesitates. She lets herself cry a little, nothing more than welling tear ducts. Then Leanne, tough nut of a woman, lets herself cry a little. "I doubt Anton is going to change," Bobby whispers. "You gave him enough chances. Only so many chances you can give a man who don't even try."

Leanne nods in acknowledgement. A split second later, her face turns mean again. She stretches out the collar of her cardigan to wipe her tears. "What does the angel say? Does the angel say to leave him?"

"The angel says you have to throw the ring again, Leanne. You have to throw the ring once and for all."

"Yeah, that's what you say. You don't even like men, do ya? Why should I listen to you? I want to hear it from the angel. Show me a sign."

*Oh, how I've been waiting for someone to ask me for a sign, to appeal to my might and solicit the gifts I've gained since you woke me up again. Watch me stop the blood in their veins. Make their skin bubble. One divine sign, coming right up.*

Etta yanks me to my feet again, and then floats me above the floor like a rag doll. She's never done this before. *We can dance on the ceiling*, she howls in my ear. The women scream. I scream. I'd kick and scream, but my legs are numb. All the candles around us snuff out. Then the lights in Rose's house, then the RVs up and down the driveway grow dark. And in the distance the street lamps go out on Cherry Street, then Vine, then Maple. Complete darkness.

I drop back down with a hollow thud. I am empty. Do I still have bones? A beating heart? The women around me must be shouting, frantic and loud. I hear a voice that might be mine or Etta's. It says, You asked for it you asked for it you asked for it you asked for it it it it it it it x x x x xx xx xxxx xxxxx.

Tamara's face is right next to mine, so close her lips bump my cheek as she repeats my name.

"Piss 'n' shit!" Hal blurts out in the distance. It sounds like he is stumbling through the blackout toward us. At least he didn't swear in front of the children, I think. Bobby hates that. Rose is crying again. I know the sound of her quickened breath without seeing her. Etta has given me eyes and ears everywhere.

Reverend Agnes asks again, "What reason have you come?"

The women around me hold onto each other in a tight and reverent circle.

# 46 Great Advice, Thanks

acon grease fills Rose's kitchen. Most of us spent the night at The Point since we were too afraid to drive or walk home. Tamara and I slept in the cabin, hugging each other tightly together on the single cot. Reverend Agnes and Reverend Esther slept in Ricky's old room in Rose's house. Leanne crammed somewhere into Hal and Bobby's trailer. We're all thinking about what in the fuck happened last night, though we're all acting normal. Or normal for us, which is pretty far from an all-American family sitcom.

Tamara fills Dolores in on what's been happening at Pure Platinum since she quit. In front of everyone, they breezily use lingo like "friction dance" and "pervert row" like they're discussing the weather. No one seems to mind. We're visionaries now—we haven't got time for prudishness.

Rose has pulled out a wooden cigar box filled with antique charms. She shows the Reverends her *nonna*'s sterling silver *mano figa* and *cimaruta*, with its little moon and sprig of rue—witchy stuff, superstitious and private, at least any trace of it was in our family. Is privacy off the table now too? What will she do next? Dip her thumb in olive oil and perform *il malocchio*? Again, no one minds. Strippers and *stregheria* together at last.

Bobby paces the kitchen, Rose's long telephone cord swaying back and forth behind her. She's on hold with a social worker from Child and Family Services, or "fucking CFS" as she's taught us all to call them. "I just want access to my original birth registry. Is that so hard?" She speaks loudly, holds the phone receiver an inch from her face. "Yeah, what choice do I got? I'll hold, again."

Hal is whistling Bobby McFerrin's "Don't Worry, Be Happy" as he cooks up more bacon.

Lucky sits on my lap. A purple Froot Loop sticks to his chin. "I love you," he tells me. It is the first time he's said this to me.

"I love you too, Lucky Star." In the five years I lived in Toronto, I doubt I told anyone that I loved them. Maybe drunkenly. Or as a zealous expression of thanks, like "You bought me a copy of Doris Lessing's *The Golden Notebook*. Wow. I love you." My love for Lucky bubbles up inside of me. I have that hot, urgent "I want more" feeling again. I want more for Lucky, for Bobby, for all of them. Who would Bobby be if she had access to her birth records, to her real family, or Hal, if he wasn't born into god only knows how many generations of violent alcoholics? Or Ricky, dare I consider it, if he had never killed himself? Or Etta, if she hadn't fallen from a roller coaster fifty years ago? It's not actually *more* I want. Not like the despairing, compulsive *more* I usually want. I only want us all to be what we could have been if pain didn't happen. Is that greedy? To want what's been stolen? I love this place, these people. I want wholeness for them.

I'm never going back to Toronto or moving to New York or Montréal. I'm going to quit chasing the dummy's dream, or whatever it was that made me think I was too good for this place. So fuck me and the horse I rode in on, I belong here. I belong with people who deserve more.

And Etta won't let me leave anyway. I'm trapped. I am both loved and trapped.

Our scene comes to a standstill tableau when Agnes briskly invites me to go for a drive. The Reverends stand up, all ready to go. She nods at Tamara. "You and your companion."

"My companion," I balk. "What are we, characters in a Victorian novel?" But Tamara urges me forward. She gives me what I interpret as a *please behave* warning look. With my hesitant compliance, the Reverends ask us to remove any jewellery and empty out our pockets. Agnes even pulls a barrette from my hair. The room bristles as we empty a small pile of personal belongings onto Rose's Formica table.

Esther picks up the Crystal Beach flag pendant. "Were you wearing this last night?" she asks.

"She's always wearing it," Tamara tells her. Jeez. She's giving away my secrets. I hope Etta didn't overhear her. I'm already waiting for Etta to grow jealous or suspicious of Tamara. But so far, my relationships have only grown stronger with Etta around. Like she's experiencing my connections, second-hand.

"Where are you taking them?" Bobby demands, her hand cupped over the mouthpiece of the phone receiver. But they don't reply.

Tamara loops her arm around me as we leave. Not wanting to let go of each other, we both climb into the back seat of the Reverends' Chevrolet sedan through the same door.

"Where did you say we're going?"

"We're not sure yet. Somewhere where we won't be heard." Agnes heads west on Number 3 Road, toward Port Colborne. Patches of asphalt thump under the tires. We turn on Point Abino Road, and Tamara points out the shoe tree. I turn backward in my seat to watch it as we pass. There must be well over a hundred shoes tacked to the trunk. When I was a kid, Barbara and I nailed up a pair of my Mary Janes.

We veer onto Bertie, then loop south back to Killaly Street to pass a few chestnut mares that reach their long necks over a wire fence to nibble sumac growing in the ditch. We turn onto narrow, gravelly Miller Road. I wish Tamara could read my mind like Etta. I wonder if she's freaking out as much as I am. I try it. Tamara, can you hear me? Buzz. Hum. No answer.

Agnes rolls the car to a halt, and gravel turns under the wheels, hitting the back bumper. Overgrown Queen Anne's lace and cone-flowers brush up against the side of the car. I reach my hand out the window and pick one of the wildflowers for Tamara. She tucks it behind her ear in a gorgeous attempt to seem calm and easygoing.

The Reverends turn around to face us. "Call her," Agnes tells me.

"The angel? It doesn't work like that."

"Concentrate."

I should tell her to take a flying fuck, but these ladies seem so assured, shrewd, and sharp. Somewhat horrible to talk to, like how I imagine most of my feminist heroes would be if I were to actually meet them. So, compliantly, I close my eyes and hail Etta. Hail again. "No response. I'm too far away."

"Too far away from what, exactly?" asks Agnes.

"From where she makes her appearances," I shrug.

Agnes has more questions that she asks in rapid succession: "Do you notice a pattern in her appearances?" and "Have you mapped the places where you can or can't reach her?" She slows down to ask her linchpin question. I can tell it's important because she claps her hands before asking. "'Angels' often have a task to fulfill. Do you notice recurring messages or tasks?" Agnes air-quotes "angels" Does she question the existence of all angels, or just Etta, I wonder.

Tamara wonders about her intention too. "Do *you* notice," she mimics, "that you're asking all sorts of questions when you've obviously formed an opinion already?" I am crazy for you, Tamara, you badass queen, I declare silently to myself. "Why don't you say what you brought us out here to say? We're listening."

Esther opens the passenger-side door, as if the additional airflow through the car will help her begin. Today she is wearing brown mascara, which is unfortunate since it's already searing hot outside. Tamara and I brace; we're about to get schooled by a woman with raccoon eyes. "You know," Esther says to me, "and I suspect you also know," to Tamara, "it's not an angel that you're dealing with. The spirit last night wanted nothing to do with me. I couldn't hear her. I couldn't feel her presence. Despite her efforts to block me, I still caught a glimpse of her. And she was not an angel."

"I get you girls are trying to do good here," Agnes jumps in. "I'm for women's lib as much as the next. You know the female to male population in Lily Dale? We got the men outnumbered. There's no domestic abuse. No pornography. No prostitution." I grip Tamara's hand, squeeze my eyes shut, willing Agnes to not go on some Andrea Dworkin-esque tirade.

"As the saying goes, the road to hell is paved with good intentions," continues Agnes. "You use the name of the divine—god, angels, the Virgin Mary—even to do what you think is the right thing—well, grave consequences come with that type of lie. Very grave, you understand?"

Like Esther, Agnes opens her driver-side door. "You mind if we stand outside? We're cooking in our own juices in here." The four of us tumble out of the car and walk a few paces into the overgrown farmer's field to stand under a nearby willow tree. Grasshoppers ricochet off my bare legs. A half-dozen Baltimore orioles chide us from high branches. I scan the treetops for their pouch-like nests. I bet they have fledglings up there—new orange balls with beaks, maybe a few downy tufts still clinging to their young feathers. I bet they're really cute. I want to be looking anywhere except at the Reverends' faces, listening to anything except whatever the Reverends have to say.

"What concerns us is that your spirit seems, plainly put, arrogant and manipulative. That's not what we, as mediums, do. We do not pander to arrogant spirits."

"And we most certainly don't condone last night's type of spooky stuff and showing off," says Esther. "The spirits we communicate with aren't seeking worship or fear." Esther notices my gaze wandering. She follows my line of vision for a moment, then turns back to me. "Listen to me, please. She only talks to you, this ghost? I've been thinking about why that is. At first, I assumed she had attached herself to you, just as she's attached herself to certain places and objects, like that gazebo she had you build, and those tokens of Crystal Beach she's had you gather. That's not all there is to it, though? It's more that you've attached yourself to her. You've latched on to her. You are holding her dangerously close."

"Dangerous? How?" asks Tamara.

"In my experience, dangerous spirits can only do to us what we're already doing to ourselves. They're attracted to sadness and grief. Strong emotions. Many mediums are battling with some kind of heartache, some kind of past trauma. It makes us more receptive. But it can also destroy us."

"Were you emotionally unwell when she first started speaking to you?" asks Esther. "Were you always this thin?"

"You have lost weight, Star. And the blackouts—how many have you had?"

"You must untangle your soul from hers." At Esther's grim warning I half expect the orioles to suddenly fly off or a swift breeze to bow the overgrown grass down. Everything remains hot and still.

"Sure, thanks, great advice. How do we do that?" asks Tamara. I notice she is using "we" not "me." Hallmark card: True Love Means Helping You Untangle Your Soul from the Undead. Glitter heart.

Glitter heart. Lip print.

The Reverends sigh together. "The truth is we don't know. It's up to you, Starla, to protect yourself and the people you care about."

Tamara turns back toward the car, nudging me to follow

"It will certainly help to find out more about her," Agnes follows. "Find public records or living family members if you can. Visit her grave. Perhaps there is one particular things she's searching for. Instead of pandering to her tricks, talk to her. Try to find out what she wants. Maybe under all this showy behavior she's looking for some kind of peace. Most spirits are."

The last thing Etta wants is peace, I think.

Agnes thrusts a business card and glossy pamphlet about Lily Dale in my hands, offering to take my call "any time." "Word of mouth is spreading about your angel of Crystal Beach," she tells me. "Please do find your way back to truth before more people get caught up in this."

On the ride back to The Point I muse over how many people might have heard about the Crystal Beach angel. I notice, on the pamphlet Agnes gave me, that Lily Dale charges a gate fee of ten dollars. Ten dollars just to enter the community. Never mind the fee to see a medium one-on-one. How much would people pay to see an angel?

# 47 Circuit Breaker

arbara returns from DC with a ring.

Barbara returns as I am packing my room—a task that shouldn't take long considering I never quite unpacked. But when every item I own begs a narrative of fulfillment and of over-spending, it takes awhile to get organized.

My bedroom looks like a tornado blew through it, scattering my belongings from wall to wall. Barbara stands at the edge of a storm, extending her hand like Michelangelo's Adam in the Sistine Chapel. The engagement ring is like almost touching god, I suppose. Good for her. I wish her happiness. I should, literally, wish her happiness. Say something, Starla, you broken daughter. Talk. To. Your Mother.

"We're still discussing where we'll live," Barbara tells me, thronging the doorway. Is it possible her boobs got bigger over a four-day weekend? Or did Rahn take her fancy bra shopping? Why must these questions snake into my mind?

"Well, now you can have this room as a den. That's what you wanted, right?" Oops. That was the opposite of congratulating her. Barbara doesn't notice. She hasn't even asked why I'm packing or where I'm going.

"He's going to retire in a year," she says. "I'm nowhere near retiring. So really, he should move here. But I worry." Barbara twists the engagement ring on her finger. "I worry that this house is too small for him, too dumpy. You should see the size of his place."

I abandon my mess on the floor, and stand to face her. The second we lock eyes, it occurs to me that this is the last time she and I will be in this room together. The emotion of it surprises me. Is there something to be done to mark the occasion? I should get my act together. I should glow over her ring. What fiancée doesn't want a fuss? The ring is a *fede*—two rose gold hands clasped along a pink diamond band. I wonder if she picked it out or if Rahn researched Italian engagement traditions before proposing. Something tells me the latter.

"Rahn is a really good guy." I don't add, *Try not to fuck it up.*

"I might move to Buffalo with him just to get away. You ever wish you could live someplace where you don't have memories?" Barbara asks.

Has she forgotten that I moved to Toronto for five-plus years? "Not anymore," I tell her. "I'm staying in the Beach. Tamara and I are getting a place."

Barbara blinks at the contents of my room as if she's suddenly noticed that I'm packing. Here is the chance for her to ask me if I am gay. The chance for her to ask where I'm moving to, when I'm leaving. Was I really molested as a kid? Is she a bad mother? Can I perform miracles? Am I haunted? Will I live to see twenty-five? To ask me anything at all. "I'll bring up a couple of Rubbermaid bins from the basement," she says. "There's no way you're going to fit all this stuff back in your luggage."

Hearing her heavy footsteps on the stairs makes me want to break something. I press my knuckles to the wall but think better of throwing a punch. These walls are so thin, I'd surely make a fist-sized hole. Instead, I imagine it—a fist-sized hole. I visualize my bedroom rife with holes. More holes in that room. Negative space. Barbara floats in the chasm. Our relationship is me imagining shit and her imagining shit. Nothing solid comes of it. I don't have the skill to make our relationship work. Or maybe I don't care. Both and neither are true.

She is having her own tantrum below me. Too many slams and thuds to be merely accidental. I imagine her wildly wrestling with the step ladder. Storage boxes crashing to the unfinished concrete floor. Guardedly, I walk to the top of the basement stairs. This could be another scene from my childhood, a loop in trembling time. I might be thankful, I suppose, that Barbara has always excused herself to have fits in another part of the house. And I have always listened to the "bang bang o'clock," as Lucky would say, from my bedroom. As a child, my job was to not interrupt, and afterward to be attentive, maybe compliment her hair or the most recent meal she cooked. What if the present can be different?

"Mama," I call, descending a few steps. "I'm coming down."

When I was a child, maybe eight, a mother skunk and three of her kits took up residence in our basement and stank up the whole house. Barbara tried tossing ammonia-soaked towels down to scare them off. Then paper bags filled with chopped onions and Tabasco sauce. In the end, it was the buckets full of boiling water and dried *pepperoncini rossi* that forced the skunks to relocate. I remember her opening the basement door, chucking the homemade repellent, then slamming the door again. For months, maybe years, I was afraid of the basement. Not so much scared the skunks would return, but scared of how upset Barbara got at the top of the stairs. Far more upset than she ever was with any of her boyfriends.

Why couldn't she have protected me the way she protected the basement?

I descend one slow step at a time. "Mama," I say again, louder.

There aren't any spilled boxes, no beat-up step ladder, but Barbara is frantic. She weaves around the three steel support poles as if she might outpace her unwanted tears. The English language is inadequate, I think. There should be a unique word to describe your mother's crying. A specific idiom used to represent the tears of a mother whom you do not completely trust or feel compassion for. Seeing Barbara cry is distinct from any crying I've witnessed at The Point.

"What's wrong?" I ask. A rarely asked question in our household.

"Nothing," she says. Also, rare. We aren't exactly WASPs. We're second-generation Italian Catholics, which means something is always wrong. Barbara quits pacing. She holds a steel pole for support. Her body jerks with palpitating sobs and wheezes. I know that kind of crying, that overloaded, circuit-breaker crying. She paddles the concrete floor with her feet. I recognize that foot movement. For me, it means I'm drifting away, that I need to plant back into the here and now.

"Sometime I spell ... a word when I'm upset," I quietly offer. "It helps calm me down. We could spell ... *grazie*," I suggest, impromptu. "G-R-A-Z-I-E." I spell again in the Italian alphabet, embellishing the accent, in fun. "Gi. Erre. A. Zeta ..." Barbara doesn't spell along with me, but she seems to be taking a deep breath in time with each letter.

"I always dreamt we would be friends," she blurts. "That you'd get over being so fucking angry, and we'd finally be friends."

A hundred responses, which range from "I love you" to "I wish I was raised by wolves," parade through my thoughts. I wish I had an angel-sanctioned task to assign us. How much easier would that be?

I say, "I suppose you did better than me. I didn't even have the dream."

If this were a movie, an emphatically hopeful orchestral music score would play now. The camera would catch an over-the-shoulder shot of me going in for a hug, then pan out. Fade.

This isn't a movie. I am the queen of a haunted campground and trailer park and I'm moving in with my lesbian girlfriend. A ragtag group of people I've only known for a few months are my closest family. My mother and I cannot settle sweet fuck-all between us. I am twenty-three years old and not a total dipstick.

From my mother's house I take one thing and leave one thing behind.

Taken: Mr Winky, the eyeless teddy bear. Technically, he's mine anyway.

Left behind: My copy of *The Golden Cell* by Sharon Olds, bookmarked with a sheet of mauve letter writing paper at the poem titled, "After 37 Years My Mother Apologizes for My Childhood." Becky McPhee was good to remind me of this book. May poetry be a catalyst for more. It was not easy to write "We still have time for that friendship" on the mauve paper.

But I did.

# 48 E is for

"o you have any brothers and sisters?" Lucky asks.
"Nope. Only me."

"Me too. Only me." Lucky jumps into my lap for a hug. I peek at Bobby, glad she's out of earshot. I don't want her to hear Lucky talk about being an only child. I wonder how often she thinks of her stolen baby girl? Hopefully, not today. Today is her birthday. She made us promise: no "happy birthday" song, no candles, no cards, and no gift-wrapped presents (and no booze).

Lucky and I spent the afternoon gathering wood lilies and lady's tresses for a birthday bouquet. At the edge of the field, we found a long tangle of thimbleberry shrubs. I ate a few berries before giving Lucky the okay to eat some himself. "Only the black ones. The reds aren't ready," I told him. We used the folded bottoms of our T-shirts as baskets and carried home as many berries as we could. Rose said she'd serve them with ice-cream cake after dinner.

Hal is grilling rabbit over one of the empty campsite fire pits. Two large metal bowls full of rabbit bits and oil and garlic salt sit on the picnic table. "Pull the kidneys off them rabbit legs. They keep falling in the fire," Hal shouts through a billow of smoke. Immediately, Bobby and Rose are at the table. Their fingers work the oily lumps of rabbit meat. I ask them to teach me. Bobby shows me the dark round kidneys and how to peel the membranes away. "We'll fry 'em up later with bacon and onions," she says.

"My ma never taught me to cook," I blurt. Bobby gives me side eye, shakes her head. "Totally serious, she hates sharing her kitchen, would yell *Vai! Vai!*"

"It means scram," Rose explains to Bobby.

"Did you get hit with a wooden spoon? I had an Italian lady for a foster mom once. She always hit us with a wooden spoon." Rose and I frown at each other, sinking our hands back into the rabbit meat.

Campers frequently wander up and linger awhile. At first, I let myself believe it's the gamey smell of grilled rabbits that's attracting onlookers. But, of course, each one wears a pleading expression on their face. They are waiting for me to return to the gazebo. I can't look at them. If I do, I know I'll be drawn out to perform whatever it is Etta might fancy this evening. I need some time in the human world. Human's night out! I maintain firm eye contact with Bobby, Rose, and Lucky. We speak loudly to each other. All of us are unwilling to be disrupted.

Hal smells like charcoal by the time he sits down. Rose set the picnic tables with real tablecloths and melamine dinnerware that I bet was a wedding gift in the 1950s. We are a party of eight: Dolores, Rose, Leanne the bus driver, Hal, Moustache, Bobby, Lucky, and me. "I never had this many people come to my birthday," Bobby tells us.

"Best thirty-fifth birthday ever," Hal teases. They kiss, and not their usual half-a-second long peck, but a kiss that goes on long enough for Dolores and Leanne to click their plastic utensils against their glasses. "To my beautiful wife." Hal raises his glass of lemonade. "And all our friends come'd to celebrate her."

Bobby stands too. The sun splits through the trees and onto her face like a spotlight. Her eyes flash gold and brown. "I never understood in the moment, and maybe it's because I'm getting older, but I haven't felt like I have a gang of friends for a long time. So, thank you all for showing up for me. For sharing food and looking after Lucky and being pretty good people."

"Fine toasts," says Rose. "Who needs wine when the company is this good?" She bangs her glass on the picnic table to scare the evil eye away from our feast. Old village superstition—there have been too many compliments paid at this table. *"Benzadeus."*

Dolores stands, clears her throat emphatically, cracks her knuckles. "'Friendship' is kind of a word I save for special occasions. Since it's your birthday, I guess I may as well admit it. I'm glad to call you a friend." Dolores and Bobby smirk at each other.

"Last winter, you remember when that bad snowstorm hit?" Rose stands now. I guess she's over being superstitious. "Worst winter of my life, without my Ricky. So Bobby, she packed us all into my car, and I never let anyone drive my car, and she drove to the Tim Hortons, and after we all got our Double Doubles and Timbits, Bobby spun donuts in the parking lot. You know that parking lot's mostly gravel. I was scared half to death. And that was the moment I realized ... I realized that life would go on without my son." Rose raises her lemonade glass again. "Thank you, Bobby. And I'll never let you drive my car again."

When the cake comes out, we clap and stomp our feet. Dolores and Leanne have to carry the cake out together—it's practically big enough for someone to pop out of, decorated with Smarties and mini Crunchie Bars, and thimbleberries scattered around the cake tray. "That's a Dairy Queen cake all the way from Saint Catharines. Angel money paid for that cake," announces Dolores. The "Happy Birthday" song seems to be poised at the tips of our tongues. Or maybe "For He's A Jolly Good Fellow"? Lucky feels the pending music; he start to hum. "I don't wanna set the word on fire ..." he stands and sings.

Swift as thought, Bobby yanks him down again. "Don't you sing that song." She throws me a dreadful glance. She knows! She knows that song is connected to Etta and that Etta is getting in Lucky's head. "How about you sing me 'Twinkle, Twinkle,'" Bobby redirects him.

*Not here.* I close my eyes. She hears me. I can tell by my sudden headache. *You better not be here.*

*Come meet me on the dance floor. I'm dying of loneliness.*

My jaw starts clacking and I clap my hand over my mouth. An ache rips into my ears and throat, like a rapid infection.

"You're not going to finish dinner?" Bobby says as I wriggle away from the table. She stands as I stand. My movements are drunken, hers are sharp. "You draw her away from my son," she whispers in my ear as she gives me a spiky hug. "Keep her clear away from him."

I want to say "sorry" or "I promise she won't harm Lucky" but I'm afraid of what my voice sounds like right now. I nod mechanically.

"Wait," she grabs me by the arm. "You being hurt?"

I'm not sure anyone has ever asked me that before. Gravity seesaws between a cruel pull and weightlessness. I understand that I'm speaking, but I can't feel my teeth or tongue. "You're a good mom, Bobby. Good mother. Good woman."

My arms thrash at my sides as I walk away, as I try to manage a goodbye wave.

Etta waits for me on the gazebo steps.

# 49 Ex-Boyfriend's Dodge Challenger

Tamara and I drink rye and ginger at Don Cherry's Sports Grill. Hockey highlights whirl across three large TVs. Out the enormous window is the Peace Bridge, the line of trucks about to head to Hamilton or Toronto or anywhere but here. In the parking lot, there's half a dozen New York license plates. Ears perked, I listen to the muffled conversations of the business-casual dressed men for any New York City-sounding accents. All I hear is the flat short and hard long a's of Buffalonians. "Think outside of the backs," a man in a dated early '80s skinny tie says to another man. (Think outside of the box.) The other man replies, "You're rate, you're rate." (You're right.)

Tamara puts her lipstick on at the table. With her other hand, she waives a black leather billfold at our server—a brunette wearing the wrong-sized bra. I stare at the lumpy place across her tight Maple Leafs T-shirt where her breasts spill over her bra cup. "Thanks, Jenny," Tamara says to her. "How's the little guy? Growing fast?" Jenny says something about first words and not getting enough sleep before returning to the kitchen. I watch her walk—she's also wearing the wrong kind of underwear for white jeans. Screw miracles. What local women need is my fashion advice.

"I have friends, you know," Tamara says to me. "Like, friends we could be hanging out with if we didn't spend all our time at The Point."

I gesture at the restaurant around us. It was her idea to go out for dinner together before her shift at Pure Platinum. So here we are—hot wing and beer mug paradise. She pulls out her compact from her purse and holds it in front of her face. Maybe to hide that she's annoyed? "It's not as if I've refused to meet your friends," I say. Tamara holds her compact closer to her face. "Okay. What are you thinking? Girls' night? A double date or something?"

"Girls' night would be fun. We could go across to The Continental in Buffalo. The Goo Goo Dolls and Gorilla Biscuits play there all the time."

I nod in agreement. Girls' night at the macho punk club—why not? Actually, I could stand to be smashed around in a mosh pit. She kisses my cheek goodbye, leaving a burgundy lip-print on me, I'm sure. I watch the men in the bar watch her as she leaves.

I flip my hair when I see the table of four young ball-cap-wearing studs seated beside the electric fireplace. Biceps and babyfaces. Newly nineteen, I bet. Crossed the border to drink legally at the first Canadian bar they could find. Nineteen-year-old Americans keep our local bars afloat. I'm glad at least the Canadian drinking age has allowed us to carry on our tradition as a party town. One boy tips his glass at me. It would be easy to get into their car, or into any one of the big rigs coming across the border. Rather, it would have been easy. Now I'm leashed in Etta's backyard. A dog at the end of its chain. I can't even imagine where I'd go. I summon images of New York City—gallery row, Chelsea, the stone steps outside the Met—my brain's become nothing but the white noise of Etta's absence.

Tamara is right. I do need more time away from The Point. And so, what now? I've successfully eaten a Caesar salad and half a basket of popcorn shrimp. I lean back in the pleather chair waiting for the nausea I wouldn't allow myself to feel with Tamara here. My stomach gurgles a human gurgle, that's all. No alien baby kicking. No *Exorcist*-like possession of my long intestine.

"Pornstar Martini," one of the ball-cap-wearing boys interrupts my wallowing. He is not a boy. It's Chris Sakokete, my high school boyfriend. Pornstar Martini was his nickname for me, not because Martini was my familial last name before it was anglicized, but because we were obsessed with Absolut Vodka ads in high school. His round cheeks are the same. Same set of perfect big square teeth. I wipe at my cheek, the lipstick from Tarmara's goodbye kiss. Hopefully, he's had enough beers to see me as pretty. My voice hiccups as I say his name.

"Been hearing weird stories about you, eh? Hell of a way to find out your ex is back in town." I wonder if I should stand to hug him. In my periphery, his friends shuffle out the door, leaving him here with me. "Let me give you a lift. Where you headed next? Barbara's? The Point?" He downs the last of his beer. His knuckles are puffy—the only sign that he's aged a day. "Two pints with lunch. You know me, I'm fine to drive."

I want to say, two beers is a drop in your bucket. An echo of the jokes we used to make about him being twice my size and able to drink twice as much. I don't know if these jokes are funny anymore, to him or to me.

He owns the same brown Dodge Challenger as he did in high school. The car has a name—Collette, after Collette Miller, the woman in the punk metal band GWAR. Collette has an origin story—she was manufactured at the Dodge plant in Windsor by one of Chris's uncles, who made a good-luck wish when it was just parts on the assembly line. The passenger-side still has a wrench clamped to the window crank where the handle fell off years ago.

I start to tear up and it feels good, like squeezing a pus-filled sliver from under my skin.

"You that happy to see me?" Chris jokes. "Waterworks and everything."

I am happy to see him. He may be the only person I've seen since coming back that isn't connected to me by Etta. Chris and my mom.

I ask him to drive along the Niagara Parkway, in the opposite direction of Etta. He's a quiet driver, no radio or conversation. The quiet gives me pause to doubt all of my relationships. Would I have read bedtime stories to Lucky if it wasn't for Etta? Would Rose have practically adopted me as the daughter she never had? Would Dolores even talk to me? I'm tempted to ask Chris what he liked about me years ago—did I have any good qualities of my own? Instead, I silently gawk at the rich people's houses, or what I used to consider rich people's houses, before I moved to Toronto and saw the Bridle Path. Still, compared to The Point, the sprawling mowed front yards and two-car garages appear grandiose. Brick is ridiculous and white fences, overblown. Chris clears his throat a couple times. He wants to talk. We hold an awkward energy between us, like we've both just lifted a heavy old sofa before figuring out who will push and who will pull.

"You married?" I ask. He isn't wearing a ring.

"No wife." He changes his speaking pitch, lisps. "Never married, just like you."

What is he up to with that voice? "Well, I couldn't get married if I wanted to."

"Sure. Plenty of guys would marry a lesbian." He waits for my comeback. We used to tease each other endlessly. Two months ago, I might have giggled or blushed or feigned shock. Now, I can only muster a numb gape. "Dolores told me you and Tamara Matveev are a thing. She's my cousin. Dolores is, not Tamara." He pokes me in the side. "We're all cousins, remember?" Another one of his jokes. I laugh, cautiously. "Yeah, I got the scoop. Lesbians and voices from beyond, eh? I know a pretty good tattoo guy." Chris hikes up his T-shirt sleeve to show me a bat skeleton tattooed on his shoulder. He shimmies his shoulder up and down, making the bat fly. "I'm sure he could ink up a lesbian angel for you."

Something about the awkward flying tattooed bat finally relaxes me. I want to sink into a bubble with him—the same bubble we spun when we were young. Collette, the car, always facilitated that; looking through the windshield is like watching the world on TV. We Sunday-drive past children running through a sprinkler. A few doors down, a similar bunch chases each other in circles with water guns. A man washes his car. Another mows grass. Chris parks in a viewpoint lot near Black Creek, and the two of us stare at the rushing Niagara River. The water is the colour of a Tiffany's gift box, but dirty with silt chop and algae. In the winter, the river turns metallic black. Men in rubber waders rush in to fish for steelies before the ice forms. If a winter gets cold enough and lasts long enough, an ice bridge will form at Niagara Falls—seducing daredevil types to the brink. Niagara Falls seduces year round. Tightrope walkers and barrel jumpers and the suicidal.

I prefer the river to the lake. The river is always moving, always offering us stories. Lake Erie is famous for being so polluted it's dead. Its story is trash. Crystal Beach banks on trash.

A pair of inner tubers bob past us—girls in bikinis. After wordlessly watching the water for so long, the tubers look superimposed. Caricatures hollering as the river carries them. I used to do that, spend all day in my swimsuit. Chris was a strong swimmer too. Maybe the strongest in our school. "You still able to swim to Grand Island?" I ask.

"Only if Lemmy is tailing me." He reaches toward me, and I unwittingly lean into his hand. He pops open the glove compartment and pulls out two apple juice boxes. "Get your vitamin C," he says, passing me one. "Cleanses the liver, eh."

"Drinking boxes? What are you, a soccer mom now?" There's my tease. I smile at myself. Chris smiles too. Big perfect teeth. We slurp our apple juice, return to our silence.

"Maybe I turned out like you," he says so quietly I almost miss it.

"You grew boobs?" I whisper back. Memory fleshes out more of him, our whispered conversations of yesterday. If I could make the prattle absurd and light, if I spoke in just the right low tone, if I reacted with just the right amount of surprise and calm—then we'd really be talking. What I enjoyed most about him is that he dubbed me the keeper of his secrets. Is this why he was the only boy I ever really fell for? Do I have that right? Have I figured out love?

"Wrong," he whispers.

"You're a lesbian," I guess again.

"No. Ahhh ..." He slurps the last bit of his apple juice and tosses the empty drinking box in the back seat. "Getting warmer."

"Oh my god. You're gay?" He sharply turns away. I ruined our game, my voice way too loud, my reaction too big. "Does your mom know?"

"My mom has nothing to do with it, Star. God, neither. That's a white dude question. Only white faggots ask about my mom."

Gobsmacked, I don't know what to say. He turns red around his ears, embarrassed or pissed off. I think about getting out of his car. Hitchhiking my white ass back to The Point. In my head, I spell "Niagara Falls." N- I-A ... Breathe.

"Barbara doesn't know either," I say. "Doesn't know or more likely doesn't care."

"Big whoop. What does she care about? Barbara never was the Carol Brady type."

"Try more like Morticia Addams." *Meno male*! We're back to

teasing again. I tentatively ask, "So, what kinda guys do you like?"

"I'm not one to kiss and tell."

"Oh yeah? Is that how come the entire Sakokete family knows I owned underwear that read 'Sitting Pretty' across the butt?"

"It was my brother with the big mouth. How many times you gonna blame me?" He pokes me again. "Shit. Still holding a grudge." Then, back to a whisper, he says, "I don't mind goatees. And, like, bad hair, I guess, like Billy Idol hair." When he smiles widely, a familiar dimple appears on his right cheek.

"Like 'Rebel Yell' Billy Idol? Or 'Cradle of Love' Billy Idol?"

"What's the diff?"

"He grew his hair a little long in the back for the 'Cradle of Love' video. Sort of punk rock mullet."

"Mullet! No! Definitely 'Rebel Yell.'" Our laughter becomes easier.

"The three gays in our rinky-dink school all ended up dating each other," I say.

"There's more than three of us, believe me. But, yeah, treat her right, Star. It's slim pickings around here." He starts the car and edges back onto the Parkway in the direction of Crystal Beach. "Plus, she's a babe."

"I think she'd going to dump me. I mean, we're either going to move in together or break up."

"Whatcha do? Sleep with her friends?"

I suppose I deserve that. I paw the wrench lever beside me. The passenger-side window is already rolled down all the way. The car's not getting any airier. I tilt my head out for the breeze.

"She's an awesome girl, eh? You'd better get to work with whatever charms you got. Fake it if you have to."

"Mind dropping me off at The Point?" I ask. I've already laughed the few laughs I have left in me. My head pounds. Can I learn to like these headaches? Look forward to them like a pervert looks forward to a spanking, maybe?

Back in Crystal Beach, my nausea returns, three-fold. Bile fills my mouth before I can ask Chris to pull over. I lurch my head out the window and watch my vomit spray the back tire. Chris swears beside me, but curbs the car slow and gentle. I've created an emptiness for Etta to push her way inside. She stuffs my acrid mouth, claws her way down my throat. I yelp as she clamps down on my stomach, my cunt. She's weak and upset, like a wounded animal. Non-verbal—she speaks to me in the language of pain. My legs spasm into violent kicks. The glove compartment door pops open and a juice box falls into the seat well. Chris swears and yells louder. He's shaking me now, one hand on each of my shoulders. His perfect teeth move in slow motion. I will black out. I am cursed. I deserve this.

When my eyes return, I am staring at the funhouse mirror. My mouth is stretched like a ribbon, saying, "The angel may light the path, but we have to make an active choice to walk it," and "Each day is an opportunity to understand ourselves better," and "Pain is just like us, it's always changing. Pain is just like us, it's always changing. Pain is just like us."

Am I ripping quotes from *The Courage to Heal* in a half-conscious state? I suppose I can finally say I read those survivor books for a reason. Who knew the reason would be an amassment of salvation seekers? Etta's appalling light crowns my head. Amusement park souvenirs stockpile at my feet. Behind me, I don't feel body heat or breathing, only desire. He wants a second child—a son. He wants to quit his job. She wants to have sex again. She wants see the place of her grandmother. He wants things to go back to how they used to be. She wants to reach whatever is next, and reach it at a fever pitch. He wants to be forgiven. She wants to be forgiven. They want to be forgiven. They want their apologies to be seen as clearly as a late-summer moon. They want atonement, to feel like a bottle shot off a wooden fence—each target shattering with a sure-fire bang.

Mostly, there's the overpowering desire to know exactly what to desire. The desire for certainty. It is these very desires—to understand why and what they are—that I have the most compassion for. It is these desires that make me too hot like a panic attack. I want to turn and face this mountain of wanting. Not to conquer it, but to bow. To bow as low and small as I can. To disappear beneath it.

Etta's version of a bow isn't about humility, but rather adoration and encores. When I turn, there's Bobby, Hal, and Lucky, Dolores and Leanne, Joe and Howie, Moustache, Leanne and Rose, Chris and Wendel, Rahn and my mother—fuck me, my mother, *non lo credo*, my mother—I can't bow to them. Not to their pain or dignity or desire. I only tower and awe. Up, up I rise, over the horrified heads of onlookers, past the trampled lawn and gravel driveway. How far is she going to take me?

Etta sets me on the gazebo roof. She appears just for me, and I'm dazed. How could I forget how beautiful she is? Her right hand rests on my back. Her right hip meets my right hip. She steps forward and I step back. Together we twirl around and around on the rooftop, delirious. *We're gonna dance until our feet fall off, 'til we're not able to stand any longer. We're gonna dance until our hair falls out. We're gonna dance until our bones are ash.*

Later I dream about Chris Sakokete, or maybe he is really standing above my slack body. It's one of those dreams (or dissociative moments—same difference) where I can see both him and myself. He thrums his fingers against his jeans, thumbs tucked in his pockets. I lie like a cadaver in an anatomical theatre, which is apt as there are also onlookers crowding the cabin door and window. In the dream, or for real, Chris says, "Fuck you, Starla."

He says, "None of it is right."

He says, "If you can cut this shit out, then cut it. Because this shit is ... is ..."

He walks out, and I hope I'll dream of him again—his nice teeth, his Billy Idol lyrics, the stories he must have collected while I've been away—but I bet I won't. I hardly sleep these days anyway.

Onlookers push in through the cabin door. "Don't crowd her," someone shouts. This someone is Barbara. *Mama mia.* Did she come to save me? Mother protect me. I don't want all these people in here. Why are there so many? Don't let them touch me. Don't let them touch me. Don't let them.

Hands on my feet and legs. My hair. My stomach. My face. It's one of those dreams where I feel too much. Or it's for real, and I'm doing my best to be unconscious.

# 50 On Top of the World

W hat do we do with it?" Rose gestures at the cash spread across her kitchen table, along with unopened fan mail and every kind of keepsake from the amusement park imaginable. "Hire Starla a body guard?" Keychains and stuffed animals. Multi-coloured midway lighting fixtures. A scuffed red glitter bowling ball from the mini-bowling lane.

Bobby, who is re-counting twenties, belly laughs at the absurd abundance of it all. Leanne does too; she scoops the bowling ball up over her head and bellows like she's Godzilla about to throw a rock at King Kong. Lucky squeals, presumably delighting in the delirium alone.

"Four thousand, nine hundred and forty," announces Bobby. "Can you say that, Lucky, four thousand, nine hundred and forty? Four. Nine. Another four. And some zeros." He's been speaking fewer words lately, reverting to squeals, giggles, and shrieks.

"How many circles have we held?" asks Rose. "When was the first one? How long you figure people will keep coming?" Rose squints at *The Golden Girls* calendar beside the refrigerator, but she can't seem to make sense of the days and weeks. And no wonder; she's still got her calendar on June. It's July.

I brood over a Dell 320 laptop. The next big thing—a computer you can carry around. It's ingenious and only $1,099. I would totally write a book if I had that laptop.

"Ricky wanted fruit trees," Rose says, finally changing the month on the calendar. "He said we should grow our own food to prepare for the apocalypse." And just like that the funny money turns sad, a reminder of what could have been.

"He was a good kid," Hal tells her. "Handy. Mended the rabbit pens for me."

"He taught Lucky how to forage for puffball mushrooms. He still knows a puffball to see one, don't you Lucky?" Bobby says. "Can you say puffball mushroom?"

Ricky plus mushrooms plus money swamps my already soggy mind. I'm the only one who's read Ricky's journal, his many excerpts listing poisonous mushrooms and berries, followed by page upon page of suicidal ideation. Sometimes I almost hear these grisly excerpts read aloud from his journals, like I hear Etta. It's a voice that's almost mine and at the same time alien.

Lately, thoughts and feelings rapidly flood in, swell my already swollen skin. Each visitor brings their secrets, and each of the secrets Etta divulges chips away at the separation between me and others. I am now made of too many people. I hold knowledge that isn't mine. I've been given tender hopes and pivotal memories—and actually, these stories weren't even given to me. No, really. It's more like story just enters my body. Weights me. Waterlogged self. That's how I feel when I hear Hal mentally reciting the Serenity Prayer or Step Number 2 of the 12 Steps: I believe a Power Greater Than Myself will restore me to sanity. I can hear the same looping hold-on music that Bobby hears when she calls the Federal Identity Program office. I hear Lucky asking "why" all the time. His vocalization may be toddler babble, but his inner thoughts are all "whys." Why are there so many people here? and Why is it so noisy/busy/scary?

This very moment, I know that Leanne is thinking about where she's going to live next. She left her husband—a move prompted by the angel—and has been crashing in Dolores's Winnebago for the last week. Her presence is marked by the arrival of a Panasonic RX 6400—the mother of all boom boxes—and an ongoing soundtrack of Canadian rock. "Rise Up" by the Parachute Club and Jeff Healey's "Angel Eyes" on repeat. Music soothes. She wants to move to The Point permanently. I recognize her attachment to this place. It's getting harder and harder for her to drive the bus. It stings to head in the opposite direction from Etta—a sting I share.

Right now, I have boxes and luggage stored under the cabin's cot, a few more piled in Rose's laundry room. I tell myself it's temporary, while Tamara and I find a place. Truth is that I can't leave Etta. Now I get a headache if I travel any farther than Derby Road. I haven't called to inquire about any of the rentals listed in the local paper. Nor have I told Tamara that I moved my belongings here.

I hand Leanne the *Auto Trader* as she heads out to work in her customary bus driving uniform—a rock T-shirt and cut-off jean shorts. I've circled single-occupancy trailers in red pen. I remind myself I'm searching for Leanne, but, admittedly, I'd like to get a trailer too. I could park it right beside the gazebo. "Check out the single wide with a roll-out Florida room. Looks comfy."

"I suppose I should buy now while the economy's shit and the snowbirds are selling. I could always resell in a year or two when things are better." Leanne squints, holds the paper close to her nose. Mother Mary, please say the town bus driver isn't developing a vision problem.

"Were you thinking about giving money to Leanne?" asks Hal. "For a down payment?" The money becomes less funny again.

Bobby backs her chair away from the table as if touching the bills alone is stressful. "We should start a whatchamacallit for Lucky," she says.

"A trust fund," I say.

"Yes, A trust fund."

I think "Laptop computer or New York City?" then, "I could bring my new laptop to New York City." I want to stuff the money in my bra and run. If I ran now, I could eat a late dinner of *frisee aux lardons* and a poached egg at The Odeon in Tribeca while making eyes across the restaurant at some up-and-coming indie filmmaker. I could smoke clove cigarettes outside of CGCBs waiting for a Gorilla Biscuit concert or some other hardcore mess. By one a.m., I'd be fucking a thrasher bitch in the filthy, graffiti-ravaged bathroom.

"We oughta pay Rose back for the salvaged boat wood. That was a lot of cash to put up front," says Hal. Rose raises her hand to stop him, her face pained. It's too late, he's unwittingly dragged her into the money debate.

"Lucky is the closest thing Rose will have to a grandkid, right, Rose? Who else are you going to give your money to?" Bobby says.

"Fuckin' hell, Bobby," snaps Hal. "A minute ago we was talking 'bout her dead son. Show some respect."

"Fuckin' hell, Bobby," Lucky parrots.

Bobby starts in on Hal with her customary hosing. "How many times have I told you not to swear? I'm trying to give our kid a better life here, and you can't even clean up your language." Lucky scoots into Rose's lap, yowling his three-year-old tearless cries. Leanne sneaks out the door and across the lawn to her bus. My gaze trails her. Already crowds wander the grounds. Some carry bouquets and others carry cameras. Some have reserved campsites and others look like they just came from church.

Rose's phone rings, and Bobby flies to answer it. She spits a few last insults at Hal before switching to her telephone voice. "Hello. Roberta Varin speaking."

Our money argument completely halts, all of us knowing that the "fucking government" said they'd get back to Bobby "any day now." She grunts out a series of uh-huhs before holding the receiver in my direction. "You wanna talk to a nut job calls himself Dr Jaguar Tongue?"

"How do these people get my number?" Rose complains as I take the call.

"Are you excellent?" Dr Jaguar Tongue asks in place of a greeting. What is his question exactly? Do I perceive myself to be excellent overall, like, am I a high-quality human being? Or is this his own peculiar way of asking, "How are you?"

"Beautiful land you've got here," he continues.

Bobby returns to the money, stacking the bills Queen's heads facing up. Rose puts a second Moka Pot on the stove. Lucky slinks off to the living room and turns on late-morning cartoons. I glance around the corner to see *He-Man and the Masters of the Universe*, then turn away from the television before I get sucked into its fantastically easy good-versus-evil entertainment. Hal shuffles out the door looking hunched like the old man he is, and then bounds back in again frantically wielding *The Fort Erie Times* in the air.

Dr Jaguar Tongue goes on, "I'm sure I'm close. So much energy—"

The front page of the newspaper reads, "Angel Craze in Crystal Beach."

"Mister, uh, Jaguar," I interrupt, overwhelmed. "Tell me what you want."

"Ah. Wow. The gift of a direct question," says Dr Jaguar Tongue. "We got lost trying to find you. Can't ask the path to be straight. We're calling from a payphone outside a country music bar. The Roadhouse—do you know it? Any directions you can give me would be cool."

"Who knows driving directions from Netherby Road?" I turn the phone over to Hal, who seems grateful to be called away from Bobby's continued death stare.

"This money is nothing worth fighting over," I say to her. "We got people calling from lord only knows where. You want money, Bobby? I'll get us money. Starting today, we make anyone who comes to the circle pay a mandatory entrance fee." I swish the back of my hand across a neatly stacked pile of bills as if it's nothing.

"The angel's love can't be monetized," Hal says, not even bothering to cup his hand over the receiver. Again, I'm thrown off by simultaneous conversations. I wonder what I'm not hearing through all the noise. Like Hal—is he sad? He looks sad, like one of those shrunken apple dolls. I should find a moment to check in with him.

"Where'd you learn the word 'monetized,' Hal?" asks Bobby. "I didn't figure you for putting three syllables together."

Rose bangs the fresh coffee on the table. Her movements are drawn out, languid. It's not just me—we're all losing sleep, losing weight, losing words, losing context, and losing time. "The angel says we're to stick together. You can stay here and fight if you want, but I'm going out there with Starla," she says.

On cue, the gathering of people cheer as Rose and I make our way to the shrine. The crush of their voices practically shoves me forward. Howie Foster thrusts a cassette recorder in my face, asking for a quote. One visitor sweeps a camcorder in a wide circle, taking a panorama shot. Bobby runs after us, the wooden donation box rattling in her hands.

*Smile. Show them your pearly whites*, Etta instructs me. My gate stiffens as I spot Tamara and her mother waiting on the shrine's steps.

"I couldn't keep her away," Tamara grabs my arm. "I hope today's not freaky. She's got pretty bad nerves. Can you not be freaky, Star?" Tamara's mother waves a timid wave, her elbow hugged close to her body, wrist barely moving. Barbara would never wave modestly like that, I think. If Barbara were here, she'd probably be loudly telling the crowd something to embarrass me, like at what age I got my period. It certainly would not be the first time she publically pronounced me a "late bloomer." But Barbara would never take a day off work for me. Not even if I'm performing goddamn miracles. Literally. She'd never lose a day's pay.

"Welcome," I say, clearing my thoughts, smiling as Etta advised. "We are strong in numbers today. I'm going to ask that each of you support this gathering, this blessed gathering, with a donation."

*You sound a lot like me, back when I used to hustle the fellas,* says Etta. *Donation is what I called my fee too.* Etta ups the ante by stirring a tiny cyclone in the centre of the shrine. Her invisible hand tosses the flowers and Park memorabilia set on the altar—flyers and ride tickets—flying. The crowd grows stone cold. She grounds the collection and people quietly open their pocketbooks.

"Who is here for the first time? Don't be shy. We only want to welcome you." At least fifty hands float up, many I recognize from riding the bus or grocery shopping in town. Etta overloads me with their stories. *He's holding unsigned divorce papers. She is adopted and looking for her birth parents. She is waiting for the results of an HIV test. He's a widower—*

*I can't do this*, I tell her.

*You already* are *doing it*, Etta reminds me.

"And who has been to one of our circles before? I know who you are. But raise your hands up and let the newcomers see you." I look for Tamara, Rose, Bobby, Hal, and Lucky. I want to know exactly where they are in the crowd. Another two dozen hands also float up. Can that be right? This many regulars? Becky McPhee and Dolores's co-workers from the hospital, Marge and Dolly I know well. But the other faces. Some of them are my age. Old high school classmates?

Why don't I recognize them? *Etta, I'm losing it.*

*Whatever you've lost, I'll find for ya later. Go on.*

"I'm going to ask each of you to choose an object from the altar," I say, adopting my deep, drawling otherworldly intonation. The gathering hesitates as I gesture encouragingly to the now flightless items amassed on the altar. "Don't be afraid. These things have power, yes, but you may also find them wonderfully familiar."

*There's my girl. Get the Park in their hands. Power them up.*

"It's all stuff from Crystal Beach," Howie says, picking an old postcard from the pile.

"Hey, check out this blank payroll cheque. God, I miss getting these cheerful orange cheques every other week," says the woman next to Tamara's mom. She has frosted blonde feathered hair, like Angela Bower from *Who's the Boss*. Wisps of this woman's bangs sway with her bobbing head. "I worked at the Floss Stand next to the Magic Carpet ride for eight seasons. My grandmother was a secretary in the Hall's main office. My grandpa, too. He started as a garbage picker, then when he turned sixteen, he got to work rides. He told the same stories about the Park for years. A real broken record. Most of my family earned a living at the Park at one time or another."

A round of "Me toos" echoes through the crowd.

"When the Park died—does that sound dumb?—it was like watching my grandpa die all over again. The Park was dying right before our eyes and there was nothing we could do about it. I didn't realize how depressed it got me. Here we are, the first summer without it and I feel like I've already forgotten so much, like these silly orange paycheques. There used to be thousands of people here. Everybody loved us. If you were from the Beach, everybody was your friend. Now you walk along the shore, and it's like the Park was never there. Nothing but an empty lot."

Another round of "Yes" and "It's true."

"It's nice to be around people. I haven't been in a crowd since the park closed. You get used to being a big deal. Now, I guess I'm pretty lonely."

*Vanessa Wilson is her name,* Etta tells me. *Several Wilsons worked the Park, all right. See if her grandpa's name was Cecil.*

She shepherds me toward the funhouse mirror. I jerk, like I might shake her unseen elbow off me. *Don't push. I know the way.* The crowd gasps as I move into place in the wheelhouse. They know it's show time. A chilling thought occurs to me: What if they don't grow tired of this? What if more come, and more, and all of them want the funhouse mirror? What if I'm trapped in this warped, continual shock for infinity? What if I watch myself grow old in front of this funhouse mirror?

My vision blurs and swells as Etta pushes her way inside, but still my eyes are clear enough to spot the strange couple circling the shrine. Are they part of my vision? The man is dressed like Clint Eastwood in a spaghetti western—a Navajo poncho and straw cowboy hat. The woman prances through the lawn in what looks to be an embroidered Mexican dress and bare feet. A large cassette recorder is strapped over the woman's shoulder; she points a microphone in my direction. The man holds a type of large, boxy camera I've never seen before. They must be the ones who called this morning. The "excellent" ones who got lost.

*You gonna let me in?* Etta complains. *Audience is waiting. Vanessa Wilson, remember her?*

"Grandpa's hands were old leather spun with blue veins. Your grandfather worked outside all his life," Etta and I synchronically moan. "If he'd been a more ambitious man, he might have been a singer in a country quartet. But he hated people looking at him. Shy Guy Cecil Gunn, he earned his nickname. He could barely stand up at his own wedding. Only a handful of people ever heard that beautiful voice. You were one of the lucky few, Vanessa. You were the apple of his eye. When you were little, he used to take you on the sky ride. The blue gondola was your favourite. And on a windy day, high above the lake, he'd sing. He's sing just for you." Etta is cruelest when she makes me sing. When she swings my limbs around or pushes, she feels like compressed air. Forceful, but still just air. As she tangles into my voice, I asphyxiate.

Vanessa begins to cry, and soon others are weeping too. Some clap their hands. I see that strange camera near my face. Flash bulb. Flash bulb. The microphone juts closer. By now I've gotten to know the distinct screams of the regular circle visitors. Tamara is who I hear before I smash into the floor.

# 51 Glorious

I wake up tucked into the cabin cot next to Tamara, but it's not her heavy sleeping arm that holds me. Etta's weight is a strange density, and I may never get up. Through the open window, the night sky crackles like lightning. The air is too still, and the crickets are too loud for rain.

*Are you making those lights?*

*Not me. My hands are kinda occupied.*

My cunt spasms. The convulsion plugs me deeper into her. We could be in the past, only a couple of short months ago, when it was just the two of us carrying fear and fascination between us, our *magnus essentias*. I heel into her divine hands, her perfect and horrifying dead hands. Laying beside her is to pray. Like holding the swathe of light from Veronica's rose-coloured glass lips in Saint George's Church on a particularly glorious Sunday. Poetry. Like reading Joy Harjo or Bronwen Wallace or Sharon Olds one careful line at a time. Then reading the poem backward, last line to first, to find the meaning hidden outside of chronology. Like racing tipsy down the station stairs in platform heels to barely catch the last subway of the night as the other drunks on the subway car nod, wordlessly celebrating the fleeting victory. Like listening to Yma Sumac or Freddie Mercury hit those holy high notes. Like when a preposterously gorgeous stranger asks you to light her cigarette. Like standing before a Lynda Benglis or Roni Horn sculpture and being hypnotized by all that burnished gold. Like the centre of a panic attack when the most catastrophically terrible possibility seems quite plausible. Like waiting at the grocery checkout to see if my credit card will be approved.

Like when Tamara—my flesh and blood love—fell fast asleep with her head in my lap and, dreaming, muttered the words, "It's a good snake. Don't kill it."

Like when I came upon Bobby and Lucky singing "You Are My Sunshine" together, and they replaced every "you" in the song with Lucky's name: "Lucky is my sunshine, my only sunshine." And I realized there is so much more to mothers and children than I personally understand.

Etta locks my arms behind my back. *You give me life. You give me twenty lives, fifty. I never felt so much, not even was I was living. I never dreamed this big, not even when I was breathing. You feel it too? Don't it feel good? You gonna cry out my name? Tell me you've saved some of that grind show voice for our love?*

Tamara shakes me. She thinks I'm moaning in my sleep. "It's a bad dream, Star. You're safe. You're here with me." I pull her into a kiss. She coos out comforts as her lips dampen both my cheeks. She tucks the quilt back over me. "This cabin gives me the creeps. Tomorrow, we'll start looking for an apartment," she says. "And we'll buy a bed. A brand-new bed."

# 52 Cancellami Means Cut Me Out

Outside, the flower child with the cassette recorder is spread on the grass reading a paperback copy of Timothy Leary's *Flashbacks: A Personal History of a Cultural Era*. I'm so glad to not be her. Several feet away, Lucky perches in the grass, deadheading red clover and tossing the flowers in her general direction.

Hal and Dr Jaguar Tongue sit across from each other at Rose's picnic table. They inspect an album of photographs. "Mornin', sleepy heads. I thought you'd never wake up." Hal waves us over to his side of the table. "You gotta look at Jaguar's photos." Jaguar smells unmistakably of Nag Champa. He wears a long white lace vest with shorty-short jean cut-offs. I marvel at the uniformity of his tan. His hair is the exact golden hue as his skin. Rose looks him up and down as she brings us coffee. I wonder if she's into muscles, young Fabio Lanzoni types, right off the cover of a drugstore romance novel. Fucking eh, Rose. When was the last time she had sex?

"Life's a beach," Jaguar reads the slogan from the one-inch Crystal Beach Park button I wear on my denim tank dress. "Cool. Cool. We say that on Centre Island too." He flips through the pages of the photo album. "Most paranormal photos are nothing more than mist or smoke. Here's how early-morning mist appears in a photograph. Easily mistaken for a ghost by the untrained eye. And here is an example of cigarette smoke."

He shows us a photo of two women standing toe to toe with a drab nimbus floating between them. The photo is intimate, neither of them aware of the camera. They look like they're telling each other a secret.

"Our angel ain't smoke," says Hal.

"True. Smoke doesn't switch lights on and off. And smoke won't set off one of these." Jaguar passes Tamara a small black device with two knobs on the top.

"EMF," she reads the letters embossed on the device. "Electromagnetic ...?"

"Electromagnetic Field Meter." He shifts a little closer to Tamara on the picnic bench. Am I going to have to keep an eye on this guy? As if I don't already have enough to do. "I track real spiritual energy by finding anomalies in the visible world. Light holes. Vortexes. Orbs. My specialized shamanistic abilities allow me to sense these anomalies through the mind's eye. That's my gift. For everyone else, I track electromagnetism, psychotronics, thermographic energy, and, as you can see, I take a lot of photos."

"How'd you find this kinda job?" asks Hal. "And where do all these thingy-ma-jiggers come from?"

"It's a shaman's calling to identify energy potential," Jaguar says slowly, putting his manly naked arm around Hal as if he were a child. "And more importantly, it's my job to ensure that these energies are in balance. The machines are tools, like a wrench in the hands of a skilled carpenter ..." Jaguar carries on. "I measure energy potential by the spirit's ability to affect the visible world ... " Hal's attention is locked. " ... Spirits appear for one of three reasons. One, being vengeance ..."

Hal silently shakes his head "yes" and also "no." He's having a hard time placing his angel into one of Jaguar's three categories.

"All this fancy stuff ain't much use to me," says Hal. "God as my witness, she's an angel."

"She might be. Out of the ninety-six photos I took—"

"Ninety-six!" I snap. "How'd you even get prints so fast?"

Hal pats my hand in a 'there, there, calm down' kind of way. "Ya seen Jaguar's campsite? It's like NASA over there."

"Out of the ninety-six photos I took," Jaguar continues, "an anomaly appears in ninety-four. Here's a series of you leading last night's circle," he says, shifting a stack of photos from the bench to the table. "A light hole or orb always appears over your shoulder. Excellent circle, by the way. Healing, sister, it's our path. I could teach you to really hone those gifts."

Tamara picks up an eight-by-ten and wordlessly hands it to me. "Yes. Here you two are walking around the quarry last night with light constantly hanging between you both."

*Tell me there's one photo, just one is all I ask, where I look like myself,* says Etta. She pokes my chest through the Crystal Beach button. *No one sees me. No one except you.*

I search through the photos more furiously than I'd like to. I don't want Jaguar to think I'm his new biggest fan. But like Etta, I need to see her image. See her manifest somewhere besides in my own comprehension. I need more proof of her being. I need proof.

To my left, Tamara fidgets in her skin. She's scratching the underside of her jaw, and I'm watching pink heat spread under her aqua-painted fingernails. It occurs to me that she never asked to be photographed. She hates being photographed—or at least I know she hates when men try to sneak photos of her at the club. These photos of us should be ours. I want the negatives. "The light intensifies whenever you're with the little boy over there," continues Jaguar. "Here's one of you standing side by side. See how the light anomalies intensify? Excellent light striations across the whole image. But the strongest anomaly is of you tucking him into bed. I sent a copy of this one up to my buddy at *Spiritual Truth News.*"

"Wait! Wait. The circle is one thing. I can't control all the cameras there. But these others, these are private moments. Private photos."

"Photos are never private, Starla," says Jaguar. "We're not private property. I've paid to be here. Like Disneyland."

"Yes, but this one is shot through the window of Bobby and Hal's trailer. How is that not private property?" Fuck. What did those art school brats teach me about photos and the law? What if Jaguar is right? "Lucky is a kid," I give it another shot. "You need permission from a parent. Bobby would never let you send out pictures of her boy."

The awful pregnant pause is forewarning. Tamara squeezes my thigh, hard. Hal confirms what I am afraid of. "I gave permission."

I try to rewind the last twenty-four hours. What private moments might Jaguar have caught on camera? Tamara asks, "Why, Hal? Why would you give permission for someone to peep through your windows?"

The word "peep" bewilders me. I hope one day I can not have to think about something unwanted coming into my childhood bedroom, something unwanted seeing me while I sleep. Taking something from me. From me. From Lucky.

"Come on, Hal," is all I manage to say. I hate myself.

"He's my boy, too, dammit," Hal huffs, then immediately softens. "Folks wantin' the truth. The almighty truth. Yer not the only one who talks to her. Lucky hears her too. He's a visionary, and I ain't keepin' it a secret. Miracles ain't meant ta be secrets."

I concentrate on Etta. My mind aches and stretches like a hand in the dark, feeling her out. *Etta, this guy's not a friend. He's here to fuck us up. Can't you do something to scare him off?*

It's not Etta, but Bobby and Dolores who intervene. "We being documented?" Dolores says, tapping her finger against a photo of her and Bobby in the circle. Both wear sour faces. "Hal, you coming for the meeting?"

"What meeting?" Jaguar asks. Dolores means the AA meeting, but she ignores his question.

Hal shuffles on the picnic bench for a second before declining. He leans over the pile of photos, laying his elbows across the table. "Jaguar and I ain't through talkin' yet."

"Well, I'm going," Bobby tells him. "I'm going, and I don't even got a drinking problem. Trying to be supportive, like I always do, hey, Hal? Anyway, Dolores is taking me to the Friendship Centre after to meet somebody. Lucky will want hot dogs and carrot sticks and dip. And make sure he washes his hands."

"Bobby doesn't know about the photographs, does she?" I say. Hal shrugs.

"Hal, you can't fucking hide it from her." I grab the photos of Lucky in his bed and bolt up from the picnic table. Tamara is already running after Dolores and Bobby asking them to wait.

"I'm going with or without Hal," Bobby barks at Tamara. Now all four of us—Tamara, Hal, Jaguar, and I—are speeding up the driveway. Bobby sighs at us. "You can't survive without me for an afternoon? I'm going to meet a lady who got reunited with her sisters. She says she'll talk to me, eh? Everybody's gotta know everybody's business round here. I'm working my own problems out, like always. So don't come running after us, slowing us down."

"She's going to talk to you about dealing with the fucking CFS?" I ask, holding the photographs behind my back.

"Yes, Sherlock. Now can I go?"

Tamara kicks me as Dolores and Bobby drive away.

"Hal, either you tell her or I will," I say. Hal clasps his palms together. He looks as if he is counting down from ten to keep from shouting at me. "Think about it. What's it going to be like if she finds out from someone else, eh? What if one of her friends calls her up because she saw it in a newspaper? How's that going to play out?"

"If it runs in a paper, then everyone sees our angel. That's a good thing. Bobby will be happy."

"Bobby doesn't even believe in the angel," says Tamara. "Neither do I. Neither does Dolores. I'm sorry, Hal, I know you want your 'angel,' but this thing is way more complicated."

"Smart women see complexities. Indian women are the visionaries of our age," says Jaguar. I smell the odour of his hippie perfume as he steps his long golden body closer to us.

Tamara smiles sweetly at him with the same smile that she uses at the strip club. She leans close to Jaguar and says, "Fuck you and the Porsche you rode in on."

I follow her cue and storm off toward Rose's house. "You kick ass," I whisper to her.

"You don't need a fake angel to speak up, you know," she replies.

"Shit, Tamara. I *was* speaking up. I was the one who told that prick he couldn't have the photos. Don't come after me."

"Who should I come after then? If it wasn't for you, pricks like him would never be snooping around here in the first place." Something in her shifts as she turns to face me, clear and foreboding as the smoke in Jaguar's photographs. We both pause, waiting for this something to take further shape. We are one word, one syllable, away from our first big fight.

"Yeah, if it wasn't for me, Hal would still be drinking, Leanne would still be getting beatings from her husband, and Rose would be losing money on this shitty campground."

"Well, thank god you came back to save us all." Tamara looks at me with such pity and disdain. I should have a response for her.

344

Say something to blow away the smoke between us. Instead, I close my eyes. I hear the screen door to Rose's house slam as Tamara goes inside. I keep my eyes shut. I can hear Rose asking Tamara what's wrong.

So much is wrong. Isn't it? *Etta, make me faint. Make this moment grow dark.* Cancellami.

# 53 Martyr

Rose and Lucky enter the cabin with Father Mario from Saint George's. My whole body smells like armpits. The priest holds folded copies of a half a dozen or so newspapers in one hand and a steaming mug of Rose's coffee in the other. He doesn't remove his *cappello romano* in the cabin, which is far better than if he took it off and placed it on the bed. Priests get to wear their hats indoors. I like to imagine priests never ever take off their hats or any vestments. That they are action figures with their cassocks and linens forever molded to their bodies.

Father Mario's *cappello romano* means business. It's like the Catholic version of a squad uniform—designed to intimidate. I bet he just wears jeans and a clerical collar on most outings.

"Was I out for long?" I ask Rose.

She holds up all ten fingers, flashes them twice.

"What? Twenty hours?"

"Yes, and your mother came. I told her you need sleep whenever you can get it and not to disturb you."

"My ma!?"

"I gave you water. You were thirsty." Lucky holds up a green plastic water gun. Bless his sweet little head, I'm so grateful I can't remember him shoving a toy gun in my mouth.

The front page of the *Simco Reformer* reads, "Angel's Light Cured my Carotid Artery Disease." Father Mario gingerly holds the front page up for me, holding the curled corners taut. I wonder if Barbara has read the same headline. They must get the *Simco Reformer* at the library.

The next paper, the *Tonawanda News,* has a pullquote as a headline that reads, "I Swear I Saw Hell on Earth. Pure Evil." Well, no one here reads the Tonawanda paper, I assure myself.

"Do you read the papers?" Father Mario asks me.

"The *Fort Erie Times*, yes. Otherwise, I don't care for the tabloids," I lie.

"A Mr Carl Redding from Simco claims that he witnessed 'a blinding heavenly light.' He goes on to recommend that 'other people should see the angel. She's a sign that there's still hope in the world for us.'" Father Mario has read the article several times, I guess, seeing the trail of pencil-mark asterisks he's made. "Do you believe he's been cured of carotid artery disease?"

"I'm not a doctor," I say. In fact, lying sweaty and bloated in this cot, I've probably never looked more like a hospital patient in my life, even when I've been at the hospital. "And even if I were, I haven't examined Mr Carl Redding from Simco."

Rose briskly opens the cabin's curtains. I'm the only one who shields my eyes from the sudden glaring sunlight. I think I hear a bird. How long has it been since I've heard a bird? My mind has been so noisy.

"Do you believe that anyone has been cured?"

"I'm not in the business of curing illnesses, Father. I was raised Roman Catholic, so I believe in both kinds of healing—science and prayer—just like any other Roman Catholic. I chose Ermina as my confirmation name, modelled my faith after Saint Richard Ermino Pampuri of the Hospital Orders. I'm all about medicine. Not practicing it. Using it, I mean. Antibiotics mostly. You don't want to know how many bladder infections I've had."

What the heck am I saying? I am incredibly lucid and articulate for waking up after two days' sleep. I wonder where Tamara is. Is she mad at me? "I used to think I was being punished for all that pre-marital sex," I blurt. Damn. Do I want to embarrass the priest before he embarrasses me? "That's what church taught me. But no. Science tells me it's about bacteria. Thank god for science."

An awkward pause dogs the room. Did I win this conversation? Father Mario traces his thumb along the rim of the coffee mug, testing its temperature. Still too hot, I assume, as he withdraws, his left hand returning to a neatly cradled position.

To end the silence, or to join in the antics, Rose says, "Starla, I'm surprised you chose a male saint."

"I was raised Catholic. I had to find feminism. Plus, I was only, like, fourteen when I confirmed. Cut me some slack." Laughing, I try to sit up. Rose and Lucky rush bedside to help me. Lucky tugs my arms. Rose's hand is firm on my back. I'm not only Etta's rag doll, I'm limp in everyone's arms.

"Saint Richard Pampuri is hardly a popular saint with the youth," says Father Mario. If I'm offending him, his tone and body language don't show it.

"Yes, but he was beatified in 1981. That's the year I was confirmed—at your church, actually."

"Yes, forgive me. I did not expect you to be a Catholic, much less a member of my congregation. I've only served at Saint George's for a year." He finally takes his first sip of coffee.

"You'll know my mother then, Barbara Martin. Curvy brunette. Loud singer. She's been going to Saint George's forever. Ever since Father James was the priest." Again, Rose briskly moves around the cabin, this time sweeping a cobweb from under Ricky's lamp. Father Mario and I both turn toward her as she continues dusting the desk with her bare hand. "Anyway, Barbara always sits at the end of the second pew," I tell him. "Closest to the Station Six stained-glass window. Veronica wipes the face of Jesus."

Father Mario's eyebrows rise in recognition. I've always been amazed by aging men whose eyebrows remain thick and black while the hair on their heads thins and greys.

"You came today because you think it's not right that devotion and miracles and whatever are taking place outside the church? I'm surprised it took you so long. Most supernatural phenomenon are debunked by the local priest within a few days."

"Is that so?"

"Sure. I've read about Our Lady of Guadalupe, and Fátima too."

"Ah, wonderful. Then surely you know the reason I have come." Father Mario places the coffee cup on the desk beside his newspapers and leans in. "You know then that the prelates of Mexico City did not believe Juan Diego's visions for some time, as you were saying. And in Fátima, the three shepherd children were subject to all sorts of criticism and ridicule. The town's mayor even went as far as to imprison the children and threaten to boil them in oil if they didn't renounce their visions. And as we speak, the Marian apparitions in Medjugorje, Yugoslavia, are under a third investigation by the Vatican commission. Those teenage visionaries have faced every kind of torment from skeptics around the world. Their little village has been turned inside out. They are all willing to suffer, even die for what they believed

"I'm an old man, and an older priest, if that makes any sense to you. I am well aware that sinful thoughts and even the occasional sinful action happen within the physical walls of the church." Father Mario notices his mug leaks a coffee ring. A small trace of brown liquid bleeds into the newsprint. He retrieves the paper and folds it in half.

"In turn, I've humbly witnessed acts of God outside of the church many, many times. When human beings do incredibly loving things for each other, it strikes me as angelic or godly. The holy spirit works through us all, everyday, everywhere. But what I believe is hardly of consequence. It's what you believe that will be tested."

"She already is tested," snaps Rose. "Look at her. You think she looks healthy? You think we don't know about suffering?"

"The Diocese of Hamilton is already discussing your alleged miracles," says Father Mario. "I would be very happy to report to the Diocese that there is 'nothing to see here' as they say. It would spare you and everyone a lot of trouble." With that forewarning, he turns to say goodbye to Rose and Lucky. Rose practically rushes to the cabin door to see him off.

"Wait," I say. "You only asked me about the healings. Aren't you gonna ask me if I'm pure evil, like it says in that other paper?"

"No. Better not to ask about evil. As I've said, I'm an old priest. I am curious, though." He lingers in the doorway. "Does your angel have a message?"

"Yeah. She says the amusement park is sacred." Again, the priest's black eyebrows touch in the centre of his scrunched forehead. "You ever visit our recently defunct amusement park, Father Mario?" I ask.

"Well, there is some debate as to whether it's appropriate for men of the cloth to patronize amusement parks, discos, race tracks, casinos and the like. But, yes, I did go to the Park a couple times in its last season. I liked the Ferris wheel, and that funny mechanical clown, what was her name?"

"Laughing Sal," says Rose.

"Yes, Laughing Sal. I hope she was adopted by a museum some-where. Things that joyful should not be thrown out."

We watch Father Mario walk across the lawn in his head-to-toe black vestments through the crowd of summer-dressed visitors, and then past the tree line. I bet he walked here in the midday heat. I bet he whistles as he walks. "Rock of Ages" all the way.

After he is gone, Rose shoos Lucky outside too. She passes me her glass. I taste a Limoncello Tom Collins. Too sweet. Undissolved brown sugar muds the bottom of the glass.

"*Grazie*," I say, passing the drink back her.

"*Alla salute.*" Rose raises her drink in the air. She sips, silently appreciates, and sips again. "I had Ricky baptized. That's the least I could do. And I sent him to Our Lady of Grace because everyone knows it's a better school than Bertie Public. Then, all his school buddies were altar boys, and kids, they have to do everything their friends do."

My gaze softens. Rose is going to reveal something to me. Where's Etta? I wish Rose would pass her glass back to me. I want another boozy sip.

"Anything he wanted, I let him do. I helped him do it. I learned all about the lives of the saints, read the Bible, helped him study to be an altar boy. He's my only son. Mama's boy."

I swear I can feel my blood sugar dropping by the minute. I'm so thirsty. *Etta, where are you?* I reach for my neck and the pendant is gone. Removed while I was sleeping.

"When I was a younger, I was grateful I had a boy. A thousand unthinkable things can happen to a little girl. What's there to do with a boy but spoil him? Boys are supposed to just grow up. No fuss, no worry. Until they become men. Then they make their own problems. I'm not saying it's fair, but it is what I wished for Ricky. For him to grow up, happy and spoiled, until he got old enough to make his own problems."

Rose empties her drink. She triple-bangs her tumbler down.

"Did something happen to your Ricky, Rose?" I say softly. "When he was a boy?" Rose sits on the wooden stool beside the desk. She reaches for me. Her hand has shrunk since the first time we briefly held hands at my job interview. The gold rings she wears are looser now. Gemstones droop to the left or the right under her wrinkled knuckles. I wonder if I should disclose my own abuse. I wonder if I should cook her something fatty to eat—Alfredo sauce with double cream and butter. I wonder if I've done anything but fuck with her sanity.

*Etta? Etta! Etta, are you hurting her? Am I?* The painting behind me is gone. I flinch when I notice its absence.

"I took it down when Father Mario told me he was coming. I didn't think Ricky would want a priest to see it. All those naked body bits. See me? I am still thinking about what Ricky wants. That monstrosity outside—that gazebo we built—I said 'yes' for Ricky. Still trying to raise a mama's boy. But look what I got instead. *Buonanotte al secchio.*"

"Goodnight in a bucket? *Che cosa vuol dire?*"

"It means the bucket has fallen. The milk has spilled. And there is no way to get it back."

I wait for her to cry one of her magnificent cries, but she doesn't. It occurs to me that crying and screaming are really good at filling silences. There's no silence left in life. Except now.

"He loved your cooking, Rose." There's not a hint of affect in my voice. No Etta. I'm only telling her what I know. "Your tortellini in brodo was his favourite. He said you never bought tortellini at the store. You made them by hand so that you could put an extra pinch of nutmeg in the filling." I start crying, hoping Rose will too. Immediately, I recognize the emotion as uncontrollable, convulsive. I want to press my forehead against the wall, against the spot where Ricky's painting is supposed to be, but I don't dare turn away from Rose.

"Did the angel tell you that? I've been waiting for her to bring me another message."

Regret crying is far, far worse than crying over something someone else did to you. Pain can be fine, if there's someone to blame. Regret is downright sickening. Like fever-ache sickening. Sick coming out of both ends. Maybe worse than Etta's sick. How many ways are there to be sick? I need to come up with more words to describe illness.

Where should my confession begin? Do I tell her that Ricky's journals sit inside the nearby trunk? The angel is a phoney? Tamara, Bobby, and Dolores already know this. Ricky was once being haunted by the same ghost that now guides me—is that the right confession? Rose is edging toward me. She touches the top of my head, motherly. I can't. I can't let her comfort me. I don't deserve her kindness.

"Rose. I have something to tell you. You should sit back down."

# 54 Lost and Found

Tamara is the only one who comes to the evening circle, and she brings her bitch face with her. I am surprised to see her show up at all and more surprised still at the slam-bang way she lights the candles and sets the cut flowers on the altar. She bends a few dahlia stems and leaves their cheerful fat pink heads bowing downward. Who knew she was the passive-aggressive type? She's usually so straightforward. Although, with a crowd of apparition seekers around us, there's hardly space for us to talk.

Bobby has joined Hal and Moustache in Rose's house to do childcare for the sweeping brood that showed up with the masses of local parents. Maybe Hal has told Bobby about Jaguar's photographs of Lucky. Maybe he feels as shitty as I do after telling Rose the truth.

Rose patrols around the gazebo a few times. I practically hold my breath watching her, but she doesn't come into the circle.

Leanne's driving the final bus loop from Fort Erie. Dolores is at the hospital, working.

I don't recognize most of the faces around me.

*I'm alone*, I say to Etta. *And exhausted. Let's take one night off.*

*You're never alone. We're a duo, and our audience awaits.*

Tamara hatefully handles the Crystal Beach memorabilia. Instead of fanning the postcards out like a poker dealer she makes a protest of dropping them to randomly scatter across the floor, then walking on them as she takes a seat. Etta hisses her disapproval in my throat, a growl that hushes the crowd. The postcards float up and hang in the air—suspended long enough for the people in the inner circle to all witness—before they settle. Dr Jaguar Tongue pushes his way to the front with his camera. He slides his long, tan body into the tight spot beside Tamara, and her unbelievably bitchy face grows even more irked.

If Jaguar's camera can indeed capture ghosts, the forthcoming photos will show Etta on my back. Not ghostly slight, but lead-loaded. Fierce as a Lake Erie derecho. She bears down and brings me to my knees. People scream. Will I ever get used to all this screaming? But not one of them comes to help me up. When I try to stand, Etta knocks me down again. The photos will show Etta pressing my face to the floor, working her fingers into my mouth. Her tongue in my left ear. She wants. Wants. *Please, don't be so rough, Etta!*

"I want," she makes me say. Her words kick and wind me. "I want." *Etta, whatever it is I'll do it. Please, don't hurt me.*

Tamara apes my name. Maybe she comes to me. Maybe she's holding me now. Yanking my arms.

"I want the locket. Who is carrying the locket?" I spit drool onto the altar. I've torn the dahlia bouquet into an eyesore of pink petals. The candles are nothing but smashed warm wax. "Bring it to me, now."

The gathering unblocks a path for a stranger to come forward. I see Jaguar urge Tamara out of the way of his camera's view. I see flashbulbs as the stranger hastily unbuttons the side pocket of his cargo pants and digs out a tarnished necklace. He wipes his hand on his pants afterward, as if he's just passed me something dirty. The locket is cold. Unprompted, the brass chain swings in small circles like a pendulum. One side is painted in enameled flowers—daisies and daffodils. The other is cracked glass—a lock of black hair tied with a red ribbon pressed inside.

*I've been looking for this.*

Etta lets go of my voice, not my mind. "This locket has a lot of affection attached to it," I say. Her elation is my elation. Her questions are my questions. "But this isn't yours, is it? How did you get it?"

The stranger's brow furrows. "No, it doesn't belong to me." He glances uncomfortably at the crowd, turns to slink away. And I want to let him disappear, this limp-gaited man. I want to watch the threadbare seat of his pants walk off without a ghostly brawl. He's not interested in a monologue, not like the others. He's not looking to transform his misery into a show. I place the locket on the altar and move on.

But Etta wants him to wait. She has me say, "You haven't forgotten your story, have you? Come." I lead the stranger to the funhouse mirror. Every night, Etta uses my voice and limbs, but she's never made me touch another person before. She's never pulled anyone but me to the mirror. The stranger's back is cold sweat and seems to beg "mercy" from each of my five fingers. We stand before the swerved glass. Can he see Etta too? Her red-painted mouth drawn horror-show wide. Her mouth is my mouth. Her whims are my words.

"You were no more than a newborn in a buggy when you first visited Crystal Beach Park. Your pop and uncles all worked at the Opus Steel plant in Port Colborne. Union picnickers. The good old days. It was the plant's annual picnic brought you to Crystal Beach." The stranger tries to take a step back. Etta and I hold him in place.

"Remember how excited you got every year on that fateful evening when your pop came home with Park tickets? Like winning the children's lottery. You could ride the swings or bumper cars all day while the adults played beach volleyball or sunbathed.

"As a young man, you got a job as a ride operator. The plant didn't work out, did it? Hard labour, Opus Steel. Who wants that kind of hard living? The burn in your nostrils. The backache. The heat rash.

The hearing loss. Not for you, no sir." The stranger grows pallid. His cheeks puff out a few times like he might vomit. In the mirror, I see Etta's arms around his waist. He flinches and trembles. *Are you really touching him, Etta. Are you inside him? You said only me. You only touch me!*

"At the end of the day, you ride operators made a game of scouring the ground and the lower tracks for things people had dropped. Coins, purses, wallets, jewellery, hats. You turned it all in to Lost and Found, of course. Right? Well, most of it." *This circle is different. We're not a double act. She's not talking to me, only through me. Etta, what's so special about this locket? Talk to me.*

"There was a sundog the afternoon you found the locket. The line of people waiting for the Cyclone all faced the sky, pointing up. You spotted something else. In one swift and unnoticed move, you jumped off the platform and scooped the locket into your pocket.

"You slept with it under your pillow and dreamt of a girl in a red floral dress dancing alone. Twirling so her dress flew up to reveal her stockings.

"The locket came to you on a Saturday. By Tuesday hand-made posters were tacked to telephone poles near the Park. The poster claimed the locket was priceless. Priceless, imagine that. How valuable a thing must be to be called priceless." *I clutch him with both hands. The flesh under his shirt grows hot. I don't want to be twisting his skin like we are. Etta, we're hurting him.* "Twice you called the phone number listed, only to quickly hang up."

*Let go. He doesn't want this.* "She became a part of you. Her recurring appearances in your dreams grew more captivating and maddening each night. When she told you her name, she became your private testament that an inconceivable 'more' existed."

"Etta," the stranger says.

Etta. Someone else besides me can name her.

Her name calls her out. The entire crowd sees her. In what exact form, I don't know, but however she appears to them, she sends them running. Mass nonsensical whooping movements. Many hurtle the gazebo railing. Many more waterfall over each other down the stairs. Some run on the spot, the worn wood floorboards slipping under their feet, like Hanna-Barbera cartoons, like Shaggy and Scooby fleeing a masked villain. Etta is delighted, buoyant. *See me and run!* Finally, I can stand up straight, her weight off my back. Even the locket feels lighter in my left hand. I see it with my own, unaltered eyes. *Is this a lock of your hair, Etta?*

*This locket is what I was missing, Dollface. Something to prove I was here. Me. Not just the roller coaster and the dance hall. But Me. Me. Me. I was a part of it. Etta Zinn. Etta Zinn was here.*

Jaguar is snapping photos and photos and photos. The clang and ache is clearing from my head, and I think, what would it be like to punch such a handsome square jawline?

*Etta Zinn died here. And my name died with me. My name.*

She becomes very angry again.

# 55 Queens

I lived at the Herbert Hotel for two years, two months, and a handful of days. Same rent. Never raised by a single penny. Five dollars a week for the European plan. I chose the Herbert for one simple reason: the owner, Mrs Abby, didn't as much as blink when I showed up at her door, a baby vamp without a steady fella in sight, carrying enough cash in my pocketbook for a month's stay.

Didn't take a whole month for folks to start talking. You bet your life, I was wise to them. I put a bouquet of roses in my room the day I arrived, and by the time the first petal fell I was the town whore. I've been called worse than a whore, and paid less for it, so what did I care?

Then one night, I remember it like the lyrics on a well-worn record, I was pointing a gentleman caller toward the door. Of course, the boiled fish had to clear his throat as he left. Couldn't tiptoe, like I asked. No. He coughed loud and phony as if he was rehearsing a part for *Men in Black* with The Three Stooges. I was standing at the top of the stairs and I heard him, so Mrs Abby and her husband surely heard him from where they were sitting in the parlour.

Mrs Abby's husband said, "What a scandal. How many men has she had up there?"

Mrs Abby—well, she musta known I was peeking down from the landing—she said to her husband, "A wise woman doesn't ask these questions," and she leaned back in her velvet parlour chair to look right up the stairwell at me. I fell in love with her right then.

Not love like I was gonna lift my skirts love.

Love like how I felt about Mama Famke. Or even Madame Fannie or Ann Montgomery at the Little Harlem Club. Any woman who could hold her own, I suppose. I loved watching these women. Admiring how they set their shoulders different depending on what room they were in. I loved how they sometimes spoke high class, and other times they spoke kitchen table. I loved that they drove cars and carried bankrolls and lit their own cigarettes. I loved these women 'cause when I looked at them, I could imagine a future for myself.

Mrs Abby always had a smart smile for me. No lipstick, her smile was all her very own character. If I been out for an hour or for a string of days, she asked, "Where have you been keeping yourself?"

I always answered, "Oh, around."

When I stayed for a long spell up in my room, Mrs Abby knew just the right moment to check in on me. "Walk with me. The salt air will do us some good." I never corrected her, told her there's no salt in Lake Erie. At some point in her life, I figure she lived by the sea. I could tell by the glum way she stared at the shore as we walked along the beach.

When I was really blue, Mrs Abby would tell me stories. "A lot of queens came from the wrong side of town," she said. "It's in the history books." She told me how a Latvian housemaid became the Empress of Russia, and a vegetable merchant from Stockholm became the Queen of Sweden.

What Mrs Abby did for me, I made sure to return. If I found her crying in the parlour while listing to the radio, I'd borrow her line, "Let's walk. The salt air will do you good." I'd put a soda in her hand faster than you can say Coca Cola, and I'd tell her all about movie stars with hard-knocks starts. Real rags to riches stories. "Did you know the great Greta Garbo never went to high school?" and "Clara Bow almost died of starvation, she was so dirt poor as a girl."

I dunno why Mrs Abby never had children of her own. She would've gotten a little girl off to a good start. But a wise woman doesn't ask these things.

On my twenty-first birthday, I gave her a lock of hair.

I wanted her to have something of me that would last forever.

I suppose I knew what the future would hand me. I read them same history books. The tabloid papers too. Empress Catherine the First died sixteen months after taking the throne. Clara Bow became a raging drunk who got hauled to the loony bin.

Is that why Mrs Abby never claimed me?

*Why'd she leave me a Jane Doe?*

*Why didn't she identify my body?*

*Dollface, wake up and say my name again.*

*Dollface, wake up. Aren't you listening?*

# 56 Fan Mail

*Dear Crystal Beach Angel and friends,*

*My name is Samantha Mills. I live in Tonawanda, not too far from the University of Buffalo. Everyone who grew up around here went to Crystal Beach Park as a kid. I wish I could share some wonderfully nostalgic stories with you. Sadly, my long-term memory isn't what it used to be.*

*Last week, I attended one of your circles. Think nothing of it if you can't remember me. I'm not known to stick out in a crowd. Besides, I was seated behind two rather large men, both of whom were openly weeping. Despite my own personal reservations, I took a collectible from Crystal Beach as you instructed. My item was a postcard from the 1920s that said, "Business Section Crystal Beach" across the top. For starters, that gave me a laugh. The business section was nothing but fast food signboards, hot dogs, frozen custard, old lager, waffles, loganberry drink and the like, with a very small sheriff's office in the middle of it all.*

*I ended up keeping your postcard to show it to my eighty-six-year-old mother. Right now she is in hospice and confined to bed. She hadn't spoken to anyone in several weeks, which is the real reason why I came to see you. I've never been a religious person. Visiting an angel circle was what you might call a last resort.*

*When I showed Mom the postcard, she switched on again. Not only could she form words and sentences, she was able to tell a little about frequenting your "business section." She said she was too scared to go on any of the rides, but she sure did remember sunbathing and dancing at the ballroom.*

*By the next day, she was humming a tune that I recognized as "Moonlight Serenade" by The Glenn Miller Orchestra. Turns out she had danced to that song at least a dozen times at the Crystal Ballroom. A few of those times must have been with my father. They got married in 1940.*

*I ran right out and bought The Glenn Miller Orchestra Golden Hits on cassette. Mom sat up at the edge of her hospice bed, and she and I held hands and danced, swinging and swaying to "Moonlight Serenade" and "In the Mood" as best as we could.*

*She died peacefully listening to that cassette.*

*I believe she was waiting to be happy one last time before she died. She was always such a happy person. I just didn't know how to reach her until I visited your angel circle. You said the Park was sacred, and while it sounded like balderdash at the time, I see now how it is true. That Park was sacred to my mother, and that's more than good enough for me. Please forgive me, but I'm keeping your postcard. I've enclosed more than enough to pay for it, and to thank you for your help. Also enclosed is a copy of Mom's obituary.*

*Tell your angel to look out for my mom. I hope she's dancing, wherever she may be.*

*Yours truly,*

*Samantha Mills*

A three-legged Betty Page hangs above me. Tamara's Butthole Surfers poster. She leans through her bedroom window, smokes a cigarette, blows a long plume outside.

"You don't smoke," I say. I'm wearing lavender teddy-style pajamas, and I badly need to pee. Tamara butts out the half-smoked cigarette on the window glass.

"How many fingers am I holding up?" She makes a peace sign.

"How long have I been here?"

I have been sleeping on and off in Tamara's bed for nearly eighteen hours, she tells me. Prior to my long sleep, she and Dolores also took me to the hospital where I communicated astonishingly clearly with the doctor and was sent home for bed rest. "Doc probably thought you were crashing from a coke binge or something. ER always sends druggies home for bed rest." Her room smells like nail polish and cigarettes and candle wax. She says she's been in the room with me the entire time, but the place beside me on the bed is smooth and unrumpled. Has she slept? Or has she been watching me sleep?

"The Point!" I say, sitting up. My left breast creeps out of the skimpy teddy pajamas. Couldn't Tamara at least have given me a T-shirt to sleep in?

She grabs a glass of water from the nightstand and puts it in my hand. There's a mauve-pink lip print on the glass. My shade. At least I've been drinking water. "Lay back down. You can't hold a circle if you're attacking people and blacking out."

"Oh my god, please tell me I punched Jaguar?"

"It was pretty cool, actually. I think he left the next day with a black eye." Tamara smirks for a second and I want her to get into bed with me. "Anyway, Rose and I decided it was best for you to have a break."

"Rose decided? Is she mad at me?"

"Duh. Of course she's mad at you."

"I've got to get back to The Point! I can fix this."

"Yeah, we knew you'd say that. But your idea of fixing everything is to be all possessed by a ghost. How messed up does that sound? Even saying it is weird—'you are possessed by a ghost.' That's why you're here. Miles away from The Point and from Etta." It stings me to hear Tamara say Etta's name. She sees me wince.

"Dolores brought your mail on her way to work this morning. I've been reading you letters as you sleep, so it's not like you're totally cut off." She holds up the newspaper clipping. "Francis 'Fanny' Mills. February 19, 1913 – July 18, 1990."

She carefully fixes Fanny's obituary to a bulletin board across from the bed. It joins the child's drawing of an angel flying over a stick-figure family, and a half a dozen other thank-you cards. "I pinned them all up so you could read them yourself when you're up for it. Really sweet letters. Fucking misguided, but sweet. Here's one from a peach farmer who says his crop recovered. He included a clipping too." The headline on *Today's Farmer News* reads "Farmer Credits Crystal Beach Angel for His Ribbon Winning Peaches." I clutch at my naked chest, feeling for the missing pendant. "No necklace, no ride tickets, no postcards. I even got rid of anything from the Park tucked in your mail. I'm serious about a break, Star. More than a break—this needs to quit."

"The locket. The locket from the last circle, I need it. That I need, I'm serious."

Tamara waves a dismissive hand at me. "Maybe later today, we can do some of the stuff those mediums suggested. Try to find her grave or go through public records again. Useful things, you know?"

"Who put you in charge?" I can't say anything but the worst, most-idiotic thing to say. Why censor it? "You're jealous."

"You wanna pick a fight with me? Let's not, and say we did. I'm going out to clear my head. You count to ten or whatever it is you do to not be an asshole. Help yourself to anything in the fridge. And there's one letter for you on the nightstand. That one's from me." Tamara shuts the bedroom door softly, but the front door to her house slams. She pulls her Galaxy 500 out of the driveway quickly and the tires squeal. I jump out of bed, but not fast enough to wave out the window after her. Pins and needles shoot up my legs. She's right, of course, I am an asshole. I'm an asshole who receives fan mail thanking me for my dishonesty. My blessed subterfuge. Icons are notorious assholes, though. Charles Dickens. Dr Seuss. Thomas Edison. Ernest Hemingway. Henry Ford. Pablo Picasso. Orson Scott Card. Jimmy Page. What do they all have in common? I really have to pee.

Sitting on the toilet, I wonder why I can't name historically famous women assholes. Like did Jane Goodall ever kick a chimpanzee in the face? Did Yoko Ono sleep with an under-aged art mentee? Did Penny Marshall torment her actors for the sake of so-called brilliant art? Did she have her crew hurl toys at Tom Hanks in *Big*? Alfred Hitchcock constantly tossed live birds at Tippi Hedren throughout the filming of *The Birds*, then threatened her career if she didn't sleep with him. Major asshole.

Maybe too few women become famous enough for the world to know about their assholery? Maybe in an equal-opportunity world we'd see more women assholes? Margaret Thatcher is an asshole. But I know dick about UK politics. Mostly, what I know is through Sinead O'Conner's "Black Boys on Mopeds" song.

I do need that locket, though. Etta will literally tear me apart if it's lost again.

In the kitchen, I drink orange juice right out of the carton. I fight the urge to spit. The juice is acidic. Tamara has left me a break-up letter, I can feel it. Feels like shit shit shit shit shit shit shit shit and also fuck. I should leave the letter unopened. Show her!

I get dressed before I read it. It's just not right to be dumped while wearing your soon-to-be ex-girlfriend's skimpy pajamas. Her bedroom feels wrong too, so I take the letter outside. Together, the break-up letter and I sit at end of her scraggy privet-lined driveway. Her handwriting is so careful. The letter must be draft two, or three.

*Dear Starla,*

*I love you. Sure, there's a lot going on for you right now, but can you just pause to realize the meaning of these words. <u>I LOVE YOU!</u>*

*I've never told any woman that before (apart from my family members). I'm out of the closet, as you know. And I've had plenty of fleeting flings with other dancers who I've met at the clubs. Then, when you came home and we started dating, I got really excited to build a life here together. I was ready for a real relationship. I guess I'm still hopeful that maybe we can be together, but I'm not excited anymore. Mostly I'm tired and worried. I'm tired and worried about you all the time.*

*Rose told me that you moved your stuff to The Point. You didn't even tell me that you left your mom's place. We said we'd move in together. Why would you keep this a secret from me? Or were you just so busy with Etta that it slipped your mind? I don't know what is worse, you ditching me for Etta or you ditching me to make sure you are smack dab in the middle of everything. Is that why you moved to The Point? So you can constantly be the centre of all this bogus attention?*

*The times we've spent telling each other tender things about our past and all our future dreams were the best times we had together. I didn't even know I needed a close "companion" to talk to until we were deep in conversation. It's like I got to go back in time and make some peace with some of my memories. It's like I got to imagine possibilities that I thought were just daydreams. I hope you did too.*

*I used to think it was the special bond we had that made you tell me that Etta is actually a ghost, not an angel. I used to think I was special because you told me your darkest secret of all. You reached out to me for help. I guess it's a lover's cliché, but that made me feel needed.*

*Now I'm more of an accomplice than a special confidant. I've been growing more and more uncomfortable with what's happening at The Point. It was hard to figure out what was wrong because so many people have claimed that their lives have gotten better after visiting. So many people have hope now. It's not easy living around here, watching friends and neighbours go broke or become drunks or bad moms or whatever other problems we have. We need hope. But your hope is fake hope. I mean, it's <u>really fake</u>. I'm surprised anyone is even falling for it anymore. It goes to show you how hungry people are for hope. But the hope people have should be in <u>themselves</u>, not in some lie you feed them.*

*I can't sit around and watch you lie anymore. I can't watch you get sicker and sicker either. You have a choice. If you want to fix this, I will help you. I will be there for you no matter how long it takes or how hard it gets. I will be there for you even if Hal and Bobby and Rose and everyone gets angry and upset (although I bet Rose will love you no matter what).*

*But if you are going to go on and on with this, then it is me that has to make a choice. Believe me, my choice will be to break up with you. Don't make me break up with you.*

*Love,*
*Tamara*

# 57 Screech Owl

I guess the going notion says the worst possible thing that can happen in a relationship is a breakup. Boy meets girl, boy loses girl. That's the hetero boilerplate, right? If I was a dude at this very moment, I would be plotting my reunion strategies. I would try to win her back.

According to Tamara, the real lovers' cliché is feeling needed, feeling special. If I follow her logic, I'm a hundred-pound, walking, talking, nonstop cliché. I am special. Fucking miraculously special. People do need me. Well, they need what I currently have to give them.

It's going to take about three hours to walk back to The Point. I start simply, by putting one foot in front of the other, and march east down Tamara's street, turn onto the Niagara Boulevard, which is as scenic of a route as there is around here, and follow the water. The sidewalks are stupidly wide. Why do we need such wide sidewalks? It's not like there's pedestrian traffic to warrant such wide sidewalks. The sidewalks are cracked and always sprouting crabgrass. Step on a crack, you break your mama's back. Kids are so cruel.

No one is around to hear me, so as I walk I sing, "Little bird, little bird, I am going to pluck you. I'll pluck the feathers from your neck. I'll pluck the feathers from your neck. From your neck, from your neck."

Then I sing, "Lizzie Borden took an axe, and gave her mother forty whacks. When she saw what she had done, she gave her father forty-one."

I'm distracting myself, yeah, no, duh. I live to distract myself from my life.

I sing, "Ask me no more questions, please tell me no more lies. The boys are in the bathroom unzipping their ... Flies are in the city, the bees are in the park, the boys and girls are kissing in the dark dark dark! Darker than the ocean, darker than the sea, darker than the underwear my mommy puts on me."

Sweet fucking Mary, kids are cruel because they hate their mothers. I really am a cliché. Can survivors be cliché? Is not being believed a survivor cliché? Is not knowing if your truth is legitimately true a cliché? I suppose a Cassandra complex lacks a certain originality. Aeschylus told that story 2,500 years ago. Phobos is the Greek god of fear. Christougenniatiko dentrophobia is the fear of Christmas trees. Christmas fucking trees! The fear of not being believed has no name. It's not listed as a phobia. There's no diagnosis, only myth and tragic plays and children's rhymes.

Showing Tamara the x's hidden behind my childhood bed was tender, as she wrote in her break-up letter, tender and fine. I wanted her to touch me then, the way she lets me touch her. I wanted one of those howling female orgasms, as loud as hers, as wet. I wanted my body to perform desire, to perform love, and maybe just maybe real desire and love would follow. I wanted to meet her on her beautiful feminine orgasming pedestal.

And I wanted a long-term relationship to follow? Or I wanted the other stuff, the other-than-sex stuff. The intimate emotional stuff.

If I was in Toronto now, perhaps walking the goddamn length of Yonge Street, I could stroll into any sports bar, any shopping mall, any subway station, any public library, any public place really, and find sex. Or, if not sex, someone would touch me just enough to remember there's blood in my body. Men, yes. Men, easy and always available. Even the men who'll decline sex want to nourish a flirtatious moment or two. And women, straight-laced women, always seem to be ready with kind shoulder taps and accompanying concern: "Are you okay?" If I was in Toronto, or any city, it would take me less than ten minutes to find someone willing to ask me if I'm okay.

Along the stupidly wide sidewalks no one passes me. No one dots the stupidly large expanse of thirsty green grass before me. Walking alone is not a metaphor. Sing something else, I tell myself. Recite a poem or a scene from a favourite film. But it's muggy hot and too bright and there's no corner stores for another few more kilometres and besides I don't have my wallet.

I could hitchhike, not that there's many cars. Should have taken Garrison, darn it.

Eventually, the stupid sidewalk ends, leaving me on a single lane road, which soon turns to gravel and dirt. I'm close to Crystal Beach. Brush thickens on either side of me. I'm quickly attuned to the particular music only heard on rural roads on hot days, a sort of chorus of insect and bird chatter and the oddly specific sound of dry leaves and bush weeds holding still in the absent breeze. Occasionally, off either shoulder, I spot something that has been left to rot in the woods. The rusted flatbed of an old truck. Coils from a box spring mattress. A grim threesome of oil drums. And a few lean-to piles of boards and plastic sheeting that must be the secret forts of children. Squirrels wave their anxious tails at me. A toad basks in the middle of the road; I almost miss it until it hops away from my footsteps.

A woman waits fifty feet in front of me. At first I think it's Bobby, then I think it's just wishful thinking, and then I realize it is actually Bobby. She beckons me with a hush-hush gesture. I slink up beside her, follow her gaze up the side of willow tree. She juts her chin in the direction she wants me to look.

"In the daytime?" I ask, spotting the screech owl looking down at us. How can something with a heart-shaped face look so terrifying?

"A young one," says Bobby. "Betcha she left her parents' burrow no more than a month ago to find her own tree. Maybe she hasn't found the right tree yet, so she ain't sleeping well. Only reason you see an owl in the day is if her sleep's interrupted. She's looking for a place to sleep, I bet." Bobby laughs, and I wonder what's funny about a young insomniac owl until she says, "Either that or she's come to tell you you're gonna die."

"Oh my god! You believe that?"

"Nope. Just getting a rise out of you." Bobby turns and walks toward Crystal Beach. I ask her where she's going. "Now that I found you, back home."

"You came for me?" I clutch Tamara's break-up letter inside my pocket.

Bobby sighs peevishly, "Yes, who else? Leanne telephoned Rose. Said she saw you walking one of your trance walks. I figured someone better get you before you wound up underwater." Outside of The Point and without Lucky clinging to her, Bobby appears younger, physically looser, almost drifting. Her toes pitch in slightly as she walks, hips sway. Shoulders so bouncy I can't help stare. I think, she must have been a hot number when she was young, a real man magnet, then I feel guilty for thinking it.

"Bobby, um, did you talk with Jaguar at all before he left?"

She keeps her eyes forward. Unwavering stride. "Hal came clean about the photos of Lucky, if that's what you're asking." That is what I was asking. Though I'm unsure of what my next question should be. What exactly did Hal tell her? Where are the photos now? Is she pissed? Is she pissed at me? Maybe it's better not to ask. If she wants to tell me, she'll tell me, right? Bobby veers in front of me, bends to pick up something in the dirt. "Found a loonie," she says, holding up dollar coin. "Good luck." She passes it to me. I slip it in my pocket with Tamara's break-up letter. "So, I tossed Hal outta the house. He's set up camp at one of the sites."

"I'm sorry, Bobby."

"Everybody's sorry."

"Are you going to divorce him?

"Divorce, ha!" Bobby hip checks me along the path, playfully. I stumble a step or two. "No, Hal needs a good long think, is all. So do I. Divorce is what thirty-year-olds do. When I met Hal, I was already thirty-nine and he was forty-four. I thought he looked just like Lorne Greene from *Bonanza*. He shaved his beard back then. Had the leather vest and everything! Both of us were as bitter as we were sweet. But our fights were always going someplace. Listen now, Starla. Our fights were always going someplace. Can you guess where we needed to go?"

Is this a question I can literally answer? I slow my steps as Bobby walks a few paces in front of me.

"Back!" she says, as if the answer was obvious. "We needed to go back to all the screwed up stuff and be okay with it. It's okay that he was in jail. It's okay, all those years I got tossed around—"

"It's okay that you were in foster homes?"

"I mean, no, it's not okay. You got to listen, Starla. Let me get there. It's not okay, what happened. But we're okay. We're okay. There's nothing wrong with us. That's what loving taught Hal and me. There's nothing wrong with us. I bet we even love harder than regular folks after all we been through."

The dirt road turns back into pavement under our feet. Soon, sidewalks reappear on either side of us. I am hanging on Bobby's every word. "When I got pregnant, Hal didn't even blink. We got married. No family came. No church—not even a cake. But we were as happy as any young couple. Happier because we knew all the things it meant, the good and the bad, when we said 'I do.'

"Everything was going real smooth until Lucky started talking and asking questions like little ones do. The bigger Lucky got, the more Hal got mean. Drinking. Kicking up all kinds of fuss. Going off for who knows how long by himself. Anything he could do to turn away from his son. You know what I think it is?"

Bobby pauses again, and I panic a little that I should have an answer ready for her. We're passing Willowwood Street—the last of the tree-named streets—and we'll be back at The Point soon.

"I think he started seeing himself in Lucky, seeing himself as a child, and that got him thinking about childhood, eh? And not being okay. And when you're not okay, nothing is. You stop loving your own, like you're supposed to. Hold a grudge against your own son."

The sidewalks recede again. The brush closes back in, wilder and buggier and noisier than it was a mile back. The narrow birch trees ahead glow a peculiar white that tells me Etta knows I'm coming. I wonder if Bobby sees the trees the way I do?

"That's what those photos were, Starla. He's more concerned about proving to the world that he's shoulder-to-shoulder with some phony baloney angel than he is about his own son. You got that Bambi look in your eye, Starla, but I know you're a good listener. This is what me and my Lucky and Hal are going through right now. I already told you: they are all I got."

We stand together at the entrance to The Point. The driveway is skid-marked from so many cars racing in and out for the last couple of months. Bobby takes my hand. Her palm is cool; mine is sweaty. She makes eye contact; I look down. She's going to ask me something that I don't want to answer; I can feel it coming.

"Are you being hurt? It's not gonna to do anything for us to watch you grow thin as a rake and sicker than a dog. You have to say it. You have to tell us. Are you being hurt?"

*You think you're hurt? I'll show you hurt.* I can't see Etta anywhere. I don't know from which direction her voice speaks to me. The driveway smells like gasoline. The tar and gravel is hot against my cheek. Maybe I've fallen, or maybe I just lay down. Bobby towers over me, she yells for Dolores, for Rose, for help. My answer to her question comes out of my mouth as black retch. Blood and sour spit, cursed spit. My raw throat swells shut.

I am being hurt.

# 58 Phony Baloney Angel

The pay phone is far away, and there are too many people between it and me. I move through their voices, their outstretched hands, like a sideways rainstorm. Bobby and Dolores intercept before too many of them circle in.

"We got Hal and Joe guarding the cabin door. How'd you give 'em the slip? You can barely stand upright," says Dolores.

"I have to call Tamara," I tell them. Dolores orders the crowd back as Bobby loops her arm around my waist. "I don't want to break up."

"Well, halle-fucking-luya! She don't want to break up with you either, dummy. Why don't you use the phone at Rose's?" Dolores asks.

"There's too much Crystal Beach stuff insider her house." The two stop dead. I just confessed again, right? 'The amusement park is sacred' was all a ploy to make Etta stronger. The boat wood, the souvenirs, all of it. I try to imagine what they're thinking. That indeed they were right all along? Or that now the money will dry up? That they should abandon me to be trampled by this crowd?

A second later, we are moving again. "Outta our way," Dolores yells like a boss. Bobby hugs me into her. She doesn't even make a face at the touch she's offering me. Is that it? Am I forgiven? Above us, the sky is the same pale yellow as the sun—summer haze. The quarry and grass are pale too. I wonder if I'm losing the ability to see colour. But the gazebo is still stained so red it hurts my eyes.

The pay phone rings before we reach it. Bobby lets go of me to answer. Dolores does her best to shush the crowd. "Who calls pay phones?" she says. "The government!"

It's Etta, I think. She's found a way to worm through the telephone lines. She is everywhere. Relentless. In the tap water, I'm sure I'm drinking her. In the grass, she is my every step. Stops at nothing. In everyone's ears, on all tongues.

Maybe it really is fucking CFS, I think. Because Bobby hasn't passed the phone to me yet. She says, "Uh huh. Uh huh." Her hand moves like she's writing in the air.

"Pen and paper," Dolores shouts into the crowd. "Gimme a pen and paper now, people!" The crowd listens, hoping a divine proclamation is going to come through a beat-up pay phone, and for a moment everyone is quiet and still. In the lull, I finally spot Etta, waving at me from the shrine steps like she is Queen fucking Elizabeth II. I hate her. And I hate her more for not being close right now. For not being inside of me. She vanishes, and I hear the crowd roar up again with their familiar questions: Is there a message?

Etta appears again on Rose's doorstep. One hand on the screen door handle, the other waving her royal asshole wave at me. *Not Rose's house. You promised.*

*Then come meet me on the dance floor. We'll scream our pretty heads off like a Laurel and Hardy show. A real Dance of the Cuckoos. One can't do that dance alone, Dollface.*

I start screaming right where I stand. I'm a tripped alarm, a possessed siren. The quake in my throat flattens the grass, sends ripples across the quarry, and clears the haze from the sky. Many people in the crowd literally drop and roll and writhe on the ground. They are desperate for the reverberation. They want my suffering and fraudulence. They want my tired empty body. They want any feeling that they themselves don't have to evoke. I understand this. But how do I un-understand it? How do I un-know?

Dolores is yelling too. And Bobby. She yells "Yes!" and "Finally!" and "Thank you." Bobby holds the pay phone receiver skyward, triumphant.

"Was it the fucking CFS?" I ask, dazed.

"It was my auntie. I have an auntie. She saw me and Lucky in the news. In one of those photographs. Looks like your phony baloney angel has answered my prayers." She shows us the piece of paper, the exuberantly scribbled words: Mother's sister. Cat Lake. North of the Sioux Lookout. Aunt Helen.

Etta blitzes beside me, a blister of divine light, too fast, too sharp. The crowd also sees her and, just like the night the locket was found, everybody moves like there's a riot.

"Run, girl," Dolores yells. But it's too late. I become as diaphanous as lace drapes, easy to tear into. Etta steps into me like a dress. She wears me. She's wearing me out. Wearing me down to nothing. I am nothing without her. I am being hurt.

# 59 Stronger

We're going to take off your clothes now. Do you understand?"
"It's just me and Rose. Hal's got the men standing guard at
the door. You're safe. Stay calm." Daylight enters from the open
cabin door and cracked window. Two silhouettes border my body. I
want to spell something, but I can't conjure the alphabet. I hear the
sound of water and pee myself. Warmth seeps under my bare ass.
Ammonia stinks up the air. Gooseflesh dots my arms and I shiver.

"Fuck," Tamara says. Then, "Don't worry, Star. It's nothing to be
embarrassed about." An enamel water basin sits beside me on the
cot. Sprigs of rosemary float in the water, olive oil pools on the
surface. A wet cloth dabs my back. Am I being anointed? Oh my
god, am I dead? Can the dead wet themselves?

"Etta?" This might be the only word I still know how to say.

"No. No more Etta, not if we can help it." My left arm is lifted.
The wet cloth circles my armpit.

"Tamara picked this out. What a pretty dress." Rose waves something magenta pink in front of me. Maybe I nod and try to raise my
own arms over my head. My movements feel drugged, dreamlike.

Tamara brushes my hair as Rose wiggles flip-flops onto my feet.
"One. Two. Three," they count as they pull me to standing.

"How—" How long have I been out, I want to ask, but I can't
make an "l" sound. My tongue is swollen and the roof of my mouth
numb. The day is too brilliant. Sun scours the horizon into harsh
annihilation. Hal waits a few paces outside the cabin. Rose and

Tamara pass me to him. Moustache and Chris Sakokete are here and maybe Rahn? Wendel and the Foster brothers close behind? Maybe the locket man and the peach farmer. Their arms are outstretched as if I'm about to be handed off again, like a sandbag passed from volunteer to volunteer along the Niagara River during a storm. This strikes me as funny, but the noises I make are not laughter.

I see it.

This is why the men are closing in, because they know I see it.

The shrine in a fallen pile.

Joe's truck is backed into Rose's driveway, and the old wheelhouse stands mostly intact in his flatbed. Dolores and her co-workers from the hospital laundry toss more busted wood from the pile into the truck. When they all stop to look at me is when I realize I am struggling, flailing my arms and kicking my feet. My forehead knocks against another head and I see blood. I bite someone's hand hard enough for knucklebones to crunch under my teeth. Etta is not here to lift me, to float me up, up. The land feels so different without her. Gravity is insulting.

"We don't wanna hurt you, Starla," says Hal. It's his meaty palm that holds my face down on the dry grass. Someone else pins my shoulders, someone else my feet, my arms. So much for my sponge bath. Tamara should have picked a black dress—the grass stains wouldn't show so much.

"Okay," I slur. I coax my thick tongue. "Yeah. Okay."

Later, I sit at Rose's kitchen table before a half-eaten plate of creamed polenta and garlic butter. It seems every very few seconds someone whispers a worry around me—"How's she doing?" and "Give her time" and "Should we call a doctor?" I'm still wearing the magenta dress and, yes, it has an unfortunate grass stain across the boobs. Hal's left hand is cleaned and bandaged now. A small dot of blood soaks through the gauze. It was him I bit, and hard.

He sees me looking. "You eats half as much as me and are twice as strong. Makes me miss the days when I could give ya a good lickin'."

I laugh a real laugh that comes out both through my mouth and nose. Hal reaches his injured hand across the table to take mine. His calloused fingertips are warm and alive. "I can feel your warmth," I say, astounded. "I can feel." I put my own hand against my cheek. I'm still here, also warm and alive. I touch my forehead. My eyelids. Each earlobe. I touch my throat and suddenly it is too much feeling, like I might choke. Like I might choke to death.

Later, Lucky and I are tucked into Ricky's old bed in Rose's house. The sheets are Garfield and Odie print. Does anyone grow into adulthood while living in their parents' house? I'm struck by the reminder that Ricky didn't grow up. He must have been depressed in this bed. I want to grab Lucky's tiny hand, pull us out of bed, and take us someplace that isn't marked with sadness. But where?

Bobby enters the room with a copy of *Where the Wild Things Are*. "Your ma brought some kids' books from the library," she tells me. She sits on the edge of the bed and begins to read as if it's any ordinary night and we are ordinary children. I am angry, at first. The simple story grates at me. Fuck Max's room turning into a forest. Fuck the wild things for being so easy to tame.

I spoon Lucky, feel his little bare butt press against my stomach. He's sleeping just in a T-shirt again. Here is a kid that's never been molested, I think. I always wore underwear to bed. Double underwear. As soon as I think it, it becomes a wish: *May Lucky never be molested.*

And Barbara—my mother and lender of library books—I wish that she'll never have to bury her child. That one day I'll make her proud. Or at the very least, I'll keep living. Those two wishes are enough. Right now, they have to be enough.

Later, the dead of night tells me that wishes are not nearly enough. The dead of night reminds me how worthless I am. My body tingles in sleepless mania. My head pounds Etta's name. I'm up and out Rose's front door without shoes or a flashlight. I drop to my knees in Rose's driveway and nose through the gravel. There must be some splinter of boat or roller coaster wood left behind. A scrap of divinity. Of my sexuality. Of my self. Of Etta. Etta. Etta. E-T-T-A E-T-T-A E-T-T-A.

Etta is nowhere to be seen, but is that a rhythm ballad up ahead? A standup bass, a croon? Her signature song, "A flame in my heart." The moon is a sliver and barely lights my path toward the fallen gazebo. My knees scuff on the ground. Dirt smears my palms as I go. There's still wood there. Roller coaster track. I feel it.

A lighter flicks in my path. Hal and Moustache stand ready to ambush me. Their stupid man mouths say, "Go back to bed, Star." I remember Hal telling me I'm twice as strong as him as I lunge at him.

More people arrive to yell nonsense at me. More and more hands try to pin me down. Hair is caught in my teeth, skin under my fingernails, feet connect with groins. My hands roughly meet throats and eye sockets. These are people I love. Why aren't they stronger? Why can't they stop me? Why won't they just rip me limb from limb?

Why isn't my love for them stronger?

Why can't I stop myself?

What have we done to deserve this?

# 60 Trust Poetry and Carpet

Outside Ricky's bedroom window, four Niagara Region Police officers escort the last of the die-hard angel seekers out of The Point. And with them, they carry off remnants of Crystal Beach. Whatever semblance of Etta's existence I had now weakens to a dull hum. How hollow is completely gutted? August heat isn't helping the defeatism. Mowed grass lies in dry mounds. Leaves—sagging on the trees—have already begun to yellow. The evictees lag in the humid air. For a moment, I feel sorry for the cops, who must be cooking in their navy blue uniforms.

When I try to leave the room, the door bumps into Hal's hulking frame. "We're gonna call a meeting, Star. You're invited. Just gimme a bit more time." He pokes his head in—he has a black eye and surgical tape across the bridge of his nose. "You want coffee?"

Rose brings me coffee and a change of clothes. Jeans and a worn tank top this time. I figure she's brought clothes I won't mind being ruined if I freak out again.

"We have no idea what to do," she says. "If we bring you to the hospital, they'll ship you to the psych ward in Niagara Falls as fast as they can look at you. Never mind what the local papers will do with you. Dolores and Hal suggested some kind of meeting, so that's what we're going to do. Lucky's going to be there, so try ... sweet Jesus, just try not to hurt anybody."

She knocks twice on the door for Hal to let her out again.

"Rose," I call. The "r" comes out rolling—I've got full use of my tongue again. "Will you ever forgive me?"

"Same thing that got to you got my Ricky. That she-devil. *Che malvagia.*" She turns her back to the door, steps back into the centre of the room. I quickly sit on the bed and shove my hands under my seat in case they feel like involuntarily swinging at her. "That's what I learned reading his journals. Something got at him. And something got you, possessed you. You know, by the time I finished reading, I felt better. It was a spirit. A spirit I can handle. What I couldn't handle was the thought of being such a bad mother, that my only son—"

"You are a good mother, Rose," I say, planting my face into the softest part of her belly. I free my hands and hug her close to me. Her crying is calm. Nothing like the rough convulsions from months ago. "It's not your fault," I tell her. "It's never been your fault."

Rose is still sniffling a bit when she and Hal lead me to the living room. I scan for injuries, look for who I'll need to profusely apologize to. Moustache has fingerprint-shaped bruises on both his arms. Joe Foster's ear is taped up. Leanne's lip is split. Bobby sits on one side of her on the sofa, Dolores on the other, her hand firmly resting on Leanne's shoulder in a gesture of solidarity. Lucky nuzzles and sprawls across the three, playing with the fringe of Leanne's AC/DC T-shirt. Leanne won't make eye contact with me, and I don't blame her. I punched a woman who recently left her abusive husband. I punched a domestic abuse survivor. Tamara is a vision of lipstick and tight spandex perfection sitting next to the TV. Barbara sits on a kitchen chair; Rahn stands behind her. I settle on the carpet in the far corner of the room.

"Thanks, everyone, for comin'," Hal says with a wide wave. "We're here to decide 'bout what do with the Crystal Beach Park artifacts anymore, and the remainin' wood on the property and how to respond to all the scandal."

"And the collection money," adds Barbara. "You need to make a sensible group decision about the money, and since Starla has not got her wits about her, I'm going to stay for that conversation."

"And the money," Hal sighs. "Before we start, we gotta agree on a few things. This here is a private meetin'. No more newspapers. No cross-talkin'. One person speaks at a time. And no violence." Everyone looks to me during this last point. The pause stretches long.

"As if I want to be violent," I say, ashamed. A longer pause spreads across the room. "Okay! If I start to feel out of control, I'll head for the bedroom as fast as I can?"

"Works for me," nods Hal. He waits for the others to agree with him, but only receives a few nods and shrugs. "Movin' on. Barbara volunteered to handle the Crystal Beach Park artifacts. Barbara."

"So, Bobby and Leanne helped me track down the Lily Dale mediums, Agnes and Esther. I guess they visited here in June, not that anyone told me about it. So, it was all news to me when they said Starla has to keep clear away from any Park artifacts and memorabilia. What did they call it? A channel? Anyway, they suspect it's this Park stuff that's acting like a channel, you see, it connects Starla to this bad ghost."

Barbara's news is not new to me, of course. My missing Crystal Beach pendant still chafes my neck and chest, and it's been more than a week since Tamara took it off me. Tamara notices me scratching my throat, or I hope she notices me scratching my throat. I cough and I want her to hear me cough. I want her pity if it draws her near.

"Every last postcard and leaflet has been collected," Barbara says, "and I brought it all to a storage locker near Niagara Falls. Agnes and Esther are going to visit the stuff ... talk to it ... I suppose. I guess this is like an exorcism. Not exorcism. Excor .... Ecto ...? They had a special word for it." Rahn rubs her back in a few gentle, circular motions, prompting her onward. "Anyway, the stuff is part of our history, and we can't just throw it out. I'm the town librarian, for christ's sake. So once the mediums say it's clear, we'll hand the collection over to the local historical society."

"All in favour of havin' the witches fix the Crystal Beach stuff, then handin' it over to the Historical Society, say aye," says Hal. I guess AA has taught him Robert's Rule of Orders.

Both hearty and half-hearted "ayes" are given.

"Anybody object?" asks Hal. Again, everyone looks at me.

"It started in my house. My own house." Barbara bolts up from her chair, then quickly sits back down again. Behind her, Rahn's eyes widen. His hands hover over her shoulders for a second before he gently places them back down with a little squeeze. "I was the one to buy her that stunt from Laugh in the Dark. I knew it was a dumb purchase, a waste of money. But who knew, night after night, it was haunting her? It was hanging over her bed all this time. What did the ghost do to her? My little girl—why didn't she tell me?" Barbara is talking about me in third person. I slump down onto Rose's carpet. It smells like baking soda and weird apple juice.

"Night after night. To think of it. I put that stunt in her room with her. I didn't know." Barbara shoots up from her chair again and rakes her fingers through her hair. Rahn takes a step back. Hal mumbles something, trying to soothe her. "I didn't know," she says again, this time looking directly at me.

I close my eyes and press my forehead. One of the women says to Barbara, "How could you have known?" Someone else says, "Should we put Star back into the bedroom?" and "Everyone relax." I know they are calling my name, but I can't look up.

"Why do these things always happen to her? What, is she cursed? Am I cursed? Where did I go wrong?"

Rose's carpet is patterned with small paisleys and geometric flowers. Staring at the carpet fibres this closely makes all the colours a muddy teal green, the same colour as algae blooms on the lake.

"I didn't know. I'm sorry, Starla." The fine fibres of Rose's carpet taste oddly salty between my lips. Rose's carpet tickles my skin. Rose's carpet can miraculously recite all the words to "After 37 Years My Mother Apologizes for My Childhood" by poet Sharon Olds. This may be the closest I'll get to validation, to closure. I press my ear down. Listening. Listening. Listening. Maybe I can trust poetry—and carpets? The carpet arrives at the last line of the poem, "... who would I be now that I have forgiven you."

# 61 Club Crisis

We talk about money. Or rather, I don't talk but keep my body flat to the carpet, my head turned toward the wall. Everyone who is not me talks about the now sizeable cache of angel donations. I refuse to hear numbers, exact amounts. There's no way I'm putting a dollar value to any of this. When exact amounts are being said, I say the word "gratis" in my head. Gratis means free—as in zero price—in at least six different languages. Maybe more. Maybe I'll study language again? Maybe I want to learn about something that exists outside this room? Every now and then I raise my arm, or my leg, in agreement with what's being said.

"'*GRATIS*' amount goes to Rose for damages to her property." I raise my arm.

"'*GRATIS*' amount will go to Bobby and Lucky to fly up and meet their relatives. It costs a lot of money to fly to Sioux Lookout." I kick up my leg, both legs. Sensation is returning to my limbs again. It feels good. I kick once more for the simple joy of being able to kick.

"'*GRATIS*' amount to pay the witches their fee for de-ghosting the Crystal Beach artifacts."

"'*GRATIS*' amount to Starla for debt recovery or counselling or both." I roll over to face the room. I want to refuse this money. Refusing seems easier than accepting it. For a split second, I allow myself to picture the bills in my hands. Or begrudgingly handing it all over to Barbara to manage for me. I remember how the ATM machine sucked up my first overdrawn credit card; the screen flashed with CONTACT YOUR BANK IMMEDIATELY. I remember buying rounds of tequila shots at the bar. I remember carrying shopping bags down Bloor Street, a.k.a. the Mink Mile. I remember paying cash for scalped concert tickets, outbidding the other punks in the lineup. I remember how dry the air seemed inside Toronto Women's Bookstore whenever I waited for my purchases to be rung up. Was I happy in those moments? What did I feel?

"Don't be a shithead," Bobby snaps at me. "Take the money. You don't even know where you're gonna live next, what you're gonna do. So take the money and do something with your damn self."

"Rahn thinks you should go to counselling. With this money you could see a real fancy therapist, at least for a few of months," says Barbara. "That's a good idea, eh?"

"Studies show that most psychotherapy clients improve after about twelve sessions, that is, depending on the severity of the problem," says Rahn. "In your case, Starla, I really encourage you to commit to therapy. Get the help you need."

"You people are hilarious," huffs Dolores. "Oh, go to therapy and you're as good as new. Girl, you're going to be dealing with this for the rest of your life. It's lifelong."

"Welcome to the club," Bobby says. "Club screwed-up-for-life." She, Dolores, and Leanne cackle and jiggle together on the sofa. Leanne clamps her hand over her mouth to protect her split lip as she laughs. Right, yes, life is not a book or a movie. No one writes "the end" when the crisis is over. But why is that funny? One day, will I get the joke? I have a terrible feeling I will.

Hal claps his hands together loudly, says, "This is a good place to break for lunch." Feet shuffle across the carpet and out of the living room. How are they handling this so well? Are they handling it well? Like normal? I think about eating a normal lunch, a tuna fish sandwich, but nothing happens. I'm not hungry. I can't stand up. I'll be screwed up for the rest of my life.

"I'm proud of you, Star," Tamara wriggles up beside me. "We all are. It's just too fresh, you know. Not everyone's ready to say it, but we all know how brave you're being."

"It's not like I tore down the gazebo. Or cleared all those people from Rose's property."

"Yeah, but in the end, you're the only one that had the power to say 'it's over.'"

"What if I don't want it to be over?" I'm queasy as I peel myself off the floor. I bring my sick head closer to hers and she touches my cheek, only for a second, but long enough to make my breath catch.

She says she has something to show me, slides a VHS tape into Rose's player. The salt-and-pepper on the TV screen turns into a woman news anchor's face. The anchor's shoulder-padded blazer is so 1986. Someone give this poor woman a wardrobe refresh, I think, before I realize she is talking about Etta. "Do ghosts really exist? Are we alone in this world? Parapsychologist Dr Jaguar Tongue claims, indeed, we are not. Dr Tongue took his photo on July 22nd, and it has been the subject of growing debate ever since ..."

The photo, evidently taken through the cabin window, shows Etta, Tamara, and me curled together on the cot. Post-coitus sleeping, though I know Etta doesn't sleep. Her ghostly eyes may be closed, but at the time that photo was taken she was whispering in my ear. *Dollface, you're mine.*

"Turn it off. Turn it off," I shout. Tamara bangs the TV power button. "I'm cool. I won't swing any punches. I just can't see her. Not even on TV."

"I only wanted you to see what they're saying about us," says Tamara. "Lesbian ghosts! Imagine the scandal. Rose had to change her telephone number. People were calling day and night to heavy breathe into the phone. She even got a few death threats. Couple of a-holes said they were going to round us lezzie demons up and slit our throats."

"What am I supposed to do?" I say.

Tamara's brow creases, she tilts her head away from me.

"I mean literally, I don't know what I'm supposed to do. I literally don't know. I don't know." I must be yelling because Lucky darts back into the living room waving a half-eaten grilled cheese at us. Bobby and Hal bound in after him. Bobby gives me a "stay calm" warning look.

"Breathe, Star. It's not all death threats. We got lots of fan mail too. Gay men and women from all over North America wrote us. I've saved every letter for when you are ready."

Hal scratches his beard, "It ain't right. First we was angel seers. Now folks thinks we're a buncha lesbian feminists."

Tamara slaps her hand against her forehead.

"For pity's sake, Hal," says Bobby. "Whatcha think's been going on here this whole time? You've been takln' advice from a lesbian, is what." Hal and Bobby retreat to the kitchen, Hal grumbling about lesbians as he goes. Lucky belly-crawls under the coffee table to keep an eye on us.

"A bunch of the letters said it's horrible to live and die in the closet. Or to lie and die all alone." Tamara inches closer to me. "That's probably what happened to Etta, right?"

I wince at her name and Tamara quickly takes my hand. "Yeah, that, and other things," I say.

"What things? The mediums told us if we learned about her life, maybe we could bring her to peace."

I touch my forehead, as if touch will make her voice vent in my head. I slap my bony sternum, as if force will dislodge her in my body. Tamara takes my hands again—this time to prevent me from hitting myself.

"She told me she ran away from home," I say. "And that she made her money hustling men, like an escort, I guess. She loved dancing and movies, especially scary movies. And she thinks no one loved her, not really. When she died no one came to claim her body. She was buried as Jane Doe in an unmarked grave."

"That's awful. No wonder she went evil."

"She's not evil, Tamara." I pull my hands back from hers, wrap my arms around myself in a solo hug.

"I saved this for her." Tamara births an embroidered handkerchief from her pocket. The curly monogramed initials read YDM. "Yuri Denis Matveev," she tells me. "That's my dad. He was a solid guy before he got sick. Like a real protector, man of the house kinda guy. I wanted to use something of his to wrap this up." Inside the folded handkerchief is Etta's lost locket. I hug myself harder, clutch the sides of my tank top, pinch my flesh through the thin fabric. Lucky squeaks from under the coffee table. I'm captured by the small swirl of Etta's black hair pressed behind the cracked glass lid. Tamara wraps the locket back up tightly and slips it into her pocket again.

"She became extra violent the day whatshisname brought it. Maybe she wants to be buried with it. Doesn't help that she's buried in an unmarked grave. I bet if we all put our heads together, we could figure out how to find her."

I feel my jaw unhinge, my mouth widen to let the first round of wails and sobs come out. I take a fire-belly breath and begin round two. Lucky throws his body into mine in a rough hug. Tamara is shushing me, telling me not to be scared. My next inhale trembles through my whole body. The living room fills again. Bobby and Dolores hover particularly close.

"You need a time-out, Star. Let's get you to the bedroom." Dolores hooks her hands under my armpits to lift me.

"Don't! She's just having a good cry," Tamara tells her.

A good cry. The noises I make are mine. The hands that have slipped under my shirt to lay bare against my chest are mine. Everyone gathered around me sees me and only me. Am I good? I am good and crying.

"Thank you for going through this with me," I bring myself to say.

"Well, the ghost said we need to stick together," says Rose.

"The one good thing she did say," says Tamara.

"Yup, the ghost did say one good thing, that we have to stick together," Leanne speaks for the first time. She looks at me too, almost smiles.

"Actually, I said that. I said that on my own. She didn't tell me to say it."

Tamara takes my hand, says, "Well, that makes it twice as true."

# 62 Scream Famously

The last photo of the angel of Crystal Beach is taken with Rahn's Polaroid camera. After eating too many sandwiches made by Rose and Barbara, the group of us blearily creep into the early-evening heat.

Leanne, still our resident maestro of Canadian rock, plays "Raise a Little Hell" by Trooper on her boom box. Our laughter is stifled but audible. Hal carries a gas can. Me, matches. It has been decided that I will burn the last of the roller coaster wood left out on Rose's lawn.

"Are you here?"

She's dim light, a watermark against the sunset bright sky. *I'm here.*

"I knew you'd come." I use words, not my thoughts to talk to her. She's not getting in my head.

*And I'll keep coming back, too. You won't be rid of me.*

"I believe you. I believe there's more to come." She surges forward but fails to touch me. I don't reach out to see if I'm able touch her. "I'll never forget you. Not how you lived or that you died too young. We're going to look for your grave. We're going to return your locket. We're going to carve a stone with your name on it. I promise you."

The dinged, yellow roller coaster wood between us is a gasoline-sopping eyesore. I imagine the scorched earth that will be left after the fire. The matchbook lingers in my left hand.

*Etta Anna Zinn. Born September 9, 1919, in Horseheads, New York. Put that on my stone.*

"First, please tell me how you died."

*Oh, that's dull*, she says. *I simply stood up, is all. The man in the roller coaster car beside me was too fresh. I asked him to stop once nicely. Then downright told him 'No.' Then I simply stood up. Except, unlike you, I didn't have anyone to catch me.*

"I'm sorry," I say. Twenty feet in front of me, Tamara and Hal inch closer. Dolores flashes me an encouraging two-thumbs up. Barbara turns her wrists in frantic circles, a "get on with it" signal I've seen many times before. "I'm going to burn the last of the coaster you died on. There's no need to keep it anymore." I tease the match head against the igniter strip.

*There was nothing special about him, the last man I rode with. Average in every darn way. Even his come-ons were middle-of-the-road. I suppose I was just done. Too tired to scream my last. Me—the scream queen—silent as falling stone. That's how I died. Without a word or a sound.*

"I'll scream with you now, if you want." The match hisses as it ignites. Flames lick the wood like they've been waiting, wanting this particular fire for a long time. *Fuoco* means fire. It also means focus, like *fuoco selettivo*, selective focus. I focus only on good.

Thank you good cry. Thank you Classical Linguistics. Thank you Violent Femmes' debut album. Thank you Barbara Kruger lenticular print. Thank you old-growth Black Maples. Thank you lightning bolt printed panties. Thank you Vivienne Westwood heels. Thank you Lemmy the lake monster. Thank you Hall's cinnamon suckers. Thank you chick-a-dee-dee and whip-poor-will. Thank you Gena Rowlands for Mabel in *A Woman Under the Influence*. Thank you Diamanda Galàs's *You Must Be Certain of the Devil*. Thank you Sharon Olds' *Gold Cell*. Thank you *The Courage to Heal* workbook. Thank you *The Serenity Prayer*. Thank you fan mail, especially the letters written by lesbians, which I will read when I'm ready. Thank you every single novel that doesn't end with "the end." Thank you pay phone, especially when the calls come from Cat Lake. Thank you Hal for measuring twice, cutting once. Thank you Rose for making bottomless coffee your love language. Thank you Lucky for your innocent, unafraid, bare-naked butt. Thank you Dolores and Bobby and Leanne for being a trifecta of beautiful formidable women who inspire me to keep living at least until my thirties. Thank you Barbara for raising me all by yourself. Thank you Tamara for loving me, or at least loving the honest messes we've made together so far. Thank you Sodom Road Exit. Thank you land and lake and fucking hot humid air. Thank you fire and ash and skyward smoke.

Etta and I scream famously. We scream exhaustively. And then it is only me screaming my shrill and clumsy thank-you to every damn thing I can think of. My unsteady key reminds me just how mortal I am. Mortal and stupid and very, very lucky.

Tamara rushes toward me, open-armed beauty. Close behind her, Barbara runs as she shakes a Polaroid picture in her hand. Maybe this picture is proof that Etta's gone. But I don't need to see it. I already have all the proof I need.

# Acknowledgments

Thank you to the friends and mentors who read drafts of *Sodom Road Exit* over the past four years. I completed this novel with the council of Vivek Shraya, Tom Leger, Torrey Peters, Hiromi Goto, Chelsea Rooney, Carmen Wiseman, Richard Van Camp, and Jónína Kirton.

Thank you to the Peoples of the Six Nations of the Haudenosaunee Confederacy, onto whose territories I was born and raised.

Thank you to the Fort Erie Historical Museum, whose collected edition *Many Voices II* provided an invaluable research text. I have both honoured and altered many historical facts throughout my novel, in particular I have treated the Crystal Beach Cyclone and the Comet roller coasters as one composite "character."

Thank you to my Dad for sending me Crystal Beach postcards and memorabilia, and for telling me stories about working at the Park as a Magic Carpet Ride operator.

And a loving thank you to my Mamma, Sandra Anna, for photographing places I needed for setting references. Thanks for jumping guardrails and hopping ditches to get the picture.